PRAISE FOR *THE DARK WORLD* SERIES

"S.C. Parris weaves a beautiful story within a world that will leave you breathless. *The Dark World* is a refreshingly new take on the Vampire and Lycan war that has slathered the dark fantasy realm since *Underworld*, and will take the entire community by storm. Xavier Delacroix could very well be the new Lestat."
– Kindra Sowder, author of *The Executioner Trilogy*

"S.C. Parris may be a young writer, but in *The Dark World* series, she reaches for something remarkable: a vision of horror firmly rooted in the great gothic tradition of vampire literature, but completely original. *The Dark World*, populated by mixed monstrosities, magically gifted humans and the descendants of Count Dracula himself, will be instantly recognizable to lovers of vampire tales but accessible to those new to the genre. Some great story-telling here, with something for everybody. S.C. Parris is a talent to watch."
– Jamie Mason, author of *The Book of Ashes*

"With intricate characters just as delicious as those from Game of Thrones, you truly can't help but become invested in the sequel and thirst for more!"
– A.Giacomi, author of *The Zombie Girl Saga*

THE
PHOENIXES
OF THE NEST

THE DARK WORLD BOOK IV

S.C. PARRIS

A PERMUTED PRESS BOOK

ISBN: 978-1-68261-251-4
ISBN (eBook): 978-1-68261-252-1

The Phoenixes of the Nest
The Dark World Book Four
© 2016 by S.C. Parris
All Rights Reserved

Cover art by Christian Bentulan
Map provided by The Noble Artist, Jamie Noble Frier

PERMUTED
PRESS

Permuted Press, LLC
permutedpress.com

Published in the United States of America

Dedication

I never knew I'd be here now, and for that I thank you.

Also by S.C. Parris

"A Night of Frivolity" short story

The Dark World series
The Dark World
The Immortal's Guide
The Two Swords
The Phoenixes of the Nest

Coming Soon: The Goblet

Chapter One

DARK ALLIANCES

The silence that passed across the jagged rocks could have been cut with several swords, the dark of the night pressing around all who stood upon them, but nothing could tear the angry glare the Vampire gave the beautiful, powerful woman.

"Xavier," she breathed, "what. . .to what do I owe this honor?"

He remarked upon her fear. . .was it fear, indeed? Her eyes were wide with surprise, yes, but she hardly seemed scared, indeed, she seemed. . .relieved?

"We need to talk," he repeated, the confusion in his gut at seeing her again palpable in its hold. *Damn.* He'd hoped he'd be free of any coercion.

Her eyes found his before he could try and look away, her gaze upon him careful. "Why?" she whispered at last.

"Your mind games," he spat, the cruelness with which the words left his lips striking her hardest across her face: her eyes widened, something of fear, confusion filling them the more he spoke, "they must end."

And before she could say a word, a great ripple of something cold pressed against his front, blowing her hair across her face. He stared as she turned, her long black hair given to him, her gaze, he knew, on the large black mountains days away.

He looked at them as well, the high building seeming to shine in the dark, the glow ethereal, strangely powerful. . . Yes, it was a power he could feel, even from where he stood along jagged rocks, dark stone walls, surrounded by various Creatures he had never been sure he could truly trust.

She turned back to him, and to his surprise, her eyes were wide with clear fear. Oh, yes, she was scared. But why?

"You know I play no games, Xavier," she said. "I've never played games with you. I offered you the truth, and you decided not to take it. But perhaps," and she turned in full, taking a small step, her boot finding a forgiving crevice in the rocks, "you've changed your mind?"

He stared at her, seeing the fear give way to hopeful desire as her attentions turned. "What do you know," he began, feeling the strange energy thicken around him, waving about the dread as if it were a wisp of wind, "of Darien Nicodemeus's state? Of the. . .creature. . .Dracula was before?"

"Before?" she breathed, her eyes darting to the Creatures behind him, but he did not turn, he kept his gaze upon her, waiting, watching. . .and then: "Oh." It was a simple breath, a giveaway to the secrets she'd kept, the secrets Dracula had kept, and with that truth her eyes retained a red hue. "I thought if Dracula shared what he did in his book, you would have come to me with this question a month ago, Xavier."

He almost smiled at her ignorance, at all of their ignorance. *They placed*, he thought, *too much on the damned Vampire.* "I learned this. . .truth from Darien, himself, Eleanor. He turned right before me after taking Lillith Crane's blood, into what Peroneous Doe said he was when they first met."

2

Pale fingers ran across the many silver necklaces atop her chest, the quiet contemplation evident on her face, a face he could not tear his stare from, indeed. Yes, the longer he gazed into the red pools of command, the more he found his questions, his thoughts fading. . .but he could not let her gain his mind, not again—

"You can see why I have quite the time believing that Darien. . .what did you say? Turned right before you?" she was saying as he pulled his thoughts back to the present.

"I don't," he said, the short breaths of the Creatures behind him reaching his ears in full. Ignoring them, he went on, "He turned, Eleanor, wings and all—Aciel and Amentias saw it as well, rattled all of us to our core." He saw her gaze move to them against the dark. "And there in that. . .transformation, a greater truth was revealed to me."

She was silent as she waited for him to continue, a strand of her long black hair blowing across her face in a brazen wind not of her own making. He knew it came from the mountains, the brilliant light on the building at its peak shining high in the sky, the sun that hovered there overshadowed by its radiance. He could barely question what was happening there when she said, "What truth, Xavier? I'm sure you didn't come all this way to waste my, no, all of our time?"

Turning back to her, he saw the fear, the impatience that riddled her brow, causing it to crease in her urgency. *What was she so scared of?* he wondered, the pulse of energy drifting from the mountains settling around him with an ease he was not comfortable with.

"I believe—no, I *know* you hold some knowledge of the Vampire's current appearance Eleanor," he said, regaining his mind, his conviction. She had to know—it was in the way her presence was in his mind, what Aciel had shared the other night. If he truly was tied to her, responsible for the Elite Creatures as well, then *she should know*.

The disappointment he felt at the utter incomprehension on her face surprised him. He had come to her seeking answers, a common ground to know that Darien was not his fault, that he was not responsible for the Vampire's. . .plight. But she had not known. It was clear in her eyes: she had no idea what he was talking about, indeed. *What the bloody hell* does *she know, then?*

He turned to Victor on impulse, knowing Eleanor had shared all her secrets with the Vampire, indeed, but the look the Vampire returned to him was equal in its bemusement: they both looked upon him as though he were deranged.

"Xavier," Aciel whispered well enough for him to hear. He turned to eye the red-eyed Creature, his pale skin a great contrast against the dark. "This is what you came to ask her? If she knows of that monster?" The incredulity clear on his sharp face.

He stared at him, knowing he desired an answer, and what could he say? What could he tell him that would quell the incessant need the Creature had for safety, protection, to remain living in this damned world where safest?

"Yes, Aciel," he said at last, seeing the shoulder slump in his disbelief and, Xavier guessed, his fatigue, "she's the only one who would know of Darien's plight—the only one who ventured through the book—"

"Besides yourself," Amentias offered. Xavier eyed him, watching as he closed his eyes and did not open them for quite a time, the pale of his skin seeming to gleam in the dark. *They needed blood*, he thought.

"Ah yes," the hurried voice of Eleanor whispered, bringing his gaze back to her, "you did go through the book, didn't you? Tell us, Xavier, what did our dear mentor reveal to you? I imagine it cannot be much at all if you have to come to *me* for answers."

He hesitated, feeling the stares of all Creatures upon him, feeling their curiosity, indeed, for he already knew they were all told or shown something different than what he'd seen, what he'd been told. . . .

"He told me only," he said slowly at first, feeling the strange energy pulse around him again, the magic thickening, indeed, "only what he deemed important at the time. And that," he remembered with an angry snarl, "was simply. . .what he desired Victor to know. . .that my father was still alive. . . ."

"Is that all?" Victor asked, sending Xavier to whirl to eye him. The violet eyes were wide with sheer bemusement. "Is that truly all he told you?"

"He told me," he said, staring upon Eleanor again, seeing the anticipation in her gaze, the hopes, perhaps, that he knew all she did brimming in her eyes, "that you and Darien were human in the book, Eleanor. Human, and you hated it."

She was silent, and it was not until another pulse of energy reached them from the mountains in the distance that she said anything at all. "I was. And I did," and she stepped toward him, a hand outstretched to grace his cheek, and despite himself, he did not step away. He felt the cold breath leave her lips as her fingers graced his skin, and he felt it, the faint pull that sparked in his abdomen, the desire to fall into her arms tremendous as he stared at her. "And that is why I moved as I did, Xavier," she whispered, her fingers moving across his cheek to run through his hair, "to claw and fight through that damned book to wrangle what little secrets, what truths, I could uncover. And there," her hand tightened into a fist in his hair and began to press him forward, her voice now a delicate whisper, "there I saw the truth between the blood of Lycans, of Vampires, the truth that mixed our blood. And I decided to do just that, mix our blood. . .it was the only way to get close enough to the truth of Dracula's real power."

He stared at her lips despite himself, feeling the cold breath press against his own, smelling without abandon the enthralling scent of lilac, fresh blood.

Damn.

He was upon her lips in the next second, their parting only allowing him deeper into her mouth, her tongue lashing desperately against his, the desire to lose himself in her lips, her arms growing stronger.

"Bloody hell," he heard Aciel whisper somewhere behind him.

"Well if they join together," Amentias said next, "we're safe, aren't we?"

"We shall see, won't we?" Aciel answered, and that was when Xavier felt it, the rush of wind at his back, blowing his hair and clothes against her, a hand grasping desperately at her waist, for he smelled the blood of the Vampires, knew what they would do—

The strong hand tightened around the back of his shirt, a strangled sound leaving his lips, vibrating against hers, and then he was pulled back, flying against the dark air, the vision of Eleanor's black hair flying about her startled face all he could see—

Aleister's green eyes glared back at him in the next second as he landed roughly against the rocks, their sharp tips digging into his back, tearing at his shirt: he smelled his blood fill the cold air, colder now as the lack of her against him, the utter absence of her cold skin brushing against his surrounded him.

"I won't even begin to ask if that was some new kind of magic Equis unleashed with his newfound control of the art!" Aleister yelled, Xavier able to see the furious anger in the Vampire's green eyes.

He opened his mouth to respond, the words unable to rise past trembling lips, when he felt the heavy wind push down from above them, laid eyes on the large, red Dragon that hovered high above their heads, the remaining number of Order of the Dragon Members settled atop its back.

"I don't even know what to bloody well say to you!" Aleister screamed, reaching out a scarred hand to grasp his shirt. He pulled him off the rocks with a strength Xavier knew the Vampire held and most well: he had been bandied about the Dark World at the scarred

Vampire's behest, after all, and with the sword all but forgotten at Aleister's feet, he sent his free fist into Xavier's cheek.

All thought of Eleanor, of her skin, her lips, dispersed with the feel of the Vampire's cold knuckles, the blood pooling in his mouth as he staggered backwards, the hand still clutching his shirt keeping him in place—

"Father," he gasped, blood sputtering from his lips as he glared at the angry Vampire before the fist was sent into his stomach, causing him to double over. A retching gasp left him, more blood spluttering from his lips to land upon the rocks. He gripped his stomach with an arm, looking slowly up into the Vampire's hard face. He had since let him go with the blow and replaced his fist at his side. Xavier stared at it. It would not unclench. "Father—"

"You turned a bloody sword on me, Xavier," Aleister said angrily, brandishing his own blade, and for the first time since he'd appeared, Xavier could see the Vampire had not fully healed from being badly burned. The red robes he wore were black in places, the smell (he had not been able to smell it before, so consumed was he in Eleanor's scent) of burned flesh reaching his nose the more he stared, the tip of the long blade pointed straight at his nose, but he no longer cared.

"Father, what happened to you?" he asked through coughs, blood leaving his lips, splattering against his shirt, feeling the pain subside at last, but still he would not dare move. The stare the Vampire gave him held him securely in place.

"Don't," Aleister spat, pressing the sword against his forehead, "don't you dare profess to care now! Now that I've a sword to your bloody skull you ungrateful, idiotic mistake for a king! You abandoned us—the bloody knights—we Creatures tricked, coerced, and lied to, to stand by your bloody side and you abandon us when we needed you—needed the king—the most! And for what?! To, to," and he turned in a frantic whirl, Xavier watching as the sword moved with his hand, his black hair billowing in the strong breeze that passed across them.

Xavier watched the sword tense in hand, and with wide eyes he rose to sit up along the rocks, disbelief falling upon his every sense, for the Vampire wouldn't be so brave, so foolish.

"Aleister?" he heard Aurora Borealis say beside the heavy wings of the Dragon as they rose and fell in the dark air, causing the wind to rise around them.

"Oh, he's not going to. . . ." Dragor's voice sounded, causing Xavier to look upon him. The Vampire stood beside Peroneous, Aurora, Lillith, Christopher, Yaddley, and Minerva, atop the jagged rocks, and he noticed the utter fatigue that seemed to find themselves in the Vampires' eyes, but he could barely question what had happened, when he felt the smaller gust of wind at his front.

Aleister was moving, his red cloak flying around him as he ran, the sword held aloft, aimed straight for Eleanor's heart.

Xavier rose to his feet despite the cuts in his back, the aches to his cheek and stomach, the cry leaving his lips before he could call it back: "Eleanor, don't!"

For he had seen her red eyes brighten in a deranged hunger, a stark bloodlust, he had seen her slender hands lift through the air, the wisp of black energy that blended in brilliantly with the dark of the night.

But the black energy froze with his voice and she looked his way, and for a moment, a wild, mad moment, she looked rather regretful, and then something happened Xavier did not believe.

The wisp dispersed with the next burst of wind from the Dragon's wings and she side-stepped Aleister's sword as he reached her, and with a glance to the glowing mountains behind her, another to Aciel and Amentias, and lastly to Xavier, she waved a hand and Aleister fell to the hard rocks, the sword clattering loudly against them, though he was not dead, Xavier knew: he could still smell his blood.

She had spared him.

He stared at Eleanor again as she whispered words he could not catch, and with another blink, was gone in a swirl of dread. Victor, not to be left behind, was gone in a softer breeze.

"Aleister!" Aurora cried, moving across the rocks until she reached him. Xavier watched her drop to her knees at his side, noticed the blood that littered her robes, face, and hair.

"Your Grace," the dark Enchanter said from beside the Dragon, and he watched as Peroneous Doe moved to him skillfully maneuvering over the rocks as though he'd done this many a time. He too was covered in the blood of someone else, his eyes black in the strange night. "What exactly were you planning upon coming here?" And Xavier heard the edge to his voice, the anger that settled just beneath the words.

He eyed the others that remained beside the Dragon, their eyes all upon him, some wary in their gaze, others bemused, all holding hints of betrayal.

Of course.

Doing his best to ignore the daggers of humiliation that struck his frame, he turned his attention back to the dark Enchanter just before him, the black eyes still awaiting his response. And what he could say? He, himself, was not sure what had just happened, though he felt, somewhere deep in his mind that he would not have been able to remain focused for long once around her, indeed.

Whatever blood, magic, curses she used to force this transformation from beast to mortal to Vampire and back, holds tinges, scents, wisps of your blood.

Aciel's words to him the night before returned with a severity he could not ignore. And as the dark Enchanter shifted his footing against the jagged rocks, he said it, no longer caring what they thought, for he knew it as truth: he and Eleanor were connected, through blood, through passion, through it all, Dracula be damned. "I came to better understand this connection that rests between us."

He expected the harsh stares the Creatures gave him, the dark one of Christopher Black that had perused the jagged landscape, the Creatures atop it with something of bemusement and disbelief, but he was mildly surprised when this very same Creature pulled himself from beside the haggardly-breathing Dragon and moved to him.

He merely watched as the black eyes, so like hers, so troubled, drew closer along the night. And once within earshot, the gruff voice said, "Was that her? Eleanor?"

He stared at him more, seeing the striking similarities the Creatures held, yes, he could see it all now. His hair fell in slight, thick waves down his chest and back just as hers had done before she'd become an Elite Creature. His eyes were terribly black, void of the life a human or Enchanter would hold, stricken with a tormented kind of grief, and knowledge, terrible constant knowledge. It was in the way the Vampire's heavy brow creased, and even through his worry, his perceived desire to know what his sister had become, he was still, and perhaps had always been, kept out. *From the bowels of Dracula's secrets*, he thought, *this Vampire had sprung. Unaware. Unknowing. And what, indeed, would the knowledge of his sister do to him? For him?*

Xavier turned from Peroneous and stared upon Christopher Black, wondering what secrets lay deep behind those dark eyes, what he had been told by Dracula that he, Xavier, had never been *deemed* important enough to *know. But apparently*, he sighed, *everyone else* did. "Your sister?" he said, feeling the eyes of all Creatures upon him. "Yes, that was Eleanor. A woman who chose, once shown what had been kept, to forge her own path."

He had not meant for the words to spill, but the moment he'd opened his lips, there was no stopping them. But how strange. He knew not where they'd come, only, somehow, that they must be said.

The tingle that overtook his lips where hers had met his next sent a small smile to lift his cheeks despite himself.

Connected, indeed.

"Xavier," Peroneous warned, the formality of king and knight somehow all but forgotten, and as Xavier looked past the harrowed Christopher, he could see the others were not regarding him as one to be respected, but one to be feared.

"I meant nothing by it," he said, knowing the lie would not muster truth. He was right. Peroneous's glare became quite troubled, and the black eyes began to peruse his face for, it seemed, some sort of answer to the strange words that spilled from his mouth. "Truly," he recovered, "despite all of our stances here, we are here, like it or not, because *Dracula* made it so. We were not given a choice in the matter to our states. But Eleanor Black, the one that causes this dread to seep into our blood, to mar our minds, our words, chose to hold the power she does. She chose to mix the blood of Lycan and Vampire. She chose, unlike us, to forge her own destiny."

Aurora cleared her throat, bringing his gaze to her, the upset clear in her dark eyes. She stared at him coldly, her black hair falling down her back as she knelt at the unmoving Aleister's side. "You sound as though you agree with what she's done," she said, spurring on hardened nods of assent from the others.

"We shared words," he said. *Words that make sense the more I think on them.* And they did. The memory of *The Immortal's Guide*, its vast landscape, curious Creatures, and limping Vampire returned, and with it he saw what he had been too preoccupied notice before: he could control what happened there, the air, the nature of the land.

And if he could, would that not mean that the others, Darien, Eleanor could control what happened? Yet the seed of doubt began to bloom, and he realized with a start that neither Creature had Dracula, not until the very end did Darien have the Great Vampire it was said, so truly, was Dracula the reason he could control all that happened? And without his presence? What would *The Immortal's Guide* look like?

He stared at the spot Eleanor had remained several moments before, mind lost on what she had seen. "...*To claw and fight through that damned book to wrangle what little secrets, what truths I could uncover....*"

What did you fight, Eleanor? he asked as her words returned on a kinder hint of dread, mind gone on the air of that place, the way the sun would emerge from clouds with his happier thoughts, the sight of the beautiful woman named Sindell... He ran a hand over the handle of the cold sword at his waist, barely remembering it had glowed profusely the past few days when lost to her dread, to her Creatures, to his mind.

And the voice answered back; he almost took the Ascalon out of its sheath to point wildly at the air: *"Come to me, and I'll show you."*

"Xavier?" Peroneous asked from somewhere nearby, his mind lost on her words, her scent. "What's wrong?"

Releasing his grip on the sword, he eyed the wary, dark Enchanter with cold eyes. "Nothing," he said, and then louder still to the others who remained watching him intently, angrily, "not a damned thing. The Enchanters, they live there, yes?" And he pointed an unsteady finger toward the mountains where the energy still pulsed, reaching them in swift, cool breezes. *Why were you scared of that energy, Eleanor?*

"Yes," Peroneous said, "but Xavier—"

"King," he corrected, mind lost on her, the real book he had been kept from. "I'm your king, and you will address me as such." He heard the bite in his words, felt the sting remain in his throat long after he'd spoken, but he did not care. *What more did Dracula keep from me? What would I have seen if I wasn't tied to the Vampire? And what—what was she scared of? What did the Enchanters have now?* He did his best to recall what Aleister had said, "...*His newfound control....*" *Newfound?*

"You have to be joking," Aurora spat from Aleister's side. Xavier eyed her across the rocks, the large stone wall at her back appearing to ripple against the waves of energy that pressed against them. "You haven't been acting like a bloody king, Vampire. You ran off to her—you raised the Ascalon to Aleister—your father, when all he wanted was to protect you, to get you to the Goblet! You are ungrateful, and you're driving us all down with you—"

"Enough!" he shouted, the anger burning in his blood, their words of confusion, righteous anger at his lack of duty fueling it further. *Despite it all*, he thought, whirling from Peroneous and Christopher in full to glare upon the woman, *I am doubted. I am doubted, and I doubt Dracula, still.* . . "I moved from you Creatures to protect you—Darien's state jarred me, as it jarred us all—she filled my thoughts—*fills* my thoughts—and I wanted to see if I could understand this connection that rests between us."

All was silent as he went on, no one seeming to desire to speak against him, the steady pulse of energy from the mountains, the white buildings atop them, reaching them every so often against the dark. "She knows nothing," he said, eyeing Aurora coldly, her black eyes steady as she watched him, "she knows nothing of Darien's state—but believes the truth stems from *The Immortal's Guide.*"

A glance of bewilderment passed across her face, as she eyed the others near the Dragon, beside him, indeed, but he would not be deterred from what he had to do, next. "Yes," he said to the weary silence, "I went through the book, but apparently, I did not truly reach what I had to know. What Darien Nicodemeus saw within those pages, what Eleanor Black saw within those pages. . .I was kept from. It is this fact that begs me to further question Dracula's. . .actions when he was alive and dead. In that book, he was no more helpful than he was alive. As I told Victor moments ago, the Great Vampire merely relayed what secrets he deemed important, only prattled on that I was not ready—that I had to be complete before the Phoenixes reached us in the book."

A slight tremble of the rocks brought his gaze to the Dragon, its long nose brushing the ground as though it searched for something, and with a second glance he knew he had seen the Dragon before.

"So what are you saying?" Dragor asked, stepping from the Dragon to reach him, sword no longer glowing its blue light. "You'd rather run off to Eleanor and learn what secrets she's uncovered?"

"She's fought through the book," he said, turning to face the blue eyes that glared upon him in confusion, "*fought*, Dragor. I *walked*. Well, limped. Either way, what I faced was clearly nothing compared to the plights of Darien and Eleanor."

Peroneous crossed his arms bringing Xavier's gaze to him next. "You didn't answer the question, your Grace," he said darkly, "will you be running off to Eleanor again, or can we breathe easy knowing that you will stand with us? Give we. . .bidden Dark Creatures a fighting chance against her, as it were."

He turned from the black-eyed Enchanter to eye the black mountains, the sun that hovered just above it, brightening its peak in perpetual day. Without turning to eye the others, he began to step forward, mostly stumbling over the jagged rocks, thinking briefly of the ones along his shore at Delacroix Manor—

"Your Grace?" the voice of Peroneous sounded again, pleading, demanding in its intensity: Xavier stilled as though bidden, knowing the Creatures would not follow if he did not say what they desired to hear. "What will we be? You cannot ask us to follow you further if you, yourself, are not willing to speak to us, to tell us the truth. Where are we to go now? For what? And why?"

The sight of her black hair whirling around her face conjured images best left to the darker parts of his mind, he knew, but the feel of her lips would not die. . .and what she held deep in her brilliant mind. . . .

"We go to the Enchanters," he said shortly, "I am sure, as my father said, we will find the answers to our current afflictions,

Eleanor's. . .power the least of our problems now." And Peroneous looked as though he desired to speak, when a harsh burst of magical light beamed from the mountains, blinding them severely.

Xavier raised a hand against it, hearing the others let out bewildered gasps, the Dragon bristling, its large wings creating a new wind to rise up around them: Xavier felt it blow up his hair. And then the Dragon spoke, her voice sharp, deep as it rang through their ears, and Xavier knew where he'd seen this Dragon before:

"The Enchanters have their wits about them," Worca said, "it would be best for you Vampires if you were to seek out their. . .assistance in the matters to come."

The light died in the next moment and Xavier turned to watch the Dragon, to see, indeed, if her mouth opened, if she had indeed spoken the words that could bend the others to his will. . . .

She was staring at him knowingly, her large eyes dark, a plume of black smoke leaving her nostrils in what seemed to be impatience.

He merely nodded his thanks, before Peroneous let out an aggrieved sigh. "I do admit the nature of my brothers' gift with the Enchanting Arts is startling, and it is vital to see what has caused this change. . . ."

"That settles it, then," Xavier said, turning from them all before they could stop him, "we move for the Enchanters." *And learn what had Eleanor so scared.*

✳

"Your Grace," one of the Lycans said, Lore stifling the growl that threatened to rise in his chest.

"What is it?" he said, not bothering to turn to eye either of them as they stepped down the dark dirt path, the cool wind of the night pressing on all around them.

"The smell of Vampire—"

"I know."

The snap of his words were not lost on the Lycan, and Lore was relieved when the man did not try and start conversation again. It was pointless, indeed.

He had known before they left Lillith Crane's manor, where they'd set up base, that something was different, that something, whether right or wrong, had occurred. But as he walked the Dark World, his remaining Lycans at his heels, he trembled despite himself. Yes, it became clearer the more he walked, following the scent, the instinct that drove him forward:

She had turned.

James had failed.

Thinking only of the punishment the man was to receive if he weren't already dead, Lore stepped forward, the heavy breathing of the Lycans still in human form behind him cutting through the low wind that breezed around them. Eleanor Black's energy pressed on, and he knew it spurred their desire to turn, knew it ripped at their throats, trembled in their chests, their desire to take the form of the beast.

But it would not happen.

Not with the moon a sharp crescent in the sky, hidden partially behind thick, unforgiving clouds, her dread darkening the sky. . . .

He could no longer smell James's blood, the blood of the woman overtaking all, but he had not released hope that he was still alive, still his heir. . . .

The thought of his son entered his mind, lost to Eleanor's madness, praised beyond all recognition for killing Dracula. The pain filled his heart, and he quickly replaced his thoughts, returning his focus to the Lycan he had bitten, the Lycan he had been sure would help restore the dominance he and his Creatures once possessed.

A shiver filled him as the woman's cold blood entered his nose, covering his every sense, and he stopped short, that blood entering his mind, wisps of her coldness, her power strong. . .and then he heard it:

"Help—help me. . . ."

"What?" he said aloud, whirling along the path, the eyes of the men behind him dark in their bemusement.

"My Lord?"

"Your Grace?"

"Help me, please. I need—need—Dracula—"

And it was gone.

He looked up from his hand to eye the bewildered gazes upon him, head still pounding, pain sharp as the words resounded in his head, fading quickly.

"Damn," he said aloud, rubbing his temples where the pain was sharpest. Although the words were gone, he could not shake the blinding pain that covered his eyes. He blinked, determined to regain his mind, remove the pain.

"Your Grace?" the Lycan nearest him said. He reached out a dark hand to grip his shoulder, but Lore glared upon him, feeling the sweat form along his brow.

As it dripped past his eyes and nose he straightened, blinking in the dark, attempting to refocus his gaze on what was important. *The boy. The boy is important.*

"We must move," he said, growls leaving his throat beneath the words. And as he turned from them, determined to move further down the road, he smelled it: death and dirt. "There," he whispered, pushing past the pain, the confusion the strange words had spurred—

"Your Grace," the dark Lycan said, pulling him from the scent.

He eyed the dark man in exasperation, seeing his serious gaze was on the road ahead of them. He followed suit, returning his gaze to the night ahead, the figure just there on the horizon, the line of trees on either side of him tall, only deepening the darkness the man remained in. Lore narrowed his eyes as the new scent grew stronger. *It could not be.*

He could see the blood that adorned the man's naked body the closer he moved, the pain that seemed to pass through his body: The man lingered on a foot before stepping forward again, his breathing slowing further with every step.

"Thomas?" Lore breathed, not understanding what he was doing here. *Could* he *have injured James?* For the smell of blood that was not Lycan grew stronger with every step Thomas took.

The brown eyes were narrowed as Thomas finally reached them on the path—the vague moonlight above shining faintly against his frame, illuminating the blood that covered his chest and legs. Lore stared, not sure what more he could do—and where was James?

He could not smell the boy in the stench of Elite, sweat, and blood that filled the air now, no he could smell nothing but the angry scent of his son, angry but weakened—

"Your Grace!" a man at his back shouted in his ear, but he needn't the warning to know what was happening:

Thomas's frame trembled before he lurched forward in a jolt, landing roughly on his knees as though bidden. His eyes were wide as they gazed upon the dark sky, searching, it seemed, for something that would aid him, help him, indeed, where Eleanor could not.

He could barely question where the thought had come when a shrill cry echoed in the sky, sending his gaze, along with the others, to the moon. Another shrill cry filled the air, and with a start he remembered where he had heard it before.

Naked in the woods before Wingdale, the strange woman just before he and Thomas. . .they had cornered her, yes, they had, but this, this. . .sound had stilled them with a brilliant sort of magic he had never encountered.

"What the bloody hell is that?" someone said in a surprised whisper, pulling him from his reverie.

He blinked, focusing on the sky in earnest, not all surprised to see the three large birds fly directly overhead, several feet above them, the strangest scent of smoke and something he could not place filling his nose as they passed.

Their tails were just as large as their bodies, trailing out behind them as though their cloaks. They seemed to be wispy, soft, the same as their equally large wings, and when the one in the middle opened its red beak, letting another shrill cry fill their ears, he could have sworn a trail of gold dust left its wings.

They swerved gracefully in the air, much like a Dragon would do when circling for a kill, but instead of diving straight for them, Lore watched as the three magnificent birds let out one last cry together, before flying away from them, lost to the darkness that was not, somehow, as dark as before.

He blinked, pulling himself from the empty sky, looking around at his men; he knew they all held the same gaze he did. Their eyes were puffy and swollen, and he dared to think one of them might cry it was so quickly his eyes were watering.

Blinking away his own tears and ignoring whatever curious sensations had bloomed in his heart with the sight of the birds, he turned to his son. Whatever the birds had filled him with dispersed as quickly as it had come:

Thomas was gone.

"No!" he shouted, not caring that his men jumped at his voice. He ran to where the man had knelt, splatters of fresh blood that had dripped from his body onto the dirt lingering there just before his boots. The smell of dread thick on the air as well. *He was here.*

For he had believed, if only for a brief moment, that he was imagining the man's appearance, that in his anger, his. . .desire to see James alive and well, he had conjured images of his son, instead, full of the fear that he had truly failed in trusting one so young, and with a task as important as killing the strange woman.

But no, the more he stared on the blood, smelled the air, the dread that filled it, he knew Thomas Montague had been here.

So where? he thought, pulling his gaze from the blood at his feet to eye the path ahead of him. *Where is James?*

"Your Grace," the voice said, bringing him around to the present. He tore his gaze from the barren horizon to eye the dark Lycan again.

"What is it?" he asked, thinking vaguely that something more had transpired. He turned, staring in confusion upon the man who trembled just as Thomas had done, his eyes completely black although tears left them in earnest. He turned in full, staring upon the man carefully, seeing the other in the same state as well. Fear gripping him in full, he tried again when neither would speak: "What? What's happening to you? What's wrong?"

"The woman," the dark man said. He looked quite uncomfortable, as though he were to transform at any moment. "The woman is here—she's—she's in my blood."

Lore gripped the man's shoulders to still his shaking, a cry of pain leaving his lips as the red light flashed where his fingers touched, the painful pressure not leaving his hands. "What—what is happening?" he breathed, pressing his burning arms against his chest, not sure what more to do, how to still the pain—

"We must go to her, your Grace," he continued, tears still leaving his black, empty eyes, "she calls, she calls. . . ." And without another word, their trembling grew as their hands and arms lengthened, growing hairier, their noses and lips forming the snout of Lycans.

A horrified gasp left his lips as he found himself on the ground, his hands instinctively pressing against the dirt to smooth his landing. Another cry of pain left him with the movement, and he quickly recovered, pulling his hands to his chest once more.

They stared down at him, their saliva dripping from their many-fanged mouths. He half-thought they were to rip at his limbs, so deep was their growling, but in the next moment they were running from him, down the path the way Thomas had come. He watched them go until they were no more, and rose to his feet, doing his best to still his shaking.

They turned, he thought blindly, staring after the cloud of dust left in their wake, *turned on a waning moon. Impossible.*

The need would overwhelm them, yes, he knew, but he knew damn well they would not be able to turn at all, and not on his orders—so what the devil?

Pain still brimming in his hands, he stepped forward after them, the smell of smoke, dread, and yes, Alexandria Stone's blood filling his nose the more he walked, fear filling him in earnest with the sight of their eyes.

She did that. Made them turn. Sent them running after her. But how?

Somewhere deep inside, he knew he should run, fly across this dirt path and reach them, see James, alive or dead, see the woman in all her pale, bloody glory; he knew he should try with his dying breath to reclaim what was his: power. The power of the Lycan breed.

But somehow he could not bring himself to do anything more than walk, the invasive dread of Eleanor bloody Black pooling in his veins at last. And as he looked around at the line of trees on either side of him, the emptiness of the path before him, he thought of Thomas, the love the man held for that damning wife of his, and whether or not he had missed something entirely in denying the humanity he had killed for.

※

The warmth of the room could not be felt by the Vampire who lay atop the small, comfortable bed, though it was a comfort he was not able to feel.

A protective barrier hovered over the sleeping Vampire's frame, his red hair pressing against his face, grown slightly longer in the hours passed.

His eyes were pressed shut and with a slight groan, he rolled over onto his side, the glare of the sun from the window just beside his bed pressing against his face in full.

And then, with a start, he opened his eyes.

The scream left his lips in a rush, the smell of blood filling his nose everywhere he dared turn, the pain the thing spurring his screams: It covered every inch of his body, he couldn't feel any part of himself that wasn't burning—on fire—*pain*—true honest pain he had never felt before, not even at the hands of the various Creatures he had fought at Dracula's side—

Dracula—dead.

Friandria—Eleanor Black killed her.

Everyone's dead—

"No, everyone is not dead, Vivery," the familiar voice sounded, cutting through his thoughts, cutting through, somehow, the endless pain.

He felt himself ride on the cool breeze the voice conjured, and then he was in the serene darkness of his mind, but he was not alone.

"Vivery, you were dying," the Enchanter said, his long black hair tied back into a hold, the rest of his hair trailing down his back, "but one of my own saved you. You have met her today—Philistia Alicia Mastcourt."

He opened his mouth, relief flooding him when there was no pain, "I have failed. That Elder has my blood—he has taken magic from Dracula—"

"A Vampire that is no longer of this Earth, and therefore has no use for the art, Nathanial. We must not be selfish in thinking any one Creature can hold all of the power."

"Then why—how did Equis give Dracula control of all magic? I thought he was *the* Enchanter."

A small smile lifted his lips, and the water at his feet rippled with a slow step forward, the hem of his black cloak treading the water.

"The Head Phoenix was eager for an opportunity to end the plight that is the Vampire and Lycan Creature," he said, "and although you, yourself, are a Vampire, you have taken well to Enchanting. But you are still privy to what has happened. Magic is back where, forgive me, it belongs, and as such you Vampires shall go back to enjoying your lesser existences—regardless of what blood you may have taken in."

He blinked. "I don't—master, you mean I'm dying right now because he took my blood—took away the magic that let me walk in the sun?"

He was silent for a moment. "What makes you think it is magic that lets you traverse the light, Vivery?"

"I know my childhood was secured because my father bit me, turned me into a Vampire before I would die a human," he said, watching the man's face. "I overheard Dracula talking one day— the spell cast upon we Vampires born from human mothers, Ancient fathers to ensure we would become Vampires, not die far too young as humans."

A small chuckle escaped him. "Observant, Vivery, very," was all he said.

He let the silence continue on before he got the nerve to speak. "Master, if all you're going to tell me is that we Vampires do not deserve magic, that I, no longer with the gift of Enchanting, cannot stand the damned sunlight, and have no advantage over my enemies, then I'd rather deal with the pain out there."

He raised two gloved hands in haste, and Nathanial narrowed his eyes. "Calm down, Nathanial, I've merely reached out to let you know nothing has changed between us. You may not understand the importance of what has come to pass, but you, who have studied in our halls, and spoken with our betters, has a greater. . .advantage than most. . .Vampires on the Arts of Enchanting and it would be wise to use this in the coming journeys."

"Your hands," he said, not thinking on all he was just told, a fear filling him that he did not understand, not yet, "you've never worn gloves. What's changed?"

He quickly placed his hands behind himself, clearing his throat, sure to say, "Focus, Vivery. I am no longer your master and yet I entered your mind to tell you what must be done even when it is no longer my duty. I am no longer tied to Dracula, no longer tied to the Phoenixes. But still—I am here, when it would be wise for me to not be. Regardless of if you understand the severity of what I do or not, you must heed my word." And he stepped forward, grasping the collar of a clean blouse Nathanial was not certain he was wearing outside of his mind. "We have power now, Nathanial, yes, we Enchanters do. But I see the importance of your mission—to help Xavier Delacroix end the Lycans' and Vampires' existences. We Enchanters regaining our power will only help this endeavor. You Vampires must stay the course—Philistia will help you—she, I believe, isn't as keen to the coming treatment of Vampires like myself. She will aid you."

"The coming treatment? What the devil do you mean?"

His eyes blackened, Nathanial seeing a severity in them he had never witnessed before. The fear flared anew. "I mean," the Enchanter whispered, despite his voice echoing on in the vast emptiness that was Nathanial's mind, "Equis plans to end all Vampires before they can reach the Goblet, if Xavier Delacroix does not get to the Goblet first. And he is confident we Enchanters can end the means of Eleanor Black as well. . . ."

He could hear nothing else the man said, despite the movement of the man's lips, very aware a small need that had been burning in the back of his throat had been growing to an insatiable spark. . . .

And now, the man so close to him, the smell of the man's blood so clear—never-mind that it was the blood of an Enchanter—was all he could smell. He could feel the pulse of the man's blood in his fingers as he gripped tight his shirt.

And all at once the darkness fell away, the water at their feet as well, and without anything to stop it the burst of blood covered them on all sides, drowning them, and the Enchanter broke away, pushed with the rush of blood.

Nathanial's mouth, open from a scream of fright when the blood pressed against him, allowed copious amounts of the red liquid to stream down his throat, but the hunger, the desire would not be quelled. It did not take him long at all to realize the blood he drank was his own.

Once he did, the rush of blood died, steaming away from them into a deeper, darker blackness, although the floor beneath them was no longer water. It was his blood, resting, waiting to rise up again when the need would overtake him.

He eyed the man before him who sat on the floor in stunned surprise, blood covering his frame, indeed, causing his hair and clothes to stick to his face and body, and without another thought Nathanial kneeled just before him.

The gasp that left the man's lips was lost to Nathanial, as was whatever fear he had felt just before the blood had flooded them: the desire surged.

He gripped the man's neck roughly, not hearing the cry of pain that left him, moving his mouth only to the vein along his neck, and he was quite prepared to sink his fangs into it when the man whispered, "*Dilenvor.*"

A whirl of fierce wind pressed against him in the next second, pushing him away from the Enchanter who still sat upon the bloody ground, a small smile forming on his face. "Do not worry, Vampire," he said as Nathanial was pulled farther and farther away, the howl of brazen wind screaming in his ears, "I will do my best to help you reach your goals in the safest ways. *It would be cruel to let you Creatures die by the hands of the Enchanting Great.*"

He smelled the blood, the snarl escaping him as he sat up atop something soft, all pain ignored as it was the desire that drove him.

Blood.

It was here. *Here.*

"Blood," he said aloud, his throat dry, the pain flaring every so often when his focus would wane from what he needed most. *Must focus on blood. Not pain.*

"Focus, Vivery. I am not your master. . . ."

"Blood," he snarled, the smell greatest to his left.

"I'll. . .get Madame Mastcourt," a soft, scared voice said from that direction.

With the voice, he found his strength. He rose from the forgiving surface he'd sat upon and moved, the smell of the blood guiding his every step. . . .

The sound of other footsteps issued just before him, but they were moving away from him, much to his growing frustration.

"No," he said, the word leaving his voice in a snarl, "come here."

"I. . . Madame Mastcourt!" the voice yelled, and for the first time he realized it was a woman who stood just before him. He no longer heard footsteps, a small smile gracing his lips. She must have hit a wall.

The smell of her blood thundered in her veins, his every sense attuned to its progression. *Heart, veins, heart, veins. Pumping. Pumping. . . .*

He smelled it strongly now, having led his body to it, unable to deny himself any longer. Whatever part had been resisting was gone, the desire all that fueled him—

He felt the blood burn in her veins, just there at her neck, yes, he felt it all, and he opened his mouth, so dry with his need—

"Symbolia Rocare," a new voice said from somewhere behind him.

He found it impossible to move, felt the blood in his own veins still, anger filling him as he felt the woman sink down and under an arm he didn't even know was pressed against the cold hardness of what had to be a wall. Focusing on the new blood that caused this, he fought the spell, doing his best to turn, to not rip forward and tear into the new blood of the meal that had entered the room.

Thick with magical energy, it was powerful, that blood, powerful enough to allow him to turn, but keep him against the wall: He attempted to move against it, but found with every attempt the spell grew stronger keeping him in miserable place.

It was with an aggrieved sigh that he relented, remaining against the wall.

"I leave for a moment and you finally decide to react to my healing," the voice said.

Madame Mastcourt. Of course.

Somewhere in his blood-addled mind, he was remembering the beautiful, dark woman who had greeted him upon his arrival to the Mountains of Merriwall. The Ancient Elder who had taken his Enchanting from him. . . .

"You Vampires must stay the course—Philistia will help you. . . ."

"Madame," the scared voice said, "is it. . .safe. . .er, smart, to keep a Vampire here? Especially when His Greatness has—"

"Enough," the serious voice interjected, "you may take your leave, Solva. I will attend to the Vampire from here on out."

"But—"

"Enough."

The footsteps were quick in their departure, and now alone with this new blood, this powerful Enchanter's blood, he found himself ravenous.

"You, who have studied in our halls, and spoken with our betters, has a greater. . .advantage than most. . .Vampires on the Arts of Enchanting and it would be wise to use this in the coming journeys."

"Nathanial Vivery," the soothing voice of the Enchanter before him said, cutting across all desire for blood, indeed. "You must be in great pain."

The snarl was involuntary as it left his lips. "*Blood,*" he whispered.

He heard the long robes of the Enchanter sway around her shoes as her heels clicked against the floor. Felt the slight wind that blew against him as he stood there, only able to smell her pulsing, energy-filled blood.

"Sit, Vampire," she said, and he felt the hand press against his shoulder guiding him down onto a hard surface, his back resting against what felt like more wood. "Now," the voice went on, "you must be in great pain, yes?"

Why, he thought, somewhere amidst the desire for blood, *did that matter?*

But when he opened his mouth to ask this, all that could leave his lips was, "*Blood.*"

"Yes, yes," she said, and he heard something clink, and then what sounded like long fingers unscrewing the lid of a jar. The horrid smell of Unicorn Blood filled his nose, and he could barely gag his displeasure when the thick, cold liquid was poured unceremoniously down his throat.

As the liquid descended, all desire for blood gently ceased into a miniscule ebb, and when the jar was removed from his lips, he spat what little remained on his tongue through the air.

"Distasteful," Philistia said, and he could hear the frown in her voice. The gentle sound of a jar being placed down somewhere nearby resounded in his ears, no longer pounding with his own blood, and then the woman said, "Now, open your eyes, Nathanial Vivery."

Gently, slowly, he opened his eyes, blinking as the brightness of the room greeted him in full. The walls were white stone, high around their heads, only one window remaining in this room and that, he saw, was beside the narrow bed he must have slept in. The window's light blue curtains were drawn, sending a generous blast of sun directly onto the messy, ash-covered seats.

Ash? he thought, narrowing his eyes upon the gray substance.

"You were carried here by myself once Equis was distracted on other things," the voice said, and he turned his head to eye her for the first time since he'd awoken in the strange place.

She was as serious-looking as he remembered, her brown eyes round within her dark face, her hair cropped short, black, atop her head. Her lips were painted red, only accentuating the thickness with which they produced their words, and when she opened them again, he found it hard to look anywhere else.

"But understand, Nathanial, there was very little of yourself to gather. What I could carry," and her eyes watched the bed regretfully, "was used to. . .bring you back, as it were."

He stared at her, trying to understand what it was she said. "I'm. . .what?"

Her eyes returned to him, and in their deepness, their darkness, their knowledge, he saw the truth.

"I was reduced to ash?" he whispered.

"Only part of you," she corrected, her gaze serious, something within them hidden, still he saw.

He turned his gaze to the bed, the small piles of ash resting atop the pillow and atop the mattress. Instinctively, he touched the back of his head, feeling the hard bandages grace his fingers. Intrigued, he searched the rest of his head, quite surprised to feel the rest of it was covered in bandages, indeed.

He turned to her, the expectant question lingering on his tongue, but before he could get it out, she strode across the room, and closed the large white door. Just before she did, however, he noticed the vast hall beyond the room, the single white couch that sat several feet away from them, and he remembered the large man that had sat atop it. The man who had taken his magic—

"No anger," she said quietly, turning to eye him once the door was closed.

He blinked, looking up at her, her gloved hands placed before herself as though she considered something, though her eyes were resigned all the same.

"We must be smart about this, Nathanial," she said, her deep black robes intricately designed around her slender body: there were slight protrusions beneath them, and he guessed she held weaponry.

Wondering if she knew how to handle a blade, for she looked every part the magical dignitary, he was taken from these thoughts, when she said, "Evian Cross has contacted me within the past hour, and he has given me faith that we can do this the way Dracula intended—with your king the one to drink from the Goblet. What Equis plans—I admit I was wary in going against him, but I cannot stand by while he. . .destroys Vampires and Lycans before they've the chance to redeem themselves—"

He stood, feeling his head pulse painfully as he did, his knees giving way, placing him abruptly back in his chair. She stopped speaking with his movement, moving to him in concern, a hand upon his shoulder. He looked up at her, unable to keep her in his sights. Her frame was moving rapidly, spinning wildly, although he knew somewhere deep in his pain-filled mind that she stood perfectly still.

"You need rest," she said, all manner of seriousness gone. He felt her gloved hands pull him up to stand, and despite his weak knees, he found he could step gingerly with her to the waiting bed.

She released him once they reached it, allowing him to settle atop the sheets, his body releasing the ash in puffs through the air.

He looked up at her, seeing the concern in her gaze, yet whether it was for him or his cause, he could not be sure. . . .

My cause, he thought wistfully, *I have no cause.* . . .

And as sleep clawed at his aching mind, a flare of fear covered his dead heart. He wondered if he would see his former master again, wondered what more the strange Enchanter would tell him.

"No, Evian," he heard her saying, and with little to stop it, he turned to watch her.

Her back was to him, the interesting design there catching his eyes. It was of a sword encased in fire, a gentle silver outline allowing it to be seen against her black robes.

A sword in fire?

". . .He needs rest. He is not ready to rise and do a thing—we are at a disadvantage. Even now Equis moves to leave Merriwall. He deems to travel to Shadowhall to seek out their Guild for his assistance—yes, I understand. . .no, we cannot move as quickly— no, I don't know where Xavier Delacroix is. . .regardless if we are to truly do this and Equis moves for Shadowhall, we need the Vampires to have power they don't currently have. . . ."

And she turned to eye him, much to his surprise, her brown eyes narrowed in deep question.

When at last he thought she wouldn't speak, she said, "Your former master wonders if we can locate Xavier Delacroix."

My former master? "I. . .I don't know where he resides, currently," he whispered against the pain that had grown considerably once he'd laid down: The desire for more of the disgusting blue liquid flourished despite the protest of his tongue.

She made a sound of discontent before turning away from him, a great heaviness descending over his eyelids, now.

And as darkness returned to him, he heard her words, a great rush of fear filling him as they were spoken along the bright air:

"We are greatly outnumbered, Cross—even the will of the Phoenixes may not be enough to stop what is to come."

Chapter Two

FEAR

Christian Delacroix stared.

Her red eyes glared back upon him with a darkness, an untouchable coldness he had never known another Vampire to possess, not even his darling brother, indeed.

She stared around at the dark trees, the dirt path beside them as though drinking all of it in, as though it would be the last time she would ever see it all, as though she would never get enough.

He remembered how different the World had seemed when he'd risen from the floor a Vampire, everything darker slightly, but holding a beauty unknown in life. There was little to fear in the sight of a Vampire, fear was different, as was touch, the lighter of emotions that would grace the hearts of warmer Creatures. Everything was subdued, darker, emotion just barely there, and no matter what it would not reach the eyes, of this he was aware only because of the fear that once existed in her gaze when she was human.

Fear, he remarked in awe, that was now gone as she looked around with the eyes of a Vampire at last.

Because of him.

"Alex—" he started before she was staring at him again, her red gaze pressing as though she'd never seen him before.

And he wondered vaguely what she saw before she was speaking.

"Christian," she whispered, and he felt the world spin under him with her voice, a slight snarl instinctively leaving his throat, "what— where are the others?"

What others?

He merely stared upon her for moments more before realization beckoned. *The Order of the Dragon. Of course,* he thought, questioning filling him next. *How could she remember them so quickly?*

"Th-They went on ahead," he whispered at last, staring upon her in sheer bemusement. She was so different, certain, cold. . . .

And indeed, all manner of cuts and holes within her person had healed with her transformation, only the torn, bloody clothes upon her telling of the battle she had endured. Her long, dark brown hair was slightly disheveled as it trailed behind her back, slightly longer than it had been minutes before, he was sure, her skin pale, void of the life he had come quite accustomed to seeing her possess.

She's a Vampire.

The woman able to still the blood of Lycans, cease the desire for blood of Vampires was finally what it was said Dracula desired. The mysterious Alexandria Stone had been found. *So what,* he wondered, staring upon her as though she would rise from where she sat on the bloody ground and destroy him, *would happen now?*

"Ahead," she repeated, sending him to blink upon her again, "and they just left you here? With me?"

Wasn't she scared? Unsettled? He watched her for moments more before deciding she was in perfect control of herself: her gaze was steady as she stared at him expectantly. *Bloody hell.* "You were. . .I turned you, Alexandria. Don't you remember?"

"I do," she said, her red eyes still unwavering in their seriousness. She eyed the sword he still held in an absent grip and a small smile lifted her lips, and he found he desired nothing more than to kiss them again, stifle the scream that wanted to pass through his lips, indeed.

For he was scared, yes, he was, rejuvenated, yes, but terrified of what sat before him, what he had done, nothing but her blood pulling him to taste her, to turn her. . . *"The blood-stiller. . . ."*

Dracula, what does this mean? he asked the air, feeling the sword pulse once in his grip as if in response.

"We must move, yes?" she asked, rising to stand, looking around at their surroundings carefully. "I trust we can't just remain here."

He stared upon her, marveling at her ability to move. *Wasn't she burdened with thirst, terribly cold, scared, confused?* The sword pulsed again and he found the strength in his legs to stand as well, his gaze trained on her as though if he looked away, she would disappear, this impossible woman, this strange Creature.

She's a Dark Creature. My God.

For he'd watched her for the better part of two months now, marveling at her humanity, her fear which was never-ending, chased and desired as she had been at his side. And now, the past few days or so lingering freshly in his mind, how her blood called him, how he could think of nothing, indeed, but its call, its scent. . . .

"Bind the blood, do what you will, repel it, remove it, accept it, destroy it. But never taint it. . . ."

That blood. Was it what propelled her so confidently now?

"Alexandria," he said, unsure of what would come next, indeed, all he knew was that he desired to continue speaking her name, speak it and she wouldn't flee in the face of what she was, she wouldn't come to her senses and beg to be released from death's numbing embrace. She wouldn't decide, ultimately, that she no longer needed him to protect her. . . .

She stared at him, her hair swaying pleasantly across a shoulder as she turned from the dirt path where James Addison still lay, unmoving, her brow still furrowed in concentration. "Yes? What's wrong?"

Unshakeable. "I. . .Alexandria—do you feel—feel any different?" *What an utterly stupid question*, he chided himself. *Of course she felt bloody different—she was a bloody Vampire.* Opening his mouth to repair the idiocy that drifted on the air, he was silenced when she answered back, and for the first time he saw the sliver of fear that existed within her before it was gone to red coldness.

"I'm cold," she said, "though I suppose that is to be expected." And the way her lips turned up in a small smile sent his own dead heart to pulse with a timid beat.

Of course she's not okay, of course she's not at peace with this. . . The scream that rent the air when her eyes opened returned to him in a wave of horror. *That pain, she had felt it, had experienced it. Had always been bidden to this*, he thought, remembering the sight of the monster-esque Dracula staring at her from a window.

Not knowing what more to do, he reached out a slow hand to grace her shoulder when she stepped from him as though he had attempted to slap her. His hand dropped swiftly to his side, and he weighed the sword in his other hand, ridicule drowning him in its maddening hold. *Of course she wouldn't want to be touched, of course she wouldn't want my touch—I'm the one that made her this, I'm the one that took her. . .made her my own.*

For he had felt it the moment her eyes opened, the underlying link that connected them deeper now. It was what scared him more than her next movement. The possibility, indeed, that she would come to resent him for this connection between them, this pull to succumb his every word, for he'd felt it whenever his father would utter a word: the irresistible need to obey.

"Christian," she said, pulling his gaze from the bloody blades beneath their shoes to eye her again; to his relief, her gaze had grown softer, much more reassuring than before, "I'm. . .terrified, naturally, but—"

And her gaze, red as it had been when she lifted from the ground, turned toward the dirt path, toward James, and without another word she stepped from the grass and moved, as though bidden, toward the dead Lycan.

Dried blood lay in a pool beneath him, and the soles of her shoes treaded the thick puddle though she did not seem to mind. Her gaze, he saw, was glowing a very familiar red.

He tore his gaze from her blood-stained back to eye the sword at his side, for it too had begun to glow the same red, the faint whisper seeming to emanate from the gem, itself, and fill his ears with its gentle command, *"Bind the blood, do what you will, repel it, remove it, accept it, destroy it. But never taint it. . . ."*

※

She stared down at the dead man below her, the words drifting through her mind. She had felt, when she had awoken, that hands, many hands had been pulling her down, down into the dirt; a never-ending coldness surrounding her as the life was pressed from her.

But then she saw him, the Vampire who was always there. Yes, Dracula appeared in-between her time of life and death, his cool brown eyes never leaving her own as she was dragged further downward, his long white hair flying about his head in the wild wind.

She had reached out to him for help, incensed and terrified when he would not lift a hand, merely smile his small, cold smile. That was when she realized he wanted her to be taken under, wanted her to die, indeed, wanted her to become this—

She returned to the present, staring down at Xavier Delacroix's servant, remembering when she had made the beast who had helped him turn flee, sparing, she had thought at the time, his life. But he had turned into a Lycan, himself.

And he held, she knew now, very special blood.

Blood akin to Dracula's.

Blood very much like her own.

The sight of the dark Vampire, Damion Nicodemeus, throat cut, gushing blood returned with startling ease, the vision as sharp as the cold air that filled her.

How all other Dark Creatures in the large hall stared upon her as though she were mad when she knelt before him, clutching his throat as he was. She had felt Christian's gaze burn against her the most, but she could not turn to eye it, much like she could not turn to eye it now: She knew she would find confusion there, confusion she could not placate, for she, herself, knew not what was happening to her.

All she had known, then, kneeling before the badly bleeding Vampire, allowing him to drink from her, was that Dracula, or something greater than him, indeed, desired Damion alive.

It was what she felt now, standing over James, an inescapable need to bring him back, give him a chance to do. . .do. . .do whatever it was her grandfather wanted. *But what that was*, she thought as she knelt at his side, *I don't know.*

She knelt in the blood, running a careful hand over his bare chest, covered in cold sweat as it was, a vague thought that she should have been scared crossing her mind, stamped down quickly with the image of Dracula's cold eyes flashing across her vision.

What do you want me to do? she asked them in frustration.

The fear that filled Christian near the trees became clear to her the more she kneeled here, but she would not turn, not eye the black eyes so filled with alarm. . . He was terrified of her, terrified of what she'd become, that much was clear, but she knew, somewhere deep inside, that it would not do to address it, not now, not when Dracula was pushing her to—to—*what?*

She blinked, staring upon James in growing frustration. There was nothing she could know to bring him back to life, the only way she knew to do so was to—

Her gaze found Christian's with the thought, and she saw, indeed, his gaze was upon her with great concentration as if he looked elsewhere he would lose himself. *Blood*, she thought, recalling the taste of his blood upon her tongue, her lips. *If he could bring me back to. . .life. . .could I not do the same for James?*

She turned back to the cold man below her. The sight of him upon the ground behind Delacroix Manor returned in a most unwanted rush of clarity: she could smell his blood in the air, see Lore, snout covered in blood and bits of flesh, look up from his feast and bolt into the trees with a burst of her red light—

My red light.

My blood.

"Alexandria!" Christian's alarmed voice sounded from the trees. She whirled in the blood to eye him, wondering what more could have happened when she saw him: The sword in his veined hand was blaring red light, trembling. Christian had his free hand on a shaking wrist as though to still the sword's energy.

She rose from the ground, the blood that stained her clothes, James all but forgotten as she stared at him, his face bewildered in the red light. It canvassed the dark bark of trees, the blood-drenched grass as it intensified the more she stared.

"Christian?" she called over the blare of red, the new voice that had begun to scream the words she had always heard, somewhere deep inside her mind.

"Bind the blood, do what you will, repel it, remove it, accept it, destroy it."

"Christian?!" she tried again, determined to hear his voice above all else. "What's happening?"

And then, quite suddenly, the blood beneath her shoes was whisked away and she found herself staring up at the sky, the strangeness of it not lost to her at all. It swirled with a terrible darkness, a thick, encumbering strangeness she recognized as the infamous dread all Dark Creatures feared.

"*Alexandria,*" the voice whispered, close by now, no longer needing to scream.

She turned toward the voice, never lifting her head from the ground, eyes widening upon the man that stood there, just feet from her, the red light blaring behind him casting his front in deep shadow.

"*Rise,*" the man said, "*we can do nothing while you remain upon the ground.*"

She did not move, could not against that voice. A voice she'd heard only in dreams, only against pillows and sheets, arms and hands, dirt and grass. *It couldn't be.*

"Dracula?" she whispered, narrowing her eyes as she sat up along the ground, still staring upon the darkened figure.

She heard the smile despite being kept from it all the same. "*Forgive me,*" he said, "*for appearing as I am. For. . .ruining what I am sure was an. . .emotional reunion, but you must do something for me, Alexandria. You must ensure that James is kept alive, and close. With your blood. . .you can make it bearable for him to remain around my Vampires.*"

She'd stood as he spoke, her head pounding against her skull, a vague need she could not recognize beating along with it. She blinked upon the Vampire, able to see him better within the night:

His long white hair lay unbound behind his head, his brown eyes seeming to shine with life, although how strange that was, the small smile upon his slightly aged, handsome face almost haunting in its presence.

But he's dead, she thought the more she stared upon him.

"*I live on,*" he said, "*through those who share my blood, share my burdens,*" and he waved a hand absently to the glowing Vampire behind him, "*my Artifacts.*"

She stared past wisps of his long hair to see Christian still staring upon her, his face stuck in perpetual bemusement. It was a moment before she realized he was not moving at all: The hand that held the sword was still, the red light the only thing moving; it pulsed steadily as though it breathed.

It was with this that she looked around at her surroundings at last, noticing for the first time the absence of wind, the lack of rustling of leaves, the utter stillness of air. . . .

"I'm asleep," she deduced, "lost in another of my strange spells." *That must be it. I'm unconscious. Blaring my red light—*

"This," he said suddenly, bringing her gaze back upon him. His smile was gone, replacing it a grimace, *"is not like your red light blaring from your blood, granddaughter—this is the result of what you are—your blood,"* he pressed a long-fingered hand against the worn, ruffled collar that dropped to his chest beneath a buttoned purple vest, *"my blood. Blessed with magic as you are, you are the key to controlling the blood of all Creatures. Because you are a Vampire at last, you shall remain awake while you gain my knowledge."*

What? she thought as the vague need that had been building since she'd awoken grew steadily the more they spoke. . . "Gain your. . . D-Dracula, I don't. . .did you used to tell me things before. . .when I was. . .a-alive?"

An uncomfortable silence pressed on when his lips would not open, his stare reaching her with something of impatience flickering in the darkness, the red light that barely reached them. *He's remarkably scary,* she thought the more he continued to stare as though her words bored him.

"You don't remember," he said at last, the words covered in telling disappointment. *"Of course. . .one can't assume you would. . . ."*

She was prepared to ask him what on Earth he meant when he frowned, a darkness that was not the absence of red light passing across his eyes. *"There will be more time to talk later, I'm sure. For now, you must prepare to feed. I am sure you are thirsty."*

"Dracula," she began before he nodded, and with a flourish of an arm gave a half-bow, before disappearing into nothing, leaving only a cold wind in his wake.

She could barely open her mouth to finish her thought before the wind began to howl again, the trees swayed, the leaves fell from their homes along branches, and Christian Delacroix was yelling, "—andria! It's Dracula! His sword! I can't—"

But his voice died as abruptly as it had started, the red light as well, and he stood there, holding the Ares tight in hand, confusion blanketing his still red eyes. "What?" he breathed. "Alexandria— you were near James—how did you get over there?"

She eyed the dead man again, remembering the cold Vampire's words as they lingered on in her mind regardless of how much she desired they go away (there was far too much noise in her head as it was): *"You must ensure that James is kept alive, and close."*

But why?

"Alexandria?" Christian called, and she turned back to him, seeing the hesitation in his frame. One boot pressed against the bloodied grass farther than the other, his stance ready, wary.

It was with a start that she realized he wanted to come to her, wanted to, but wouldn't. *He is truly scared of me,* she thought with a sliver of pride, sadness. She had to admit it was a curious feeling to be the one in the position of apparent power, remembering with far too great an ease when she sat in the white sitting room of Delacroix manor, a steaming cup of tea just before her, his black gaze unyielding as they surveyed her, her fear. . . .

"Christian," she said, after a long time of staring, desiring nothing more than to snap him out of his reverie, "I. . .I felt the strangest compulsion when I. . .awoke to—to save James."

He took a step along the ground and the thought entered her mind swiftly, "*How brave.*" Shaking it away, she smiled her most comforting and said, "Dracula. . .desires it, though why—*how* I'm to—to—"

For he had reached her in two steps, the sword all but thrown to the ground, his lips upon hers, his arms tightening around her as he drew her close. She could barely think what on Earth was going on when she saw it as clearly as if it was happening just before her:

She knelt before James, breaking the puddle of blood once again, although she remained on his other side, a pale hand against his forehead, caked in cold sweat and dirt as it was, another on his chest, just over his heart.

She continued to feel Christian's lips upon hers, feeling his hands travel through her hair, race against her back, pull her closer still as though he could not possibly get enough—

She was glowing with the red light, now, and with a small smile upon her lips she was sending the red light into James, the red light seeming to breathe as it pulsed around them both.

And then, with a sudden intake of breath, James opened his eyes—

He pulled away hastily as though burned, and even she felt the slight tinge of heat against her lips despite the utter cold that had claimed her since she'd taken his blood. "Alexandria, I—" Christian began, stopping short upon eyeing something behind her.

She turned, eyes widening upon the red light that covered James Addison, but he was no longer on the ground. She pulled from the lingering hands that were still gripping her waist and turned in full to watch the red light completely cover the man who was definitely no longer dead: his skin was no longer pale and blue, but now held the rosiness of life, warmth. . .blood.

A slight growl escaped her throat, though she hadn't meant it at all, but yes, the more she watched the man return to life, indeed, the more she was able to smell the one thing she had not been able to since she awoke, the one thing, indeed, that had been rising steadily in her chest, her throat, a thunderous need—

She moved for him against the wind, and the moment she did so, the red light around him died, and he fell back against the ground, a slight cry of pain leaving his lips. She was halfway toward him, a foot in the puddle of his blood, when he opened his eyes against the night and rose to sit up, a strong hand upon his head, his brown eyes wide with confusion, terror—

"Alexandria," Christian called, pulling James's head in her direction.

She stopped her movement with his gaze, unable to press on any further for there it was: The man was alive. Because of her.

But she had done nothing, truly, Christian was the one who had kissed her, he was the one who had moved from the grass, the shadow of trees to. . . .

The vision.

Was it possible at all that what she had seen while they'd kissed allowed the red light to travel to James? To save him? *Save him where I didn't know how?*

Then how, she wondered, turning a confused gaze to Christian, now that the desire had subsided, *did Christian know the kiss would give me the vision? Had he known?*

She studied him within the dark, marveling at the look of perplexity upon his face, the same need from before filling his red eyes. *Did he desire blood?* she wondered, marveling at the state of his eyes, how they had not turned their normal color since she'd awoken.

But then, weren't my eyes the same?

A stifled groan sounded from the path and both she and Christian followed it, although she stepped toward him first, the desire for his blood surprisingly gone from her mind. It was as though it never existed.

Before she could remark on this strangeness, he was pulling at her leg, almost pulling her down with the strength of his grip, but she remained standing, remembering the words of Dracula from before. *Why James? What was so special about him?*

She looked down at him, the dried blood sticking to his back as he stared up at her, fresh sweat beginning to form atop his skin, above his brow.

His cheek was pressed against the soiled fabric of her breeches, his new sweat staining it further, but he did not seem to care. She noticed he shook as he forced himself to look up at her, an anger, a sorrow deep within his eyes. "You should. . .have left. . .me dead," he whispered, the words reaching her ears as a pained growl.

She knelt down, gently prying him off her clothes, allowing his head to rest against her shoulder. He was far too weak to put up any sort of fight, she knew, could smell it in what little blood would reach her nose, what little blood that would not make her ravenous with hunger.

This man torn from his aunt's arms just as she was torn from her home to be here, amongst Creatures, beasts, monsters. This man who she felt terribly responsible for, seeing his leg get torn off by Lore those weeks before. This man who was far too young to get caught up in what he had, to turn into a Lycan, and she had not known, had not known at all if he were alive or dead until he'd shown up at the white manor in the woods speaking of escape and fear.

This man, she remembered with a sudden coldness, who had held her in his hairy grip, had pierced her with his claws, had tried to take her from the others, from Thomas Montague, in order to kill her—

His cry of pain reached her ears dimly, as though it came through a rather long tunnel, and she blinked, realizing with a start that she held his throat in her grip, had been squeezing what little life she had just given him clear from his body.

A new hand was upon her wrist, pulling her hand from his throat, and she looked up into the red eyes of Christian Delacroix, a darkness there she had seen in Dracula's gaze. A secret he knew that could not be spilled deep within them.

"Enough," he whispered, pulling her up to stand.

With her movement, James fell over to the ground, the side of his face getting lost in his old blood, covering it messily. He did not attempt to rise from it as he coughed and clutched his throat with a shaking hand.

"The sword," Christian said, bringing her gaze to him. He still held her wrist, his other hand holding her waist as her back pressed against him. He was looking down at James as he continued, "The sword is a connection to Dracula, Alexandria. I heard him—I heard him when I gave you my blood and I heard him just now. . .it was why I moved to. . .kiss you. . .why I moved to stop you from harming James. Dracula. . .wanted me to stop you from hurting him."

"What?" she breathed, mind racing with confusing possibility on top of possibility. She looked back toward the path where Christian had remained and saw the sword lying atop the dirt, the red gem glowing, shedding a low red light across her dried blood.

"He is important to him," he whispered, and she turned back to look at him, his gaze troubled despite the glare of red in his eyes, "why, I cannot say, but being that you just brought him back, I gather it would be. . .best if we keep him that way. I think it will be easier, since you are keeping his blood subdued."

He was a different Christian, she remarked. He seemed sure, a far cry from the confused, seemingly afraid Vampire that had been within the grass just several moments before. She blinked at him as his words reached her at last. "I—what?"

He released her wrist as though he'd done something indecent though his hand still stayed firm around her waist. She thought he felt she was to attack James again if he let go. "Your blood," he repeated, slightest traces of confusion gracing his face, "it is keeping his blood suppressed, yes?"

She stared down at James who had long since stopped coughing, but still clutched his throat. He had rolled over onto his back and stared up at the sky, anger lining his hardened face. "I. . .I didn't believe I was. I merely meant to console him, and then I," she paused, recalling what had happened, indeed, "I remembered what happened before. . .before I died. It was so vivid. Even though I was unconscious I could see everything—I could see him reach for me, take me, I knew his intent was to kill me and it made me angry. I was so very angry of everyone always trying to kill me."

His hands moved to her arms, rubbing them consolingly. "A Vampire's memory," he said quietly as James shallow breathing reached them along the air, "is sharp. Some might say it is sharper than life. What you have experienced in your life. . .you will always revisit. In thoughts, in dreams. Your life, all you've done, alive and as a Vampire will stay with you, easy to recall should you ever choose to. Along with this, are the emotions they spur.

"You might have realized this already but we cannot. . .feel as easily as humans do. True emotion is kept from us. We feel joy, relief, anger, sadness, yes, but it is removed. To truly feel. . .well I have heard from others that to break this threshold is to cease to be a Vampire—it breaks whatever is in us that cannot stand human emotion and releases it. I have never seen a Vampire who has taken this that far, but it is widely spread: The tears of a Vampire, are the tears of the permanently dead."

Something akin to happiness rose deep within her with his words, for she had never heard the Vampire speak to her so softly, as though she were his bloody equal. It was a surprise, indeed, but she found his words soothing. What little confusion had remained as she'd stared down at James was now completely gone. She felt a strange peace, despite standing in a puddle of blood with a former man-turned

Lycan at her feet, Christian Delacroix, human-killer extraordinaire at her back.

And that kiss. . . .

She opened her mouth to ask him just why he'd kissed her when he asked, "So are you suppressing his blood?"

She looked down at James, his brown eyes filled with tears. It did seem as though something was being kept from him. He was weak, but she had just assumed it was because he had been brought back from the dead, but what if it was because of her? The swirl of voices that would not die roared louder in her mind still, and she bypassed Dracula's, slipped past a voice that seemed to yearn for something she could not understand, and focused on the one voice, the quietest of them all, that seemed to be telling her what was best:

"Protect the Dragon and spare all."

"Well?" Christian asked, pulling her from her reverie. She looked up at him, his jaw tensing the more he stared down upon James over her shoulder. "Are you subduing him or is he just this weak?"

"Morbid curiosity?" she wondered aloud. "Or are you concerned that he will rise and attack us?"

He did not tear his gaze from him as he said, "A bit of both, honestly. I didn't trust him when he showed up at Cinderhall Manor. His blood reeked of Lore, of anger. I figured there was an ulterior motive there, but your blood. . . ."

She stared at him as his voice trailed, waiting for more. When it was clear, he wouldn't continue, she probed, "My blood?"

And with this, he tore his gaze from a most despondent James to eye her fully for the first time since she'd awoken. His gaze made her heart pulse just once: He had been holding onto this for quite some time, it was there in his red irises, the silent hunger, the need she realized at last, that was for her.

"Your blood. . .did such things to me, Alexandria," he whispered as though he didn't want the words to leave his lips, but could not stop them all the same. She felt his hand tighten on her waist the more he spoke. "I believe it made me half-mad," he said with a short chuckle, though it would not reach his eyes. He was serious, confused, terribly bothered by this, whatever it was, she saw. "I could not. . .get your blood out of my mind after you. . .saved us from Eleanor Black. Your blood. . .well, you probably know since you seem to be able to recall what happens around you while your red light blares."

She searched her mind for whatever it was he spoke of, but could find nothing. Her blank stare must have given him his answer for he sighed, pulling from her much despite her desire to continue to feel him against her, and he stared at the sky much like James did now, although his gaze was not despondent in the least. He, in fact, looked rather like a young boy unsure of how to share his feelings.

She felt she would blush if she could, instead she turned, giving James her back, her attention on the entirely bashful Vampire before her. *What a turn*, she thought in slight amusement.

"Your blood. . .consumed me," he went on, staring upon her, wiping the small smile from her lips, "I could see nothing but your veins, your blood. It. . .called me, Alexandria. You were *allowing* me to smell it—and only I could. And I was ravenous with thirst, but you wanted to save me, you wanted me to drink your blood, to be the one to turn you.

"At least," he whispered, a great hope in his eyes, "that was what I told myself ever since you brought us to my father, the others with your red light. I hoped all of that was the truth, that you *did* want me to drink it—turn you. Everyone else. . .they didn't believe me; felt I didn't know what I was talking about. . .but I believed. I. . .I stayed true, Alexandria. I listened to your blood, your red light where no one else could, and I did what Dracula desired be done."

She merely stared as his words hung in the air, heavy on her shoulders, atop her head. How similar he sounded to a crazed

Thomas Montague, and in a flash, the memory returned, the sight of the obsessed Elite Creature in the tunnels of Eleanor's home:

The red light covered his entire frame as he turned on a heel away from them, darting down a hall into a bemused crowd of Elite Creature. *His focus on was the sword*, she recalled with a fresh knowingness as the image changed, showing her an unconscious Christian in the hard grip of stern-looking Elite Creatures before he was dragged away down a sparsely lit tunnel, astonished Elite Creatures allowing them to pass, their gazes betraying the bewilderment they felt, that she had felt as well. . . .

"Alexandria?" Christian whispered.

She blinked upon him, focusing on the desperate need in his gaze. *How could I not see it before?* Yes, he was staring upon her with that same frenzied gaze Thomas Montague had given her. . .and hadn't the Elite Creature been hoping to gather the sword for her? Hadn't he gone on and on about her ability to give him back his dead wife? And all to get the sword to her.

Her eyes narrowed upon the sword just behind the Vampire. How easy it would be for him to grab it, to stab her, or fall into a state of madness just like Thomas, ranting and raving about his lost ones being able to have life again because of her.

She glanced toward James who still lay on the ground staring up at the sky before turning back to the Vampire who seemed to hang onto her every movement, every wisp of wind that would perhaps send her blood to his nose.

Of course, she thought with a dull hurt clawing at her dead heart, *he wouldn't want* me—*it was my blood he was always after. Well he had it at last*, she thought with a snarl, *so why hang around?*

Her gaze found the sword again and Dracula's gaze passed across her vision, taunting now in its appearance. *Everything was to get his bloody sword*, she thought in anger, remembering the way he had motioned to the sword in Christian's grip when he'd appeared those moments before.

"What," she began before she could stop herself, not daring to betray the complete humiliation that filled her cold body, "what is it that Dracula desires, Christian?" *Besides his bloody sword, using maddening Creatures to reach it. We were all pawns—*

"Protect the Dragon and spare all," the words returned in a rush of cold wind, and she felt the many hands return as well, their cold fingers and sharp nails beginning to drag her down into lonely sleep, the disconcerting sight of a terribly needing Christian Delacroix her enduring image as all went black.

※

He had felt something was wrong, and he'd moved before she could truly begin to fall. He caught her in steady hands, marveling at how quickly something had changed.

Her eyes remained closed as he held her, the ends of her long hair brushing the ground, confusion falling in waves upon him. What could have happened? She had seemed so happy whilst he'd held her, content in what she was, even, but then she grew cold as a cloud of remembrance fogged her gaze. Yes, he had seen it, but what she could recall, he could not know.

And now. . . .

He stared down at her, the familiar unease reaching him as it had many a time before. She was lost to him again, gone in her red light, gone where his words would not reach her. . .or would they? He had thought, and foolishly so, this whole time she could not hear him whilst she slept, but she admitted she could see what happened around her. So was she lying when she said she could not see what had happened whilst she remained encumbered at Eleanor's home?

"The mystery thickens," he whispered, eyeing the sword over her body. It still lay in the dirt, and as he stared inspiration struck. It would not hurt to try, he decided, then.

Quickly he moved with her still in his arms, glad at how effortless it was to move when several hours before he had been badly burning, in dire need of blood.

This is beyond rejuvenation, he thought, shifting her in one arm to reach down with the other and grasp the leather handle of the sword.

The moment his fingers grazed it, the dim red light of the gem grew greater, overshadowing all, and once again red colored his vision. He stared blindly, his hand wrapping around the rough leather as though tied by strings, the compulsion returning in a sickening wave of need that was not his own.

He stared down at her in the great haze of red, repositioning the hand that held the sword underneath her knees as to better cradle her. She still slept, her skin pale, tendrils of her brown hair falling across her delicate face. He had not known when it happened, but his desire for her blood, as mad as it had pulsed within him those days before, had not overshadowed his desire for her, alone.

He desired nothing more than to see her safe, to see the rare smile that would light up her lips much more than he ever had before. She had not fled with the connection that had formed between them, blood amongst blood, and for that, he was eternally grateful. It was not like when she was human and to flee was to face certain death out of his sight, no, now, as a Vampire, she was far more capable of defending herself, Dracula's red light securing this formidability as well.

And her stare.

The focused gaze she bade him as a Vampire far outweighed the interesting gaze of concentration she would give him whilst human. It was different, colder, yes, but somehow terrifying. She was no longer maddening, no, he admitted to himself, she was radiant, a horrifying knowledge deep within her eyes, in the way she moved, the way she spoke that had him questioning his own ability as a Vampire.

She moved with the grace of one who walked as a Creature of the Night for centuries, spoke with a tongue as hypnotizing as one who turned many, and the tiny growl that had left her lips when she seemed moved by James's blood had sent a stirring of equal terror and desire to boil his own blood.

He wanted her, damn it all, but it remained to be seen, indeed, if she wanted him as well. . .or at all.

The sword, which had been pulsing in his grip began to tremble violently, and before he could utter a word of alarm, the ground took up the thunderous rumblings of the sword as though the sword's power had grown.

"Bind the blood, do what you will, repel it, remove it, accept it, destroy it. But never taint it. . . ." Dracula's words went on in his mind, as though the Vampire himself stood close by and whispered them into the strange air.

And all at once the red light dispersed with a dull sound, and as he blinked on the new darkness that greeted him, he was astonished to see two rather large Lycans standing on the path blocking the way the Order of the Dragon had gone in their search for Xavier Delacroix.

"Bloody hell," he whispered, an involuntary snarl leaving his lips as the smell of Lycan reached his nose at last.

"Vampire," a voice behind him called, causing him to turn.

He eyed a standing James Addison, the man's shaking, profusely sweating frame glistening in the vague light of an unseen moon. "James," he said warningly, daring to turn his back on the two waiting Lycans, their long snouts dripping with thick saliva, though they did not move, "don't you dare. She just saved your life!"

"And I," the man said before his arms grew hairier, the bones beneath lengthening to those of a beast, indeed, his scent hitting Christian's nose in full, "intend to return the favor." And before

Christian could stop it, the half-formed James started forward, leaping clear over his head, to clash with a black-furred Lycan that barred their path.

He stared in astonishment as the three Lycans did battle, James fully formed now, a large claw slashing into the black-furred Lycan's snout causing it to whine in pain.

He wasted no time in rising from his knee, securing Alexandria in his arms, the sword in a hand, before he ran past the group of Lycans doing battle, the strong need that he knew as Dracula's to consume him, pushing him to keep her safe above all else.

James, this need knew, would be perfectly fine.

It was his duty, after all, the need responded as he wondered just why Dracula desired the Lycan alive.

Chapter Three

THE VAMPIRE IN THE DARK

Arminius stood still as the darkened skies appeared, if however briefly, to lighten, revealing their violet depths underneath the black thickness of Eleanor Black's dread.

He stared at the moon, its baleful crescent shape reminding him of a time there was no dread, but peace, tranquility, clear skies, fresh waters. . . .

The thought carried with it the reason he had left the moderate safety of the cottage in the first place: Xavier Delacroix.

He had had no such luck moving south beyond Cedar Village, and he had thought it strange to not feel the Vampire's blood any longer, the red light of the Ascalon, but this had not caused him to hesitate in his venture, no, it was the sight of the three very large birds that had just flown overhead that had done it.

He had wondered what they were, having never seen Creatures like them before, and he had been so moved to an emotion he could not place that he almost forgotten just where he was, and what he should do.

Now in the right frame of mind, he stared at the Vampire City of Role several miles beyond where he stood on the grassy plains, saw its dazzling shine emanate from the heart of the tall glass buildings, themselves, and sighed.

He remembered his Guild before he was unceremoniously removed for the foolish actions of a younger Xavier Delacroix, and what he wouldn't give to return to such a time. . . .

Another sigh left him, and he turned on a heel, allowing the cane to press against the soft grass, the distant cottages of Cedar Village several hours away.

"I move where bidden," he hissed to the wind, stepping with the cane back toward the Vampire he had left, the knowledge that Xavier Delacroix would not be found unless he desired it firm in his mind.

※

Nicholai Noble opened the door against the darkness beyond it, and inhaled the cold, dread-filled air much against his best wishes. *Still weak,* he thought with a frown, closing the door a bit too forcefully: The hinges groaned as the door swung shut.

An exasperated scowl upon his face, he turned his back on the door, the merciless dread, to eye the small cabin he had remained in for a full day; the old armchairs still sat before the fire, weathered books floated above shelves placed against the walls, cobwebbed corners gleamed with dust in their darkness.

Small, he thought coldly, *far too small.*

For he had wanted to leave the damned cottage, yes, by the Phoenixes, he had, but the sun had kept him from moving farther than the weathered steps. Now that the sun had long since set, he found it was something else that kept him here.

With a low sigh he moved for the chair closest to him and sank deep within its old fabric, the filling used to stuff it slightly deflated from overuse. He knew he could do nothing but wait for Arminius to return, for he could not step foot in that World. Not when that familiar dread was everywhere.

Dracula. The sight of the monstrous black eyes, the feeling of mortality ever present whenever Dracula was around. . .and in *that* form.

"And bequeathed unto we, his children, endless death and desire," he whispered to the dark air, the crackle of flames in the low fire that burned before him.

No, it would not do to leave this place, for that Creature. . .that thing that Dracula was, had always been was out there. He knew it mad to think it, for Dracula was dead, indeed, but he could not deny this familiar dread that seeped beneath the door to claim his heightened, frazzled senses. He had felt it long before, after he had moved to save the woman. Save her from a life bidden to the true Dracula. Save her from being a prisoner just as he was now. Just as they all were.

But she had been found, hadn't she? She had probably already turned he reasoned with himself, had probably already moved to disperse the blood of the Lycans, had probably, and this he thought with the lowest of hopes, already moved to take the crown from a most maddening Xavier Delacroix.

And as he glanced toward the black door, eyeing its frailty, the old, chipping wood that formed it, he felt it in full. Clear, unrestricted fear. There would be nothing to stop her or Dracula from breaking it, not with their power, power he was sure had been passed to her blood. And he, he grimaced, would be left, once again to their whim, tied by the dread-covered shackles that were his duty to the former King.

He tore his gaze from the door to eye the medallion at his chest, black and dull, sharply offset by the gold around it and along the chain. *She was losing this war,* he thought, feeling the dullness of

Eleanor Black's dread swarming against his dead heart where the medallion fell. *She was losing it and it did not matter who won. We would cease to be no matter the outcome.*

Chapter Four

ELEANOR BLACK

He walked through the high hallways, their nature unnerving. Something was wrong with the Elite Creatures, the dread here stifling, more so than it had been before she'd left to go "take care of matters," as she'd called it, but that was not all that was wrong here.

Javier Theron slipped down a darkened corridor, sparse torches here and there along the walls barely small enough to light a useful glow. Hood upon his head, he moved quickly, the dark of the dirt tunnel not troubling to him at all, for here he had studied in silence, here he had sought what secrets she had kept. . .here he would find solace where the well-lit tunnels were crowded, obtrusive.

"Where is Eleanor?" he heard a Creature far behind him ask to another.

Where is she, indeed, he thought, focused intently on the piece of the page he had ripped whilst he underwent his transformation, the Creature that had appeared within that room. . . .

The end of the hallway greeted him in darkness, and with a knowing movement, he pressed for the old wooden door, opening it swiftly, feeling the fresh, cold wind of the small room brush against his skin.

Out of darkness appeared a great light from the center of what he knew to be the small room when the door remained closed. He eyed the great light for a long moment before stepping onto the hard stone floor, closing the door behind him, allowing the light which had been expanding the more he stared upon it, to engulf him in full.

Before long the light died, in its place a steadier light, golden in its glow. It sat in the sky high above his head, sparse clouds lining the horizon, for the room had disappeared as he knew it would, the wide, green field before himself rustling softly in the faint clear breeze that had blown up from, he knew, the depths of nowhere.

As he was feeling quite content, he had expected the room to show itself in some semblance of this face: normalcy, quaintness, an air of peace the world beyond the door no longer possessed, but as he took a step along the grass, he found the sky to darken ever the slightest, and this brought the question that next filled his mind to the forefront of his thoughts: *What is wrong, here?*

For he had undergone the transformation quite painlessly as it was, and he knew it had everything to do with the fact that Dracula had been right there beside him, patient, unyielding in his service, his multitude of voices, of actions to ensure he, Javier, knew what the true power of the Elite Creature was. What, indeed, would befall him if he went down that route, what would await him if he, and did this intently, listened to Dracula's every word without fail.

He *had* failed spectacularly when faced with Eleanor's grace, her beauty, her commanding word. He had let her energy, her strangeness enter his mind, stick to the parts of his brain he would need to be smart in his work. But he *had* succeeded in moving for her truth, the secrets she'd divulged, if only at the cost of becoming the thing he had been told would end him, nay, the lives of all Dark Creatures, indeed.

But what, he thought darkly, seeing the sky darken and thicken with impending storm, *more could I have done?*

Reminding himself hastily why it would be best to leave these thoughts to darkness, he turned his attention to the faint cottage appearing along the horizon the more he stepped toward it, its straw roof placed haphazardly atop its wooden body, the stone spout of the chimney jutting out from beneath the straw depths as though most misplaced.

He eyed the thick, black smoke as it billowed into the air, and smelled the fresh scent of what had to be death as a large Dragon flew slowly overhead. He paid it no mind as he stepped up to the oddly placed wooden door, its rectangle form not fitting into the stone frame made for it, and knocked with a pale fist.

The door opened before long, the disheveled-looking Vampire appearing in the door's frame in the next moment. His brown eyes were sunken, dark circles sat heavy beneath them, and his normally pleasantly kept white hair was wild and messy as though he hadn't brushed it in days. With a snort the Vampire stepped back, allowing him entrance, and moved to an old chair before the fireplace. In its mouth, over the high flames was a human head never burned as it floated within the fire, where its neck once was now dripped with endless blood. Javier moved for another chair just before the fire, although he did not sit, and when the door closed, he smelled the scent of blood clearly. It was far too much for one human head to produce at all.

"As you've reached your Age, my young protégé," the old Vampire said, waving a hand absently through the air, sending a book from an old, crooked shelf, flying toward him. As it landed in his lap and opened to a page, he went on, "We can discuss what more would benefit you."

When Javier eyed him in question, the brown eyes appeared to shine, although they still looked terribly tired. "You are an Elite

Creature, and pleasant though these visits have been, you are under her hand. Though her influence cannot extend into this place, it still. . .pains me to be near you, Javier. But all the same I find we must share what must be shared with no time to share it."

"What do you mean, my Lord?"

"In my death I've had the. . .privilege of maintaining this form— what you see now," and a long-fingered hand was waved across his frame, "but as my grasp of magic fades from the World. . .so too will the Potion that keeps the blood of Vampires somewhat human in feature."

He squirmed ever the slightest in the uncomfortable chair, knowing full well what the Vampire meant. "You will return to that. . .that thing?" he asked.

"I will return," Dracula said, his exhausted features appearing to darken ever the slightest, "to the form I held at birth. But nevertheless," and he smiled as best he could: it looked to be a grimace to Javier, "we will forge ahead. The progress made will not be faltered. Eleanor— what more have you learned?"

"The woman," he began, stopping short when he rethought her significance. She left the tunnels to focus on matters most secretive, but he knew from overhearing whispered conversations within her halls that her very Creatures had begun to doubt her power, had begun to see things that had them scared, questioning her sanity, indeed. "The woman appears to be undergoing a process most dangerous, my Lord."

He sighed, a low needless sigh, and settled back into the high armchair with great relief. His tired eyes closed as he let another needless breath leave his old lungs. Before long he opened his eyes, and looked, not at Javier, but at the fire, the head that still hovered within it. The eyes were opened wide in a state of permanent horror, the blood, Javier realized for the first time, fell from the bottom of his head into a large brass pot at the base of the flames.

"She is becoming a terrible mixture," Dracula said at last, sending Javier's gaze to him, "I told her she was a curse, a plague on this World, and I meant it. I had my thoughts that she would desire to mix the bloods. . .mix the truths of what we, Lycans and Vampires, are at our cores, but to actually succumb to the intoxication of perceived power. . . ."

Javier said nothing as the slightly shaking voice faded, nothing but the crackle of the flames licking the stone sides of the fireplace reaching his ears. It was a while before he decided to pursue the unspoken words that had lingered on the fading lips of his creator, but the old Vampire continued before he could voice his decision:

"She is becoming a mixture of my true form and the Lycans' form. A true hybrid in every sense of the word." And then he smiled, although it was small, never reaching his eyes. "She will be a force. . .unimaginable. That is why, Javier, you must proceed with the plan, regardless of the state of the World. Is there anything more you can tell me about her?"

"Not her, but Victor Vonderheide, my Lord, seems to be gaining quite the. . .attention amongst the other Elite Creatures."

At this Dracula stiffened, all the weathering age within him appearing to disperse with the words. He had turned to eye Javier so suddenly, Javier rather felt he had said something quite wrong. "Victor?" he breathed, the breath cold as it reached Javier's face.

He could only nod.

"Tell me," he demanded.

He began, sharing what he knew of the old Vampire in surprise, for it seemed Dracula had had no idea that Victor had joined her at all. And when he got to Victor's unwillingness to abandon a previous mission assigned him in order to locate an Elf and a Vampire that was not Xavier, Dracula let out a sound much like a groan.

"He is truly at her side?" he whispered long after Javier had finished, staring again into the fire.

"Yes."

"But he seems. . .unhappy, indeed. Surely he will leave her, surely he will not—not transform."

"There is no telling what he will do. I barely see him, myself, my Lord. The more despondent he grows with Xavier, with Eleanor, the more it can be believed that he is prepared to leave her."

These words seemed to strike Dracula with question: He turned in his chair to watch him, a glare Javier found most unnerving within his old face. "But he still bears his ring, he can still die, can't he?"

"I. . . ." Javier began, not knowing what more to say. *What was he talking about?*

"It matters not," Dracula said, his disturbed features disappearing, "regardless, Victor's purpose is beyond my plans. We must refocus on Eleanor," he waved a hand through the air, "Alexandria. She has claimed her blood-right, Alexandria—she is a beautiful Vampire. Her power knows no bounds. I have comfort in the fact that one plan has met its end wonderfully."

The tinge of gray on the back of the Vampire's hand could not be hidden in the fire's light the more he stared at it. It was translucent, the veins dark, almost protruding through the skin, the skin itself appearing thin, showing the dark blood beneath. Javier shifted nervously in his seat once more.

"Dracula," he whispered, unable to tear his gaze from the hand that now sat plainly atop the book within the Great Vampire's lap. It was not until Dracula hummed vaguely in response that he thought it safe to go on, the vision of Dracula's true face flashing in his mind's eye. How small the room seemed now. "Your hand," he finished dully.

The brown eyes stared at the thin skin atop the book's many pages, judging, it seemed, the severity of reaction the sight warranted. It was a long moment before he sighed, and with a smaller smile waved the same hand, rising from his chair. The book fell to the floor completely ignored.

Javier followed suit, staring still upon the hand, chancing a glance toward the head in the fire, its eyes still blank and wide, trapped in perpetual horror.

"This is enough for today," Dracula said, bringing his gaze back to him, "you can return to your World, Javier."

"But, my Lord," he started, "your hand, Victor—what of Eleanor? I'm to stay behind her walls moments longer?"

The Great Vampire looked remarkably ancient, Javier thought, the dancing shadows the fire cast upon his face rendering him terribly old, not a Creature, no, but a man haunted mercilessly by his secrets, his truth. Indeed, he looked ready to keel over at any moment.

"You are," Dracula said, turning from him in a graceful sweep, his long white hair flying behind his head as he moved around the chairs and for the door, "there is much to be gained by keeping eyes on our enemies. Alexandria, I believe, will provide eyes beyond Eleanor's dread."

He stepped around his chair to reach him, staring up into the brown, weathered eyes, the open door letting in a blinding sun that did not diminish his ability to see the Vampire before him. A *resilient man, if only hanging on by the single thread that binds him to life, through us, his chosen few.*

"And Xavier, my Lord?" he dared ask the more the brown eyes bore down upon him.

And it was with a wave of this gray, translucent hand that Javier found himself pushed as though by invisible hands through the doorway onto the dirt ground, the door slamming closed before he could make out the words that had drifted on the air as he was moved:

"Xavier is lost, and I fear it is for good."

※

A breath of disturbed wind passed across the old, black trees, their roots twisted as they rose from the dark, barren ground, and from these trees they appeared, the woman clad in darkness, her long hair unbound around her head, the man's long black cloak, bloodied and torn sweeping around his boots as he stepped beside her.

They moved wordlessly on the wind, stepping toward the wide mouth of the low cave just before them when the man spoke, his words trailing the air with a fear, a coldness she could feel in her blood.

"What was to be gained," he began, "by the kiss?"

She let a cold breath escape her before turning to eye him, his violet eyes shining tiredly upon her. A slight wind blew, picking up his long silver hair, blowing it across his lips, and she blinked. "Reaffirming a Curse," she said, watching his eyes for any sign of bemusement. There was none. He glared upon her seriously.

A gloved hand graced the handle of the sword at his waist. "The *Calling of Void*," he said. "He came to you freely, however. Scared were you that he wouldn't return again?"

She closed her eyes, feeling the coldness of his voice surround her mind, *"Eleanor, I need to know more."*

"Come to me, and I will show you all."

Opening her eyes, she focused on the old, terribly worn Vampire before her, still waiting, the seed of anger, grief still within his violet eyes. . . The smile lifted her lips. "He will return. He always does. We can take comfort in the fact that he appears to have begun doubting, greatly, Dracula's. . .endless schemes. They could not keep his soul from what I have unleashed."

The grip tightened around the sword. Her brow furrowed. "What you've unleashed," he repeated, and she could feel the anger grow within his blood, swirling within his mind. *"Victor doubts just as you do. . . ."*

"We must discuss what it is you've truly unleashed."

She opened her mouth to ask just what it was he meant, when the hurried footsteps sounded from within the cave. She turned to eye its entrance, eyes widening as the Enchanter and two Elite Creatures climbed the steps to reach them. The woman in silver robes, glaringly red hair down around her face, bowed low. Eleanor smiled in sheer pleasure. *Wonderful, the woman survived.* "Friandria," she said, "what a pleasure."

The woman said nothing, her eyes shining a strange silver color, and Eleanor smiled, quite pleased the spell was ever the success. To know she could, indeed, return Creatures from the dead without giving them any shade of her blood was a powerful knowledge to hold.

"Your Grace," an Elite Creature at the Enchanter's side said, pulling her gaze to him: his hood remained upon his head, hiding his features in darkness, "we have been infiltrated by a Vampire."

"What?" she breathed, thinking of a clawed, winged Darien Nicodemeus swooping through the mouth of the cave, straight through the barrier—

She eyed Victor, his gaze returned in equal shock, though she knew not if he truly cared for the state of her cave as she did. There were terribly valuable things deep within certain rooms that could not be touched, *should not be touched.* "What happened? Who was this Vampire?" And she pressed past them all, moving down the stone steps to stride into the long tunnel before them, lit only by several torches high above her head.

She heard them step hesitantly after her, the same Elite Creature to speak continuing on with a panicked frenzy, "He was a Nicodemeus, your Grace. We believe him to be Damion. We found him in the. . .well, *the room*, your Grace. He awaits you in the throne room."

Damion? she thought, moving past him. She reached the end of the hall, rounding the corner to the right, almost gliding to the throne room, eagerness, alarm, pulling at her mind.

She said not a word to other Creatures as they passed, their placating stares boring into her frame, a thrill of excitement rushing through her blood at the sudden thought of Xavier's blood filling the air, here. Blinking away the thought, she returned her mind to why Damion Nicodemeus would move so brazenly for her home—would move at all for the place she held the precious truths which enabled her and others to transform at all. *Damion wasn't that smart*, she thought, dead heart racing the closer they neared the long hallway. It began to slope slightly downward toward the large stone door whose magic kept what powerful Artifacts beyond it from being discovered, and as they neared it, the silver-robed Enchanter seemingly found her voice.

"There was great magic cast, here, your Grace," she said quietly, her voice dull as it spread through the air.

"Yes," Eleanor said, "there was. But who, my Creatures, is the caster?" *For surely Damion Nicodemeus would not harbor the arts of Enchanting. . .* She pressed from their bemused gazes, stepping for the door, and with the wave of a hand it swung forward, scraping against the fresh dirt, disturbed as though the door had already been opened.

A cold burst of death pressed against her face, blowing her hair and clothes away from her, and behind her they gasped, but she stepped into the darkness, moving effortlessly over the bodies of the dead to reach the wall. She pressed a hand against it, feeling its coolness, the hard of the stone beneath her skin, and she whispered the words, *"Aperire, malach et pol."*

The wall parted and there stood the two stone stands; they were bathed in the red light of the necklace atop one—

"Are you sure Damion was the one to enter the cave?" she asked the hooded Elite Creature, the light of the necklace illuminating further the utter absence of what should have been a plain-looking goblet. Disbelief pooled through her. *There was no way the damned Vampire would have been able—!*

"Yes, I am sure," the Elite Creature responded quickly, the voice of Victor sounding next.

"What was taken?"

She whirled to eye him in the light, his expression cold, morphed further by the anger in his violet eyes, the anger, she knew, that was directed at her, the things she had not told.

"A very important Artifact," she said, ignoring the look of disbelief that next graced his face.

"Dracula's, I presume?" he asked, not missing a beat. "Who would have been able to gather such a," he chanced a glance back the way they had come, the beginning of bodies shining in the dark light, "well-protected. . .Artifact? Surely not the likes of Damion Nicodemeus."

She managed to smile feeling all eyes upon her, watching her intently, waiting, she knew, for her response. "Surely," she whispered after a time, "never him. As it stands we have been infiltrated—the barrier must be hardened, my secrets—our secrets must be protected." She eyed Friandria, wondered more on her state, if she knew, indeed, where she was, why.

"Work more on the barrier, my girl," she said kindly, the dull eyes staring upon her expectantly, "strengthen it. Ensure no Creature can enter it. And you Victor," she eyed him, pushing all thought of his anger to the back of her mind as a new anger took hold, "how dare you think it your duty to have the barrier released!"

He raised a cold eyebrow. "Oh? I was under the impression you would have been thankful I handed you the woman and Christian Delacroix. Or did you find that meeting. . .wanting?"

A laugh left her throat before she could call it back. *How he played the game. Played it well.* "Dear Victor," she whispered, her voice unable to rise higher, indignation keeping it low, "you cannot know what that meant to me. It was. . .illuminating having the woman here. . . The truth of her power. . .it is truly as you said. But do not think me so grateful as to neglect your clear dislike of my duties for you.

"Yes, I saw your anger at being moved to track down the Vampire and Elf, taken from Xavier Delacroix, I saw your hesitation at being tasked with what you must have deemed a lesser journey. It is why I cannot help but wonder if you have not had the barrier lowered for this very reason. To allow my Artifacts," and she waved a hand behind her to the empty pedestal, "to be taken."

All Creatures besides Victor and Friandria tensed with these words, the implication of it not lost on him at all: His eyes widened in shock, then the familiar anger took its place, remarked coldness coming next, and finally a blankness she had come to regard as his trademark glare found his face.

"I have no reason," he began, "to betray you, Eleanor. You, who have taken me from a life of doubt." But even as he spoke his violet eyes roamed behind her to where the necklace sat, the glimmer of question in his eyes once more. "You, who have shown me, told me things Dracula never desired."

"But there are things," she said, "you cannot possibly understand unless you are one of my Creatures. There are so many things you will never gather unless you bear the blood of both Creatures."

"Like the curious longing to gather Xavier for your own."

Her lips pursed. "Yes," she said after a time, "that very longing. It is why I need you to prove yourself to me at last. I've only kept you on this long because of our history together, my dear, old friend."

"Have I not proven myself enough?"

"Oh yes, you have. But with Mister Gail's death at our hands, my defenses currently down, and a dear. . .object in the hands of Damion, I need another at my side. One who can do what has to be done. One who won't be swayed by Dracula's maddening. . .presence."

"And you think that is me?" And again, the glimmer of doubt bathed his eyes. "But what of Xavier? You just kissed him, cursed him again as you said. Isn't he the one you want to stand at your side, Eleanor?"

Oh yes. More than you know. "He is not ready. Not ready to take the transformation."

"And I am?"

She stared at him, seeing the fear in his eyes, the desire to run from her, from all she'd shown him in his old face, the perpetual grimace that had seemed to shape it ever since Dracula's death. *No,* she thought, *no you're not, but I can use you yet.*

"Tell you what, Victor," she said, resuming her kindly expression, sure to placate him as best she could, "as I am more than generous, I have a proposition for you."

His brow furrowed. "Proposition?"

"Xavier Delacroix," she said, seeing the confusion in his gaze, "his home could not be touched in the destruction of London. More power I am sure Dracula put in place. I need you to destroy it. Perhaps if you give the Vampire nothing to return to, you will be more at ease in his place in this World. He will be tied to me even more than he already is, and you, through your deeds, will be the same. Perhaps you will come to understand the comfort I can afford those lost. . .and your position in this World so rapidly changed."

He looked as though he wanted to object, that he felt it would not be wise to bring the Vampire he considered his enemy to her door, but when he opened his mouth, she was surprised to hear, "All of our homes were protected, Dracula saw to it we were well compensated for our time on the surface. I may," and his chest heaved with a great breath he did not need to take, "have peeked over his shoulder whilst he wrote his notes on what he did to place the spells.

"And I am rather versed in the Enchanting Arts. It would not be hard given I had an Enchanter at my back to remove the spell." And his gaze traveled to the dim Vampire at her side.

"My," she breathed, despite herself, "I was not wrong in plucking you from the bowels of that dreadful city, was I? Excellent, Victor," her hands clapping together as they often did when pleasure was at her fingertips, "when do you feel able to leave?"

"At once if it pleases you. . .your Grace," he said feeling the words turn around over his tongue.

"Brilliant," she said, nodding, knowing he desired nothing more than to stay, to know just what was lost, what more she had not desired to share. But there would be time for that soon. . .if he truly fulfilled his end of the bargain.

And she watched with great joy as he stepped from them, bowing low as he moved, before he reached the first body along the floor and turned, stepping gingerly over them. It was not long before his broad back was lost to the darkness of the room, only reappearing once he entered the torchlight of the tunnels, moving further away until he was seen no more, lost in the bowels of her halls.

"You would burden him with such an impossible task, my Queen?" the Elite said from beside the open wall.

"Burden?" she repeated, the word foreign on her tongue. "Whatever do you mean?"

This Creature stepped from his place against the brighter stone, but only by a step. The red light did nothing to illuminate the shadow that was his face, indeed: the hood still rested atop it, hiding it from view. "Delacroix Manor is untouchable, this all Elites know," he said, "one can only wonder if you truly plan to bring the Vampire aboard as one of us. Respectfully, naturally."

Her finger grazed the many necklaces along her chest. "And who are you?" she asked at last, staring upon him, truly unable to see even a glimmer of eyes beneath the veil of dark. *What magic was this?*

"Just one of your humble Creatures, my Queen," he said with a bow, "one that cares what happens to our home. And to our Queen."

Her eyes narrowed. "Do you feel Victor will betray us?" she asked.

"Perhaps," he whispered, sending a small chill to descend her spine despite the blare of red light at her back, "he already has."

"If there is something you know about my home despite it being breeched, Creature, I desire to know what it is."

"I know as little as I have said. But because I am still on your side, your Grace, I will tell you this: there are the beginnings of discontent within these halls. And many are beginning to look to the Vampire. It is only natural to wonder if his true intent is to pay heed to your word. . .or indeed, ever become one of your Creatures."

She said nothing as the Creature bowed low, following in Victor's footsteps as he moved away from her, stepping quickly over the corpses in the darkened room before reaching the sparse light of the torches and just as the Vampire before him, disappearing beyond the door's frame.

"My Queen," the dazed voice said, reaching her ears in something of a strained whisper.

She turned in the red light, eyeing the woman who stared upon her as seriously as she could muster, although her gaze was immensely unfocused.

"The potion has been created," she repeated expectantly as though that was all that mattered.

And to Eleanor, staring at her creation in the red light of a medallion Javier would never wear again, a tomb where the bodies of her own Creatures that had betrayed her in some form or another, or merely outlived their importance, the fact that this long project had finally, it seemed, been finished, it was all that mattered, indeed, Victor and Xavier be damned. *With this*, she thought, motioning for the Vampire to lead the way out of the room, *I will have an edge no Creature will be able to overcome.*

※

Victor Vonderheide walked the halls, mind most gone on Eleanor Black and her. . .lies. He was not certain he could call them lies, but there were definitely secrets she deemed to keep hidden.

Yet, instead of the self-righteous anger he believed he should have been drenched with, he found himself quite calm. For one, whatever was taken seemed to have rattled her greatly and this brought him considerable pleasure. For another (and this he could not help thinking about with glee), she accused him of releasing the barrier on purpose.

How hilarious!

He had seen her fear at things she could not control, oh he had, but this was beyond anything he had witnessed before. She was terrified of something; he had seen it whilst they stood on the rocks several days from the Enchanters' city. The fear in Eleanor's eyes when the white light blared, he was sure Xavier had seen it as well. *She was scared.*

And for some reason this pleased him, to see her fear, her indecision. *"We see your indecision, your grief, and we welcome it."* He recalled the words the late Joseph Gail had uttered to him whilst in the dark, dreary office of the Vampire City.

Saw my grief, did you Eleanor? Did you desire my company?

For now, on the other side of this cruel, maddening World, he was aware things were not much better at the hands of the one ultimately powerful Creature in the World now that Dracula was dead.

Things were, he thought, as he stepped along the dark tunnels, nodding briefly to lingering Elite Creatures as he passed, *not much different at all.*

"My Lord, Victor," a voice said as he walked, distracting him at last from his thoughts, "a word?"

He turned, eyeing in surprise the Creature in Vampire form, his blonde hair long as it flowed down his back, the black robes he wore distinguishable only from the others by the white traveling cloak settled atop it, draped around his shoulders.

Javier Theron stepped up to him and when just before him, the other Creatures turning to leave now that their view of the Vampire had appeared to be taken, he said, "There are talks, my Lord, of your. . .victory in acquiring the human woman and Christian Delacroix for Eleanor. It is being passed about that you are looked upon as someone who has done more for her than anyone would ever dream."

Victor stared at him. The scent of Eleanor's stifling dread flew off him in droves, yes, but there was something else, something so very familiar, the scent almost teasing him in its appearance, forcing his mind to a place it could not go lest he be broken in full, the tears allowed to fall.

Regaining himself, his brow furrowed. "Victory?" he repeated, exhaling sharply to try and expel any dread that would dare seep past his nose, but it was far too late. He could already feel her dread in his blood, tangling in his veins, her words trailing on in his mind.

"I need another at my side. One who can do what has to be done. One who won't be swayed by Dracula's maddening. . .presence."

So I am to be swayed by yours, Eleanor?

Focusing on Javier, some of the lingering stares of the Creatures that still filled the hallway, he spoke again, finding his voice amidst the suffocating scent of lilac and blood, the new scent that would not seem to leave. . . But how impossible it would be if it were true.

"Whatever victory you believe that to be, I was merely doing my duty, Mister Theron." And with that, before the tears could begin to leave his eyes, he turned away from the Elite-Vampire, the eyes so wide with judgment, he knew, for he was not like them, not like them and perhaps, he would never be regardless of what she said.

He began to step over the stone ground, his footsteps not making a sound the more he moved and he wondered what on Earth would possess him to think that strange Elite Creature would ever hold Dracula's scent. *Delirium*, he mused, *madness. Perhaps*, and with this thought he chuckled aloud causing a woman in tattered robes to jump, a delicate hand bracing a wall in her fright, *I am falling to her hand faster than I would like, the grief, the madness of this week alone causing me to recall his blood.*

But even as he thought this he could not deny the sharpness of the gaze that held his frame as he moved further down the narrow hallway, the sudden heaviness of the round stone he had gathered but hours before in his pocket, but he would not turn, no, he was certain it was just his mind playing tricks, his grief marring his senses further.

For it felt as though Dracula surveyed him through the eyes of the Elite Creature, that the Great Vampire knew he held this strange stone deep in his pocket, but he was not fool enough to believe it, no, matter how he wished it to be true.

Dracula is dead, he thought, feeling the gaze burn a hole into his back, *no amount of desire, of mourning will bring him back.*

But it was for the briefest of moments as he walked, that he felt the stone seemingly burn within his breeches, but as fast as it had come, it was gone, and he once again chided himself on his absolutely wild imagination.

Chapter Five

THE SAVIOR

The low wind seemed to press against their bodies alone, the high stone wall to their left doing nothing to still the burst of white light that blinded them the further they moved. The madness of the World around them seemed dim here, lost in the cool energy of the Enchanters' magic, and the curiousness of this fact spurred the dark Enchanter forward, his eyes never leaving the soiled clothes of the Vampire that led them.

His long black hair swirled in the wind, and through flashes of light Peroneous Doe could see the tenseness in Xavier Delacroix's shoulders. *Tenseness born of Eleanor Black?*

He was not certain at all how much they could truly trust the Vampire, not anymore. It was enough that he'd been dragged along for the maddening ride, his dark secrets being revealed through regrettable lips, now the very Vampire that was supposed to be their leader was wavering, and fantastically.

He stepped carefully over a large rock, watching as Xavier and Dragor Descant stumbled slightly, their grace falling: Morning was fast approaching, indeed.

With a slight frown he eyed the sky, the faint blue that was beginning to form above the sparse clouds causing him only the smallest hints of worry: *The Vampires would burn.*

"Aurora," he whispered, not desiring to draw the others' attention. She stopped short sending a thoughtful-looking Lillith Crane barreling into her back. With a small smile and low apology, Lillith stepped around Aurora, the hardened Christopher Black pressing a hand against the small of Lillith's back as if to reassure her.

Aurora side-stepped the Caddenhall siblings as they stepped past, their equally hollow features hardened only on the black mountains in the distance, and she hung back until Peroneous was at her side. Once she was walking just beside him, he said, gesturing to the heavens with a dark hand, "The morning shall harm them. And the sun at Merriwall Mountain. . .what shall we do?"

"I had thought of that," she said, the dried blood that stained her face now black along her chin, "we can perform the *Nubilosus* again, just as we did on the Gibbering Elves' Path."

He could not still the sound of disapproval. "*Nubilosus* takes equal concentration, Borealis," he said a bit too coldly, "if we could not hold it back then, what makes you think we will be able to hold it now?"

"We've magic back now," she said, her eyes on the large figure of Aleister draped across Yaddley Caddenhall's broad shoulders. His eyes still remained closed and her brow furrowed in clear worry.

A small frown began to form at the corner of his lips but he quickly released it, returning his mind to matters more important. "Yes, we've magic back, but do you really think I want to spend my time back in Merriwall catering to a group of Vampires? I'm banned there as it is, I don't want to miss anything before they decide to send me hurtling back to Cedar Village."

"Miss?" she repeated, eyes moving from Aleister to watch him in grave question. "What on Earth do you feel you'll miss, Peroneous?"

"Whatever's happening, of course!" he almost shouted, and with bemused glances from Christopher and Lillith, he went on, quieter now. "The magic that pools from that place is concentrated, far more powerful than we've felt in a long, long time, Aurora. Whatever Equis has uncovered. . .it clearly. . .it clearly quells Eleanor Black's dread. Can you not feel it? Her dread is far lesser than it was only hours ago."

And he watched her look around at the wide passageway, an understanding blanketing her dark brown eyes in the next moment. "I hadn't paid attention to it. . .when she attacked Aleister I. . . ." but she didn't finish, her words fading into the recesses of unspoken thought.

He did not press the point, knowing her growing affinity for the scarred Vampire had numbed her mind to all else. She would not be able to work, to move, indeed, until the Vampire was safely revived.

Turning his mind to the growing morning, he waved a hand, resigned to covering the Vampires as best he could. He felt her start at his side, waving her own hands, solidifying the heavy dark cloud above their heads, though he noticed it rumbled with thunder, and he eyed her warily, hoping she did not allow it to rain down upon them.

He did not much desire to be wet.

The city let out one quick burst of blinding white light, brighter than all the others that had come before, and he covered his eyes with a free arm, hearing the Vampire at the head of the group let out a cry of pain. Peering over his arm he saw Aurora had faltered with the burst of light as well and as such the large cloud had lightened considerably, the warmth of the sun pressing down upon their heads: The Vampires' skin sizzled where the light touched.

"Aurora!" he cried, waving both hands despite the light that still blared in front of them, and the large cloud solidified further, the woman at his side letting out sheepish words of apology, righting herself, raising both hands in the air as well.

The Vampires had turned to eye them, their gazes moving from them to the cloud above their heads and back, their burned skin healing in the shadow of the veil.

Xavier snarled with clear displeasure, the sound sending shivers of fear and guilt down his spine. "We cannot survive in this World like this," the green-eyed Vampire said, anger ripping at his throat.

Peroneous knew the Vampire was not used to being weakened, not used to it at all.

The thought made him smile, if only slightly.

"No matter, your Grace," he replied, "we will keep the sun from your heads as best we can."

"But it is clearly few days' travel to the Enchanters' City, Peroneous," Dragor said next, his large hand on his sword. Peroneous narrowed his eyes upon it: it no longer glowed its steady blue color.

"We will keep the spell aloft," Aurora said with a touch of finality, "trust us, Dragor."

The look that graced his face was telling: no Vampire that dwelled upon the surface, that basked in the glory of Dracula's protection, had ever felt so subdued, or at least, had not felt thus in a very long time. It was all Peroneous could do to stifle a great laugh. *How the tables turn.*

The wide smile quickly fled his lips, however, when the thought of the other Enchanters, the ones not tied to a dead Vampire's dying wish as he was, surfaced.

Would they, indeed, react so triumphantly to several Vampires showing up at their door? Would they pardon the Enchanters that traveled with them? Especially if he showed up with the very Vampire that, he knew from his many travels about the Dark World, was the cause of many Dark Creatures' ire?

A sliver of unease creeping along his back, he cleared his throat, wondering at all if he had been smart to ignore Xavier's absolute strangeness regarding Eleanor Black in lieu of the Enchanters' reclaimed power when he knew not at all what they would do.

※

Christopher Black watched the Vampires turn from the Enchanter and step, with something of sobering realization toward the black mountains again.

He, ever curious to the state of this World he had been kept from, had watched the Creatures' interactions with each other and had found it disturbing. For one the Enchanter, the dark one, had come across as nothing but condescending in his manner, his speech with the Vampire supposedly chosen to rule them all, and the woman, well she only truly cared for that badly scarred Vampire across the large Vampire's shoulders, hadn't she?

A motley crew of Dark Creatures if I ever saw one, he thought, wondering what Dracula ever saw in their faces to warrant them, as far as he was concerned, quite an enormous task. For now, out of the tower, he could not deny the severity of his sister's threat to the Dark World: he had seen Dracula's worry begin to form through the brief visits the Great Vampire bade him at the beginning of her training with him, but now, with the woman having fully embraced the completeness of whatever she'd uncovered, he began to wonder, if these Creatures could stand to it. If Xavier, and he eyed the hunched shoulders of the Vampire ahead of him, could withstand her allure.

For he had seen the way they kissed, he had seen the way she had faltered in striking the scarred Vampire, he had seen the look of great longing in Xavier's eyes, one he knew well, for he was very aware he stared upon Lillith the same way.

But what was that? Why would the Vampire move so recklessly to her? Get swept up in her hold? Do the exact thing the other Creatures, it seemed, did not want him to do, could not allow him to do? For she was the enemy, wasn't she?

She was to be destroyed, wasn't she?

The threat that she held had to be eliminated, hadn't it?

So why on Earth would their new King run headlong into her arms, oblivious, it seemed, to the World that fell around him?

Christopher narrowed his gaze upon the long black hair of the Vampire as it whirled in the sharp wind. The Vampire commanded authority in that gaze, but it was misplaced, not anything like Dracula's had been, reassuring, commanding in its feverish, almost crazed glare. Driven mad, Christopher knew, by his secrets.

Yet Xavier. . .the Vampire seemed to be driven mad, not by any secrets he kept, though Christopher suspected there were many, but by what little it appeared he did know: the way he had moved to Eleanor, demanding to know what happened to a Darien Nicodemeus was telling enough.

But with quick glances to the other Creatures that walked around him, the uncertain air that claimed the morning sky, he had a sinking feeling that no other Creature who bore a medallion wanted to follow behind him.

And Christopher, bidding another glance to Xavier's long dark hair as it was momentarily lost to a blast of white light, could understand why as Eleanor's dread, fainter along the air now, was blown away by the Enchanters' power once more.

❊

Morning pressed against the tops of the trees but still Lore stared. He had faltered when his men had moved, fully grown against the fading dark of night, and had not moved until the sky had lightened considerably, snapping him from his morose reverie.

She had taken from him the last two remaining Creatures that had afforded him what little protection he had been able to muster, she had taken from him his son, and, the more he peered around the tree he'd stood behind now for the past several minutes, his hands still burning from touching his own Creature several minutes before, it appeared she had taken from him James as well.

The Lycan was bruised heavily, still retaining his form, a limp hairy arm hanging loosely at his side. He let out an aggrieved roar before charging for the only remaining Lycan left standing in the middle of the wide path, its black fur shimmering with fresh blood in the morning's light.

The other Lycan had long since been disposed by James: he lay in a pool of his growing blood, reduced to his human form, his skin already pale. His eyes blank as they stared in his, Lore's direction.

"I knew you were weak, boy," the dark-furred Lycan roared to James, padding the road with large paws, sending clouds of dust to rise from the sky, momentarily obscuring Lore's vision to what transpired.

He heard James laugh, and smelled the death on the air. The man was ready to kill, but for who?

"Weak?" James said as the dust died, allowing Lore to see the beasts in full glory. They stared upon each other, both on hind legs, as though daring the other to attack next, but Lore was not sure which one would dare. They were both badly bloodied whether it was from wounds inflicted or received; their blood littered the ground, blending in nicely with the mess of blood that he knew was not Lycan at any rate. It smelled too thickly of *her*.

"I am not weak," James went on, a low growl leaving his large throat, "and you will cease calling me 'boy!' I am a man and one that damned woman deems important enough to bring back to life!"

It was clear these words brought the Lycan a great swell of pride. His large chest protruded as he shifted his footing atop the Earth, a seemingly wide grin encompassing his hairy face, though it was hard to tell for sure. All Lore saw were many rows of large, sharp teeth.

The darker Lycan fell to his front paws, the claws ripping at the Earth, leaving five long, large gashes within the dirt. "What?" he growled, sounding shocked.

"You heard me," James went on, much to the darker Lycan's growing displeasure, "she brought me back to life and you bet your arse I will still all who deem to harm her."

"Harm her?" the dark Lycan almost whispered. It left his throat in a harsh sound barely lower than a scream. "I do not wish to harm her you fool! She called us here!"

At this James began to shrink, his fur disappearing as glistening tanned skin replaced it. When at last he stared back upon the Lycan with human eyes, hardened with a desire Lore had never seen before, he said, "Called you, did she? Why would she do that?"

It let out another growl as if in irritation. "She needed our blood, you fool!"

James's expression mirrored the utter confusion Lore felt falling down upon his shoulders. *Needed their blood?* he thought, willing himself not to laugh. But he recalled with a terrible suddenness the look the dark man had given him back on the path when he was still at his side..still his Creature. It was a look of desperation, of madness, of longing, indeed. *To give her their blood?*

Lore stared, a sliver of hope filling his thundering heart the more the thought solidified in his mind. Were his men moving to give her their blood in the hopes of killing her? It was known far and wide that the blood a Lycan would kill the blood of a Vampire if their blood merely touched one another. Would they move to such an ingenious plan?

"Why would she need your blood?" James asked, his voice having lost the prideful edge; it now sounded lost.

The Lycan growled again, padding at the dirt with his front paws sending yet another cloud of dust to cloud Lore's vision. He heard the Lycan roar, felt the ground rumble greatly beneath his feet, and then nothing at all. It was as though everything on Earth had ceased to be. The cloud of dust remained within the air, obscuring all sight of the Lycan and James, the birds did not chirp, and the clouds, he saw, looking up at the sky past the ceiling of leaves, were terribly still.

He could barely wonder what on Earth was going on when he heard the familiar sound again, the high-pitched screeching filled his ears, and at once his hands flew to his ears, for all the good it did not do. The sound still pressed against his eardrums just as clear as ever, sending a great, crippling pain through his body.

He fell to his knees, but only before glancing once more up at the sky, able to see the flash of red feathers as the large bird passed quickly overhead.

The moment it was gone, the shrill sound ceased, the birds continued their song, and the plume of dust along the path rolled to the other set of trees just opposite him until it was no more than a wisp of its former self. It was here he stared in earnest, seeing the dark patches stain the grass, and he barely wondered whose blood that was before a cry of pain issued from the road.

James was being shaken violently by the darkly-furred Lycan, his shoulder and chest in the larger Lycan's mouth, his blood spilling from the holes made. And with one great ferocious twist of its entire body, James was thrown from the Lycan's mouth, sent flying through the air toward the row of trees further down the path away from Lore.

He stifled the growl of frustration that threatened to rise past his lips and watched in anger as the dark Lycan stalked toward the line of trees eager, it seemed, to finish what it'd started.

Growling now, Lore trembled with his anger, but he would not turn, he would not bring any attention to himself, indeed, for he knew not what the Lycan would do. And as for James. . . .

He dug his nails into the Earth as he eyed the limp legs of the man that, even from this distance, were not moving.

A lost cause, he thought angrily.

And as another shrill cry filled the sky some miles away from where he kneeled in grass, he lifted himself up to stand and turned from the dark Lycan as it descended on James at last.

※

Christian had long since disappeared from the straight path in a haze of her red light upon being pierced with the thought to return home, that perhaps there he could recover, place her somewhere safe. And now he walked, never tiring, toward the large piece of land that was his home.

He'd gravely ignored the wayward glances and glares of passing humans as he stepped along the crowded sidewalks, and he very nearly yelled at a drunken man who had tried, with surprising haste to pull the wrongly-clothed woman from his very arms.

He had, instead, shown great restraint, resorting only to a simple glare. The man had scurried away, dropping his almost empty bottle along the sidewalk where it had splattered loudly against the stone.

Mind fuddled on her state, what had rendered her unconscious again, he had not stopped in his venture to reach his home, his steps quickening with an ease he knew he would have never had in the daylight before he had taken her blood.

Before he had become the one whose words clung tight to her ear, guiding her, controlling her.

He shook his head as he reached the high gates to his home at last, not bothering to swing them wide. They already remained open along the dirt path, the high doors within the tall white structure shut against the morning.

Wondering why his gate was open at all, he stepped up the stairs, not bothering to drop the sword or shift her within his arms as he reached out a free hand to push down on a golden handle.

It swung wide with his push, the rush of fresh blood reaching his nose with little abandon.

"Bloody hell," he gasped, shaking his head again as the smell pressed against his mind, for he had forgotten the number of help he had hired when London had been restored to its former glory. He had forgotten, with the woman unconscious in his arms, a bloody Vampire, that he had needed the humans to feed. How long ago it all seemed.

He faltered on the doorstep as the cruel memory of the last time he had been here resurfaced, the sight of Alexandria blazing with a dignified anger had caused him to scowl with her precise ability to keep him from feeding.

He stared down at her delicate face, tufts of dark brown hair falling over her cheek and felt the small smile lift his lips.

"Master Delacroix?" the voice said in a relieved whisper from somewhere in front of him.

He tore his gaze from her reluctantly to watch the woman further down the hallway, her brown eyes wide with water, a lip, even from the distance, trembling.

He shifted Alexandria in his arms as he stepped over the threshold, willing the door to close behind him the moment he'd done so, his eyes still upon the young woman. Her blonde hair lay unbound along her shoulders, against her back, and she wore, not the required uniform that afforded him great sight upon her neck and shoulders, but a long, white dressing gown, slightly frayed at the ruffled collar and hem, rumpled as though she'd just fallen out of bed. Her feet were bare, quaint as they pressed against the cold floor, her steps long as she neared them.

It was dark here, the many candles and torches along the hallway's walls not yet lit for the day, and he realized with a start that she must have been terrified when they had not returned.

She stopped just before them, her arms folded across her abdomen as though to still their trembling though Christian thought it fruitful: her entire body shook, whether it was from fear or relief he could not be sure.

"I feared Miss Stone dead," she whispered, the words leaving her in a rush of shaky breath. She stared at the woman in his arms, a tear leaving an eye. It was not until she stared back upon him that he realized the girl had thought he had possibly harmed Alexandria.

The pit of anger bubbled in his throat. "She is alive," he said, somewhat defensively, "she just needs her rest."

"Does she, my Lord?" she said, her voice rising as a kind of terse anger appeared to cover her tongue. "Why is she c-covered in blood? And she's white as a sheet—" Her lips closed abruptly as her eyes widened further, though Christian were not sure how it was possible at all. "Y-you," she gasped, "y-you took her b-blood, didn't you?" And she raised an accusatory finger toward him as she stepped backwards, fear clear in her eyes.

"Wait," he said, beginning to step for her, "I didn't—it's all very hard to explain—"

"It's all quite simple!" she said as though lightning had struck her skull. And much to his growing horror, she opened her mouth wide and yelled at the top of her lungs, "Murder! Murder! Lady Stone is dead; Master Christian is a murderer!"

Oh for goodness sake.

Doors opened, footsteps pounded toward their location, and they did not have to wait long at all before the number of help had appeared in the long hall, many of them rubbing at red eyes, others tense with alarm, all of them staring in horror upon the pale woman in his arms.

And a woman Christian had seen a few hundred times since he and Xavier became what they were pushed through the crowd of new help, a large dark scar jutting down her right arm as she moved for him, the folds of her many grey skirts swishing around her ankles. She had her blond hair pushed haphazardly into a grey cap atop her head, her brown eyes narrowed upon Alexandria as though Christian didn't matter at all.

She stepped farther than anyone else, plump arms extending as though to take Alexandria in them. "What's happened?" she asked as she pulled Alexandria roughly from his grip. He eyed her in alarm as she shuddered upon feeling the woman in her arms, the cold of her skin, he knew, shocking to a human's warmth.

"My word," she gasped, trembling slightly, a dark understanding filling her brown eyes as she looked from Alexandria to him and back. "My *word*."

"Is—is she dead?" the maid from before asked as murmurs from the others flowed along the hallway toward them.

Christian stared, wondering what the woman would say, indeed, for her brown eyes so similar to James's darted back and forth from him to the maid as though she could summon unspoken thoughts to either of their minds. It was with a deep breath that she turned to him and said in a low voice so the others could not hear, "Wait in the white room, Master Delacroix, there are things we need to discuss."

He blinked, unsure he had heard her correctly when she turned from him in a whirl of skirts, Alexandria's hair and legs swaying around her arms as she did so. "Amelia, my dear," she began, addressing the young maid Christian remembered at once as the one he had failed in biting only days before, "accusations such as murder can get one in serious trouble. We must be far more careful in divulging dark fantasies, yes?"

He began to move for the double doors where the white living room waited in all its silent glory, when he felt all eyes upon him,

Amelia's as well. He had just made it but two steps before the crowd of frightened, confused humans when Amelia said, a sob ripping her throat, "But he tr-tried to kill me, Misses Alston! The day he and Lady Stone left, he—he—" but she did not go on, her voice dying with the look the plump woman bade her over Alexandria's body.

Christian's eyes narrowed upon her as well: Her glare was far too practiced, why, it was as if she'd have to give such a commanding look before. And then he saw it: The deep well of knowledge in the woman's eyes.

A Dark Creature? he thought in wonder, trying to remember if at all he smelled anything peculiar from the woman, but nothing would come to mind.

Eager to hear what James Addison's aunt would have to say about her state in all of this, for there it was, a whisper in the back of his greatly changed mind that she knew far more than she was ever letting on, he turned from them and pushed open the doors, the rush of energy within the white room greeting him as though impatient for his arrival.

Of course, he thought, stepping through, closing the door behind him to the continued stares and whispers of bemusement, *there was magic here.*

The white couch sat where it always had, several feet from the double doors. It faced the unused fireplace, the chandelier high above it glistening as the many candles placed just above the couch burned eternally.

Behind the couch remained the high bookshelves that reached the ceiling, the books upon them now appearing to glow with a low, golden light.

He stared at them for a few seconds, the spells seeming to pool before his very eyes, and why hadn't he seen it before?

"Bind the blood. . . ."

Of course, he thought, stepping for the long white couch. He sank into it as Dracula's words repeated in his mind, begging his obedience. Pushing them aside, he did his best to focus on what truly bothered him: Alexandria Stone.

Though she was just outside the doors, he had to admit it was utterly strange to be without her. He felt quite alone, now, far more than he had in months, and he found it amusing how much this did not startle him. *We are bound*, he thought absently, eyeing the sword as it pulsed in his hand, *by blood, by Dracula.*

"Enough of this nonsense! Lady Stone is fine! Now, you Amelia, I daresay your mind is heavily troubled!" the startlingly loud voice of James's aunt sounded from beyond the doors. "Get dressed and head on to your duties for the day! All of you!"

There was a scurry of footsteps, a sound of approval, and then a door opened.

He eyed it, watching as she stepped through the doorway, Alexandria still in her arms, her eyes alive with a passionate kind of fury, but she smiled slowly as she eyed him. He rose, the sword falling out of his grip onto the couch, and then he was just before her, reaching out to grasp Alexandria once again.

She relented, closing the door behind her once Alexandria was out of her arms. Shaking them, she did not look at him as she stepped swiftly past, moving for the back of the room where, he noticed for the first time the small table, upon which sat several plain cups, a silver pitcher beside them.

She poured the clear contents of the pitcher into one glass and downed it whole before wiping her mouth with the back of a now-trembling hand and absently patting her robes as she turned to him.

He had moved to the couch and lay Alexandria across it carefully, though he knew she didn't need careful anymore. Pulling his gaze from her, he stared at the human, his gaze narrowing. She had not moved from before the small table, had not once stared him in the eyes since she'd entered.

"Well Sarah?" he said, breaking the silence. "What do you know?"

She took a great breath as though heavily burdened with a great many secrets, and then closed her eyes.

"I know," she whispered, her eyes never opening against the chandelier's glow, "I know what you—what you and," she gasped with a great wrenching sob, "Lady Stone, a-are."

He did not dare betray his surprise. In the back of his mind, Dracula's voice continued, "*Repel it—*"

"And I know," Sarah went on, brave enough to move from the small table, stepping closer to the couch, the Vampires beyond it, "I know what Master Xavier is."

He merely stared, not desiring to leave Alexandria's side. "And how do you know what we are?"

"I would have to be a fool to not know what the Masters of the House are. I daresay," she sighed, wiping a tear, "I would have figured it out even if I hadn't been told."

"Told?"

"The rather handsome Count. Dracul, I believe his name was. He. . .rescued James from his father—"

Christian had let out a small snarl, pushing her into silence, confusion clouding his mind. "Dracula," he asked, unable to feign disbelief, "he's the one who told you what we are? How? When?" The Vampire had his nails deep in their home, this Christian had known, but why on Earth would he move this woman and her nephew here?

She smiled though it was weak, he noticed. "Far before I'd ever set foot here, I assure you, my Lord," and she waved a hand distractedly, sniffing. "It was because of James—his family—my sister, were prominent in London. James's. . .father," and her stare darkened upon him, her bottom lip still quivering, ". . .I'd long since told my sister he couldn't possibly be human. I had my suspicions of course. . .but I knew for sure when I met Count Dracul. He was not. . .natural. He moved with the same grace you and your brother do. . .held the same. . .ghostly glow."

"James Addison came from a prominent family?"

"Yes, yes, he did," and she sighed, her tears seemingly losing their ability to fall, "and it was his father who caused the unease in Count Dracul. Like I said, I'd told my sister he wasn't right, but she, blinded by his riches, his good looks, got swept up in his tales of adventure, of leading his 'pack,' whatever that meant.

"But when I met Count Dracul. . .I had my fears realized. It turned out Lord Reginald Addison—turns out he'd killed the original Lord Reginald and took his place—was a *Lycon* or something like that. The Count told me the man turned into a beast—I thought it outlandish, naturally, I didn't pay heed.

"It was not until my dear sister bore a child that I saw Lord Reginald's true colors." And her face paled greatly with a new thought.

He did not want to disturb the woman and her memories, but he needed to hear what low thought had begun to take shape in his mind, had to have it confirmed. "Misses Alston?"

She blinked, a tear falling from an eye as her gaze focused. "H-he. . .he was a beast, truly. Count Dracul told me to go to their manor on a particular night, he accompanied me, of course—but the reason he wanted me to go to their manor was to see the monster Lord Reginald was.

"I. . .knocked, per his request, and, I admit, curious to Count Dracul's motives for leading me there that night, I allowed myself a great skepticism. My dear sister was well endowed with child, and though kind, I saw the protective glare the man gave her when within my presence."

"And where was Dracula—er, Dracul?"

"It was odd. He was there when I knocked but he was gone when the door opened. Another of you. . .Vampires' gifts, I imagine. But it was the strangest thing. . .well, perhaps not so strange, but while I shared a cup of tea that night with Lord and Lady Addison, I felt the strongest of gazes on me."

A thoughtful silence pressed on between them, nothing but the steady glow of red causing anything to move.

It was not until she wiped at her cheeks that he said, "You saw something in this Lord Reginald that warranted reasoning to think him a Lycan, Misses Alston?"

"Oh yes, yes," her hands wringing above her skirts, "it was later that I saw his true face. Several months later. James had just been born. . .but a mere babe, the most beautiful child. I had had no contact with Count Dracul for all this time, but when James was just a year, he emerged with a letter, suggesting rather nicely I go with him to Lord Reginald's manor one last time.

"I cannot tell you why I agreed to go, Master Christian. . .but I realized only in hindsight that Count Dracul had an uncanny knack for willing others to do precisely what he wanted them to. Nevertheless, I was most surprised when he did not disappear when I knocked on the door."

She began to pace before the couch, her hands continuing their nervous clasp as she went on, "The moment Reginald saw him he. . .he became a beast—a monster, Master Christian. And the Count. . .he changed as well."

"What do you mean, changed?" he asked, thinking back to when he had grasped the sword after taking her blood, had seen the young Alexandria before the empty fireplace, the large winged Creature just outside her window.

"He changed," she said simply, "his face was no longer handsome but contorted in a kind of sickening anger. They attacked each other, destroyed the manor—I hid with the baby in a cupboard until it was over.

"The Count came to get me. . .covered in blood," she shuddered, "it was ghastly. He told me that I would be taking the boy with me— that I would work for a man who would protect me from more. . .what did you say, Lycans? That James would be safe."

"And his mother?"

"Dead, unfortunately. He'd killed her in the battle. I saw the claw marks on her chest—Count Dracul, whatever he is, you are, wouldn't have been able to make those marks. . .and he's been so good to me and James. . . ."

They fell into silence once more, a deafening number of questions pulling at Christian's mind. *Dracula provoked the Lycan in order to get James. James must be protected. But why?*

Alexandria's light brightened for a moment as if in answer before dimming to its usual steady glow causing his gaze to fall upon her. Her eyes still remained closed, her chest no longer heaving with the need for air. She no longer looked as though she slept, but that she was dead, and he found the sight immensely troubling.

Taking his stare from her, he eyed the full woman. "When Eleanor Black attacked London and the rest of the help were pulled from the manor, why weren't you?" He recalled with a terrible vividness the sight of the manor as they'd approached it amidst the destruction those weeks before. It remained upright, unlike all other buildings in London, but the windows had been broken, the furniture within overturned, but there had been no sign of anyone inside besides her.

She had been wrapped in a soft, white circle of light within her bed, had apparently not heard any commotion at all, and when questioned by Christian on just what had happened, why she had been unharmed, she had only been able to look at him in dumbfounded bemusement.

But she lifted a shaking hand to her face again and he saw it, the small golden ring around one of her fingers, within it a single black gem, terribly tiny, but quite obvious what it was the longer he stared.

She opened her mouth to respond when he said it for her, "Dracula."

She nodded.

The lengths he would go to ensure all those who help him stay alive in some form. . . .

He stared down at Alexandria, marveling once more on her state. A bloody Vampire. And what was James meant to do? The son of a Lycan. . .how curious it was that he had not shown any signs at all until bitten by Lore. . . .

"Sarah," he said, causing the woman to jump; apparently she'd been lost in further thought, "why would this Count want to save James? Why would he be important?"

She blinked. "I cannot say, Master Christian. I never asked. I merely counted my blessings and never looked back as one does when a. . .strange Creature protects them and keeps them alive."

"Of course," he agreed.

They said nothing more for quite some time, both lost in pressing thought, and it was not until she drank her fourth glass of water, barely paying a mind to where she poured it, that she excused herself, leaving Christian to an ever-growing world of disturbing thought.

Chapter Six

THE MAGICAL ADVANTAGE

Equis Equinox waved a hand, smiling as the swish of blue and green light appeared atop his fingers, trailing in the air as he moved. The sense of peace that had filled him when he'd taken the magic back had been profound; he'd known the moment he taken the blood that he would never need to sleep again. He had slept, he knew, for far too long as it was.

Merriwall glowed with the regained, magical air, the burst of light from above his home sending out is periodic spark, telling all Enchanters, all magically-abled Creatures, indeed, that magic was once again where it belonged.

It will be a matter of time, he thought, staring out the high window that overlooked his city, *before this awful dread is dispelled.*

For he already had his men on it, had already sent word to the other towns and cities, reserves and guilds. He was coming.

He had known it would be the only way to regain the true power needed to preside over the Vampires, the Lycans; show up, and the World would fall at his feet.

He clicked two long fingers in the air, the man appearing in the next moment, hands pressed together before himself, his robes long, deep green as he kneeled atop the silver carpet of the room.

Equis turned to observe him, noticed the way his long shoulders were no longer hunched, his long blonde hair no longer unkempt, and when he looked up from his kneel, Equis was pleased to see his black eyes were shining with freedom, power unmatched.

"Your Greatness," the Enchanter said.

"Cleaner," he said, waving a hand, bidding the man to stand, "you and your cohorts must begin to cleanse the World for me. No longer shall you clean the blood-drenched messes of those Vampires, nor will you remove the debris left from those dreadful beasts—you will, as per my desire—only mend what must be mended, save what must be saved, that is your fellow Enchanters, the humans, Syran rest their souls, and yes, the Elves. For I believe their. . .beauty shall return when they are not clouded as we all are in this," he sniffed distastefully, "dread."

"Yes, Lord Equis," the Cleaner said, and already his hands were weaving expertly through the air, sending, Equis knew, the new orders to every corner of Merriwall.

He moved from the window, leaving the blinding light of the two suns, the artificial light created that still blared periodically from above his expansive home. He stepped slowly for the man, wiping away a strand of his long black hair from his shoulders, and with a smile, adjusted the glowing silver crown atop his head, long since cleaned and placed, he felt with absolute pride, where it should have been all these miserable years.

"And Cleaner," he said once the man had stopped moving his hands in an odd flourish, "you shall accompany me to Shadowhall. I desire to see what more my brothers have. . .accomplished there. . .what they shall think about the excessive power given to them."

At this the man looked quite affronted, and Equis thought he knew why. Nevertheless, he let the man open a hesitant mouth, if only to say, "But, your Greatness. . .is not Madame Mastcourt to attend this trip with you? I am but a mere Cleaner. . .I do not have the importance, nay, the *means* to travel to Shadowhall. . .their Arts are far above my head, surely."

"Philistia, dear sweet Philistia. An asset to my hand she has been these years. . .running behind my back as she will to keep dear Merriwall afloat. . .but no," and he allowed the folds of his black robes to sweep across the soft floor, "she is not what I believe I need now. She has done a great service to me, yes, but I fear her intentions lie. . .elsewhere. And Shadowhall is not so bad, truly," he said, bidding the man a most comforting stare, "the Enchanters there are merely versed in the most wonderful Arts of concealment, brilliance, and my personal favorite, assassination."

At this the man paled further and Equis rethought his importance on the trip at all, but not before the man was saying, "You plan to *kill* the Vampires, the Lycans?" As if it were impossible. . .as if, Equis thought with a slight smile, it should have never been believed.

"Yes that is what I said when you first appeared, have you not been paying attention? The Vampires, the Lycans, they will fall to the might that is magic, dear Cleaner. And the best way to reassert our dominance over these. . .monsters is to remind them who can cripple them, remove from them their 'gifts,' and render them immobile! Us!

"You may not be privy to the true extent of our power, young one," he continued, "but do know, your great leader was a force in his day before the Phoenixes grew. . .adventurous. We will spread this force just as they have taken it from us. Now come, prepare your things—we leave for Shadowhall immediately."

And he watched with further amusement as the Cleaner disappeared from the room, his eyes shining with excitement, but also fear of the unknown. But Equis knew, deep in his rather large heart, that this was just what his people needed. *Excitement. Fear.*

And he turned his gaze to the window where his city shined far more brilliantly than it had in many, many centuries.

Adventure.

⁜

Philistia Mastcourt had watched the Vampire sleep, his fitful stirrings alerting her to the force with which the Vampires had ruled.

They had been most at ease, she'd noted, the red-haired Vampire turning atop the rather uncomfortable bed. It was clear in the way he murmured his need for blood every several minutes or so. *Accustomed to their access*, she thought, wrapping a long leg around the other within the incredibly hard chair the Vampire had vacated almost an hour ago.

But Mister Vivery, she recognized, bore another access most Vampires would never understand. And to have it removed. . .ripped from his senses. . .it must have been dreadful.

Yes, he had grown in his ability as an Enchanter, this she could tell from her remarkably brief meeting held with the Creature several, several years before. He had been beaming with pride, then, joyful, to be at Dracula's side. *Confidante, helper. . .pet.*

She closed her eyes as the thought returned, and with a slight shift in her chair the air grew dense, so immensely thick she rather felt she would never be able to breathe again, but she waited, waving a hand periodically to assist in the air returning to this room. Assist, but it would not do a thing. Not a thing against his anger.

For he was angry.

Angry she escaped him shortly after his power had returned.

Angry she had revived the Vampire at all.

For she was very aware Equis knew what she had done, after all, magic had returned to him, every spell, every curse was now tied directly to him, and he would know when they were cast. . .if only eluded to the where.

But that, she grimaced, *would come in time as well*. For Equis and his gifts were his very joy, and to have it all back—all of it, indeed— would bring him a thrill unmatched. And she knew he would not rest until it was all truly returned to him.

No, she thought, rising from the chair at long last, her bottom sore from sitting for far too long an hour, *he would be brilliant, again. Mad. . .yes, but brilliant.*

And she, and the few other Enchanters not stricken with anger at the Vampires' waning hold, the few other Enchanters who remembered Equis's. . .iron-clad rule and did not wish to return to it, would ensure his power never resumed its prominence. The World would suffer for it in a different way. . .Eleanor Black's. . .madness be damned.

"Mister Vivery," she said, rapping him on a shoulder, the thin curtain draped across the window doing a rather poor job of hiding the many suns from view. The light still filtered through the worn fabric and reached the Vampire, though it was not enough to cause burning.

"Nathanial!" she said louder still when the Vampire would not rise. "I wish I could let you rest longer, but there is little time for it! We must begin your training!"

A groan left his lips, his eyes fluttering against her sharp taps, but still they would not open in full. "Nathanial! The fate of the World rests on your shoulders—you—must—get—up!" And with those four significantly harder taps, his eyes flew open, a frenzied kind of despair filling them as he sprang upward, hands outstretched, clawing for something she could not know.

She stepped away, his fingers curling into fists as an angry snarl left his lips. He stared at her, his gray eyes hidden in the shadow the light created, inscrutable thoughts filling them. "Fate of the World, now, is it?" he whispered, his voice strained.

She took another step away; his eyes no longer gray the more he glared. They were red.

"Yes," she said, desiring to keep her wits about her, "you must be trained how to withstand the increased magic that fills the World. . .in order to better fight against it."

"Without," he said, another snarl leaving his lips, "having any of my own, is that it?"

She knew the answer would anger him further, her lips remaining closed against his stare. And how ravenous it was. But it made no sense; he'd just downed a whole jar of Unicorn Blood but an hour ago, could he truly still be so rapt with thirst?

"Yes," she whispered at last.

True to her thoughts, he moved from the bed with ease, tufts of gray ash falling to the floor at his feet. When he stood, it was upon both legs and she felt a sliver of relief that the blood worked, yet also a trill of fear; he was staring upon her as though she were a rather glorious meal one devoured only on the most special of occasions, and she did not desire at all to be his food.

"How," he croaked, licking his lips, "will this training play out if I am to defend myself against magic, having none for my own?"

She swallowed, allowing the fear to dissipate, quite sure it would do little good to indulge it, especially before a Vampire most keen to its nature. Staring him head on, she said, "Having known the Enchanting Arts, you stand a better chance than any Vampire to successfully defend yourself against our wills. You will be able to use your abilities to deflect, and perhaps even resist whatever spells we throw at you."

He surveyed her as though she were mad for several moments, and she thought he were to step forward and play on his bloodlust when he sighed deeply, the wind reaching her in a cold flurry, sending the scrolls held stop the small table to roll to the floor. They skittered across the hard surface, but she barely noticed them, he was speaking.

"And blood?" he asked, though to her it sounded much like an impatient snarl. "Will I be allowed to feed during this training?"

"I have ordered my connection in Lane to send you vast amounts of Unicorn Blood. It should have to do until we leave Merriwall. . .until you are ready."

He seemed displeased by the idea of having to rely on the beautiful Creature's blood, but the words that left his lips belied the confusion she felt, "Leave Merriwall? Where are we going?"

Of course, she reminded herself, *he has no idea.* Squaring her shoulders, she took a simple step to him, allowing the snarl that escaped him with her movements to wash over her. Instead of spiking her fear, it merely subsided; if he had wanted to harm her, he would have. Would have when he first awoke.

"To Lane," she whispered, seeing the way his burrowed brow rose in surprise, "Mister Cross has convinced his Guild to embrace the madness that surrounds our World. They will aid us. . .aid you in your commitment to seeing Xavier Delacroix to the Goblet."

The multitude of questions swam in his eyes, no longer red, but a chilling gray. *Curious. But of course, his eyes would no longer glow with the magical wonder.* "Cross," he said, the hunger subsiding just the slightest in light of his bemusement, "that is the Enchanter that has been my master, isn't it?"

She frowned. "You never knew his name, Nathanial?"

"No."

"But why—" *Ah.* "Dracula desired it as such, I take it?"

He merely nodded.

How curiously the Vampire treated his projects. Enveloping her mind with focus, she eyed the purple light as it floated before her eyes and then seeped into her irises, her thoughts sharpening, tunneling until the only thought that mattered was front and center, keeping her immensely aware.

She stepped for him, ignoring the instinctive snarl that left his lips, and placed a gloved hand upon his back, turning swiftly for the door.

The leather did not still the cold of his skin from reaching her beneath the glove, but, the spell cast, she gently pushed him toward the white door, eager to see his skill against the greater magic, though it was not hope that spurred this eagerness.

Hope was for fools.

It was, and perhaps it was merely the spell working itself upon her mind, the satisfaction she would achieve when this was all over, action the thing that made betraying the most powerful Creature in the World almost. . .endurable.

⁂

He tensed beneath her hand, snarling with the desire for blood. Oh, how he needed it. How it tore at his brain, his throat, his veins. . . *Damn!*

He did not remember the desire being this. . .overwhelming when magic ran through his blood, filled his mind. Was that why it was unbearable, this thirst? Or had he merely forgotten—forgotten what it meant to be only a Vampire, burned by the sun, pushed to the dark, cast to the dead, the blood, the damning desire?

Stifling the urge as best he could, he felt her hand press harder against his back, pushing him toward the door; Nathanial allowing his mind to wander, hoping it would distract the great need that burned through him despite the waning taste of the blue blood still on his tongue, for all the good it did.

Blood. . .blood. . .blood. . . .

"Vampires hold the art," the beautiful woman at his side was saying as they stepped into the larger room where he had been driven to his knees by the exceedingly tall Creature several hours before, "of repelling, consuming, attracting. . . ." She swept her free hand lazily, the large windows immediately getting covered with their thick curtains, casting the large hall in complete darkness.

He had but a second to blink upon the dark before many long, thin candles were hovering in the air, lit as though summoned to life by a powerful will.

He turned to her in the orange glow about the entire room, a gasp escaping his lips, for her eyes, once brilliant and brown, were now glowing a strange golden color. "But are not familiar with the art of subduing, truly attacking. . .gaining power from their opposition without needing to take their life. We," and her hand rested upon his shoulder now, glowing a faint green, "Enchanters. . .we are able to hold the gift. . .and so much more. You, Nathanial, will learn how to look past these instinctive traits of your kind and think with the precision, the logic, of a magically-abled Creature, although you, yourself can no longer. . .house these gifts."

If she had any idea her words stung heavily on his already pained soul, she did not show it: Her glowing gaze held his strongly, and for a brief second he thought himself to float on a cloud it was so light his body became.

"Allow this desire for blood that holds you in its grip to move you," she was whispering to him from somewhere. . .somewhere beyond here, "move you beyond the need, feel the pain. . .embrace it, but do not let it take you."

He did not know when he closed his eyes, but the light of the many candles had vanished from his vision, the floating sensation strengthening the more her voice reigned on all around him, comforting, soothing. . .and yet, the great need to drink would not be quelled.

"You must use it, Nathanial. Use your bloodlust, but focus on what it gives you, focus on that drive and place it beyond you, beyond your need for blood. . .do this. . .and defend yourself because I will attack."

He fell to the hard ground with a slam, his eyes widening as the pain surged through his spine, the snarl leaving his lips. Confusion pulsing through him, he jumped to his feet, brow furrowing. She wasn't before him, indeed, looking around the large room, steadily illuminated here and there, brightening parts of the long couch, sparse tables, high shelves, she didn't seem to be anywhere at all.

He tensed, the ever-present need for blood gnawing at his brain, but what had she said? He found her words drifting from his mind, the light feeling leaving his body, a heaviness replacing it, consuming it—

He fought the insufferable urge to be driven to his knees once more, for there was no powerful Ancient Creature here to take his blood, but there was a highly-skilled Enchanter. . . .

He smelled the cool air, unable to gain a hint of her scent, her blood. But how strange. She couldn't be able to simply disappear from his traces. . .physical or otherwise. He'd never known a Creature to be capable of it before; there was always a scent left, always a whisper of energy to be sought out. . . .

He frowned. *Energy won't help me, now.*

"Vampire," the voice whispered, and he whirled on the spot, eyes widening upon her long, slender frame. She was draped across the couch, her head propped up in her hand to stare at him over the tips of her shoes. They hung over the armrest closest to him.

"Madame," he began, the sudden smell of her causing a snarl to leave his throat, "what is this?"

"What?" she responded coolly, never rising from her position atop the cushions. "Haven't you been listening, Nathanial? In order to beat the Enchanters, you must be able to repel them, and I'm sorry to say that an Enchanter at their true power will be able to still a Vampire. Now, *pay attention*. What has happened since we entered this hall?"

He stared at her, a candle most near her head casting a small light over her piercing, vibrant eyes, her dark skin, red lips. . . He blinked as she shifted atop the couch, and then remembered what she'd asked.

"You closed the curtains to still the sun from entering—"

"For your benefit. . . ."

"—you cast candles to let me see, no, no for yourself to see—"

"Yes, yes, what more?"

"—and you. . . ." he remembered the feel of her hand upon his back, "you cast a spell on me—an Enchantment, I believe—"

"Oh? And what does this supposed Enchantment do for you, Mister Vivery?"

He hesitated, racking his mind so overwhelmed with the desire for blood, he could feel it start to pound with a maddening pressure. *At this rate, I will die for good.* "It. . .it," but he could not recall the Enchantment, nor, he realized with a terrible sinking feeling in his gut, any other spell of any kind—it was all gone.

Damn, damn, think! Think!

He eyed her smile, wide as it was, refusing to be tricked, to be taken under, indeed, but hadn't it already happened? Wasn't he in the midst of her spell right now? But why—why would she spell him? For what? And what had she said before?

And the words returned, her voice cool and steady in his ear once more: "*Use your bloodlust. . .focus on what it gives you. . .place it beyond you, beyond your need for blood. . .do this. . .and defend yourself. . .I will attack.*"

"Attack," he said before he could think of anything else, "the spell you cast prepares me to be attacked."

And she was gone.

He dared to blink, figuring his sight—so dizzied with the ravenous need for blood—had waned for a moment, when he felt her behind him, her presence strong, though she laid not a hand on him, and he quickly sought his memory for anything to do against a rear threat.

His time training with other young Vampires did not seem to want to be recalled, no, it was rather much like it had never happened, indeed, the blank space where the memory of Enchanters and Vampires training should have surfaced, drew a great sense of horror to canvas his body. *All of it, gone.*

He heard the whisper at his ear, the spell a number of letters he could not recall ever knowing, but deep in his mind, he *knew* he had, once. Should have known. It was why he was moderately surprised to find himself face down upon the hard floor, a pressing wind all around him, blurring his cold and the sudden cold of the room together in a rushed mess of pressure that held him flat, unable to move at all.

Why can't I remember?

"Don't bother," the voice from above said, though it was not cold, it was rather calm, even welcoming, "it is kept from you because you must get used to being a full Vampire again. You will never hold the magical power, now focus on what *matters*, Mister Vivery. *Your* power."

How the bloody hell am I supposed to—

A hard weight, much like a rather large foot was upon his back, and he felt his spine shift out of place ever the slightest. A shot of pain rang up his spine, his chest suddenly burning against the weight. Before he could utter his surprise, blood left his lips, spilling down the side of his mouth to rest messily upon the floor.

"You must understand the weight of what it is you will undergo," she was saying from the same spot within the darkness. *So what was upon me?* "And you must come to terms with the fact that you are clear fodder for the Enchanters of this World, now. Easily," the pressure grew heavier, a low groan escaping his throat, "reduced to your natural state—dead."

And with that, the need for blood grew terribly prominent. It was all he could feel; all he could smell—

He was before her in the next moment, his own blood boiling in his veins, the sight of her, tainted red and smiling looming before him through the punctured dark.

And there it was. The voice of Dracula, soft and unyielding, a far cry from the voice he had heard when the Vampire was alive, ferocious, scared.

"Nathanial, my magic-child. Clear the path for me to the cup—let us end this, end this for good."

The image of the brown eyes so darkened with grief, with guilt filled his mind next, the memory of the old Vampire, the very first, indeed, standing just before him atop the mountain, white hair whipped wildly in a torrential wind as they looked down, down upon the sleeping Dragons, white, red, black, green, clouds of black smoke leaving their nostrils, oblivious to the fresh cold the Vampires had carried there in their wake. . . .

He remembered Dracula jumping off the mountain to land without a sound upon the black, soft Earth beside a Dragon's talons, fear full in his dead heart, then.

But hadn't the Vampire looked back up at him with, of all things, a wide smile, begging him forward with a simple nod of his head?

And hadn't he, against all greater judgment, indeed, followed in the Vampire's maddening footsteps, wherever they led?

"Well, Nathanial," the voice of Philistia said, pulling him from his thoughts; her smile gone, instead she looked regretful, as if she had made a mistake, "do you understand what you must undergo?"

He cracked his neck, the blood surging through his veins, the need strong at his throat, but there, always there, was the Great Vampire, silently, pleadingly, begging him forward. Always forward.

"For the preservation and peace of the World, Vivery," he had said one weary night in his office after they had just returned from escaping several angry Elves and Enchanters, who had not liked them attempting to free their captured Fae, *"we always do what must be done."*

And with this thought, it all became quite clear, despite the pain that thundered through his skull: Dracula chose Xavier Delacroix in his place, and these Enchanters far beyond their best wishes were seeing to it that the Vampire reached the Goblet before Equis or Eleanor could. And he, forever bidden to Dracula's side. . .was it not his duty to see the King, nay, the Dragon, to his rightful place?

"For the preservation and peace of the World, Madame," he said, wiping the blood that dripped from his chin, "I understand."

Chapter Seven

THE CREATURES OF OLD

Eleanor Black had not moved for Damion Nicodemeus until the morning. She had not desired to see the Vampire again—indeed, she had never thought she would *ever* see him again. Not after seeing him in the woods before the entrance to the Vampire City. And now, having given her orders to the budding armies that remained, seeing Victor Vonderheide off, she knew she could not put it off any longer.

She stared at the dark stone double doors, smelling his blood on the air. *Breached*, she thought in wonder. *Let us see how he pulled this off, shall we?*

And she placed a hand on the cold stone, prepared to push against it when the thought occurred to her to gather Javier. She had not seen him since she'd returned to her caves, and now in his absence did she realize the strained comfort he'd afforded her. True, he was not a full Elite, but he was enough in the way his sycophantic air would remind her of what it would be when Xavier would return to her side.

Return, she thought, directing it on the air toward him, *and be mine.*

With a sigh, she pushed against the door and it slid against the dirt ground with ease, the fresher scent of weak, cold blood reaching her nose along with the new wind of her throne room.

She blinked in the light of the ball above the dark throne, and stepped into the room, the torches light shedding their orange glow across the wet stone, the muddy ground. To the right of her throne was Damion, his head down, black hair hiding his features, but his cloak, his clothes were badly burned, revealing his dark skin through their holes, and in the white light above his head, the faintness of the orange glare of the torches most near him, she could see the blood in the golden thing he held in a trembling dark hand atop his lap.

Amazing. Stepping deeper into the room, she closed the door with a foot, not desiring to take her eyes off him. He had proven himself much more formidable than she would have dared believe him capable by merely being here—but to *take* the Goblet?

Clasping her hands before herself she stared at the weak Vampire and wondered why he did not lift his head. "I never thought we'd see each other again," she admitted.

The shudder was visible through his shoulders with her voice, and he slowly looked up, a gasp leaving her lips. He'd been badly beaten, that much was apparent. There was a great gash across an eye, and many bruises along his face, but she was able to register a look terror as it passed across him. "El-Eleanor," was the whisper that passed his bloody lips, "pl-please."

The blood in the Goblet swayed against its golden rim but it did not spill over. She narrowed her eyes upon the way his hand shook around it as it clasped it. Seemingly unable to release it. "Please, Damion?" she asked, stepping closer. He stiffened atop his knees with her movement and she smelled his blood, sickly, weak. *Scared.*

"Don't," was the muffled reply, and he shuffled backwards against the stone dais and she heard the jingle of chains.

Ceasing her steps, she stared at him closer still and saw the black chains fastened to a leg of the throne, the shackle rusted and bloody around an ankle. Her eyes widened. "I won't. . .come any closer," she said, staring at the Goblet, its blood that never spilled, "but what—how did you get in here? How did you get past the barrier—get your hands on that. . .on the—"

A low breath left him and it reached her in a cold wind. "Darien. . .left m-me here," and he licked his lips, "I-I can't drop this bloody cup."

"Why," she tried again, eyeing the way he would not meet her gaze, "did you come to get this. . .cup?"

"It wasn't the cup," he said, a harsh cough leaving his throat; blood splattered against the dirt at her boots, "I came to find my bloody ch-charge."

What? "Charge? What are you talking about?"

He looked up, his eyes appearing to water in the light. "Lucien," he hissed, blood flying through his lips, "I searched for him. I ran into Xavier—the others—*your*. . .Creatures. And then Darien came. Took me here. I s-smelled Lucien here within your walls but I never—he never. . . ." He looked down at the Goblet in his hand and let out a weak snarl. "This bloody cup!" And with all the ferocity of a man lost to his mind rose to his feet, straining against his shackles, and lifted the Goblet above his head, bringing it down with force. It merely clashed against his thigh and he wailed in pain, the blood within never spilling over, indeed.

As he sank to his knees in futility, she touched the many necklaces at her throat, wildness reaching her. "Damion," she said once his whimpers died. He stared upon her once again with the look of one who stared upon their idol, yet there was great fear within his brown eyes as well. "What you hold in your grasp is a very powerful Artifact I succeeding in taking from Dracula—"

"Then why," he roared, much to her surprise, "can I not release it? Why does it stick to my hand? *Why does it burn?!* What, Eleanor, is this *accursed* magic?" And to her further surprise, as she watched, he cried. Deep and loudly he cried, wailing at the top of his lungs, his sobs resounding against the walls and her ears, and she closed her eyes.

Of course, she thought in wonder, *of course he would be reduced to this, a sniveling mess when faced with the Goblet's power.* Indeed, she did not even feel he knew what it was he held. *The gift of my transformations.*

She opened her eyes before long, his sobs long subsided, and she smiled, a confused expression passing across his own battered face. Before he could ask what was wrong, she said, "You hold the key to my power, my dear Damion, in your hand. You cannot remove it because," she sighed, stepping closer to him, ignoring his shift away, the chain keeping him in place, "it is bound to you, now."

She was just before him now, and he'd shrank against the throne, shivering with his fear. The chain rattled as his legs, now free from their place beneath his behind, scraped against the ground, and much to her bemusement he wrapped his hands, and the Goblet, around a leg of the throne as if he were to be whisked away should he let go.

"Are you truly so scared of me?" she wondered aloud. When no answer came on the strangled air, she went on, "Why would you be searching for Lucien Caddenhall in my home, Damion?"

He softened just the slightest, and with his needless breath, she smelled it. The faintest traces of Alexandria Stone's blood. She narrowed her eyes as he said, "We know you have Dracula's sword," he said, coughing against the stone of the throne, "I had the boy move here to gather it—he never returned."

Dracula's sword? "What would you want with the Ares, Damion?"

His eyes turned red in the light, but he did nothing more than snarl. "Its power, Eleanor," he said coldly. "I know you remember it just as I—that power we stumbled across in his training room! Just there—the gem glowing in that red light—I know you remember."

She smiled as it returned. Yes, she had seen the sword glow with the Vampire in the bowels of the Great Vampire's bloodied room. It had spurred her desire to further uncover his secrets, but she had not been as surprised by the sword's glowing appearance as Damion had been. Why, she'd thought him shaken, and not in a way that inspired further inquiry; how interesting it was that he'd harbored the idea that the sword held power—power more than what he held in his own bloody grip, surely?

"What. . .of the sword, Damion?"

At this, he slunk off the throne, the Goblet clattering against the floor as he straightened himself to sit upright. "It's power—that gem. Surely, you remember! Did you not hear that power, those voices?"

An eyebrow rose in question as she stared down at him. "Damion. . .you heard voices when you laid eyes upon the sword?"

At this he shuddered again though she knew not the reason for it, and looked up, his red eyes shining in the light above the throne. "Yes—those voices—they said, they said, 'Protect,' 'Protect,'" and he sighed, "I cannot remember. But what magic do you know that projects such. . .resounding voices, Eleanor?"

Many. Aloud, she said, "I did not hear any such voices when we laid eyes upon it. I thought it merely an interesting. . .weapon. But for you to come all the way here, indeed, it must have moved you incredibly."

He said nothing but snarled, and she focused her thoughts on Javier, willing him to come forward with the sword. And it was not long at all before one of the stone doors flew open and Javier stepped to her side, but when she turned to look at him, she was surprised to find he held no sword in his hand.

"Where is it?" she asked.

His gaze was on Damion as he said, "Thomas Montague left with it about two days ago, your Grace."

She blinked in the light, unsure if she were seeing him clearly. "I beg your pardon?"

He turned to her, his blue eyes shining in the light of the torches, a glimmering knowing within them. *What an excellent Lycan he would make.* "Thomas Montague has the sword last I am aware," he said.

"And you did not stop him from moving with it?"

"He moved with it to stop Alexandria Stone. I don't know what he did with it. He has yet to return."

She stared at him in disbelief. "Find him," she said after a while, "and bring him to me." *Lost. Again. Damn.*

Javier bade Damion one dark look before stepping from the room, the large stone door closing behind him.

At the air that blew into the room, Damion's hair lifted from his shoulders, revealing his red eyes. He was staring at the Goblet in his hand, and Eleanor wondered what she should do with him exactly.

If he drank from the Goblet, he would surely render all her plans obsolete. *All of us human,* she thought. *Disgusting. Weak.* And a shiver that had nothing to do with the Vampire's cold glare descended her spine. And then the static returned, an abhorrent nothingness in her mind, and she did her best to push it out, dispel it, indeed, but it grew, and she felt it leave her mind and drift down to her heart.

As it touched it, her mind grew hot and she felt it again, felt her arms begin to grow—

She turned from Damion at once, holding her hands in front of her before it could get worse, before he could see it. "I will be back for you, Damion," she said to the doors, "and we will talk about these voices you are hearing." *For I hear none.* And she stepped from him, his scream of fear, rage, perhaps clawing in her ears.

※

He shuffled to the old door, his cane tapping loudly atop the stone steps, and he knew the Vampire heard, but if he moved forward, Arminius did not know it. All was silent beyond the black wood.

With his free hand he pushed down on the long handle and stepped over the threshold, the sight of the large Vampire within the armchair most near the door welcome, if only uncomfortable. He knew the questions were coming, knew they were just beneath the Vampire's blood-deprived tongue.

He allowed the door to close and closed his eyes as the first question reached his ears:

"Any luck on locating the Vampire, Arminius?"

"You know it better than I, Noble," he answered, limping toward the other armchair before the steadily burning fire, "Xavier Delacroix does not want to be found."

"That may be true after all," Nicholai said, and Arminius raised an eyebrow as he sank into the chair with a grunt, but before he could ask what the Vampire meant, he went on, "he arrived here shortly after you took off. With two of Eleanor's men no less. He stood over Joseph Gail's body, smiling, Arminius. I told him to wait for you here, but he flew off toward the rocks without a word."

He sat forward in the uncomfortable chair, a low wheezing breath leaving his chest as he did. Ignoring the pain that blanketed his unharmed leg, and the undoubtable fact that he was much too old to run about the Dark World for the Great Vampire anymore, he said, "Do you feel him hopeless, Nicholai?"

"Hopeless?" he repeated, the word appearing foreign along his lips. Arminius knew the Vampire, bathed in Dracula's protection as he had been, had perhaps never truly felt hopeless, had never had a reason to doubt the old Vampire's word. . . "It is hard to say—we need to reach the others at any rate, and I grow most tired of sitting here, Elf."

And there he could see it. The Vampire's blue eyes were darkened slightly in the orange light of the cottage, the thin curtains before the windows blocking what little sun desired to leak through. He could see the listlessness the Vampire held on his shoulders, on his face; gone was the formidable Vampire risen to secret ranks of greatness within the Vampire World, here sat, Arminius knew, a Creature most lost in damning thought, perhaps for far too long. And Arminius could not blame him, for what he knew, what he had endured. . .it would have been enough to make any lesser Creature end their life for good.

And he recalled, with all too great an ease, the sight of the winged, many-fanged monster that was Dracula, in truth, standing before an utterly horrified Nicholai, the terribly large claw stretched forth to grasp the Vampire. . .how he had shouted in his anger, "*All of you—disappointments!*"

Disappointments. All of them? All of us? For that was what, he was sure, the Creature had meant. All the Dark Creatures picked and chosen for their special skill in various undertakings, all had failed him in some form, hadn't they?

He recalled in the new silence what he had gathered about the remaining Creatures of the Order of the Dragon: Peroneous's potion; Dragor's hand with the Nicodemeus brothers; Aurora Borealis's spell upon the Delacroix brothers to keep them unaware their father had turned them. And indeed, with the thought of Aleister, he recalled how he had discovered the scarred Vampire's position with Dracula's Enchanter-Vampire project. All Creatures tied to the Vampire's hand through some way of trick or spell to ensure he had countermeasures for his bloody countermeasures.

And how, he thought, staring upon the flames, *were we all disappointments?*

Yes, they had not moved at once to guide Xavier back to Evert, yes, they had been removed from each other for the greater part of a month since Dracula died, and yes, Xavier had been acting strangely if Nicholai's words from earlier were true, but where was he moving to? And were the others with him?

"Disappointments," he breathed, wondering what on Earth Dracula had meant. It was known far and wide by now that he desired the Goblet of Existence to drink from, to help his Creatures, the Lycans regain humanity in full, to end the needless death and darkness that fell over the land, but he had spoken in the memory, then, of giving the Vampire a chance. . . .

"I granted you the bloody name Noble, hoping that you would be the one to help! You would be the one—can I rely on no one?!"

Rely on? Who on Earth, he wondered, *did the* Vampure *desire to rely on? For it must have been Xavier, surely, or any number of* Vampures *at his disposal in that city of his, so what? What was he truly getting at? What,* he thought, opening his eyes to find Nicholai staring at him coldly, *was the original* Vampure's *true goal in all of this?*

"It would not do to riddle your mind," Nicholai said, his voice rough along his throat, "trying to understand the Vampire, Arminius. He is no more a Creature of sanity than he was a Vampire of true merit. He was a tyrant, ensuring all obeyed his orders or succumbed to his wrath."

"And why do you still move to fulfill his orders? He is dead, you truly do not have to move forth with all of this if you truly do not desire to." But the moment he had said the words, he heard the irony within them, for wasn't he doing the very same, continuing in footsteps left behind by the monster that placed him here? And was he not tied, just as the others, by the damning medallions at their chests to fulfill the Vampire's orders, regardless if he walked the World or not?

Nicholai seemed to have understood this as well for he merely smiled, although it was rather weak, Arminius thought, and said, "We were the ones who moved first to journey to Evert's dwelling place where the others remained behind, eager, I imagine, to be lost in their lives. They tried to avoid it, their truth. Yes, even I tried to keep it at bay, in my own foolish ways. But there is one thing I learned once this necklace graces your body, my old friend."

He merely inclined his head.

"It's the light, his voice," the Vampire went on, though Arminius had known what his words would be before he said them, "it sticks in your head forever, rendering you unable to do little else but heed its call. The Call of His Red Light. Nay, it goes beyond him," and he rubbed his large hands together atop his bloodied lap. "The Call of the Phoenixes to protect their chosen *Dracon*—their Dragon, their claim to the old World before we tainted Creatures graced it." His hands untangled themselves and settled tensely atop the broken, worn arms of the chair, a great, unnecessary breath leaving his chest, sending a cold wind to press against his skin, and with a start, Alinneis realized the Vampire needed blood.

The slight shiver escaped him, and he clutched tighter the collar of his traveling cloak around his neck with a long hand. "Have you been here all night?" he asked, knowing, indeed, what the answer would be.

"Aye," he breathed, the snarl drifting along the word, filling the small home with a maliciousness Arminius did not fail in recognizing: it was the mark of a Vampire, this terrible coldness, this fear that had begun to plague his heart... Stamping it down with a shift in the uncomfortable chair, he focused, instead, on the Vampire's words.

"It is but morning," he offered quietly after a long moment, "we can go out under cover of a spell...acquire what you need... Tell me, did Dracula's blood I gave you yesterday help? You shouldn't need more so soon, surely?"

He watched the Vampire stand, yet another snarl leaving his lips, and how this one seemed to reverberate around the small cottage, filling his soul with its viciousness. He rose to stand as well, taking a step away from the Creature, his cane's prominent click against the old floor sending the Vampire's head to turn in his direction, his eyes, Arminius saw now, a calculating red, almost appearing to glow beside the fire's orange glare.

He could barely conjure the correct spell to mind when the Vampire had a hand to his throat, lifting him up toward the ceiling. "*Vampure*," he whispered harshly, pressing a hand to the cold fingers, the nails that dug into his skin, threatening to rip into his veins, "still yourself—please."

What could have gotten into the Creature? he thought, struggling within the hand. He chanced a glance the red eyes, alive as they were with hunger. . . *Hunger that should not be!* He had fed the Vampire from the medallion, had *seen* the Vampire shrink into the shadows, still scarred, but well-fed, and it had only been at least twelve hours since then—so *what*—why was the Vampire acting like he hadn't fed in weeks?

And the more he stared into the Vampire's red eyes, the more it was he saw the tinge of darkness within them, so very similar to black smoke, and all at once, inspiration struck. With as steady a breath he could muster beneath the Vampire's grip, he began the spell.

"*Reparilis Nam Emmolis-Cora, Nam Emmolis-Cora Cora,*" he thought repeatedly, his tongue caught in-between his teeth, gnashed as they were as the Vampire's hand pushed his mouth closed so he could not speak, could not whimper. "*Reparilis Nam Emmolis-Cora!*"

And with another snarl, he drifted on blackness, the red no longer there in the medallion, the feel of the Vampire's cold hand fading away as he landed softly within a dark room.

It was, he knew, the Vampire's mind, but something indeed had tainted it, but no, the more he looked around at the empty space before him, the slow breath leaving his chest, he gathered it was not Eleanor, was not Dracula at all. No, as he breathed, the darkness solidifying before him, before dispersing to reveal an impossibly large hall that seemed to have no ceiling, he knew it was not either terribly scarred Creature, but something much more terrifying, indeed.

A shaking hand rising to his lips, he watched as the darkness melted away from the corners of the large place, golden walls shimmering in an eternal light, here, no torch or candle lit to make this illustrious glow possible, but there were windows, as high as the unknowable ceiling, narrow within the walls. As a sharp breeze blew past him on all sides, he narrowed his eyes upon one just before him, and although no curtain billowed into the room, he knew they held no glass.

As he stood in this impossible place, he became painfully aware he was not alone: the feeling of sharp eyes upon his shaking frame could not be ignored nor willed away. He whirled on the spot, his cane sliding along the pristine golden floor, making not a sound as it moved. Thinking this odd, he was torn from this thought when he saw Nicholai Noble standing in the center of the large hall, nothing else within it besides him—

But that was not true.

No, the more he stared at the Vampire who looked around the large hall with a wonder Arminius was all but familiar with, he realized they were not alone.

From behind a most bemused Nicholai walked a terrifying man— no—Creature, Arminius could not believe existed.

He was remarkably tall, towering clearly over the Vampire, and as he stopped just before him upon large black boots, Arminius noticed he appeared to shine with the same gold that adorned the walls. His hair was long and black, silk-like as it fell down his back, and over broad shoulders rested a black cloak, unfathomable clothes beneath it, Arminius was sure.

Simply staring upon the man proved far too much for Arminius's eyes. He continued to blink repeatedly, waiting for the Creature to disappear (for he had the strangest feeling the Creature did not exist), but when he did not after several hundred blinks, he resigned himself to the worst: Nicholai had really met this Creature, had truly kept this memory a pleasant secret from his, Arminius's mind, for he must have been sure if Arminius had known this, had known the Vampire had met a Creature such as *this*, he would have asked endless questions, questions, perhaps, a particular Vampire did not want asked.

He blinked, returning his mind to the present, rubbing a hand absently along his throat, the faint ache just there sending his eyes to water. *I've not much time—*

"Aberration," the man said, pulling Arminius's attention to the scene before him with that voice. He took several steps backward, almost stumbling over his robes; the voice was terrible, truly, smacking against his every sense as though a vicious attack, and with a marked wonder, Arminius wondered how on Earth the Vampire did not move beneath it. "You are the one Primus has chosen to take his place when his current form betrays him. Do you feel yourself ready for this venture?"

Arminius watched in complete bemusement as Nicholai merely said, his voice timid against the booming peculiarity that had just filled the hall before it, "I have followed Dracula's word for years, Caligo Manus—if this is what he desires from me—I shall do it."

The Creature named Caligo appeared to smile, but it reached Arminius as a sneer: His face was terribly dark, jaw strong as it tensed with the slightest hint of contempt, the completely black eyes not appearing to shine at all despite the glow about his tall frame, the large hall. Arminius felt if there were white within them, they would tear through one's soul. *What the devil is going on?*

"You speak like one unversed in the truth. Has Primus not told you everything he has undergone to give you the form you hold now? Has he not," and a harsh laugh escaped dark lips, a thousand voices pressing against Arminius's high ears with the sound, "bothered to tell you beings what is true?"

It was clear these questions troubled Nicholai, for it was so silent he became once that endless voice disappeared, and Arminius did not blame him. There was a great and terrible darkness within this. . .Creature. . .but what was he? And what the hell was he on about? *Who was Primus?*

Just when Arminius thought Nicholai to lose his voice, the Vampire spoke, his silver hair ruffling in a sharp, cold breeze that once again blew into the large hall on all sides. "He has told me what he deems me necessary to know. I do not doubt his greatness at all, Caligo. And the fact that I am here," he said a bit louder now, seeming to gain confidence in what he had been told by this person, "speaks volumes to my magnitude—my readiness. I am ready. . .because Dracula has said it is so. So. . .it is so."

The gasp that escaped his pained throat left him the moment he had heard the familiar name. *Dracula sent him here?* he thought, looking once more around the terribly bright hall. *But where on Earth* is *here?*

The laughter from the Creature's dark face had fled as quickly as it had appeared. He now looked positively murderous, and Arminius almost raised his cane to defend himself, but before anything could happen at all, another tall Creature appeared in a hail of blinding light.

The cane fell uselessly out of his hand as he stared at this newcomer, his eyes unable to find anything else, and indeed, even the dark Creature appeared to dim against the brilliance this Creature held.

He was the same height of the darker Creature, though his robes (he did not don a traveling cloak like his companion) were white, his skin lighter, his hair short, ruffled to the top of his neck, blonde, almost seeming a halo atop his head. His eyes were a piercing blue, normal, compared to the black-eyed Creature he stood beside, and instead of standing quite a distance from Nicholai, he, much to Arminius's surprise, stepped closer to the Vampire, but he never did touch him. Arminius felt he did not need to. Nicholai swayed as the Creature stepped up to him, as though he were to fall unconscious at any moment, but he never did.

The tall Creature looked down at him as the darker one merely wore a resigned expression, and said, "You truly believe the Primus. . .your. . .*Dracula* to succeed in his endeavor, Nicholai Nobilis?"

The Vampire appeared the slightest bit shaken in his resolve being stared down by the unbelievably gentle Creature, but he said, "Yes— I-I do, Syran Regium, I must—I d-do."

Syran smiled and Arminius felt the tears flee his eyes, and all at once he remembered when he had been bidden to cry upon seeing the three terribly large birds within the dawning skies. . . But it could not be.

"Then," the Creature named Syran whispered, clasping a large hand upon Nicholai's shoulder; his knees sunk to the floor, "Nobilis, we look forward to seeing what it is you can do for the World below. Don't we, Manus?" And he turned his blonde head to the silent Creature behind him as though expectant.

It was a terribly long time before Caligo spoke at all, and when he did, it was to say, "Indeed."

And then something happened Arminius found impossible.

Syran looked down at Nicholai who still remained upon his knees, his blue eyes soft, though the softness, Arminius felt, could not be known by any Creature that was not what they were; to him it only appeared strong, hard to stare directly into. And then, with a small smile, the hand atop the Vampire's shoulder twitched and Nicholai went up in bright blue flames, a scream never leaving his lips, and before Arminius could shout his alarm, incredibly large wings or orange fire sprouted from Syran's back, flapping restlessly within the hall, sending a sharp breeze to buffet the high flames—and Nicholai was gone.

Arminius could only stare as the Phoenix's hand remained where the Vampire had kneeled, and then, somehow, the blue glare turned to him, and with a harsh intake of breath, he felt the ground disappear beneath his feet.

✳

He released the Elf at once, alarm filling him as the memory had returned in a flash of painful pangs, surpassing even the great need for blood. He turned from the Elf, barely hearing the cane and body hit the floor. He was far too preoccupied on the pain canvassing his temples, a thousand daggers stabbing his skull.

"No, no, no," he heard himself groan amidst the darkness of the cottage, the shuffle of robe and cane at his back, "I can't—" But he could barely get the words out before he was staring up at those damning blue eyes, feeling with certainty the utter insignificance he held against what *that* Creature was. *I can't remember, not now, not now!*

But the more he thought it, the more he knew it was useless. They would feel it, they would know where he was—they would arrive.

He felt a hand pull him back along the collar, and he let out a cry of alarm before he was on his back in front of the fire, the murderous eyes of the Elf holding him in place. The end of the white cane was pressed against his chest keeping him pinned for good, and he could barely utter a word before the Elf was saying, his every word sending a new trill of painful pounding against his aching head, "The *Phoenixes*, Noble?! You *met* them? Never bothered to share this most *necessary* piece of *damning* information? And what was *that*? Dracula chose you to take his place? Had you meet the Phoenixes because he believed in you, did he? Then why on this *damning Earth* is *Xavier bloody Delacroix* out there getting lost in a galling dread?! *For what?*"

"Arminius," he could barely hiss before the cane was slammed against his cheek, pressing the side of his face down against the floor, a fresh burst of pain to light his eyes. He blinked upon the dirtied armchair the Elf had sat in but moments before.

"You have me go out there to search for him, perhaps even knowing he would never be found, only to tell me upon my return that he was here, that he just flew off somewhere, didn't bother to come in—to join you, and you expect me to believe—*with what I have just seen*—that you didn't plan that? That you didn't want the Vampire to just fly off? What am I saying?!" And Nicholai could feel the Elf's boot press into his side as he teetered upon them. "That was all probably a lie!"

"It wasn't a lie; Xavier was here—"

"But *you* were the one Dracula *chose*—you were the one who got the meet our *Gods*—you were the one Dracula believed in enough to stand within the bloody Nest and take the claim of chosen for all the sake of the World—and you would have me truly believe that you did not want the *Vampure* to go off and get lost in this World? That you did not want the glory? That you did not want—what was his name? *Syran's* honor upon your head should you succeed?! Is that why you were the only one there with me, the only one willing to stand at my side—to do what must be done for that monster of a *Vampure*?!"

"Monster?" he breathed, willing away the pain that destroyed his mind now, when he remembered with a low snarl that he could no longer do magic. He felt his dead heart grow colder as the Elf's words reached his ears. *He knew.* "H-How can you know?"

"I went into the medallion while you were under Dracula's hold—saw. . .that. . .*Creature* admonish you for keeping Alexandria away from him. And *why* did you do that, Noble? Surely, it wouldn't grant you favor with your buddies up above, would it?"

A cry of fright left him at the thought of the Phoenixes. *Damn. Damn!* "There is no time to explain, Arminius," he breathed, feeling his mind burn, now, burn with their tracking fyre sending the pain to grow to even greater, blinding heights. "They are coming."

These words seemed to bring the Elf great pause, for even with the end of the cane pressed against his cheek, he could see the Elf's orange eyes widen in bemusement and then narrow in suspicion. And then, with great difficulty, Arminius knelt at his side, and Nicholai could feel, much against his will, the haggard breath upon his face as the old Elf said, "Another lie, *Vampure*?"

Still the fyre burned, the heat of it sending his eyes to shut, and through his great need for blood, to escape the Elf's cane, he felt the trickle of cold liquid descend out a nostril, down his cheek. There was a great gasp and the cane was promptly removed.

Free of the weight, he rose, although the moment his head left the wooden floor, he found himself unable to lift his back. "Damn," he cried, the greatest inkling of fear pressing against his chest. *They will know I lied*, he thought in this fresh fear, staring up at the bemused Arminus, *they will know—and they will kill me. Dracula preserve me—I am a coward.*

For he knew he was. Only a coward would stand before Syran—the King of all Ancient Creatures and say they could preserve humanity. *But I had believed it, then*, he thought as all began to darken around him. *I had believed in Dracula's trust—I had truly thought I would do the right thing.*

But as the memory returned, he knew in his darkest of hearts that he had failed in that simple request.

"Get the woman and bring her to me, Noble," Dracula had ordered, no sliver of remorse upon his tongue, for it was then Nicholai realized what the Great Vampire was prepared to do—what he had already

planned without relaying any of it to his supposedly favored chosen. *He was a liar, a mad Vampire*, Nicholai thought, feeling the pain recede at last.

And he recalled, as the Elf's grimace dimmed in the vague light of the fire, the sight of Alexandria Stone, felt her power, Dracula's blood within her, and a fresh anger had overtaken him, and once she had slept he had done what he could—he had placed the spell of Impeding upon her so that she would not be able to reach Xavier Delacroix. Would not be able to have the new Vampire rise to Dracula's ranks as his true chosen. For Nicholai hoped beyond all else Xavier would never have to meet the Phoenixes—never, indeed, be touched by their hand, graced by their fyre. It was, he knew, as Arminius began waving his long hands over his darkening eyes, the mark of death.

Chapter Eight

PLACES OF POWER

By late midday the group of Creatures had reached halfway toward the looming white city, and from here Xavier could see the large jagged lines embedded in the black rock that formed the mountain. They jutted from the mountain's white, flattened top and extended all the way down to the snow-covered base below, and he narrowed his eyes, seeing the small holes around the base where the lines disappeared, seemingly within these holes.

This sight was curious enough to tear him from the almost waning thoughts of Eleanor, of his unconscious father still across Yaddley Caddenhall's shoulders, and he, for the first time since they'd agreed to journey to Merriwall, spoke.

"Enchanters," he called over his shoulder, never tearing his gaze from the holes ahead.

There was a pressed silence as he waited for their reply, and when it would not come in far too long a time, he turned fully, still stepping backwards, feeling for each jagged rock before he planted his boot for good. The Enchanters' eyes were black, their hands held aloft in the sky that was now a significant orange he saw from beneath the large, dark cloud. *Afternoon, already?*

With his gaze now upon them, it seemed they could not feign their ignorance at his call and Peroneous answered with a most dour, "Yes, your Grace?"

"Those holes at the base of the mountain," he said, throwing a thumb over his shoulder, "what is their significance?"

They chanced the smallest of glances toward each other before giving him their most unwanted attention, and he narrowed his eyes upon them. "So there is significance," he said jovially, glad his thoughts had been right. "Well then, what is it? What do those lines mean?"

Neither Enchanter said a word and with this, the surge of dread just at the back of his mind, never truly disappearing, returned in a great gust of indignation, but he was just about to open his mouth and let them know of his displeasure at their lack of immediate answers when Aurora spoke from Peroneous's side.

"They are lines meant to channel the energy from the Earth into the city."

Her voice was curt and low, and beneath the black gaze she gave, he could see the lines of great resentment along her brow. *"You ran off to her—you raised the Ascalon to Aleister—your father, when all he wanted was to protect you, to get you to the Goblet! You are ungrateful, and you're driving us all down with you!"* Her words from the night before returned in an unwanted rush of cold wind only his brain could feel, and he stared upon her most seriously.

Her fingers twitched through the air and with every twitch he noticed the cloud above their head appeared to brighten with flashes of lightning. *She was still upset,* he remarked, moving a hand to the sword at his waist, *and it would not take a thing at all for her to wave her hands and disperse the cloud, sending us all to burn.. . . .*

He turned from her cold glare, its implications sending an uncomfortable chill down his spine. She and Peroneous held dark power at their hands, and they had full reign of it, indeed. It, of course, begged the question just how it had happened. He had not thought on it whilst they walked, so preoccupied he had been on Eleanor's action not to harm the scarred Vampire, but now, the closer they drew to the magic-containing mountain where the white light blared less-periodically, the more it was he could find it a most curious thing to be heavily questioned. Hadn't Aurora said the Elite Creatures' magic grew stronger, making it harder for her to use her own back in the Vampire City? So what happened whilst he was kept from them during his journey for Eleanor? What happened to keep him—*him*—bidden to the shadows like a common Vampire?

He had just opened his mouth to ask the group this at large when he decided against it. It would only lead to more hatred spewed on their part, for he had messed up his allegiances to them fantastically, he knew. But he had thought it necessary to seek her out, instead, to uncover what more secrets she'd kept—what Dracula deemed it necessary to keep hidden. . . .

But she had not known a thing had she?

Or she was lying.

"*Never to you*," the voice whispered, a heady promise that almost sent his knees to buckle. Quickly recovering, he turned his thoughts to her, quite glad the others could not hear it.

That kiss.

It was the reason her words found his mind without him having to go under to keep them. It had to be. Beyond the utter inescapable sensation of completeness that had filled him with the feel of her lips, her tongue, there had been something more that passed between them, unspoken words whispered on the feel of her skin beneath his hands—

He gasped, the thought sending him to stop dead, a boot lingering in the air, his eyes wide as the thought gained prominence, visions of times past passing through his mind with a rapidness that could not be contained.

The sight of her in the woods just beyond the Vampire City those many weeks ago, the kiss they'd shared. . .Dracula's insistence that he, Xavier had been cursed by her. Cursed. . .so what was this?

He touched his lips again, the dread swirling in his mind, and there she was, ever beautiful, ever powerful, ever. . .*his.*

Her pale hands wrapped around both wrists, pulling him into her, and as their bodies met, he felt her hands sliding across his back, pulling him closer, indeed. *Nothing else mattered, nothing truly,* he barely thought as he smelled her hair with quick kisses to her shoulder, the smell of lilac and sweet, sweet, blood filling his nose. Filling him.

"Xavier?! Bloody hell, get up!" the rough voice sounded, and with a start, he opened his eyes, quite surprised to find himself atop the jagged rocks, their painful tips prodding his backside. He quickly stood, shrugging off the rough hand of the Vampire that had stood over him, blue eyes wide in their bewilderment. "This rate, we'll need to get you a cot to plant behind you before you fall."

Ignoring this jibe, he touched the hilt of the sword again, feeling its steady cold engulf his hand, and he frowned. *Dracula has left me,* he thought, regretting it as soon as it passed across his mind; the Vampire wouldn't do that, wouldn't abandon him completely. There was just far too much not being shared, and why was he to be punished if he sought the full truth from those that held it?

"My Lord," the soft voice said, a stark contrast to the fading sultry allure that was Eleanor's, "are you alright?"

He looked up from the Ascalon, the slightly darkened stare of Lillith Crane reaching him in something of mock question. She knew the answer to that question; they all did. But there was something else in her gaze, something that harkened back to the clearing just before Cinderhall Manor where he had held her while Darien Nicodemeus had transformed, and the small smile lifted his lips. *Sweet Lillith Crane.*

"I just remembered something is all, Miss Crane," he said, his gaze moving to the gruff Vampire at her side, the smile falling. *Just,* he thought, squeezing the handle of the sword, *all of his secrets.*

Dragor placed a hand on his shoulder, but he did not turn to eye him, his gaze still on the remarkably protective Christopher Black. *What more he must have known.*

"What did you remember, your Grace?" Dragor asked, pulling his gaze from the haunted black eyes that stared upon Lillith as though if he were to look away she would vanish at last, his words holding an impatient edge.

"Hm?" he hummed, seeing the others were all watching him, waiting for an answer. "I. . .remembered," he stalled, saying the first thing that came to troubled mind, "that my brother was to retrieve Dracula's sword—did he?"

At this question, all Creature's gazes moved from him, and he heard their disconcerting silence, saw their complete lack of desire to see what more would happen lest they anger him further, and he sighed.

"He is not here," he said, doing his best to keep his voice level, though the dread was fast at work, keeping his mind bent to anger, deserved respect. . . But that was not, he knew, the way to go—the way to handle these Creatures. He had to keep their trust, whatever little he still retained. "He is not here so I imagine," he continued, "he is elsewhere. And with Alexandria Stone?" These last words offered as a hesitant suggestion. In truth, he had not thought of the woman since he'd left Cinderhall Manor. Surely she was a Vampire by now? Thinking it curious if his brother had indeed succeeded in turning the woman at all, he focused on the Creature that was now speaking, dark eyes alive with a strange kind of sorrow: it was as though she mourned the dead.

"She got badly hurt in a scuffle with Thomas Montague and that man, James Addison. Peroneous. . .must have sensed something I didn't—he grabbed her and took her straight to Christian," Aurora said, hands still raised above her head. She stared upon no one but him as she went on. "He. . .like all the others were. . .badly burned— but Christian was ravenous—he looked like a Vampire possessed. He was—"

"Dying," Peroneous finished shortly, bringing all eyes to him. "The Vampire was very near death and it was clear something in Miss Stone's blood was pulling her to him." He shrugged, the weight of his words seeming to lay heavy across his shoulders. "She was bleeding to death, I merely moved as I will—further the damned thing along."

Xavier stared at them, realizing for the first time they had stopped moving. "Something in her blood?" he repeated, incredulous, and he stared at Aleister, remembering when the scarred Vampire had spoken to Christian on this very matter. *Was Christian right?*

Peroneous opened his mouth to respond, another burst of light from the mountain's peak momentarily blinding them. When it passed, Xavier saw the Enchanter blink rapidly before proceeding with, "Yes, something in her blood. The very same something I felt in Dracula's blood when I first gave him that potion—I knew he had interfered with it—I could feel it as I held her, as it dripped down my arms, my hands. Whatever it was," he sighed as though tired, "Christian needed it. The last I saw a Vampire in that state was Dracula shortly after he'd finished the potion—it was the look of stark need, Xavier. Your brother was truly dying and that woman saved him."

He could not speak. Christian had been right, had tried to tell them all, but had been largely ignored, ridiculed. . . The shame that filled his cold heart sent his brow to furrow; the number of questions that occupied his mind riddling him with a different kind of dread. *Was the Vampire well? What of Alexandria? And the sword?*

But he could barely open his mouth to inquire upon any of this when a particularly jarring burst of light left the mountain's top and Xavier was flung forward off the balls of his feet, his hand already firm around the handle of the sword, pulling it out of its sheath with the movement. He landed atop the jagged rocks with a painful crash, the sword clanking against the rocks as well, and he could hear the others reduced to their backs as a scalding pain burrowed against his hair, eating through his clothes.

A cry of alarm left him as he looked up from his place atop the uncomfortable ground, felt the unbearable shards of fire reign down upon him.

But it was impossible.

Peroneous and Aurora lay several feet away from the tip of his blade, their eyes closed against the setting sun, their spell lost with them.

Fresh cries of pain met his ears, the others alight with fire as well, and several steps to his right the large Caddenhall Vampire lay atop the ground, a large arm draped over his eyes, shielding the sun from them, but even as he burned, Xavier could see the black hair of Aleister strewn across the rocks just past Yaddley before it too burst into high flame.

"No," he whispered, attempting to rise; the sun's heat kept him against the hard stone, and he wondered how on Earth Dracula survived the World before he was given a more human face, before all went miserably black.

※

Darkness pressed against her on all sides, but there was also cold, bitingly cold. . .what? What was this? For she was very aware something else clawed at her, here, something sharp, pulling at her every limb, pulling her down—down, but where else could she go?

I'm already dead—

The gasp pulled in her lungs, the thought burning against her mind so dark, unbidden here, no true outlet but to continue to burn, the unfinished sentence a rallying call that echoed against her ears. . . But what it sought to bring together, she could not be sure.

"I'm dead, I'm dead. I'm already dead—I'm dead. I'm dead. I'm already dead—"

A strangled sob scratched at her throat, an awareness joining it as well.

I'm upon something. Cold. No, I'm always cold, now. Scared? No, not scared—not anymore—I'm already dead—

A fresh burst of wind brushed against her face, and she opened her eyes with a start, a white light greeting her, and in a ridiculous moment of wild hope she almost thought she'd truly died, that she was no longer a Vampire—

"Sorry," the voice said, pulling her from her thoughts, "for waking you, Alexandria."

She did not rise to sit, merely stared up at the white stone of the ceiling high above her, the chandelier's candles lit, the flames shimmering with a touch of something more to her eyes. Perhaps it was because she was now something more. *Or perhaps,* she thought with a small smile, *it's because the last time I was here I was clouded with fear—*

"Alexandria?" the voice whispered, closer now.

She turned her head along the couch (for she knew that was where she'd been placed), and watched him step to her amidst the impossible glow of light that surrounded him. . .no, filled the entire room.

He wore a clean white shirt unbuttoned at the collar, a red, silk cravat tied at his throat, deep red breeches at his waist that stopped at his knees, the white stockings beneath pressed to perfection, the black dress shoes shined to utter prominence. And his hair, no longer unbound as it usually was, was tied up into a long hold, the same silk of his cravat appearing to be the ribbon that tied held his hair together. She only saw this when he turned his head to eye the doors as though scared someone would come through them.

"Christian," she whispered, not at all used to her voice. . .how strange it sounded to her ears, "you look. . . ."

He rubbed a hand self-consciously against his shirt when the words would not find her tongue, something of a smile pressing against his lips. "Debonair, I hope?" he finished quietly.

She could not help but smile despite herself.

Protect the Dragon and spare all.

The smile fled with the thought, and she cleared her throat, shifting uncomfortably within her seat. *What more must happen?* "What's— why are you dressed—is something—?"

"Is something wrong?" he cut across, his brown furrowing just the slightest. "No, no, nothing is wrong—" and with a great, needless breath, "we've been invited to a—a Ball."

She blinked, thinking greatly that she had misheard. "A what?"

He looked immensely uncomfortable, as though he desired nothing more than for the floor to open up and swallow him whole. "A b-ball," he whispered, his gaze no longer meeting hers, "it's in the Vampire City. Apparently Dr-Dracula held it yearly around this time. A Vampire by the name of Westley Rivers had the invitation sent yesterday."

She merely stared.

"I understand," he went on suddenly, "if you are not up for it—but I figure it would be safe there, at least. After all, we would be remiss not to expect other Dark Creatures to hear of you—seek you out, and to be underground with other Vampires, Vampires Xavier knows—I daresay I can't think of a safer place."

And before she could say a word, he said, "And it's only for the night—if you decide you would rather leave—we needn't stay."

And in the stare he bade her now, she could see that there was more than just a need for her blood—more than just a need that was Dracula's—he was asking her to a Ball under the pretense of protection, but one would be a complete fool, she thought, if one could not see the stark need in his eyes for her to come with him. For the simple pleasure of her company.

She felt utterly ridiculous, then, having dared thought the Vampire a needy monster like Thomas. *He's stood beside me through it all, saved my life where it counts, just as I've saved his. . .Dracula couldn't manufacture that no matter how powerful he was.*

She stood then, feeling the slight weight of the bloody, soiled clothes she still wore, and she curtsied her best, feeling the soles of her feet squish against blood-filled boots. When she rose, she was not surprised to see him staring upon her as though he'd never seen her before but desired nothing more than to continue to eye her. "Yes, Lord Christian Delacroix," she whispered, smelling the relief that trailed on the air that was his blood, "I shall accompany you to this Ball."

He smiled wide, his fangs showing themselves in the glare of strange light that surrounded them, and she thought his eyes no longer looked cold, unfeeling, but full of life. Darker, yes, colder, but still life it was. She wondered vaguely if her eyes looked the same before he stepped to her in two steps, a gust of wind traveling with him, embracing her tightly in his arms.

"Christian," she gasped, her hands automatically pressing against his arms, though she stopped herself when she saw the prints of dirt they left, "you'll ruin your clothes—we shouldn't—"

"Forgive me," he whispered, the light upon him flaring to a deep red, and before she could stop it, he'd bent forward and sank his fangs into her neck.

"What the?! Christian!" She felt his hands clawing at her back, ripping through her destroyed blouse to tear at her skin, the blood leaving the marks left in droves, spilling with little abandon along the couch, but still he drank; she could feel her blood leave her, pour willingly into his mouth, her red light filling him, causing him to glow with the great power.

Her eyes opened and she sat up as though pulled by her heart, the large white room stretched out before her in sheer normalcy, no strange white light, no glowing illuminance foretelling of desires, of needs. . . .

Without thought she looked around, the white couch she sat upon just as she remembered from her last time here, the room looking the same as it had, though a pitcher sat on a small table to the back of the room she hadn't remembered.

And she was alone.

"Christian," she breathed, the name a whisper of fear and warning all in one, for she could not will away the feel of his hands upon her back, the sharpness of his fangs as they pierced her, nor could she demand the smell of him to disperse, for it was all so clear, as though he had just been here.

The silver steel of the sword caught her gaze next, and she eyed it warily, its leather handle appearing plain enough, yes, but there was great power embedded in the blade, she knew. Power forged by desire, by greed. . .blood.

Why, she asked herself, never taking her gaze off the Ares, *did he have to make me this—this thing?*

For she knew if she had never of been born she would have not had to live a life most maddening, abandoned by her mother, lied to by suitors, indeed, left at the altar holding her head in her hands, wondering why indeed it seemed since her mother disappeared her life had taken a turn for the worst.

And then he appeared.

Not in way of appearance, of course, but through the myriad river of letters he would send almost nightly, arriving at her doorstep with an almost impatient timeliness, as though demanding to be read, and they were. And she had been compelled, strangely, to reply.

Until the one night the letter arrived desiring her presence at his manor. And of course, a Count, the lesser of all titles, would surely afford her a change from the glaring depression that was her life. So she had agreed to meet him that very night, but of course she'd though nothing of the horse-drawn carriage that had appeared at her estate out of nowhere, for she'd had her mind set. Either she was to be married to this Count before her next birthday or she'd run off into the country, remain a spinster the rest of her days. For she had known, had heard, the whispers and glances bade her direction whenever she was about town, had felt the stinging glares of ridicule. For she had surpassed eighteen—and not a husband in sight! And what was worse, she had been outed from court upon her mother's abandonment—it seemed a girl without Lady Hatfield's name beside her own would not do in the Queen's eyes. So she had been shunned, all respective suitors turned away against her will, and forced into a most unwanted solitude. . .only to be revived—a small hope in life— by the mysterious Count's letters.

She'd often wondered what would have happened had she met Dracula before meeting Damion Nicodemeus or Christian Delacroix. Perhaps she would have gotten to know him, before being turned into a Vampire, that is. Perhaps, and this she clung to almost nightly, he would have spared her the death that would have befallen her.

But no, she knew that was not so. Not with the concentrated, eager gaze he had given her whilst she'd turned. Dracula the Vampire had wanted her to become what he was, had wanted her to call others to the sword. . .had wanted someone to help him fulfill his goals. . .whatever they were.

And here I am, she thought with a sigh, eyeing for the first time the long dress that graced her body.

She immediately pressed her hands to the fabric, feeling the same silk that had been pressed up against her in dream-Christian's cravat. Hell, it was even the same color. *What on Earth?*

She pressed a hand to the lacey white bodice around her abdomen, soft though it was, she knew whale bone helped it hold its shape. She was grateful for this. She would be able to move easier for it, would have been able to breathe easier, as well, if she were still human. . . .

Tearing her thoughts from this, she focused, instead on the equally red boots that adorned her feet, their heels high and pointed, only, she had known from the very few times she had seen her mother wear similar, for going out somewhere immeasurably elegant.

"*Debonair,*" dream-Christian said again, his wide smile sending her to grin at the thought of it.

The smile fled as the recollection of what he'd done after returned in a whirl, and she stood, willing it away with a breath. *Everything is a battle of will, now,* she thought, marveling at the way the dress's many skirt flowed about her legs. Soft, soothing almost, a breath of fresh air compared to the normal dresses she would have worn before. *But who made this?*

She turned, the small table to the back of the room almost pulling her gaze there once again, but this time she saw the small piece of parchment beside a round silver tray topped with empty glasses.

She stepped around the couch and moved to it at once, snatching it up, and with narrowed eyes, read:

Alexandria,

I desired to let you sleep. Let whatever's happened to you run its course. I suspect you'll be up sometime tonight, so I'm moving to prepare what I can while I am able.

A Vampire by the name of Westley Rivers is throwing a Ball in the Vampire City beneath London within the next few days. It would be my highest honor if you could accompany me. I know it sounds remarkably strange. Me asking you to a Ball after all that's happened, but please, I feel we will be safer there than upon the surface.

Westley has outlined how well he knows my brother, spoke most highly of him, in fact. He knows of you, and I feel a great deal more than he is letting on, and part of my reasoning to journey there is to figure out what he knows.

I have had a dress made for you by the finest tailor in London. He was able, with some persuasion on my part to fashion it in extremely fast taste. I desired it be ready before you awoke. And if you are, and it is near nine o'clock, I will be returning with a carriage that will take us to the edge of London where we will have to journey three days to the Vampire City.

My apologies, I wished to make this trip as easy as possible for you. Funnily enough, I have never taken it, myself. I would think of no one else I would rather see it with for the first time besides you—

A Ball? she thought incredulously, feeling the strangest sense that she had been able to see more than just his desires in the dream. But it was clear, his words were lined with immense emotion, regret, most notably, and she almost laughed, for hadn't she been feeling the very same as she'd awoken?

—and I know it will afford us time to talk about all that has transpired between us. I know you feel the same as I do;

*confused, out of place, even, seeking answers to all Dracula
has rent upon our heads.*

It is my great hope that we will find these answers together.

Yours repentantly,

Christian

Mine repentantly.

She folded the letter carefully, letting those words linger on her
mind so filled with, not confusion anymore, no, but a stark coldness.
*All Dracula has rent upon our heads. Yes, he was the answer for all
of this, wasn't he? He was the one who'd pulled at my life so I would
come running, nay, leaping into his hands—and I did just that, hadn't
I?*

She recalled with anger the memory of a particular suitor, Jeremy
his name was, as he'd stood upon her doorstep, unwilling, nay, not
desiring to enter her home. Oh, he'd done so several times before, so
what, she had thought, was the matter this time?

But now, still lost in the memory, she focused on the things she had
not noticed before: how pale he had become, how dark his normally
bright brown eyes had appeared, how brightly the golden ring on his
finger shone in the light of the afternoon sun. . . .

Of course, she sighed, bringing herself back to the present, the
parchment she held in a hand, *he'd been turned.*

Wondering who else Dracula had turned, she was in the midst
of perusing all her memories, *"What you have experienced in your
life. . .you will always revisit. In thoughts, in dreams. Your life, all
you've done, alive and as a Vampire will stay with you, easy to recall
should you ever choose to,"* when one of the large white doors opened
and she turned on the spot, balling the letter into a fist.

A young maid stood there, a jar of Unicorn Blood in her slender hands, and she curtsied as best she could, her gaze never falling upon Alexandria's frame.

"Amelia," she breathed, marveling at the dark gaze the woman gave her at last. *Why, it's as though she's forgotten me.*

She watched in silence as Amelia stepped into the room, placed the Unicorn Blood on the floor just before the couch, and turned to flee, her long blonde hair no longer spilling freely down her back, but up in a very familiar hold; it was one all help wore in the manor, this much Alexandria remembered.

"Amelia," she called, taking a step forward, quite surprised when she appeared just behind the woman whose trembling hand had been reaching out for a silver handle.

Before she could press down, a shriek left her lips and Alexandria watched her hair and clothes blow up in the wind she knew she'd created.

"Amelia," she breathed, seeing the shiver her voice created, but knowing not how to still it, "it's me, Alexandria—can't you at least look at me?"

She said nothing and it was not until Alexandria dared to place a hand upon the woman's bare shoulder that Amelia did anything at all:

She jumped as though scalded and pressed forward for the door, pushing against the handle with an urgent fear, but not before her voice, shaking with tears reached Alexandria's ears, "Lady Stone is dead—*you're the devil*—you and Lord Delacroix. Together you shall burn—demons cannot walk this Earth for long."

And the large door was closed with as great a slam the young woman could muster.

She merely stared after it, unable to do any more than let out a sound much like a whimper and snarl, for the whole time the woman had stood just before her, she had been fighting the very alarming urge to tear into her neck and drink her blood just as a certain Vampire had done to her the night before.

With a cold sigh, she bent low, picking up the jar of Unicorn Blood, understanding at last why Christian had been driven mad with the stark need for blood those two weeks before—her own blood for far longer, still.

※

Victor Vonderheide pointed pale hands to every other dark alleyway, sending one or two of his Elite Creatures through it, their orders to convene at Delacroix Manor in the next hour or so, but they weren't to do a thing to it, of course. Not that they could.

He touched the stone in his pocket for the sixtieth time. No, he would take care of that. What little. . .power the stone held (for he felt it was plenty, the way he it flared to life every so often when he thought of Dracula) was power enough to still the protection around the manor, of this he was certain. What he did not know, however, was how he was to destroy it to allow his Creatures to get inside, whatever lie he'd told Eleanor.

He gestured for the Enchanter who strode just behind him, and when they were level, he said from beneath his low hood, "Do you know a spell for removing Protection Enchantments?"

The Enchanter raised two hands before himself as though in peace, his white robes garish against the unsteady darkness. Victor had wondered why he'd been so oblivious as to wear white on this venture when introduced to him back in the tunnels, but the more they walked through London, the more he was aware the Enchanter appeared a bit out of touch. He'd taken to muttering to himself here and there when he thought no one was looking or listening, muttering things about 'the ills of magic,' and 'great power.' It had been enough to warrant Victor little to no interaction with the Creature until now.

As it was, there was darkness, strange darkness permeating the World. . .but not Eleanor's, no, not anymore. It was different, Victor noticed, different and dangerous in the power it held. But what could it have been?

"Removing Enchantments, my Lord?" the Enchanter answered back as they passed several carriages in the crowded streets. "I—yes, there appear to be quite a few such spells. But for the protection around Delacroix Manor. . .I was there when we tried to destroy it—it wouldn't budge under any of our magical prowess."

He ignored the last few words. "But there *are* spells of such a manner?"

"Yes," he said, his voice almost lost against the thundering of boots as several Elite Creatures took off into darker alleyways, screams of fright from humans and those not renting the air, "there are. . .but none, as I have just said, of destroying the chain of protection that rests around that manor. My Lord, it is gravely protected—I believe perhaps by powers greater than those on Earth—"

"But were you Enchanters," he interrupted swiftly as he passed a Vampire whose top hat was blown off his head in a fierce wind, "not given. . .lease with your magic?" For he had heard the small tales once he'd left the cave, tales of the Enchanters atop their mountain regaining what they had lost. Something about Dracula's death. . .greater power the magical Creatures had been afforded. "Were you Enchanters not granted such power? With Dracula's death I hear you magic-folk have been given a great. . .lease on life. And we Vampires," he eyed several Vampires who stood within the middle of the street, not seeing the badges that gleamed on their cloaks until they drew closer, the light of a streetlamp illuminating them, "are bidden to the dark in truth."

He thought of the whispers he had heard from Eleanor's men, that the light burned Vampires that were not Elite Creatures, no amount of Dracula's trinkets and provisions protecting them any longer. To test this, Victor had scoured his chambers for one of his rings just before leaving, and when he had found it, he had placed it upon his finger, the metal clamps finding his skin in a painful stab of remembrance, and he had sighed heavily, feeling what little Vampiric power he had possessed retreat into the reaches of unknowingness. *More of his magic,* Victor had thought.

And now he ran his thumb across it, still keeping his free hand around the stone in his pocket, both things born of Dracula, both things, (and although he had no proof, he could not deny the feelings they gave him) born of the Phoenixes.

"Hold!" one Vampire said, throwing forth a white gloved hand.

Victor stilled in surprise, the sudden movement pulling him from his reverie, and he heard the others stop behind him. Their mutterings of alarm reached his ears just as a few officers stepped forward, effectively blocking their path, the lingering humans, Vampires, and Enchanters that traversed the cold, London street now giving the line of Vampires in uniform a terribly wide berth, their eyes on Victor and the darkly draped figures behind him.

He appraised the first Vampire, still running unsteady fingers around the stone in his pocket, not saying a word, and how it seemed the entire World stopped, until the Vampire dropped his hand and took a small step forward. "How brave," this Vampire said, his voice deep, rich with a mocking song wrapped along his tongue, and he narrowed brown eyes, his gaze held only on Victor, "for Eleanor's Creatures," he waved a hand to the Enchanter at Victor's side, "to roam the streets with no pretense for cover."

"Brave?" an Elite Creature from behind Victor's right shoulder whispered harshly. Victor had not the mind to stop him. "How dare you—we destroyed all of London in a single night!"

"And we rebuilt it in but a few weeks—far better than it was before," the Vampire said coldly, and a gloved hand moved to the scabbard at his waist, "now I ask you again," and Victor felt the Vampire's eyes burrowing into him though he would not lift his head, would not reveal himself for the Vampires knew not who it was he walked with, not yet, "what brings you bloody plagues into London? And where are you sending your men?"

Victor stared at the others in the line behind this officer, their gazes trained on him, and he wondered why on Earth he commanded such attention—he smelled nothing like the others—But what was it Joseph Gail had said a mere few days before?

"Vampire though you may be, you have dwelled in her cave, you reek of her scent just as any of us."

Ah, yes. That was it. I have dwelled in her cave. . .I reek of her scent. He stifled the smile that dared curl his lips just as the aforementioned officer took another step forward, this time large: Victor was able to smell his scent; blood and fear along the wind created.

The Vampire's stringy blonde hair was pushed back by the wind that had arisen in protest to his own, though Victor had not had the thought to conjure it, and he pressed a gloved finger to Victor's chest, eager, Victor thought, for provocation.

"He wants a fight, my Lord," the Enchanter whispered from the edge of his mouth; a gnat buzzing dully at his left ear.

Of course he does, he thought dryly, eyeing now the others behind the Vampire, their hands all on their scabbards, eyes wide with their bloodlust, their fear. He took a moment, however small, to notice the exact fear that filled their eyes, and the thought beckoned: *Was I wrong in doubting Eleanor. . .the fear she inspires?*

For however ludicrous her methods, (a kiss—a curse?) she did have all the hands of the Dark World shaking in anticipation of her next movement.

And he, he realized with a harrowing blink as the officer jabbed his finger again against his chest, led her men in the dark of night to destroy the home of the Vampire he despised. . .feared. Was he, then, not to be feared just as she was?

But what she kept from me. . . .

He had just resolved to focusing on the glaring fact of her kept secrets, instilling the anger that would surely arise once more, when the officer said, impatience clear at its end, "I beg you answer me now, Creature! Or you shall see your heads on pikes!"

He looked up with this dreadful threat, droll in its ferocity. The Vampire's voice shook as though the stone beneath his feet bid him to lose control of his bodily functions, had he any, and smiled, seeing the Vampire's gaze of bewilderment drown in incomprehensible fear the next moment.

And with a flourish, for the Enchanter at his side had not stilled in his whispers of warning, his men at his back had not stopped their angry snarls, their low growls, he removed the low hood from his head and closed his eyes as the gasps of the officers permeated the now empty air. All other Creatures, humans had long since had their fill of the event and had dispersed into the night.

"*Victor?!*"

It was a stunned whisper, burdened by great surprise, immediate fear, for Victor could easily see the brown eyes darken, flashing red in a cold breeze, and all Vampires on the line snarled their anger.

"Victor Vonderheide," the officer spat, almost shaking in his furiousness: his red eyes were wide, the sword drawn from its scabbard at his waist, a vicious snarl curling his lips, "*traitor*! I have heard—oh by the Birds I have *heard* you were with them—with *her*, but I didn't dare believe it! I didn't dare pay heed to the numerous claims about the Dark World that you, first of Dracula's line, would *betray* the Vampire Creature—betray your brothers!" His mouth opened and closed as though more threatened to pour from it, but when a long moment passed and nothing more was uttered, Victor decided to quell the uncomfortable silence.

"Dear," he eyed the badge atop his chest, "Randall Jameson of the Eightieth Division of Powers, Scotland Yard, your words are not things I have not heard before. It is to be expected with my. . .place before that Vampire's death. But come now, Randall, let us face facts, hmm? There is dread in the World, oh yes, there is, madness, even, but there is also," he felt the stone burn, and curiously, the ring as well, though he did not look down at them, no, he remained focused on the incensed Vampire before him, "truth. Whatever that truth may be. We merely seek different ways to pursue it, yes?"

Randall Jameson stammered mindlessly for several minutes, and Victor thought it would be quite a time before he spoke again, wondering, indeed, if his face was truly that much of a surprise to warrant such disbelief, such complete indignation. *It's as if he feels personally betrayed. Of course he would*, he thought, *I was the patron of Vampires, Dracula's first. I have never belonged to myself.*

Something like anger threatened to rise in his chest, but the thought of Dracula stamped it down as grief swiftly took its place. *Ugh.*

"My Lord," the Enchanter said openly, drawing all eyes to him. Victor saw the Enchanter was running a finger over his collar continuously, and he would have thought it a nervous tick if the Creature wasn't staring at him with the utmost seriousness, a certain glow within his black eyes. "I sense grave power on your person. Curious. . .power." The black gaze narrowed in clear interest.

He closed his eyes. *Not now, damnit.* "It does not concern you, not yet, Enchanter—"

The blade cut the air just before his face, and he jumped back, barreling into an Elite who disappeared in a cloud of black smoke as he was touched. Regaining his footing, Victor bent his knees, releasing the sword at his waist, feeling the stone burn scalding hot through his clothes. With a burst of cold air, he flew forward just above the cobblestone, the cries of resistance from the Enchanter blaring loud in his ears, as was the shouts, the collective air of the Elite Creatures at his back, finally moved to take action now that he was prepared to defend himself.

He reached Randall in the next second, pressing the blade into the Vampire's stomach, watched as he let out a grunt, a gasp, his own sword falling to the ground with a shattering crash drowned only by the sound of battle ahead, the Elites squaring with the Vampires with relish.

"My Lord!" the Enchanter's voice sounded loud over the sound of battle, but Victor dared not turn. He pressed the sword into the Vampire to the hilt, feeling the blood pour from the Creature's wound and slide down his hand with little abandon, and he snarled, the heat of the stone like fire now, and it was all he could do to keep from screaming his pain.

He pressed from the Vampire, staring at him as he fell to the road, anger clear in his eyes, but he did not rise and Victor wondered why. The strike was not enough to kill a Vampire, this Victor knew well, but the Vampire lay atop the ground as though he could not rise from it, as though—

"My Lord! We must leave!"

He pulled from the gaze of the stricken officer whose red eyes were still held on him—they would not close—but he turned as the hand clasped his shoulder. "What is it, Enchanter?" he asked with something of a snarl. The heat from the stone was blinding now. He half-wondered why it did not burn a hole through his cloak.

The Enchanter's gaze was fear-filled, his white robes swaying about him in the harsh breeze that had blown up from nowhere, indeed. "The skies! The skies!" And he pointed a shaking hand to the swirling clouds that lined the sky, though it was no longer dark.

The sky was a strange light in places, darker still in others, and it puckered and rolled as though something threatened to pass through its surface, something of great, terrible power that could not breach the dread of the skies. . . .

And then he felt it. The burning pain on his hand intensified with a terrible surge, and he lifted his hand to his eyes, the blood that covered it glowing in a steady, hot, red light, but the ring itself was the source of the light, for its golden shape, was glowing, not only red, but all colors, indeed. A rainbow of light.

And just when he felt as though the pain, the fire at his hand and at his thigh would burn forever, it stopped, the strange light upon his hand dispersing with a cold wind, the heat from the stone fading to its natural cold as though it had never burned.

"What the devil?" he breathed, just as the Enchanter gasped, his gaze on the sky.

Victor looked up from his hand and narrowed his eyes.

The hole was gone, the thin clouds shifting back to their normal faces, the sky darkening back to its Eleanor-filled dread, the ethereal light that had just been there gone. It was as if nothing had happened.

"What was that?" he asked no one, the sounds of battle behind him vanished as last. He knew without a glance back that his Creatures had won; nothing but the smell of Eleanor's dread filled the air.

The Enchanter had turned to eye him with his words, his scared expression widening into alarm. "The blood," he whispered, transfixed, "that jewelry."

"What of it?" he asked, just as the others moved closer, now free of their respective battles.

"That is the ring the old Vampire had spelled in order to allow you Vampires to walk the surface—but this one is bedded with incredible power. . . ."

"Pardon?"

He stepped closer, his black eyes narrowing upon the bloodied ring in great concentration; Victor could feel his breath on his hand.

"Yes," the Enchanter whispered, grasping his hand and bringing it closer as to better observe the ring, though Victor could not see how he could see through the blood as thick as it was, "that is the magic of the Phoenixes, if I am not mistaken."

He thought back to the ball of fire that had appeared in the strange manor in Scylla, the ball that had exploded, sending the doors of the manor to open, allowing he and Joseph Gail freedom at last. . . .

The Phoenixes? Truly?

He felt the hard stone again, eyes wide. *Could it be?*

"What I wonder is," the Enchanter went on, much to his bemusement, "how did you come across such a. . .potent Enchantment?"

"I've no honest idea," he whispered, feeling all the more uncertain against the Creature's focused gaze. "But nevertheless Enchanter— we've a duty to see through for Eleanor, don't we?" And he cleared his throat, wiping the blood on his hand against the cloak of the still-bleeding Randall, whose eyes were now fluttering weakly though he would not die. His lips parted periodically as though he desired to speak but could not find the words.

And before anyone could say anything else, he stepped past the body of Randall as the Enchanter whispered urgently behind him, demanding to know more of the ring, the strangeness it spurred, for he was certain it was the source of the hole in the sky.

But he could not turn and face him, not when the many questions teemed in his mind, thoughts that scared him, rattled him, for he dared not think the ring he held, the ring Dracula had created him for him was different than the rest, strange. . .powerful. For it would mean Dracula had thought more of him than he'd believed, and in the weight of Eleanor's dread it was a harder burden to bear. *And the Phoenixes?*

He did not stop as he walked, doing his best to ignore the Enchanter, waving, what he was sure, was large white sleeves through the air as he tried his hardest to get his attention. "My Lord! Please! What power do you hold?! Why do you keep it from Eleanor?!"

He lifted hands, sending his Creatures into alleyways once more, determined to put at ease the seeds of hope that had begun to bloom in his dead heart, for he bore a ring *of* Dracula, of the Phoenixes.

And he knew somewhere deep in the trenches of his mind that he had power Eleanor, Xavier did not, the image of the large hole in the sky returning as he stepped over the ash that littered the street, before they were blown away in a warm wind.

※

He clutched his ribs, the pain from walking endlessly in any direction he could sending his breath to hitch in urgent protest, his right shoulder aching where the Lycan's sharp teeth had pierced skin. *The Lycan.* He stifled a growl, gritting his teeth against the pain that filled his entire body, the anger of the transformation, the heat, not gone entirely, no. Still there. . .still—

A flare of burning liquid filled his stomach and rose steadily up his spine, dousing his beating heart in its warmth, and all at once, he found himself staring upon Alexandria Stone.

She stood before him along the path, her eyes bright with the same warmth that filled him now, the darkness that wrapped around the trees and path dispersing into a beautiful glow about her. She was pale, the red silk dress she wore swaying in a cold breeze, and when she opened her mouth, he found all his pain to leave him.

"James, you must return to me." Her voice a lilting song; it burrowed deep into his mind, forbidding him to dare think of anything else. *"Return and be the first of your kind to show this World that Vampires and Lycans can exist side by side, the need to harm dispersed from the blood."*

He blinked against her ethereal glow: it gleamed brilliantly against the dark. "Vampires?" he breathed against the pain that still burned his shoulder and arm. "Lycans? What are you—?"

She took a simple step toward him, her ghostly foot not making a sound against the dirt, and she smiled. *"You were saved by my blood,"* she whispered, the scent of something more along her words, *"and you must be protected."*

"Protected?" he repeated, the pain piercing against his skull, a burning in his throat, his eyes. "What are you talking about, Vampire—?"

She moved on a cold wind to hover just before him, a vision of long dark brown hair and fangs, her eyes a fierce red, and then she was speaking, a sharpness to her tongue he had never heard before, *"My name is Alexandria Stone, descendant of Dracula, keeper of the blood, and you, Lycan, are the hope of my Grandfather to still the needless war between the Dark Creatures. Return to me and take your place, James. It is your duty."*

And before he could say anything at all, she had gone in a fierce, cold wind, the image of her eyes, so red, so commanding unable to leave his own. He blinked rapidly desiring their presence to leave him, so rattled she had left his already aching heart. In the cold of the night air, he stared blankly down the dirt road where nothing lined the horizon but more trees, more dirt, and he blinked back the sting of tears threatening to spill from blurred eyes.

All had been taken from him, indeed, he recalled in sudden sorrow: *Where the bloody hell was Lore? For surely,* James thought, staring around at the line of trees on either side of him, *the man would have known I had failed, that Alexandria was still alive. He would be furious—he would be here, ringing my neck. But he wasn't.* And this fact scared James more than he cared to admit. He had not been sure he could trust the Lycan, but he had shared more about his nature than the Vampires had, he had not tried to subdue his power, in fact, James remembered, rubbing the blood that still poured from his broken shoulder, he seemed to know far more about it than anyone else. *Except,* he thought, *the truth of my blood.*

A low growl rumbled in his chest, the strange glow of warmth still within his heart, burning softly, and with it appeared a faint pull, a small need to walk, to move, though he knew not where.

And her words returned just as he was prepared to take another staggering step against the cold ground.

"Return and be the first of your kind to show this World. . .Vampires and Lycans can exist . . .the need to harm dispersed from the blood."

Return, he thought dimly, wondering just where she was, the faint need to continue on growing just the slightest the more he lingered on her words. *But where are you?*

Chapter Nine

DELACROIX MANOR

Nathanial wiped the blood from his mouth and straightened, pressing his free hand against the coolness of the floor to brace himself. She was in front of him, her eyes glowing gold against the dim, and she opened her gloved hands as if to beckon him forward.

"Come, Nathanial."

He let out a cold breath, feeling his lungs fill with his blood. He spit out more, a snarl leaving his lips. "We've been at this for hours, Madame," he breathed, rising to stand; he dipped as his knees buckled. "I don't. . .understand what. . .you're trying to do."

The glowing eyes moved to his face in the dark. "You've gotten the hang of using your bloodlust to your advantage—you nearly dodged my last spell," she said, stepping toward him. "But you must be famished. You must drink."

He attempted to stand once again, and found he could though his legs shook: he shifted his footing to regain balance, staring upon her as she stopped just before him. "I do grow thirsty. But I thought you said my former master would be having Unicorn Blood sent. Surely you would not have any. . .any. . . ." But his words left him as he realized she was pulling back the sleeve of her robes, her dark skin illuminated in the sparse light the floating balls cast. "What are you—I can't drink your blood!"

"But you have a need for it all the same, no?" Philistia said, holding out her wrist, and indeed, he could not deny her smell, strong though it was as it filled the air, the magic in her blood reaching his nose as strange.

Strange, but still blood.

He stepped to her and touched her wrist, feeling the blood pulse beneath his fingers as he gripped it, and before she could change her mind, he lifted it to his lips and bit across a vein. The slight gasp that left her lips was music to his ears, his mind drawing blank as her blood, tinged with magical prowess, slipped past his lips and flowed down his throat. At once, he felt himself rejuvenated, her blood spiking his own to healthy, glowing heights, and with a sound of satisfaction he removed himself from her and released her arm.

Finding her gaze, he averted his eyes: she looked bothered, in a way he had only seen on the scarce human should he allow them to remain alive once he'd finished feeding from them. Heated, sensual, delirious with the thrill of having their blood taken. It was a thrill he had allowed them to feel, but that was what was strange. He had not allowed her to feel pleasure at all.

She cleared her throat, and he felt it was safe to return his gaze to her. She rubbed her wound with her hand, its leather smearing with her blood, but before long a green light appeared over her wrist, and the blood disappeared, the holes closed.

He could barely say a word before the curtains were ripped back, the balls of light were extinguished, and the loud voice filled his ears beyond the instant sound of fire: he'd gone up in flames with the sun's light and stumbled back toward his room. "Philistia. I never knew *you* would be the one to betray me. If you had *any hesitation* about me receiving my long lost power, you should have *told* me instead of saving this Vampire!"

Nathanial had reached the door, had rolled across the floor to suffocate the flames, and now stared through the doorway, the Ancient Elder's long finger pointing to him. He watched beneath the pain as Equis advanced on Philistia, his tall frame formidable against the light. He could not see Philistia as Equis's long robes hid her from view, but he heard her voice against his own cries of pain. "You plan to kill them—all of them! What would you have me do? Stand by and let you rule with an iron fist—"

"An iron fist?" the angry voice replied. "I never ruled—I gave all of you prominence! Power unmatched! Everything was in accordance with my desires—our desires! Until the bloody birds above took it from me and bestowed it upon those abominations!" Another finger was pointed toward him and he snarled his pain, the blood he'd just taken gone with the suns' rays.

Damn.

"We could not live freely," she said, "we were burdened to your madness—your ways of ruling—the Elves did not have all knowledge of the arcane arts. What was it you said, 'They were not *worthy* of the right?' You are tyrant, Equis, only driven to wake up when there's a chance for you to regain this so-called power!"

A sound of annoyance left the tall man, and he raised a hand in indignation, the long fingers pressed together, palm open, and he swung it forward as if to slap her.

Before it could connect, a new voice sounded out of view and Equis turned, his long black hair swaying down his robes. "Your Greatness," the voice said.

"What?" Equis snapped.

Philistia took a careful step away as his attentions turned to the out-of-view newcomer.

"There's just the matter at hand," the newcomer said as Equis rounded on him, "the Shadowhall Guilds are prepared to move at your word."

Philistia's eyes widened in the light. "Shadowhall? Equis—"

He turned to her, his brow furrowing in his rage. "Shut up, Mastcourt! I'll deal with you when I'm done with this matter. The preservation of magic is more important than your feelings."

Her mouth opened and closed, and through his lowered lids, Nathanial saw a tear run down her cheek. Terror filled her brown eyes, and before she could get out of her stupor, Equis had turned to the Enchanter. "Where are they prepared to venture first?"

"Well, the Vampire town closest to them is Devanger, small though it is. They did not specify through the spell cast whether or not they would venture there first, but the message was clear: complete destruction."

"Excellent." And he turned to Philistia once more, raising a hand to point at her. "See Mastcourt? My plans have already been enacted. No amount of. . .of. . .whatever this is with Mister Vivery shall stop it. And what can the Vampire do? Sizzle to death? I trusted you, Philistia. Trusted you, made you my right hand, had you at my side for all these years—and this is how you choose to betray me? At the crux of my power, my infinite power, you would choose to side with the bloodsuckers? The nightwalkers? The abominations?"

"I side with the Creatures that deserve a chance to right the wrongs their existence has created, yes, but they did not ask for it," she responded, tears still falling. "Dracula was the one who burdened them, burdened us all with his presence—but he's atoned for it," she said before he could say a word in protest. "By preparing what he has to have his creations become human, Equis, is a noble quest. We cannot deny the Vampires that chance!"

Nothing was said for quite a long time and Nathanial closed his eyes, the light from the sun much too bright to fight against any longer. And as he did so, he smelled his burning flesh, yes, but also the curious scent of an Enchanter's energy, the static that is their magic, and he realized, as all went black, that it was Philistia's energy, her magic, and he chanced a glance to her from where he lay.

She was staring past Equis, toward him, and her eyes were still golden in color, the white tainted red with her tears. And he wondered what she was doing when he could no longer keep his eyes open, the pain, sound subsided, and all went black.

✳

Christian Delacroix had left the carriage some blocks back when Eleanor's Creatures had appeared, spreading their strange dread throughout the air. He now ran through back alleyways, eager to reach his home. *She was there. She was alone.* She was all he could think about. Her and her formidable Vampire blood.

He cursed himself for leaving the sword at her side; if he'd had it, he would have been able to know if she were safe, he would have known what to do next. *But that was stupid,* he thought, stilling in-between two tall buildings as cloaked Elite Creatures marched past, *I should know already, she's my charge, mine through the blood.*

But he didn't. He found it most troubling. He couldn't connect to whatever he had felt when she'd first awoken as a Vampire, but it made no bloody sense. He had left her while she slept, and he'd been able to feel her presence, her blood even as he left to gather what they would need for the trip to the Vampire City. It had only died when he'd acquired the carriage, and that was some hours before when darkness had freshly fallen.

He stared at the road ahead of him, the backs of the Elite Creatures getting lost in the thick darkness they conjured from nowhere, and quietly he moved onto the road, his home just there beyond the other

161

row of buildings. He smiled in slight relief: he could smell the salt of the water on the air.

No humans remained on the road he realized with a start, and he stepped forward, slipping into another alleyway just across from the one he left, and as he pressed through the dark, he smelled a familiar scent amidst the dread.

Victor?

He moved into a streetlamp's light, however darkened it was, and narrowed his eyes. There, standing before the black gates to his home was a slew of darkly cloaked Creatures, the mingling smell of Elite and Vampire reaching his nose.

Lights flickered in the windows here and there, but he focused on the white living room where she must have still remained, dismayed to find he could not penetrate whatever magic had been placed around it. *How much magic had Dracula set in place?* he wondered as he stepped onto the road, doing it best to focus on her. *Where was she? Why can I not smell her?*

"What keeps us, my Lord?" a voice within the crowd before the gates asked.

Christian blinked against the voice that responded. "Thoughts," and Christian knew that it was Victor at last, "ah, it is no matter. Do your thing, Enchanter. Let us through the gates."

He watched as gloved hands waved through the air overhead the many hoods, and from the gloved hands appeared a dimmed orange light. Uncatchable words whispered through the dark and the light pressed against the black bars, a brighter, whiter light appearing around them, repelling the orange. There was a flash as the lights fought for power, and then a brilliant white light, a burst of wind, and all Creatures on the road held up their arms to shield their eyes.

When the light died at long last, Christian heard a snarl of frustration, and saw Victor's silver hair blow up in a strong wind. He had turned to the Enchanter at his side, shouting profanities into the air. Christian was not able to hear what transpired, and found this odd. It was as though a bubble remained around the group keeping anyone who was not with them out of their affairs.

Slinking back into the safety of the alleyway, he rethought what was best to do. He wouldn't stand a chance against so many Elite Creatures, even with Alexandria's blood coursing through his veins; he just knew it. But he could barely plan his next move when something blared red from the gates and a strong wind picked up along the street. He watched from the safety of the buildings on either side as the wind howled around the Elites, and then with a sound much like thunder, a great hole opened up in the dark sky, a swirling darkness filling it.

"It's something you hold on your person, I'm sure of it!" the Enchanter was shouting within the howl.

As the wind whipped their cloaks and hoods about their bodies and heads, Christian watched in alarm as another red light appeared in the windows of the manor, and he clutched his heart, feeling his own blood pulse with the familiar energy: she was awake.

"Vampire!" the Enchanter was saying, his arms waving wildly above his head. "Look at what you've rent! Show us what you keep hidden in your pockets!" There were sounds of struggle and then the red light shot up from the gates and straight into the swirling sky. All heads looked upward and hoods fell onto backs, all of them bathed in the red light.

Christian raised his hand against the glare, but stared over it all the same, a hole opening in the sky where the red light pierced it, and he almost thought he saw a large golden wing appear through the hole. But in the next second it was gone, and an angry snarl sounded from before the gates once more.

He looked back down at the street, surprised to see Victor's shaking hand raised toward the sky, the ring upon a finger blaring red. And before anyone could do or say anything else, a great bolt of fire left the sky and crashed right into Delacroix Manor.

He jumped, his heart rising to his throat, and it was not long before the dancing flames could be seen through the windows, screams here and there filling the air.

"My Lord!" the Enchanter cried in astonishment.

But Victor was already pushing against the gates. They swung open and Christian watched, urgency filling his stomach, as the silver hair whirled in the wind and the Vampire stepped through, the Elite Creatures filing through the entrance behind him.

He watched in trepidation, unsure of what he should do, as they began waving their hands in the air, colorful beams of light leaving their fingertips, crashing against Delacroix Manor's white walls, burrowing holes into its face, filling the rooms where crashes and more screams could be heard through the night.

Alexandria!

With one last look toward the backs of the Elite Creatures, Victor who stood in the middle of the winding path before the marble statue of a horse, did not move, or say a word amidst the chaos. And indeed, as Christian stepped out of the alleyway and onto the street, he could see Victor's tall frame shake with telling power. A power he could not handle, a power that consumed him, or was beginning to. It was a sensation Christian was familiar with.

He took another step forward when yet another ball of fire left the sky and roared toward the manor again, its high flames already licking the dread-filled air. He watched it crash into the side of the manor and his heart leapt to this throat. *The white living room.*

Without further thought he ran forward, sprinting through the open gates, sure to keep his footsteps quiet, his every thought on Alexandria and if she were safe. Indeed, he could feel her blood within the air, feel it within his veins, but would not relax until he saw her unharmed. He remained near the gates, pressing himself against them as he moved to the right, toward the corner of the gates. They moved to the side of the manor where the beach remained.

He hesitated for but a moment, Victor's attentions still placed on the burning manor, its resoluteness now beginning to crumble and blacken with the damage it had taken. The many Elites that had been at his back now within it, further screams and shouts filling the air every so often amidst a deafening crash. . . .

He took but a simple breath, alarmed that he could not hear Dracula's voice, have any semblance of guidance at all, for it had been a comfort for the short while he had heard it. It had been a relief, for once, to know that James would be okay, that he had to get Alexandria to safety. He stared up at his home once again and doubted the thought. Was it truly safety if this is what would happen?

He turned his gaze to the swirling sky, the red light still billowing from the ground where Victor had stood before he'd opened the gates. Another flap of large wings appeared for a moment within the hole and then it was gone. He blinked, unsure he had seen it.

And then a raucous scream filled the air and he stiffened. It came from some ways in front of him, the sight of the sand, blackened and covered in sparking flames sending his heart to drop, the words lodging themselves in his throat.

Moving swiftly, he pressed forth, hoping against great hope that Victor did not get the sense to tear his gaze from the manor. He stepped silently over the blades of the grass, rejoicing when his worn boots graced the sand-laden path that led to the beach. And here he could smell the fire, the black smoke, and see better the beginning of a gaping hole in the manor's side. *Bloody hell.*

※

Victor Vonderheide was terrified. The stone in his pocket burned something fierce, but the fire it had caused. . .that scared him more.

Such power, he thought, staring up at the home he'd ventured to in times of joy and crises alike, *my power.*

But what he was to do with it he hadn't the slightest idea, all he knew, indeed, was that he'd accomplished what she desired be done. *Even if it were not my hand that accomplished it.* He tore his gaze off the burning manor to eye the ring on a finger. How it still glowed red.

As screams from the manor filled the night, the Enchanter at his side said, "Regardless of whatever trinkets you hold, she will be pleased." He lifted a gloved hand toward the blackened building now. "You have proven yourself her warrior."

Hmph, he thought, *her warrior.*

A large flame leapt toward him as the front doors were burned. *No*, he decided, then, *not hers.*

He turned from the sight of the burning hallway beyond the doorway, and looked toward the swirling sky. The red beam of light still remained. Its base was at the open gates, burrowing into the ground, leaving a burning circle, and without preamble, he stepped toward it.

"My Lord?" the Enchanter called.

He did not turn. The red circle loomed just there, and yes, when he reached it, the stone in his pocket let out a searing flash of heat and then grew cold. And just as it did, the red light died, the sky roared with a deafening sound, and as he looked up, it closed. It was, once again, as though nothing had happened: the dread-filled sky was calm.

The Enchanter's hurried footsteps drew near. "My Lord," he breathed, "what's happened?"

Victor eyed the Enchanter at last. "I don't know," he said, "I don't—" But he heard the slight footsteps to his left, and smelled the familiar blood on the air, and moving the Enchanter out of the way, he saw the tail end of a black cloak disappearing behind the side of the manor.

"Christian!" he roared, moving swiftly for the Vampire. He rounded the corner, the back of Christian Delacroix venturing toward the large hole in the side of the manor. The chandelier still hung from the wall, its brilliant light still shining.

Magic. Of course the room would be unharmed, he thought, running over the sand to reach the Vampire who had rounded the hole into the living room. He reached it before long, ignoring the crash of waves against the rocks at his back, and stared at the back of Christian. The Vampire had reached Alexandria Stone, who stood beside the couch, her eyes red, skin pale.

My word, he thought, staring at them as Christian touched her face, perusing her for any sign of injury. Victor knew he would find none: he could smell it on her blood, now. *She was perfect. A Vampire. At last.*

Before he could say a word, she had raised a hand toward him, bringing Christian's gaze as well, and in their red gazes, the red of the sword that leaned against the front of the couch, Victor swore he could smell Dracula's blood. *But of course*, he thought, before reason could give way to madness, *she held his blood.*

Christian stepped in front of her, an anger Victor had never known to grace the Vampire just there. "How could you?" Christian yelled, fangs bared.

And through the barrier placed around the room, Victor heard the Vampire's words as though muffled, but hear them he did. He touched the handle of the sword at his waist. "I did what had to be done."

"You've killed them—all of them!" Christian screamed, and Victor thought the Vampire would cry it was so distraught he looked. "For what? For Eleanor bloody Black? What, Victor, do you have to gain by being at her side?"

He tensed, his hand upon the sword trembling, but the ring's heat would not die. "This is for the benefit of the World, Christian," he said, despite the doubt that clawed at his back just as the salt waters' spray did, "if you would just come with me, you would understand!"

Alexandria placed a hand on his shoulder as Victor watched, and Christian noticeably relaxed: his shoulders sank, his eyes returned to their deep black, and he growled softly. As screams filled the air beyond the white door at their back, Alexandria stepped from Christian and grasped the sword.

The stone pulsed in his pocket but Victor would not tear his gaze from her. She was even more beautiful than she'd been alive. Her hair darker still, fell in slight waves down her back, and her eyes, red despite her serene nature still captivated his attention. *She was all that was left,* he realized, *of Dracula's legacy. His blood flowed through her veins. His power.*

His grip on the sword tightened and with no other thought, he released it from its sheath. Both Vampires tensed, but she handed the Ascalon to Christian who took it without a glance her way, and in a blare of red light, the voice filled Victor's mind: *"Protect the Dragon."*

The stone in his pocket was suddenly all he could feel, its deliriously strong heat almost akin to fire, and as he fished it out of his pocket, letting it fall to the sand at his feet where it sizzled, still red, he felt the gust of wind from within the room.

He looked up just in time to see Christian close his eyes, hand clasped with Alexandria's, as both Vampires disappeared from the white living room. And with their departure, it seemed the magic that protected it was gone as well, for the ceiling caved. Victor watched in disbelief as the chandelier crashed atop the couch, the burning ceiling crashing atop it all soon after.

He sank to his knees just as the Enchanter reached him and placed a gloved hand atop his shoulder. "My Lord, what's the matter? It's as though you've seen a ghost."

He did not tear his gaze from the destroyed manor until the red light from the stone dimmed. He stared down at it atop the sand, and knowing it was cool now, picked it up, and before the Enchanter could say another word, he returned it to a pocket of his cloak.

"My Lord?" the Enchanter asked carefully.

Victor would not eye him. He could not. Not after what he'd seen. *The sky, the red light, the stone, the ring. Alexandria Stone. Dracula, Dracula, it was always Dracula. Plans in place, perfectly executed, meticulously planned.*

And just as the beach was flooded with tattered cloaks, the Creatures who wore them congratulating themselves throughout the night, Victor remembered the sky, how it had opened, and he recalled the Phoenixes. *No,* he decided, as he rose to his feet, the Enchanter at his side releasing his grip on his shoulder, *not all was because of Dracula.*

And he managed a smile as he stared at the burned foundation of Xavier Delacroix's home, glad to know, at least, that the Vampire would never return to it, indeed.

Chapter Ten

ABOMINATIONS

Lillith Crane stared at them, long having had her fill of Enchanter blood. The others had taken from the Enchanters hours before, healed just the slightest, and now they stood several feet before the large mountain that housed the magical city as night fell.

The sense of dread filled her as she eyed Peroneous Doe whisper anxiously to himself, stealing furtive glances to the city high above them every few minutes. But she felt his fear was not her own, for she thought on Darien Nicodemeus, still, and what, if anything, had happened to him.

It had been days since they'd seen him fly away from before the doors of Cinderhall Manor, and in that time she had not been able to ignore the feeling that he searched for something of extreme importance. . . .

"Lillith," Christopher Black said from her side, then.

She stared at him as, at his back, Aurora placed glowing hands over a still-burning Aleister Delacroix, the only Vampire not able to take blood: he was still, mysteriously, unconscious.

"Yes?" she asked.

His black eyes narrowed in the dark. A blast of white light pulsed from the mountain's peak. "Are you well?"

She thought of it, not sure she'd ever known wellness, and the memory of her blood entering Darien's system was all she could conjure as another blast of white light lit up the sky. *He would never be human*, she thought, a sadness filling her heart, *Dracula be damned.*

She felt Christopher Black's waiting stare on her, his eagerness for an answer, a hunger she could not describe. *He looked at me as though regretful*, she thought, and with the straightening of her clothes, she smiled coldly. *He should be.*

"I am never well," she said at last, "why do you care?"

He looked hurt, and she found it curious, though a miniscule tug of regret pulled at her heart. "I merely wish to see how you are," he said, and the two Elite Creatures nearby let out snarls of frustration as they whispered amongst themselves. "I do not mean to—"

"Whatever you mean, Vampire, you are under no position to request anything from me. Not after what you've done."

"Lillith, I have apologized—"

"And I have not accepted," she said, bristling, anger burning in her blood, "you've made me this—this monster! And how am I to believe that you did not kill my family as well!"

"There was a fire!" he screamed, sending all gazes in their direction. "Your manor was gone, as was all inside. You were there—on the ground—and I could not let you die—"

"You had no right!" she said, and she saw red. "You had no bloody right! You should have let me stay dead!"

A hand was on her shoulder in the next moment and she turned in surprise. Xavier Delacroix, only slight burns left on his face and hands, stared down at her, concern dressing his green eyes. "Lillith," he said, moving the hand down her back, gently pushing her away from Christopher, "I understand your anger, but you may want to keep your voice down while you argue over what transpired."

She looked up as they stumbled over the sharp rocks, away from the others, surprised to find a smile upon his face. She did not think she'd ever seen him smile. "I apologize, your Grace," she said, "it just angers me. He has no bloody right to request anything from me."

"But do you not feel the unquestionable loyalty to the one who turned you?"

She stopped, planting her boots in forgiving crevices. "If I do, it is vague. I feel more connected to. . .well, to Darien, your Grace."

He turned to her and against the base of the black mountain his front was cast in shadow. She stared only on the glint of green in his eyes. "Darien. What do you feel toward him?"

"It is hard to say, your Grace. His blood compels me. . .I want nothing more than to. . .be at his side, I suppose. Help him. But at the same time. . . ." and her voice fell, the words ones she did not want to utter: embarrassment filled her.

But the Vampire would not be deterred. "Lillith?"

She stared at him, narrowing her eyes against another burst of white light. "I'm scared."

She could barely see the smile line his face. "Naturally, we all are." And he flexed a hand that had been badly burned that morning; the scars still remained. "But what exactly has you scared? I know Darien's new. . .visage is one to be feared. What else troubles you?"

How perceptive, she thought, holding up her hand as yet another brilliant light blew past him. Once it died, she stared upon him. "The state of Vampires," and she eyed a forlorn Christopher Black nearer the mountain's base who stared at her seriously, "if what Darien is. . .if what he is. . .is wh-what—is what we. . .we really are. . . ." She sighed as Aurora and Peroneous's voices could be heard nearing them. "We truly are monsters, aren't we?"

"Your Grace," Peroneous said before Xavier could respond, "we must begin our journey up to Merriwall. It will be morning by the time we reach the top if we wait any longer."

His gaze moved from her to Peroneous and back, and then he looked upward, and Lillith followed the gaze. The mountain's black rock jutted out haphazardly all along the mountain's body, its top not as narrow as most mountains: it was larger than its base, and flat. Atop it the beginning of tall walls could be seen, and the white light blared past it again.

"Fine," Xavier said, bringing her gaze back to him, and with a wink at her, he stepped up to the mountain's base, and pressed a foot against a jutting black rock, prepared to propel himself upward when another voice said, "Wait!"

They turned. Aciel stood beside Amentias and Yaddley, Minerva staring at the dark sky next to Dragor and Aurora, who still kneeled at Aleister's side, glowing hands running over his body. Aciel went on, "That power is immense. Eleanor had good reason to be scared, your Grace. If the Enchanters have regained control over magic—"

Amentias grabbed his arm. "You do not know this is true!"

Aciel bade him a glare, but said all the same, "We have to tell them!"

Lillith felt Xavier's sleeve as he brushed past her, mountain all but forgotten behind them. "Tell us what?" Xavier asked.

"The truth of the Enchanter's power," Aciel said. "It is all consuming. And with the bit of knowledge Eleanor bequeathed me, my time in her stead, I learned the brilliance that is the Enchanting Arts. She told me—us," he said, looking at Amentias, "that Dracula held magic for himself, that he kept it contained. It was why he was able to have the Etrian Elves' swords taken from them, their magical gifts restored, but just barely. He'd encumbered them, reduced them to lesser. It's what he's done, I've understood, for all Creatures.

"Eleanor's. . .gift to her Creatures was the true extent of this power. And with Dracula's death it seems the balance has been restored."

Lillith stared at him, not understanding. It was not until Christopher stepped forward, did anyone speak, and it was Christopher to do so. "It is as I told you Vampires back at that building. He had control of magic."

Xavier said, "But what does this mean, exactly, Aciel?" He pointed a hand at the mountain's base, the holes within it beginning to steam. "Is this why Eleanor was scared?"

Aciel nodded, but Amentias interjected with, "Nonsense. This is all conjecture, your Grace. Aciel is not certain what truth magic holds on the world, only that we were bequeathed the gifts from Eleanor. But it has waned, now that we are out of her service."

Peroneous stepped forward. "Our magic has been restored, your Grace." He waved a dark hand to Aurora who had abandoned Aleister some moments ago and now stood, staring at them. "As you have witnessed, time and time again. But I believe what the Elite Creature means to say is that the Enchanters. . .they may not be welcoming."

"So what?" Xavier asked, a hand on the Ascalon's handle. "As King, surely, they will be understanding to our plight—"

"Equis the Ancient Elder is not known for being understanding, your Grace!" Peroneous snapped.

Aurora stepped forward. "Peroneous. . . ."

"If Eleanor is scared," the dark Enchanter said, "it is for good reason. They are at their full power—and they do not favor Vampires. . .not after what I did. Enchanters do not like being the Vampires' pets—"

"That is not true!" Aurora shouted.

"It is known!" Peroneous retorted. "Just because you took a fancy to the scarred one doesn't mean the rest of us have been at ease with what we've been forced to endure!"

It happened before anyone could see it: Aurora strode the length between them and threw a punch at Peroneous's jaw. It landed with a much-too-loud crack. As the Enchanter staggered back atop the rocks, Aurora said, nursing her hand, "Don't you dare! You were the one that helped Dracula get to his state of—of muddled perfection, turning the tides of the world out of our favor! And now they are here, Peroneous. The Vampires are here! And th-they're doing something to end the torture they have rent on our lives—the lives of all Creatures! They are not Dracula! They are his creation—his children, yes, but *they are not him!*"

Dragor had a hand on Aurora's shoulder in the next moment, and when she turned to look at him, her dark eyes were wet, tears rolling down her face.

Lillith eyed Xavier. He too looked shocked. What the woman had said. . . *"The torture they have rent. . . ."* She remembered the way Darien looked against the tree, limp, lifeless, until she'd given him her blood. . . .

As Dragor consoled Aurora, Peroneous rose to his feet, a hand rubbing at his jaw. Narrowing his eyes against yet another blast of white light, he started forward for Xavier. Aciel appeared just before the King in the next moment, keeping Peroneous at bay. "What is the meaning—" Peroneous began.

"You must think, Enchanter. Anger toward all here will do you no good," Aciel interjected. "You were correct in saying the Enchanters will not favor us. What do you propose we do about it before we move forward?"

And to all that watched, the smile lifted the Enchanter's face, but it was not kind. He looked rather sick, as though what he would propose he would never dream of considering. And then he said, "We send the ones most able to handle that energy."

Aurora let out a sound much like a wail. "I won't leave him!"

All eyed her. With their stares, she seemed to remember where she was, and said, quieter now, "I won't leave Aleister."

Lillith eyed the unconscious Vampire near Yaddley Caddenhall. His eyes would not open even as the blares from above continued on brighter in rapid succession, bathing his scars. How many there were. . . .

"And I'm going up there!" Xavier said next, pulling Lillith's gaze from Aleister. The King turned on a heel, stepping past her up to the mountain's base once more. He placed a boot onto the mountain's side again, and lifted himself up, pressing a hand on another rock above him.

Peroneous rushed past her, a dark hand grasping the tail of Xavier's cloak. He pulled him down, and Xavier stumbled back, falling to the rocks below. "You can't, Xavier!" Peroneous said as the Vampire glared at him from the ground. "He'll kill you!"

And before anyone could say a word, yet another white light blared, this one brighter than the rest, and a bundle of black robes fell out of the sky at the mountain's base right beside the dark Enchanter, shards of sharp rock and dust flying up into the dark air.

※

Peroneous Doe waited until the rain of rubble left his back, before he moved, lifting himself from Xavier, turning toward the source of the crash. His eyes widened in his medallion's glow, for it was a woman in the crater that had formed, her dark skin littered with cuts, eyes closed, black robes adorned her limp body, lined with daggers. They gleamed in the red light as the dust dispersed with a harsh wind, and Peroneous stepped closer to her, able to see the trail of blood that left her red lips.

"Who is that?" Amentias asked.

Aurora, who had been wringing her hands together beside Dragor said, "That's Philistia Mastcourt. She's. . .well, it's simply impossible. She's Equis Equinox's right-hand. She wouldn't be seen without him—"

Another burst of brilliant light blared and from the sky appeared a man in green robes. He fell feet first, just inches above Philistia's body before he hovered, the wind billowing up, blowing his green robes up around him. He held numerous daggers on his person, held in place with leather sheaths, and his black eyes glowed as he eyed them.

Peroneous heard Xavier withdraw his sword, heard the arrows both Christopher and Lillith aimed in their quivers, and he raised his hands, prepared to cast the next spell that would enter his mind.

"His Greatness is not allowing trespassers upon his sacred home," the man's voice boomed through the passageway. "You must leave."

Fear ran through him with the man's words. *Trespassers. We did not have favor here, not at all!*

Aurora said, "We are here for his Greatness, Equis. We seek—"

"I don't care what you seek, woman. His Greatness has spoken," the man said. "All non-magical Creatures. . . ." But his voice trailed as he eyed the Vampires present at last. His glowing gaze moved to Peroneous. "Enchanter. . .why do you journey with the abominations?"

"Abomina—" Xavier started.

Peroneous raised a hand, bidding the Vampire silence. "Cleaner," he began, for he recognized the Enchanter as such: the green robes were spelled with light to keep the darkness of the world at bay, "we journey with these Vampires because they. . .they have been chosen by Dracula—"

"Abominations!" the Enchanter said, and he threw forth a hand, blowing them all back against the rocks.

Peroneous landed with a groan, a large rock's sharp point stabbing his back. With a cry, he dislodged himself, rising to stand, keeping his focus on the still-hovering Enchanter, who had now lifted his hands again, sending red and black lights through the dark to strike various Creatures.

He was not able to tell who it was, nor did he desire to look. The Enchanter was striking them with little remorse, indeed. *They truly do not care for the state of the world*, he thought in fear. The venom in the Enchanter's eyes would not die, and as the screams filled the dark air, the smell of the old blood filled his nose, Peroneous felt the medallion at his chest grow hot with that unbearable heat.

And without another thought, he lifted his hands into the air, the Enchanter continuing his tirade of encumbering spells, and he sent the blast of black energy straight toward the Enchanter's heart. *"Sacrade Elipsum!"*

All at once, the Cleaner's hands folded into fists, the spells died, and the black energy overtook all. From his heart onward, the black spread like a sickness, until at last, and finally it reached his hair, hands, and feet, and with a scream, he burst apart.

Blood, skin, and chunks of bone splattered against his face and robes, the rocks and walls on either side of him, but wiping it away, he turned to eye the others.

They all lay atop the ground, swords and daggers several inches from weak hands, but it was Xavier Delacroix that held his interest the most. The Vampire was shaking violently on his back, the Ascalon barely in his grip. His eyes were wide, staring up at the dark sky in horror as though he saw something he wished to deny, and from his mouth spilled blood, though much to Peroneous's growing terror, it was black.

"Xavier!" he shouted, kneeling at the Vampire's side, a hand on his chest.

Xavier would not eye him; it was as if he wasn't there.

"Damnit! Xavier!" he screamed, fear flooding through him in earnest. *If the Vampire died, we would be at the mercy of Eleanor's Creatures*, and he eyed the black mountain whose top was bathed in light, *and the wrath of Equis Equinox*. For he knew he had crossed a line by killing the Cleaner, and he knew Equis knew he had done it—had known they were venturing here, for the Ancient Elder held control of magic again. This much could no longer be denied.

Tearing his gaze from the mountain, he eyed the others once more. Eyes stared at him blankly, and not a soul moved atop the ground. He almost feared them permanently dead when a strange growl left the Vampire at his side.

He eyed the King again and hastily shuffled away, eyes wide in disbelief. The Vampire's hands were clawing against the rocks, growing larger just as Darien Nicodemeus's had. . .

What on Earth—no!

He moved to the Vampire again, avoiding his sharp claws. He dragged his palm against a nearby rock, and pressed it against Xavier's lips.

The Vampire drank as though starved, the complete black of his eyes seeming to regain sense: They appeared red through the dark, and he sat up, much to Peroneous's bemusement, grasped Peroneous's hand with his claws, much too large still, and squeezed as if to pull out more blood.

The scream left his lips, a rush of energy pooling through his veins in attempt to keep the Vampire from feeding more than was necessary, as it should, but he was alarmed when the energy met the Vampire's lips in a red light then died, useless.

Tears left his eyes as the Vampire continued to drink, the pain unbearable. "Xavier! Enough!" he shouted, the Vampire's claws finally dispersing, his hands returning to normal. But still he gripped the hand with no means of releasing it. "Enough!"

But the Vampire merely glared at him with red eyes, and it was not until a loud bird's song could be heard somewhere overhead, that Xavier released him at last.

Wrenching back his wrist, he glared at the Vampire who paid him not a mind, for the Vampire stared up at the sky, and following his gaze, Peroneous saw the large black bird glide across the dread-filled darkness amidst a burst of white light before swerving serenely over the large stone wall that kept the rest of the world from view.

The moment it was gone, he fell to his knees, the sting of the rocks registering, yes, but he was far too tired to care. He had used *Sacrade Elipsum*, though he knew he shouldn't. The energy it requires is vast, and it is quite looked down upon, indeed, but he had no choice—the Enchanter was going to kill the others. . . .

He looked around at the narrow passageway once more, the unmoving bodies of the Caddenhall siblings, the Order of the Dragon, and the two Elite Creatures striking him, beneath the weakness, as strange. *They should be awake, by now*, he thought, his still-bleeding hand gracing the rocks as his ability to kneel was taken from him. He turned to Xavier, who had stood, and was staring down at him in thought.

"Sorry," Xavier said, and before Peroneous could ask what for, he kicked him square in the head with a bloody boot, and all went black.

✕

He stared at the dark Enchanter as blood left his ears, and grimaced.

"*Come to me Xavier,*" she said, as yet another white light blared from above.

Brushing it away, he focused on what just happened. Staring at his hands, he recalled how hard it had been to focus on anything else but the sky, how it had swirled with Eleanor's dread, but also Dracula's light. He'd known nothing else, then, but the pain, the screams filling his mind, of the Enchanter's spell as it struck him, removing, he knew, the very essence of what made him a Vampire. The many times he had shared blood with Eleanor, with other Vampires returned within that pain as though bringing it forward.

That was when he had felt his blood boil, his body shake, the claws. . . .

Darien.

It is true, he thought then, staring up at the mountain's base, its white light shining permanently now, *the blood of other Vampires turns us into. . .into monsters.*

He stared at the bodies of the Order of the Dragon, of Lillith Crane, and his heart sank. *She truly wasn't given a choice*, he thought, seeing the body of Christopher Black almost atop her as though he'd moved to shield her from the blasts before he'd fallen. *No one was given a choice.*

"*Xavier.* . . ." the voice breathed, silk against his ears, and he wondered what more secrets she held in her mind, though he wouldn't dare ask through way of the mind. Not anymore.

He had felt a sickening screaming in his ears whilst he lay atop the ground, fraught between this world and another, one he could not fathom, but it was darker, worse than the dread that existed, here.

With a snarl, he turned from the others, able to smell their blood. *Alive, but injured.* Relieved with this fact, he stepped to the mountain's base and began his ascent, unsure whether he had made the right decision in moving for Eleanor.

She was, after all, the reason he was lost in this world. But, he reminded himself, catching a rock and propelling himself up as the large bird circled back overhead, letting out another cry, she was also the reason he was able to go on.

Chapter Eleven

NATHANIAL'S SAVIOR

Equis kicked the Vampire across the room, watching as he slid against the hard tiles, the wall cracking as he slammed against it.

The blood that left the Vampire's lips was the elixir to his supreme happiness, and he waved his hands through the bright air, smiling when the red light reached the Vampire and lifted him against the wall.

"Die, Vampire," he said, stepping toward him, "it will be the most honorable thing you've yet done in this world."

A snarl left Nathanial's lips despite the spell that held him in place, and Equis raised an eyebrow. "To resist *Symbolia Menta*," he whispered, curious, "is impressive. How are you able?"

He waved another long-fingered hand through the air and the Vampire's head was freed from its invisible binds. Equis watched as he shook his head as though dispelling burdensome thoughts, and said, "Madame Mastcourt. . .taught me how to use my bloodlust—"

Equis laughed. "Use your—come now Vampire, don't be daft! A Vampire's bloodlust holds no power other than to propel your afflictions to get your acquired sustenance!" And he waved a hand, Nathanial once more unable to speak.

"Now Vampire, let us try this again, where is your new king? This Xavier Delacroix? Tell me, or die."

The gray eyes merely glared at him beneath the red light, and Equis grinned, pleased the Creature was choosing to die, for all the good it did. He would find out where Xavier Delacroix was on his own.

Mind set, he waved both hands prepared to reduce the Vampire to ash for good, when the presence swept over him. Absolute and damning, he gasped amidst the suddenness of its nature. *The Cleaner is dead.*

Ignoring Nathanial's continued confused glare, he eyed the rest of the great hall. He had meant to leave it a few days before, but doing away with Philistia, torturing Nathanial had held his attention. The woman had moved to attack him when his back was turned, and he had protected himself as he should. He had waved a hand and pressed against the blue light that left her gloved fingertips with his golden light. It sent her barreling back through the air, and despite her valiant attempts to thwart him with counter spells, he'd overcome her, sending her toppling over the mountain's side. The Enchanters were horrified, but they dared not say a word against his reclaimed air of power.

As it should be.

He'd stepped back into his home, surprised to find Nathanial Vivery still alive, glowing with a golden brilliance, grey eyes hardened in their anger as he'd gazed up at him from the floor.

The sun's light had pressed upon him, brightening his red hair, but he would not burn.

Equis had found this most curious.

Now, Equis recoiled, sinking into the long white couch, hand over his heart. For that was where he felt the pain the strongest. The magical center that tied all who did magic to his heart, the seat of his infinite power.

He ignored Nathanial as the Vampire slid down the wall, the spell placed upon him all but forgotten. *The Cleaner. Dead. How. . . .*

Sacrade Elipsum.

He felt it then, pressing a long hand atop the cushion at his side. Someone had cast that most powerful spell. But who?

He could not tell, could not know—his senses of the art were not all reclaimed. But that would come with time. . . .

"Your Greatness," a voice said from an open doorway.

He looked up, a tall Fae standing there, her white dress flowing freely about her. Her blonde hair lay unbound against her back, her feet bare. Her blue eyes glowed with knowing as she eyed him. Never once did she look upon the Vampire.

He stood from the couch despite the pain that still filled his heart.

"What is it, Propheta?" he asked, stepping closer to her. The light from the suns bathed her in their immense glow.

She did not look down while she eyed him, and he figured she was Seeing. It was so intense her gaze was. "A Vampire—Xavier Delacroix. . .he comes for you. He will see Nathanial injured and he will question you. You will try to placate him, for you will see the power he holds in his death. And your Greatness. . . ." she breathed, blue eyes still looking beyond him, "he will call upon them."

He blinked, the pain in his heart growing with fear. "Them? Propheta, come now. Speak plain. Why on Earth would I ever be scared of the Vampire? What power could he possibly hold?"

She took a slow breath, vision still moved beyond the room they remained in. "He will call upon the Phoenixes, your Greatness. They will rain down fire from the sky. Destroy Merriwall. Destroy you."

His lips pursed. *The Phoenixes? Syran? Nonsense.* And yet. . .he could not bring himself to say this aloud, not when her blue gaze still glowed, her Sight still claimed her. The vision of a Fae, he knew, was damning. Changing, but damning still. That she appeared to him at all was worrisome enough, but this. . . "Syran would not—would never destroy Merriwall. And he cannot touch us, anyway, Propheta. The Dark World is off limits. Is kept. . .kept from. . .from. . . ." But he saw the way her glowing eyes focused on him, and he knew even that had changed.

"The World is no longer 'dark,' tainted, your Greatness," she said seriously. "With your power your own again, with Alexandria Stone's. . .unleashing, the World is seeing a reprieve from Eleanor Black's dread."

He stepped away. "They *can* appear *here*? They can l-land? But they can't! The Vampires—the beasts are still here! Is their. . .wrongness not enough to keep the Phoenixes at bay?"

Propheta's blue eyes lost their glow and her plain face was only brightened by the light pouring in through the windows now. "The Vampires and Lycans, your Greatness, are lesser in their forms than they used to be. The dread they instill now, is nothing compared to what they once were. The World is free to the Phoenixes once more."

"But that's impossible," he said, glancing at Nathanial. The Vampire still remained against the wall, still glowed faintly with a golden light. *Could it be?* "What would Syran want. . .should he ever. . .return to land?"

She shrugged, her blonde hair flying out behind her as she stepped to him. "I could not See his desires, your Greatness. Only Xavier Delacroix's. And yours. And you are worried that Syran will grant the Vampires pardon for their attempts at repairing the damage their existence has made."

He said nothing, his mind lost to all the new damning possibilities. *Syran, here. Not again. Not yet. My power has yet to be completely reclaimed.*

She touched the sleeve of his layered robes and he blinked upon her bravado. Now drawn out of his mind, she took the chance to continue to speak:

"You needn't worry, your Greatness. I will help you reclaim what was lost. I will help you end the Vampires' existences, and keep the Elves from ever regaining control over the Enchanting Arts."

He stared, her plain features becoming beautiful the more he stared. "Propheta. . . ." How she knew it all.

Wondering why he had never used her abilities to his advantage before, wondering why he had kept the intelligence of Philista Mastcourt close at hand and never the Arcane knowledge of a brilliant Fae, he smiled. For here was his answer to all his problems. And he needn't say a word for she knew it all. Knew it, and wanted to help him regain it all.

Rethinking the lesser status held by the Fae under his rule once before, he vowed he would never discount their abilities again. And leading her out of the room, the weakened Vampire letting out a snarl as they passed, he focused on just what he could do to keep the Phoenixes from ever stepping foot back on Earth again.

※

Nathanial Vivery heard them step deeper into the large manor, and at once, he tried to move. His hands would not lift from the floor; heavy they were with a weight he could not see. The sun pressed against him, and through his pain, his weakness, he was surprised he did not burn like before.

Philistia. She had done something.

Yes, he remembered the gold of her eyes as she stared at him before Equis sent her flying through the large room.

She saved me, he thought, staring around the room with bleary eyes now, blinking as the brilliance of the two suns beamed through the tall windows. *Where was she?*

He had not seen what Equis had done to her when they'd left the room. He had only heard the gasps from the remaining magical

Creatures outside the large manor, the stifled cries of disbelief. He recalled the way Philistia's gaze darkened as she'd glared upon Equis when he'd first appeared. *Scared. She was scared of him. Scared of his rule. But didn't she have every reason to be?*

"I will help you reclaim what was lost. I will help you end the Vampires' existences, and keep the Elves from ever regaining control over the Enchanting Arts."

The Fae. Nathanial attempted to sit up properly against the wall, straining against the pain that coursed through him. He struggled to hear anything more from the other room, for a Fae at the Ancient Elder's side was dangerous. Never given proper credit for their power, it did not surprise him that one would take advantage of the current state of chaos and attempt to gain greater favor than their kind ever had before.

He could hear nothing at all but the wind as it pressed against the windows' panes, an air of something more keeping anything from reaching his heightened senses. *Magic. Of course.* Gritting his teeth, he pressed a hand to the ground, attempting to rise to his knees when he remembered what she'd said about Xavier.

Xavier was coming to rescue me.

But was it true? Yes, her eyes had glowed with the Sight all Fae are privy to when the Vision takes them, but it could have all been an elaborate trap. No one knew the truth of the Fae's power, indeed, besides their own, their gift was one not many desired to discover mainly due to the nasty side effects their blood held for Vampires.

It was known far and wide the blood of a Fae taken by a Vampire resulted in rapid visions all but gained before the mind could process it and then ultimately permanent death.

He made it to his knees before he heard the wind press against the windows' glass again, and he looked up. The clouds had disappeared. The brilliance of the suns' light almost blinded him, but through the golden rays, he could just make out the figure of a tall man hovering within the sky.

As the light brightened, the man's silhouette seemed to glow all its own, a brilliant white cutting sharply against the gold. Nathanial tore his gaze from the tall windows at once, eyeing the doorway Equis and Propheta had walked through. He wondered if they would believe him had he mind to yell.

"Abomination. . . ."

He looked back toward the window, the voice thick in his head. The man still hovered, and unable to see his eyes, Nathanial felt the man not real until a brilliant light shined from the figure and Nathanial was able to see what hovered there in full:

He was light—his skin filled with life, black hair settled at his shoulders, and he wore long black robes. His eyes were black amidst the golden light, and he stared upon Nathanial as though angry.

Before Nathanial could say a word, the man said, his voice rippling through the window and piercing Nathanial's ears with ease: *"You are lucky. . .Creature. Syran. . .is amused by you. Your life is spared, for now. Do not fail your father."*

And in a burst of brilliant fire, a screech of ethereal music, the man was gone.

He blinked against the light, trying his best to see through it, see the strange man once more, but when the unearthly cry left his ears, a harsh buzzing swiftly replaced it, and he stared suddenly upon the brightly illuminated sky.

A needless breath escaped him, and he stared at the ground trying his best to regain his senses: everything swam before his eyes, a blinding red hue overtaking all, but he knew it was not his lust for blood. Something else was there, something he could not begin to understand. His head pulsed with his pain and he stared blindly at his hands, surprised to make out the gold light still there amidst the red.

And then footsteps were upon him, and before he could turn, the gentle hand was upon his shoulder, and he almost thought it to be Philistia when the Fae's voice sounded overhead:

"What magic do you still hold, Vampire?" Her tone was dark, the danger in her voice clear.

He could say nothing as the buzzing continued, a maddening call that had not left with the man's strange voice.

Something hard was pressed into his back and he found himself held against the floor, a fresh cry of pain leaving his lips. It felt like the business end of a wooden staff.

"I said," she repeated, venom in her voice, "what magic, Vampire? You reek of it."

"I mold mo magish," he sputtered, tasting the cold of the floor.

The staff was pressed deeper against his spine, a strangled cry leaving his lips once more. "Then why has Equis's future changed? Xavier Delacroix's?"

What? he thought, the pain issuing from the staff's end. He still saw red, his ears still buzzing with the penetrating sound.

Propheta made a sound like a grunt and the staff was released from his back. "Stay where you are," she said. He heard her step away, and then nothing more.

The buzz was a dull ache now, his vision still red as he eyed the floor, and it was a while before he heard the footsteps approach: there were many.

". . .When I returned, he wasn't coherent, your Greatness. I left him, thinking he merely needed his rest, but that's when I felt it. The visions changed." It was Propheta, and thankfully she did not press her staff into his back again.

A great shadow crossed over him, darkening the red ground, and he knew, somehow, that it was Equis.

"What did they become?" Equis asked. "Your visions?"

He heard soft footsteps pad the cold floor closer to him, and smelled her blood. "Darkened, regrettably. All changed. I can no longer see Xavier, nor your future, your Grace."

"So he does not move here?" Equis asked, and relief dressed his voice.

"That is safe to say. Things can change in several hours as we know," she responded.

Several hours?

There was a hum of approval from the Ancient Elder, and then he said, "But you feel Nathanial Vivery has interfered with these visions?"

"I do," she said, while another voice, one Nathanial did not recognize whispered something unintelligible, the buzzing quite dull now.

✳

Equis turned to the man and shook his head. "No, we cannot move for Shadowhall now, not until Propheta has had a vision on it."

The Enchanter appeared lost, his hood low over his head. "But your Greatness, they await you there. They have just sent the seventh letter. Arrived by Fairy just now." And Equis watched as he pulled out a small note from a pocket of his cloak and read, *"We are eager to work with you, your Greatness. We await your word."*

Equis stared at the paper in the Enchanter's gloved hand. "We simply cannot move," he said, resolved to see his power restored, indeed. "Not until Propheta has a vision telling us it would be best."

The Enchanter looked as though he wished to protest, but ultimately decided against it, bowing low before turning, leaving the room.

Once gone, Equis stared at her, eager to know what truly caused her Sight to change. "Well?" he asked. "What has the Vampire done to release your vision?"

"I cannot truly say," she whispered, her eyes downcast, and he thought she were embarrassed. "But I assure you, Equis, if you leave me with him, I can get to the bottom of it."

He blinked. "What? I cannot just leave you alone with the Vampire, Propheta—"

"Well why not?"

"He's a Vampire! No matter if he's weakened—" heading her off, "he's still a bloody Vampire and I won't have a Fae with your. . .courage bitten!"

She looked cross. "They cannot drink my blood, your Greatness! They would suffer for it; we all know it! So why can I not get from him what I need?"

He stared at her, seeing the darkness in her gaze. *Perhaps I was too quick in thinking she would truly help.* He sighed. "You say the Vampire stopped your visions. . .yet he is clearly weakened by something, still, perhaps, the bout faced with me. Now, if you say Xavier Delacroix is to come here, I find it in my best interest to stick with that until anymore. . .visions surface. And I," he said before anything else could change his mind, "*am* heading for Shadowhall at last. I cannot forget my actual plan, whatever your visions tell me. Unless you see my exact plan changing anytime soon?" And he appraised her seriously, her downcast gaze telling him all he needed to know.

With a cold smile, he stepped from them, heading toward the door the Enchanter had walked through. Trying to remember the Enchanter's name, he decided the Enchanter would journey with him. After all, he had not been awake for centuries, it was necessary to know just how the World had changed, even with the strange Creatures running about. *And,* he thought, never chancing a glance back, knowing they were watching his protruding back, *I will see it for myself, not from the mouth of another.* He frowned. *Philistia had the freedom to tell me all while I slept and she betrayed me at my brightest hour. Never again.*

※

Xavier Delacroix pressed a burning hand into the snow above him and pulled himself up with a great heave. His chest brushed against the snow atop the flat stone of the mountain's top, and he eyed the large stone wall ahead of him through the flames. There was no door, no gate, no entryway, indeed.

He shimmied forward until his feet were on the ground as well, his entire body afire, but he'd long since gotten used to the pain: he'd started to burn with the sun's heat halfway up the mountain, the real sun rising as well.

Ignoring the fact that he should have at least brought along Peroneous or Aurora, for they could have shielded him from the sun, surely, he rose to his feet. The wind was ferocious, and he found himself pressed back, teetering on the edge of the mountain. Regaining his balance as it passed, another loud cry issued from above and he looked up, the same black bird that had been circling the mountain as he climbed it, hovered directly overhead.

It was terribly large, he realized, its beak black, long and slightly curved. Its wings were large, about twice its body's length, which was already long in itself, and it seemed to be staring down at him with its strange black eyes.

He still burned, but he could no longer feel the flames, could only see them leap and dance from his skin, and then nothing.

Before he could utter his surprise, the bird let out yet another cry and flew off toward the Mountains of Cedar.

He watched it go in wonder, knowing he had never seen a creature like it before. And before he could think any more on it, the sound of doors opening reached his ears and he turned toward the high white walls.

Large, gold-embroidered doors had appeared there sometime he had not known, and were opening against the light of the suns, that miraculously, no longer burned him. He tensed as the incredibly tall man stepped forward, at his side was a regular Enchanter with black robes (for he felt the first man was not human at all).

The tall man with long, flowing black robes, a red traveling cloak around his shoulders, stared at him in disbelief, and Xavier stared at him in bemusement, unsure of what he should do.

"Your Greatness, it's—"

"Yes," the tall man said irritably, heading him off, "I know who it is."

Xavier released the sword at his waist, shaking his head of Eleanor's voice. "Who are you?"

The tall man smiled, and Xavier thought him quite worldly; it was as though he'd lived for many years, much like Evert, indeed. "I am Equis Equinox, Vampire," the tall man said. "And you, badly burned walking dead you are, are Xavier Delacroix, are you not?"

The sword twitched in his hand. "I am," he whispered, Peroneous's words rushing to his mind: *The Enchanters. . .they may not be welcoming.*

"Oh goodie," Equis whispered, and he waved a gloved, long-fingered hand through the air, and Xavier found himself unable to move. The Ascalon fell out of his hand, and Equis stepped toward him, moving on a trail of blue light. "I was told I could expect you, here, but I brushed it off as nonsense. It seems the Fae are not entirely useless. I was rash, yes, but no matter." And he pressed a large hand atop Xavier's head.

There was darkness suddenly, and then fresh pain, terribly fresh. It felt as though he were being ripped apart, and somewhere in his burning mind he recalled the time Eleanor had done the very same to him, begin to pull the muscle from bone—

There was a horrible screeching sound off in the distance, and then, "What in the bloody hell is that?"

The hand was removed from his head, and he opened his eyes.

Both Equis and the Enchanter were watching the sky behind him in horror. He turned to their gaze, and his eyes widened, for there was Darien Nicodemeus, large black wings flapping brusquely through the bright air.

He was headed straight for them, his black eyes within his long black face glistening in the light of the suns. A thrill of fear swept across Xavier as he watched the Creature near, and when it was just before him, he ducked on instinct, felt its wind blow up what remained of his clothes and hair, and turned on his knees.

Darien's long talons clawed at Equis shoulders as he swooped low over the tall Ancient Creature. Xavier watched in bemusement as Darien lifted the Creature into the air, back over the wall of Merriwall, much to the bewilderment (for shouts and screams filled the air) of the Creatures within the city.

He watched as Equis was dropped over an immensely tall building within the walls, and the Enchanter who had lingered behind in abject horror let out a scream, and ran back into the city, toward the tall manor at the end of a long, glowing path.

Xavier rose slowly to shaking legs, the Ascalon in hand, unsure of why Darien had saved him—for he had felt, strangely, that this is what the Creature had done: He was certain Equis was prepared to reduce him to ash.

He blinked in the light of the suns, wondering why indeed he did not burn, and refocused on Eleanor's call, for it remained beneath all else: *"Xavier. . .Xavier where are you? I cannot reach you. I cannot see you. Return to me. . . ."*

In due time, he responded, stepping with badly burned legs toward the high open doors. His thoughts turned to the Ancient Creature he had seen. What had he said? That the Fae was right after all? What Fae? Narrowing his eyes in the light, he pressed forward, much to the alarm of watching Enchanters, Elves, and Fae, all of whom had turned from the skies with Darien's swift departure.

He limped forward, his sword's metal shining brilliantly in the light, but it was not red, and he half-wondered if Dracula's light could reach him here. Yes, it was so dim any of the Great Vampire's influence appeared to have become when he'd ventured for Eleanor Black those few days before.

He has just reached the middle of the large city, a heaviness descending upon his shoulders, a weakness, when, through the crowd of bemused magical Creatures, he saw the Vampire striding toward him.

His eyes were no longer gold but gray, unfamiliar through the brilliance of the suns. His red hair was doused in darker blood, his face bruised, numerous rips and tears at his clothes, and he limped as he approached, but there was no mistaking who it was.

"Nathanial?" he coughed, blood flying from his lips and landing on the shining ground. Others moved away hastily as the blood fell, but he ignored them and dipped to his knees once more. *Weakened, greatly. . .need blood.*

Nathanial reached him in the next second, though he winced noticeably as he descended to a knee right in front of him, and placed a glowing golden hand upon his shoulder. "Your Grace," he breathed, and Xavier could smell the terror, the weakness on his voice, "you were a fool to come alone."

"I was a fool to come at all."

"Glad I am that you did, you should have come with Aurora—the better to save me and all that."

195

He narrowed his eyes. "Save you?" He covered his mouth as more blood left him with yet another cough.

The gray eyes widened. "You did know I was here, didn't you?"

"I had no—" he began when a thunderous boom sounded through the crowd.

All heads turned toward the large manor at the end of the road, a radiant blue wall appearing just before the high doors. It was translucent, rippling against the light, and beyond it, Xavier could just see Equis, the anger terrible upon his face. *A face,* Xavier thought suddenly, *that should be older than it was.*

"Vampire," Equis boomed, beginning to step down the many steps of the mansion, the blue wall moving with him, "you have trespassed upon sacred ground! You have corrupted our world, rendered we Enchanting great lesser in our brilliance!"

Silence dressed the city, despite Equis's loud footsteps the closer he drew to them, and as the crowd parted in full to allow the Ancient Elder passage, Xavier could see the looks of fear upon their faces.

Nathanial stood hesitantly and turned toward Equis before Xavier could say a word of protest. He spread his glowing, shaking arms wide, and Xavier's eyes widened.

"You won't harm him, Equis!" Nathanial yelled.

"Stand aside, Vivery!" the Elder yelled, but still the blue wall remained, a resolute shield keeping anything, be it a spell, or a fist, from reaching him.

"I will not!" Nathanial breathed, and Xavier wondered how the Vampire was still standing, a sudden wave of guilt crashing against him.

He did this for me—thought I was to save him—and I'm only here to find out what has Eleanor scared. He snarled his frustration, staring around Nathanial to eye the impressive figure of Equis Equinox. *Now I know.*

A great ball of light appeared before Equis, a hole the size of the light appearing in the blue wall. Xavier watched with narrowed eyes as the ball zoomed to Nathanial and hit him square in the chest with no sound at all.

The Vampire began to fall, but he caught him before he could hit the ground, the Ascalon falling out of his hand. His head rested on Nathanial's shoulder as he tucked his arms beneath the Vampire's armpits, and in his ear, he whispered, "Nathanial, I'm sorry. I didn't come for you. You don't have to die for me—"

"Then who," Nathanial breathed, eyes fluttering with great weakness, ". . .did you come for?"

He hesitated, realizing how ridiculous it would sound if it were uttered aloud. *Eleanor was scared of the Enchanters' regained power*, he thought darkly. *I should have listened to Peroneous. He knew more about this world than I—*

The blue wall disappeared and Equis, in a rush of blue and purple light, waved his long-fingered hands through the air. From them streaks of blue and purple light emerged, aimed straight for them, much to Xavier's growing horror, and then, quite suddenly, a figure appeared before Nathanial's limp feet.

Her black robes billowed wildly about her slender frame as her hands, raised to head level, were taut with practice, several streaks of red and gold light leaving them, and with her scream of determination, Equis's eyes widened and he dropped his hands, taking several steps back.

Gasps and cries of alarm left the Creatures around them, but before Xavier could wonder why, the woman turned her head toward him, and his eyes narrowed.

He recognized her as the woman who lay in the crater at the base of the mountain, and yes, blood still pooled from a corner of her red lips, and her dark skin was perhaps, made slightly darker here and there along her face through bruises, but she was not dead at all.

Doing his best to remember what Aurora had said the woman's name was, he watched in surprise as she cast Nathanial a sad look, and then turned back to Equis, hands raised again.

A slight gasp escaped his lips, and it seemed true fear filled his eyes, but he waved a hand to those around him and said impatiently, "Someone—anyone—do your duty! Defend your King!"

No one moved.

And then, quite suddenly, several Elves who had been standing behind Equis stepped forward, their golden staffs raised high over their heads, and with their movement several Enchanters and Fae stepped with them, a great line of Creatures blocking Equis from view now.

The dark woman let out a sound like a sob, but when Xavier eyed her again, he saw her gaze was angry, perhaps even hurt: a silent tear left a brown eye.

"Tippior! Ranir! Tiffingly! Can you not see he deems to throw the world asunder on his mad quest for power?" she yelled at the line of waiting, buzzing, glowing Creatures.

They said nothing, their eyes hardened with anger, and behind them, Equis smiled.

And before Xavier could wiggle his arm from Nathanial's to grasp his sword, Equis waved a hand through the air, and a brilliant haze of colored light filled the sky.

Chapter Twelve

THE PHOENIX

Nicholai Noble hid behind the weak wood of the cabin as the magical fyre licked the wood outside, never burning it.

My protection will fade, he thought in panic, daring to raise his head just enough to peer past the thin blue curtain.

The large blue bird still hovered low over the ground, a high fyre spread wide at its back blocking the remaining cottages and mountains in the distance from view. Its orange beak opened wide and a burst of fire left its mouth, heading straight for the door. It met it with a deafening sound, and the door flew open, the flames spiraling against the armchairs, setting them aflame.

He let out a curse, fear gripping his cold heart. "Arminius!" he yelled as the fyre dispersed in the stuffy air, glitters of golden light shining around the flames as they ate the old cloth upon the chairs.

The cane clicked overhead and soon reached the top of the small stairs to the back of the room. "Nicholai! What's that smoke?" He began to descend the stairs, his white cane appearing the more he moved. On the last step, Arminius stared in horror at the burning chairs, and then past them to the open door. "It's a bloody bird!" he shouted in mingled disbelief and apprehension.

How could he not sense it before? Nicholai thought, staring at the Elf as he waved a long-fingered hand, the flames leaving the chairs. *He had fallen asleep sometime after I'd passed out—but the moment I awoke, I'd felt them.* So why hadn't the Elf felt their presence as well?

Nicholai could not voice his bemusement, for Arminius had just waved another hand through the smoke-filled air, and the door closed with a slam. As Nicholai rose to trembling legs, and the feeling of eyes burning holes in his back faded slightly, Arminius strode passed the chairs and reached him with four clicks of his cane.

"What the *devil*, Nicholai, are they doing *here*?" the Elf hissed, his eyes angry and tired through the dim cottage.

He glared at him in indignation. "I told you, Arminius—I have lied to them—but I did not lie to you! Xavier Delacroix was here, but they will not go for him! They come for me because I believed in Dracula—because I believed him when he told me I could do this!" He glanced back toward the window. Nothing beyond the blue curtain appeared, the flames gone as well. He only turned back when he felt the hand on his shoulder.

"*Vampure*," the Elf began, and there was a solemnness upon his countenance that Nicholai found troubling, "what, truly, is going on here? The Phoenixes are coming for you?"

Yes, he thought, unable to whisper the word. Staring into the Elf's black eyes, he said, "I told them, told the Phoenixes that I would preserve humanity. But when Dracula—when I knew what he wanted for the human, Alexandria, I could not, preserve me, I am a coward, yes! But I could not let. . .Dracula. . .what he really is, infect another."

Arminius's brow furrowed. "But. . .was the woman not already destined to die once she reached the Age in which she no longer grows?"

"Yes. She was. But you do not understand, Elf. Once in the presence of Dracula's true face. . . ." he turned away, unable to go on. "It is a darkness. A truly horrible darkness that I, a Vampire, cannot face." *Could never, truly face.*

He heard Arminius's cane click toward the burned armchairs, but as he looked up, he saw the Elf did not sit. "This darkness. . . ." Arminius said, his gaze held far beyond the cottage he stood in, "you talk as if the darkness Dracula holds and the. . .darkness you *Vampures* hold are not the same."

He attempted to push himself away from the window with shaking knees, but he did not make it but two steps before he was upon his knees again. Fear had consumed all, indeed. "They. . .they are not," he managed to whisper before the burning heat filled his mind once more. The scream left his lips in a rush, and his head pressed against the old floorboards as the burning continued, growing greater with the passing seconds.

"*Vampure?*" the voice of Arminius called overhead.

He could not raise his head to eye him. *They're coming back! Damn!* His brain seared with the heat, a terrible inferno now, and then colors pooled before his eyelids and he stared upon seven large birds, backlight by a blinding light, all different colors, all quite large. Their eyes, black, red, blue, green, or gold were placed upon him, and their wings flapped with foreign grace as they remained airborne.

He felt horribly uncomfortable with their stares, the burning now gone, and before he could think to utter a word, they all went up in golden, sparkling flames, and with a thunderous pulse of his brain, he was back in the old cottage, the worried eyes of the Elf staring down at him.

"Nicholai! Pull yourself together! Get up! Get *up!*"

The old hands tugged at his cloak, pulling him up to stand, and on shaking legs he stood, holding onto the Elf's outstretched arm for support. "What's wrong?" For he noticed the way the Elf's eyes were wide, wet as though he were prepared to cry, but he merely turned from him and looked toward the covered window.

Nicholai followed his gaze, and wearily stepped forward, still gripping the Elf's arm as he reached out and pushed aside the curtain.

Beyond the dirtied pane, the village looked normal, yet as he left the Elf and stepped closer to the window to gaze upward, a slight gasp left his lips.

The sky was dark despite it being the middle of the morning, and it swirled in a large circle over the mountains in the distance. The Dragons had long since abandoned their homes and circled the tops as though agitated, their large wings blowing up a terrible wind that mixed with the churning sky. And then, as he stared, the sky flashed as though thunder would follow its light, but it never did. Despite the terrible visage of darkness and wind, the sun nowhere to be found, Nicholai realized he could hear nothing, not the flap of Dragon wing, nor the call of birds. All was far too silent.

"We need to leave," Arminius said, and Nicholai heard the fear in his voice: it trailed on the air just as long as his hiss.

He turned to eye him, and his eyes narrowed in the light. The Elf was glowing, a brilliant light all about his body, and his medallion flashed gold in the dark. "Wh—" Nicholai began, but Arminius waved a hand.

"I don't know if they can land," and his voice shook with the very implication, "but I'm not waiting to find out. Quickly, while they afford me this power. We'll get to the bottom of this once we're safe." And he stretched out another long-fingered hand.

Nicholai stared at him, glowing as he was, and realized the burning pain in his mind was now gone, replaced with it a great numbness, but if it were from the Elf or the birds, he did not know. Recalling the giant hole in the sky behind him, and feeling the gazes of the seven birds ever upon him, he exhaled a great, needless breath and took the Elf's hand.

※

She spun on her bare heels, a ferocity to her being Christian could not believe: she looked crazed, dirt and leaves strewn throughout her hair, dress only just fashioned for her a few days before now badly torn. Her blood stained it in places where the Elite Creatures had managed to land an attack.

"Fall back!" one wild-looking Elite said, his thick hair long and black as it fell in locked spirals down the back of his ruined cloak. His skin was dark against the morning's light, eyes red in his Vampire form.

"But we have her, Derek!" another shouted angrily at his side.

The ones that had lingered behind them began to step away warily, and Christian smelled their tainted blood. *They're weak and scared*, he thought, and with renewed vigor, he stepped forward, the Ares raised high, prepared to strike the closest Elite.

He could step no farther than Alexandria's side, however, before she began to glow with red light, and in his astonishment, he eyed her.

The light pooled from her in droves, powerful in its brilliance: he held up an arm to keep the light from his eyes when a terrible scream filled the air.

He turned his head from her to eye the two Elites that had remained behind. They were sizzling as Vampires did when faced with the sun's light, but they did not appear to burn.

The red light graced their bare skin, a smoky darkness rising from their pores, and Christian narrowed his eyes. They were still screaming, clawing at their heads as though threatening to pull their hair from their scalps.

What is she doing to them?

"Christian, now," she said quite suddenly, her voice causing him to jump.

He blinked in her light, staring directly upon her now, just able to see *her* past the blare: she was staring at him, her hair lifted from her back, her eyes glowing a similar red. And in that stare he saw a desire.

A desire for me to what?

"The sword," she said after a time of staring, the screams of the Elites still filling their ears.

He started, lifting the sword in his hand, and with a glance toward it, and then to her, he realized what she wanted him to do.

Bracing himself, he moved, the glow of the sword immense, blinding as he raised it, its power causing the blade to tremble greatly. He managed to see Derek on his knees just before he lowered the sword, sending the metal through the Creature's open mouth. A sickening sound filled his ears as he pressed it down through the Creature's throat and heart, and then lifted it with ease: the red light seemed to afford him greater power than he would normally have.

"Quickly, Christian," Alexandria said, and he looked to the other Elite who had seen him kill Derek, and began to rise to his feet, hands still pressed to his head in his madness, his gaze on Christian in wild determination.

He swung with the Ares before the Creature could do little more than snarl, and watched as the man fell at his feet, his top half limp while his legs kicked madly against the dirt.

The red light left the shadowed morning, and he whirled to her, sending the blood upon the sword flying through the air. She stared at him with darkened brown-green eyes, and she looked remarkably tired, as though whatever she'd done had drained her of power.

Slowly, she stepped to him, placing a hand upon his shoulder. "Thank you," she said, her eyes appearing kinder in the sparse sunlight though they were still weak.

She needed blood, he thought dimly.

He suddenly felt awkward with the sword, her touch, and cleared his throat. "I. . .think nothing of it. So. . .can you. . .sense anymore of them. . .out there?" For he could not, but perhaps she could, with her special blood, her immense power. . . .

He shook the fear that was beginning to climb through him with the thought: *She had just rendered Elite bloody Creatures maddened messes of their former selves—how did she know she could do* that?

She removed her hand at last and he blinked, returning to the here and now, and he marveled at the way she seemed to soften. Her face appeared immeasurably relaxed, even more beautiful than usual. And all at once he found himself desiring to taste her blood again, to touch her, hold her. . . .

"I can sense nothing, Christian," she said, and his name upon her lips caused his heart to pulse just the once with the sound. "Do you still think we can reach the Vampire City if we turn back?"

He stared around at the empty wood. "We know we are south of London. . .and though I have never been here before. . .I'm sure if we return to London we will meet more of them. . .especially at. . . ." But he could not continue. The image of his home ablaze, Victor's gaze, cruel and hard as it was before she'd whisked them away would not leave his mind's eye.

"We can face them," she said, and he stared at her. "While we ran. . .Dracula. . .spoke to me. Did he speak to you as well?"

"Dracula?" He recalled the pulse of the sword as he ran, her at his side, but could not remember, truly, any voice as haunting, as intimidating as Dracula's resounding in his mind.

She seemed to sense this, for she said, "It doesn't matter. Are you sure the Vampire, Westley Rivers will have a place for us in the Vampire City?"

"In his letter, he seemed eager to have us. Mentioned repeatedly that we would be safe even amidst the ball."

"And you still believe it the safest place for us to be?"

He willed himself to stare at her brilliant gaze at last, unable to look away. "It must be," he said at last, remembering that he had been spoken to, "Westley, himself, mentioned that Eleanor had not returned since Xavier took his place there. They believe it to be untouchable. And with you there, I daresay it will be."

She smiled, although it was uncertain, as if she weren't sure she should.

"So it's back to London, is it?" she asked, regaining herself: she suddenly looked quite serious and he wondered if it were her Vampire blood that caused her to appear so different.

She had been different the moment she'd awoken, yes, but the way her eyes had reddened, had become murderous when she'd turn to face the Elite Creatures. . .he had never known her capable of it.

He knew she held power, guessed they had not seen all of it, but the extent of her power the longer he remained near her seemed to have no end. Once they'd left Delacroix Manor and she had placed them in the woods south of London, they had been surrounded by Elite Creatures, a vast number of them, and even with Dracula's red light upon the sword, within her blood, they found they could not fight for long.

They had run through a burning city, and now stood within a thin wood that had begun to clear into a large field, a thin stream of water most nearby, but through all of this, her. . .demeanor, her headstrong capabilities had not waned. She never once cursed the air, shown confusion or fear, indeed, she seemed a warrior every bit of Dracula's ranks, his standing, his blood. Or at least, what Christian thought the Vampire would appear to be.

He pulled himself from thoughts on her strangeness, prepared to respond to the question asked, when the smell of Lycan reached his nose.

At once he snarled, though he was bemused when she did not, and he raised the bloody sword, fear propelling him more than anything else. "Alexandria," he said instead, eyeing the trees about them carefully, "you don't smell that?"

She did not respond.

He looked to her much against his will (a beast could come bounding through the trees at any moment, after all), and dropped the sword.

She was on the ground, eyes fluttering as though she were to be taken under any moment. He crashed to his knees at her side, placing a bracing hand on her hair. "Alexandria?!" he cried, and it seemed she did not know she was there: her lips opened and closed though no sound protruded past them. *Was I too quick in assuming she was in control?* he thought, willing himself to see past her skin, into her veins, and yes, all was normal, her blood still. . .delicious, he was sure.

The smell of Lycan so thick and horrible was upon him suddenly, and before he could turn or say a word, indeed, he was thrown sideways through the air, landing roughly atop the dirt and dried leaves. *What the devil?*

Snarling at the pain surging through his arm, he rolled onto his back, placing a hand on his left shoulder; the bones loose under his fingers. Snarling, he cracked his arm back into place, rising to his feet, blinking upon the large Lycan that had appeared from nowhere and was staring down upon Alexandria as though to feast. He stepped forward, despite himself, despite his pain, his lack of knowledge at how to properly fell the beasts, indeed, and snarled in anger. *Not again.*

The beast turned its large head to eye him, but it did not move, it merely stared in what seemed disinterest before turning back to Alexandria, and it seemed to Christian, waited. But for what, he could not know.

He eyed the sword at the beast's large paws, partly covered in dirt, and he tensed. But it did not seem to mind the sword, for all the attention it paid Alexandria, the sword could have been a twig.

Snorting the stench of dog out of his nose, he took a careful step toward the beast, remembering his previous bouts with the large Creatures. He did not desire to have his spine broken, his arm ripped off again, and yet, as he drew level with Alexandria's feet, he found he did not have to worry: the beast simply was not interested in him at all.

Chancing his luck, he stared from her to the Lycan, and then said amidst snarls, "Her blood called you to her, then?"

"How did you know?" the beast asked, its voice deep, maddening to his ears, but still he listened as it continued. "I lost her trail somewhere around a strange town of. . .Elves, but picked it up shortly upon entering these woods. She called me to her. Needs me."

He blinked. "Lycan, you speak as if—as if you know. . .her. . . ." For the Lycan had just begun to shrink, reverting to a human man. Christian closed his mouth abruptly as the fur was shed, the eyes no longer black, for there was James Addison, staring up at him from his knees, completely covered in sweat.

He hesitated for a moment before stretching out a hand with his good arm, helping the man to his feet despite the surge of madness that filled him with the man's touch, his smell.

Appraising the man for moments more, he decided he was harmless. James seemed weakened, tired, but there was a determination in his brown eyes that could not be denied.

They released hands, and Christian, wary at giving his back to a Lycan, never mind if he were his brother's servant, knelt at her side once more, eager to see her state. Her eyes were closed, her lips barely parted now, and he wondered what had befallen her—

The sword.

Dracula.

He probably spoke to her, probably desired she carry out another one of his crazed schemes, like reviving James Addison from death.

And with the thought, inspiration struck. He stood from her and turned to the Lycan, cradling his shoulder in his hand.

"Why would Alexandria call you? Why does Dracula want—no, need you alive?"

"She appeared to me after you left, and I did battle with the Lycans. They once regarded me as a brother. . .but her blood. . .her way. . .seems to render all of that meaningless. They were there for her. The dark one told me while we fought, that he had been called to her to give her his blood, that she desired it greatly." He paused as though a new thought entered his mind, and Christian waited but two minutes before he pressed, "And? You said she appeared to you? What happened then?"

James sighed, and for the first time Christian saw the dried blood upon the man's shoulder, the holes where many fangs had pierced his flesh. *Not healed. Interesting.*

"She said it was the hope of her grandfather that I return to her to help," his eyes appeared reminiscent in the light, "to help stop the bad blood between we Creatures; Vampires and Lycans."

"But what can you do?" he wondered aloud and James crossed his arms as though slighted, though he winced. Backtracking, Christian began again. "I meant how can you stop the. . .bad blood between we Creatures?"

He frowned. "I don't know. I was hoping when I saw her, she would tell me everything." And he stared down at her.

"Indeed." Christian said, thinking how many times he had thought the very same, but for very different reasons.

He turned from James, hoping the Creature would not harm him, though how he spoke of her. . .it was clear he held her in high esteem. *A result of her blood bringing him back to life?* Brow furrowed, he pulled his mind from James, and knelt at her side once more, the sword's metal gleaming in the sunlight. Thought reaching him, he grasped the sword near her head, and exhaled cold breath as he allowed the red light to fill his mind.

He stared upon a young Alexandria Stone again, though this time she appeared slightly older: Her hair was up in yet another unfathomable creation as she sat at her desk, illuminated by the faint candlelight's glow atop it, engrossed in the writing of a letter. The room she sat in was modest, and would have been considered lavish to him if he had seen it whilst human. There were thick peach curtains draped about the windows, a lush rose-colored carpet blanketed the floor, and her bed was large, pushed up against a back wall, its four posts tall and silver, around them equally peach-colored curtains were wrapped.

She folded the paper with satisfaction, pushed back her chair, and stood, the letter folded in a bare, small hand. He watched as she strode past, not able to see him, and disappeared behind a plain, wooden door. With her absence, even if she were human, he found himself aching, and he thought of following, but the moment the thought reached him, it died—he suddenly felt as though he was not able to leave this room.

And that was when he felt it, the stare burning a hole into his back, and he turned towards the window most near the desk and stepped back. The silhouette of a dark figure beyond the curtain was ominous enough, something akin to fear rising in his gut the longer he stared. But it did not move, though the feeling of a terribly strong gaze upon him would not release itself from his back, although he stared directly at it. And with no further thought, Christian stepped toward the window and lifted a hand to push the curtain aside.

There was a gasp and his hand fell to his side as he turned to see her staring upon him in fear. He could barely say a word before she let out a shaking breath, and said, "You. Why have you come back?"

"I," he began when a new voice, one he recognized as Dracula's sounded from behind him. He turned. The dark figure still remained beyond the curtain, and his shadow seemed to dance against the fabric as the candle's light shook.

"Hello, Granddaughter."

With another breath from Alexandria, the candle was extinguished, and they both watched in bemused horror as the window was opened from the outside. The curtains billowed up with the wind that seeped past the window's bottom, and Christian was able to see the dark expanse of trees far below them. *We're on the second floor*, he thought in wonder, taking a step back as he eyed the Vampire that must have been Dracula.

He hovered in the window's opening as though he stood upon solid ground, his hair long and white as it whipped at his face and back in the harsh wind. His eyes were placed only on her, their brown color somehow warming but equally commanding, and with a wave of a sharply-nailed hand, he begged her entrance.

He tore his gaze from the Vampire reluctantly if only to stare upon Alexandria, sure her gaze would be fear-filled indeed, but to his surprise, she looked calm, as though she had seen him many a time.

He watched as she stepped to the window, just inches from his face, the fangs that sat sharp and ready in his mouth, and Christian thought she was either terribly brave or remarkably dim.

He never did bite her, instead he smiled, revealing his fangs, but the smile reached his eyes, and Christian blinked in the fresh dark, quite sure he had never seen a Vampire smile so truthfully before.

"Do let me in Alexandria," Dracula said, his voice oddly kind. It was a voice that sounded as though it seldom was.

"But grandmother said you are a monster—to never entertain your visits," she said as though pressed.

At this his smile widened but there was a darkness in his gaze that had not been there before. Christian felt his blood grow colder with the sight.

"Come now," Dracula continued, his voice not betraying the anger he must have felt, "I am no more a monster than your mother." And at this quip, Alexandria stepped away, affronted, but Dracula sighed, his eyes smoothly dancing to a deep red in the dark.

She gasped.

"Please," Dracula whispered, and Christian felt a great need to obey, "grant me access. Every time your mother revokes it we must do this dance. I will not harm you—you *know* I will not harm you. Now, please."

And Christian held himself from stepping forward as Alexandria did. She stared him straight in his red eyes, miraculously unafraid, and Christian thought wildly that this was where she'd learned to not show her fear as a Vampire. How excellently it remained hidden, if indeed she felt it at all.

And that was when it reached him.

He could not smell her blood.

Staring upon the scene with renewed wonder, he watched as she stepped from the window toward the end post of her bed most near her bedroom door. She held it tight as he, with a grace Christian had not seen in his death, perhaps, only in Alexandria, placed a hand on the window's sill and climbed through.

Christian stepped away, fighting the need to kneel. *This is only a memory*, he reminded himself, but the more he stared at him, the more he was glad he had never seen Dracula whilst he still graced the Earth.

His long white hair reached the middle of his back, slightly frayed, windswept, and his eyes in the dark of the room appeared to shine with great relief though it was hard to tell. They had not left their red hue. He wore black breeches, a black buttoned shirt, endlessly ruffled at the collar and cuffs, and upon his waist was a golden-embroidered black sheath, the silver handle of a sword Christian knew quite well protruding from it.

The Ares, he thought.

Alexandria did not leave the bed post, the lace layer of her dressing gown wrapped around the silver post as well as both her arms. Now that she had allowed him in, she seemed reduced to immense regret, fear even: a large tear left one of her brown-green eyes and slid, uninterrupted, down her cheek.

Fighting the urge to stride forward and wipe it away, Christian eyed Dracula again, fear sweeping over him in a rush of cold wind. The Vampire was staring directly at him.

"Mother says you are. . .a demon."

They eyed her together, Christian unsure if Dracula had truly seen him or merely stared past him, deep in unfathomable thought.

"Your mother says a great many things, I'm sure. Things her grandmother has whispered into her ear about me," Dracula responded, his voice cool, cold, and so close to it, Christian could not help but allow his gaze to turn red as well. "But we must be smart, Alexandria. Your mother is just scared. She would not take me up on my offer to better the Dark World. . .but you. . .your blood is the perfect candidate for what I must do."

The young Alexandria removed herself from the bed post, and Christian willed her to stay put, but nothing he desired or thought would change anything, truly.

"You spoke of my blood last time, Mister," she said, and Dracula's eyes widened.

"You. . .remember?"

She made a face as though she thought he were being funny, but when his shocked expression did not change, she frowned. "Was I not meant to?"

He said nothing, and Christian knew Dracula had attempted to wipe her memory of their last encounter. Something akin to sadness filled him as he eyed her in her dressing gown, pale pink slippers upon her feet. *She's just a bloody child. She could have been no more than eight—what the bloody hell had Dracula done to her, was doing to her?*

"...*A Count Dracul*...." the voice of the human Alexandria returned. *Her special blood*, he recalled suddenly. *This must be how he made it so.*

Not sure if he wanted to continue to see more, he felt the sword pulse faintly in his grip, a ghost of the true weapon that was not here, in her memory. He suddenly felt entirely helpless to stop what would happen, whatever it would be.

When Dracula did not respond, she went on, her voice high as though a child eager to tell a long held story. "This...Count Dracul from a faraway land. He sent me a letter," and she waved a hand enthusiastically to the desk to her right. "I just sent my response!"

At this, the genuine smile returned. "And your grandmother, your mother, do they know about these correspondences?"

"No," she said, a tinge of pink appearing upon her cheeks. "It's my...well...*our* secret."

"And you are comfortable with sharing secrets with me? Essentially a stranger?"

"Well, yes," she said matter-of-factly, "you are kinder to me than grandmother...and though I don't see her often, when I do she is...angry at me. I don't know what I could have done—mother is no better." She looked at him curiously suddenly. "You've mentioned them before. How do you know them?"

He shifted his footing and for the first time looked shaken. It was clear he had not expected her to be so forthcoming, to remember him at all. And then he sighed, and took a careful step forward. Christian found himself moving toward her as well, as though he could keep Dracula from moving further.

"I am your Grandfather, Alexandria. And I am here to tell you your grandmother has died," he said, waving a pale hand through the air. And with its movement, Christian narrowed his eyes: it was far too fluid, even for a Vampire. As the hand was dropped to the Vampire's side, Christian thought he saw a tinge of green light trail on the air before dispersing. "An. . .unfortunate accident, I'm afraid, but she wished you the fullest life you could muster before she passed."

She merely stared, and there was a flash of prominent green in her eyes. They were large, water-filled, and as Christian watched in new confusion, a red light appeared over her heart. And then she began to cry—and to his further bewilderment, ran to Dracula and gripped his legs tight, sobbing deeply.

And Dracula, much like Christian had done whilst in Victor's room, placed a pale hand atop her head and said, "There, there, little one. You will indeed live the fullest life you can muster. I will see to it."

The red light grew until it was all he could see and then in a flash it was gone and he stared down upon a glowing Alexandria Stone, very pale, surrounded by dirt.

He blinked, unable to erase the image of Dracula's fingers trailing with the green light in the darkened room. What had that been? Some kind of spell?

He heard the dirt rattle at his side and looked down. He still held the sword, though it trembled greatly in his grip. Most of the blade shook atop the forest ground. Releasing it, letting it rest atop the dirt once more, he returned his focus to her.

She was still lost in the throes of her encumbrance, her eyes closed against the morning's light.

"What the devil happened to you, Mister Delacroix?"

Christian looked up, almost surprised to see the Lycan still staring down upon him, brown eyes dark with what looked to be fear, confusion.

He blinked, and stood from her, mind still rattled with what he had seen. *Dracula did something to her to cause the red light within her blood—but what?*

The strong hand was on his shoulder in an unnerving sweep of rage, he turned abruptly to face the Creature, surprised the hand was not dropped as he did so. He stared with wide eyes upon the man, feelings his fingers curl and release at his sides. *The blood of the beast was prevalent as ever*, he thought, wondering again why the Creature was there.

"You both glowed with that red light," James said, finally releasing his hand. And in the light Christian noticed his eyes narrow with question. "What did you see?"

"Nothing," he said at once, not desiring to share her memories, her thoughts with one certainly not of their blood, no matter if he were the one chosen by Dracula to 'bridge the ties,' as it were. He was still a Lycan, the heat his blood caused in one's blood could not be willed away, could not ever be denied.

Christian turned from him, and picked up the Ares, the sword now dull in the shade of trees. It did not burn or glow, but was merely cool, and he stared down at her again. Her eyes were opening in the light, as he felt they would, but it remained to be seen if she recalled the memory in full. . .or at all.

They watched her sit up atop the ground, and stare around as though in a daze, before whispering something Christian could not catch, rising to her feet.

He stared at her, unsure if she were truly okay, but she blinked upon them and said, "James? What are you doing—oh." She smiled uncertainly. "My blood. Of course."

He nodded. "Led me here past a group of angry Elves, Miss Stone."

"Please, James," she said, "call me Alexandria." And she turned to eye Christian much to his surprise. "I went under because James appeared?"

"I believe so," he said, staring at her carefully. "Alexandria. . .did you have any memories. . .anything troubling?"

She opened her mouth to respond but James said, "We shouldn't stand out in the open." And Christian stared at him, his gaze hard on the sky past the leaves. "Something's coming."

And they looked around, Christian attempting to search for whatever it was he sensed. He smelled it before long: dread.

Turning to Alexandria, he saw his fear mirrored in her eyes. "We need to head back to the Vampire City."

And before they could whisper a word, he turned from them and began to step back the way they had come, willing his hands to stop their trembling at his sides.

He saw again the sight of Dracula, the cruelness, exactness with which he spoke, moved, surely unable to be seen by her at the time for what he truly was. *A master manipulator*, he thought, snarling in frustration. The Vampire, distinct in his grace, his power. . .his damned command had made it so she would feel great sadness, had *caused* the red light to begin its blare from her heart, then. Christian could not see how it could have been anything else. Whilst she was scared on the streets of London as the few Elite Creatures in Lycan form charged for them, her power allowed her to see their whereabouts, alert him to the coming danger. Her emotion, it seemed, caused her power. He almost ceased walking as he rethought her anger thirty minutes before as she rendered the Elites immobile with her light. "*I was so very tired of everyone trying to kill me.*"

She had been angry. And terribly so.

But how, he thought, as he continued his walk, *did Dracula make it possible for a Vampire to feel so strongly—to use their emotions to great benefit?*

As they walked behind him, an unnerving silence pressing against their ears, though the dread was thickening, indeed, Christian hoped Westley Rivers was as celebrated in the Vampire City as he had heard. He needed answers, desperately, to the meaning of Dracula's nature, Alexandria's brilliance, for what Creature would cause a girl such distress? Manipulate her blood? Just to cease the bad blood between Vampires and Lycans?

Brow furrowed, he shook his head, unbelieving that that could be the only reason. With all he had seen the past few months with her at his side, and because of Dracula. . .his secrets, Christian knew Dracula had done something immensely strange to Alexandria to give her such power, and even as the sword pulsed in his hand again as though angry he questioned the former King of all Creatures, he heard the strange sound far overhead, a bird's call, and blinked in the light, only just realizing he had been snarling.

※

The throne room was dark and damp, the Vampire within shivering despite his inability to feel the cold. He stared into the Goblet, the desire to drink its contents still never reaching him. He had found this strange two days ago, but now it was. . .normal. More strangeness that blanketed the World so completely, now.

"Protect. . .better plans. . .protect. . .Damion. . . ."

The voices continued despite his best attempts to will them away, and it was with the fiftieth utterance of their nonsense that he understood they only arose when he stared straight into the Goblet, eyed the blood he could not drink.

Who makes a cup that one cannot drink from? he thought in disdain.

And once again, pressed to the madness that surrounded him, a violent surge of anger rose up within him, and with all the ferocity he could muster, which was not much at all, lifted his arm, and brought down the goblet, set to smash it against the black stone he kneeled upon.

And still nothing happened.

When the side made contact with the stone, it merely clanked and bounced up, sending his hand to do the very same. He cursed as the vibration continued up his arm, the blood never spilling past its weathered brim.

"Damned Dracula," he thought in renewed anger. "Damned cup!"

And he snarled, wishing for his brother to somehow enter this wretched place, reduce him to ash, slash him to pieces. Anything was better, surely, than being reduced to this. Unable to move, to act, to defend, to stand-up to the one Creature he knew he could never truly face.

Yes, he had seen her, had felt great fear with her presence, but it was not the fear of her being, however terrifying that now was, it was the fear that she saw him, weakened, pathetic, clutching a useless cup, chained to her throne. Though it was funny, she had said the sword was not Dracula's source of true power—what he held was. *But how could that be*, he thought for the hundredth time, *how could that be when it did nothing but irritate me so, cling to my hand, elicit no light, no power—but it did give me voices, did it not? It did spark the strange tones that would fill my mind. . .just like the sword.*

Intrigued, but not entirely sure, he knelt a little higher, resting his arm and shoulder against the side of the throne for support, and turned the goblet right-side up, and with a needless breath, looked directly into the blood.

Almost at once the voices returned, Dracula's, another's he could not recognize, and most surprisingly, the more he listened now, the unmistakable voice of Victor Vonderheide:

"What power do I hold in this stone? What can I truly do? Call down more fire from the skies? But why? Because Dracula blessed my ring with Phoenix power? Does this stone come from them? Have I been granted greater power by them? To what end?"

A piercing screech sliced through his ears then, and he looked away at last, a cry of pain gargling past his unused throat. Recovering, he stared at the cup, not looking directly into it anymore, focusing on what he'd just heard.

Victor's ring was blessed with Phoenix power? he thought in confusion. *Blessed with—but why?* He stared at the plain goblet, unsure what he truly held.

It was power, that much he was now certain of. But if all it did was give him the thoughts of those tied to Dracula's. . .hand what good was it truly?

The door opened suddenly, and he tensed, prepared to see her appear, beautiful, cruel, warped with immense power. . . .

But he blinked, and it was the young Vampire that had arrived at her behest a few days before. His blond hair fell loosely around his shoulders and back, the tattered Elite Creature robes he wore sweeping around his boots as he took a confident step into the room.

"Damion Nicodemeus," the Vampire said, a cold grin upon his face, "the Queen wishes you be kept. . .sustained while she is away."

He eyed the man warily. "Wh-Where. . .is she?" he croaked, clearing his throat.

"Attending to important matters," he said, pulling back a sleeve of his robes.

Damion eyed the pale skin that shone in the sparse torchlight as the Vampire stepped closer, kneeling once he reached him.

He tensed as the Creature extended his arm, and pressed it up to his mouth, and at once, he turned away. "What the devil do you think you're doing?"

The man took back his arm, but did not replace the sleeve. Damion eyed it with bemusement, as the Creature said, "You must feed, Damion Nicodemeus."

His eyes widened, and he looked upon the Elite Creature in full, the cold grin still upon that pale face, the eyes now red in the dim.

"H-How?" Damion asked, voice low. "How do you know my name?"

At this the Creature smiled in full, and it was somehow kind, familiar. "I saw you once before in your office in the Vampire City, my Lord," he said, and Damion's mind spun. *My Lord?* "It was after you got sent across your desk, I'm afraid. So you won't remember me."

He narrowed his eyes at the Creature's sudden change in demeanor. He almost seemed truly friendly. But why would that be?

Licking his lips, he shifted slightly, the chains sliding against the floor with his movement. The Creature eyed them, a grimace replacing his confident smile. "I am Javier Theron. I was being trained with Dracula before he died."

Damion's eyes widened and he sat up straighter against the throne. "What?" he whispered, remembering Lillith Crane entering his office to ask if he had seen a Vampire by that very name. *What on Earth?* "But why are you here? With her? Should you not be with Xavier and the others?" He said the words before he could regain himself; excitement filled him now, ridding him of the emptiness, the dread, at least for the moment.

Javier Theron chuckled and his gaze darkened in the light. "True power, Lord Damion, is not held by any one Creature." And he shook back his sleeve once again and held out his wrist. "Now drink, my Lord."

My Lord, Damion thought again. *He keeps calling me that. But I am no Lord, not anymore.* He eyed the Vampire's wrist, not feeling the desire to drink reach him at all. He looked back at Javier's face. "I cannot drink from you. . .you're a. . .you're one of hers, aren't you?" And how he refused to become one of them. They held power, yes, but it was strange, that much Damion could admit.

"I am. . .partly," the Elite said, "but I will never be, fully. I cannot." It looked as though he wanted to say something more, but could not, and instead, he shook his extended arm. "You must drink before you truly grow thirsty," his gaze moved to the goblet, forgotten in Damion's dark hand, "before you get the idea to drink from that cup."

Something is different about this Elite Creature, Damion thought, eyeing his wrist once more. His demeanor was cold, confident, yes, but there was something undoubtedly. . .normal in his nature, uncorrupted by Eleanor's power. He suddenly blinked in the light of the torches. "How can you be partly her Creature?" He recalled the daggers of smoke thrown most near his head just a week before, and eyed the frame of Javier closely for any sign of black smoke, any static-like dread upon his countenance. . . .

Nothing was there.

But how?

Is this a trick?

He blinked wearily upon the Creature for moments more, deciding at last, somehow, someway, that he had to be telling the truth. . .some version of it anyway.

He eyed Javier's wrist once more and grimaced. "I'm not thirsty," he said in slight protest. Yet he knew it would be pointless. Didn't hurt to try.

"But you will be."

"Won't I. . .become one of you if I do?"

"You need to enter the room fashioned from one of the pages of *The Immortal's Guide* in order to do that, my Lord. Please, we're running out of time. *Drink.*" And there was an urgency in his stare, in his voice that Damion found catching. Thinking only of Eleanor returning with anger in her eyes, fire in her hands, he reached forward with his free hand, and hesitating for only a second, opened his mouth and pressed down with his fangs.

The blood gushed up at once, and he did his best to catch it all, the taste absolutely strange. It was not good, not in any sense of the word. It was rather stale, and he immediately thought that Eleanor's blood had never tasted so wrong whilst he took it when she was still a Vampire.

A haze of red light blanketed his vision, and he gasped, pulling away from Javier's wrist at once, though he no longer saw the Creature. The throne room was gone, in its place an open field, a small, haphazardly-shaped cottage just before him, the goblet no longer in his hand. He flexed his fingers in relief.

Not sure what was happening, he stepped forward, toward the small cottage several feet ahead beyond a small stream. It was morning here, the sky bright, and he blinked in the light, unsure of why he was here at all.

Black smoke issued steadily from the stone chimney that peeked through the cottage's straw roof, and he stood just before the oddly placed wooden door seemingly jammed into the stone frame.

Somewhere above a black Dragon flew: he could smell the thick smoke, the fire, and the scent of cold water they all held on their bodies.

Yet he could barely ponder what kind of Dragon it was when the door opened and Dracula appeared, his eyes sunken and distant, hair disheveled against his shoulders, the clothes he wore appearing as hastily sewn together rags the more it was Damion stared.

He could not speak as the Great Vampire surveyed him with exhaustion, before turning, walking deeper into the small cottage.

Damion chanced a glance back, unsure of what he should do—if he should follow at all, when the familiar scent of Alexandria Stone's blood drifted to his nose.

He turned back to the cottage, mind blank, resolved to let things unfold as they would. He knew, somehow, he could do nothing against whatever this was, indeed.

He stepped into the cottage, closing the door behind him, and Dracula waved a completely gray, weathered hand from an old armchair, bidding him forward.

He obeyed, stepping up to the set of armchairs, and at once saw the fireplace—a human head hovered within the fire, its blood falling into a pot just below it, placed in the bed of the flames.

"Vampire," the voice of Dracula said, and Damion jumped, squeezing the back of the weathered armchair closest to him. *That voice.* He never thought he'd hear it again.

"Y-your Grace," he whispered, staring at the white hair.

"Sit down," Dracula said.

Slowly, shakenly, Damion maneuvered around the old armchair, the green fabric atop it faded to gray, and he sat, staring at the absolutely ancient-looking Vampire next to him.

The silent room was odd, at least to Damion, for he realized this was the absolutely first (and perhaps only) time he had ever been alone with the Great Vampire. Though he wasn't quite sure the Vampire deserved the title of 'Great,' anymore:

His eyes were brown, yes, but darkened, as though the color had been almost completely taken from them, and his frame was less sure, less confident. He hunched over slightly in his chair, as though his spine no longer afforded him the luxury of proper positioning. Indeed, something was terribly off about the Vampire.

Damion did not remark on this, for just then Dracula opened his thin, cracked lips, and said, "I am disappointed in you."

He stared, unsure of what he should truly be feeling. It was not as though he cared for what the Vampire thought. In reality, he was dead, permanently, so what did it matter at all what this. . .vision of Dracula said, indeed?

"I fail to see, your Grace," Damion began, "how that matters anymore."

At this, Dracula turned his head to stare at him, and it was with that distant gaze that Damion felt fear in truth: Dracula looked no longer a shell of what he was, but something more monstrous, indeed.

A terrible likeness to Darien, Damion thought vaguely.

With a snarl, Dracula waved his gray hand lazily through the air, and Damion felt his tongue curl in his mouth, forbidding him the notion of speech. "Do not interrupt, Nicodemeus," he said, his dark glare illuminated by the orange flames dancing in his eyes. "You have been a thorn in my side for years. I only let you into the Vampire Order to keep you close. Watch you. Hopefully use that Caddenhall of yours. . .but there is no need for that now." And before Damion could say a word, Dracula went on. "You are in Eleanor's home, now. You hold the Goblet of Existence in your grasp, and yet. . .I feel you do not understand what this means. But as it is, she is scared of you. Terribly scared, I imagine. So we shall use this to our advantage. When you return to your prison, you are to stare directly into the Goblet's mouth and listen to the voices. It is not until you hear mine above all else that you will recite the words, 'Protection, Preservation, and Peace. Always,' do I make myself perfectly clear?"

He blinked in the light of the fire. "I beg your pardon?"

"The oath you took upon entering my office as my Invader, do you not remember it?"

"I. . .of course I do, but I thought we were to never say the oath again. . .unless. . . ." His tongue curled once again in his mouth, only just freed to respond to the Vampire's question, and he understood that the former King was not looking for conversation.

Dracula nodded, and his eyes were colder than usual. "Unless you were to defend the state of the Vampires from threats greater than Lycans, yes. There is a grand possibility of permanent death, but I think, Damion, that you, especially in your current predicament, have little to fear in this regard." And his stare would not leave Damion's, and how small Damion felt then. "You will become a Knight, branded by Alexandria's blood, rather than my own. But the bond should be no less capable. Once you say the words, you will be freed from your chains, the Goblet, and you will, hopefully, move to aid the others."

He could not speak, could not say a word, for what truly was this?

More magic? More spells to be cast while true power—the Ares—surely went about unclaimed? For he had heard Javier tell Eleanor that they no longer held the sword—but could that not be a trick? Could Javier have not lied to Eleanor? For if he were still working with this. . .vision of Dracula, wouldn't he renounce Eleanor, her power? Could he even do so?

As he sat there, a sensation quite like being cold claimed him, and he sat up straight, staring upon the silent Dracula in renewed wonder.

He was no longer staring at him, indeed, his eyes seemed quite blank though his head was still facing his direction. His mouth lay partly open, a drop of darkened blood beginning to peer over his bottommost lip, and Damion watched in confusion as the blood rounded the lip and dropped onto the Vampire's old robes.

"Dracula?" he whispered, unnerved when silence reached him.

What. . .what's happening?

He pressed a hand into the arm of the chair, bending toward the unresponsive Vampire, desiring to see a glimmer, a spark in his vacant eyes. Inches from them now, he narrowed his own, unable to see a thing within them, why, he could be lost in a trance of sorts, but Damion knew better. . . .

"Dracula?"

The blue lips remained open, nothing surpassing them, and Damion sat back in his chair, dumbfounded.

"Bloody hell."

And he had just decided he would rise from his chair, and head for the door when he blinked and he was back in the throne room, staring upon the smiling Vampire whose eyes glowed red in the dim light.

Damion gasped, blinking hard, trying to keep the Vampire's gaze within his sights: he saw double. A rush of pain blanketed his vision, and pressing a free hand to his head, he heard the Vampire's voice come from far away:

"Damion Nicodemeus, you have been chosen. . .where Xavier Delacroix has failed. You hold the Goblet of Existence in your grip, my Lord, that makes you the Dragon. The chosen."

He could barely hear what the Vampire said, it all came through as rather rushed. "I. . .I can't be the bloody—just what the Devil is going on—what the hell was that—that vision? Bloody *Dracula*?!"

Javier stood and turned from him before he could realize it happened. New light from beyond the throne room blazed against his eyes, and he blinked, attempting to keep it from his gaze, and then it was gone.

He stared at the stone door, the pain of the shackle against his ankle burning against his skin. He stared down at it, remembering the old voice of Dracula against the crackle of flame, how clear it sounded now.

"Once you say the words, you will be freed from your chains, the Goblet, and you will, hopefully, move to aid the others."

The words.

He lifted the goblet upright, and attempting to keep it in his vision, he stared into the blood, the reflection of the ceiling hovering on its calm surface. And with a tired, rattled breath, he said, "P-Protection. . .Pres-Preservation, a-and Peace. A-Always."

A strange sensation, much like being doused in cool blood covered him, and he suddenly felt powerful. Able. Strange, but sure.

The gold of the goblet burned against his hand and he released it, shocked when it landed atop the dirt floor, free from his grip.

He flexed his hand, massaging his fingers and palm, and stared at the old, worn shackle, wondering if he could pry it open with his bare hands now, now that they no longer shook. And just as he thought this, the shackle broke at his ankle, and hardly believing his luck, he touched it. It was hard, cold, real. *Dracula was telling the truth*, he thought in astonishment, and, rising to his feet slowly, he stumbled slightly, gracing the arm of the throne for support. Surprised when his knees did not shake, he stood straight, amazed at how clear everything appeared now: the throne room was in focus, the doors just there, and he was thinking just how in the World he was to get out of the caves, when the blood within the brim glowed.

He stooped, and picked it up.

"You are not the Dragon," a deep, menacing voice said the moment his fingers made contact with the gold. He almost dropped it, when the voice continued. *"You are a farce, Abomination. Give the Goblet to the true Dragon—to that Vampire, Xavier Delacroix. He can still help. He can still make things right."*

Xavier Delacroix is the rightful Dragon, whatever that means. Xavier, Xavier, always bloody Xavier. He appraised the glowing blood once more, waiting for more words to reach him.

When none did, he ripped the remains of the cloak from his neck, and wrapped its frayed, burned fabric around the goblet. Tucking the oddly shaped bundle under his arm, he stepped for the doors, somewhat prepared to face the tunnels of her dread, which somehow, he noticed now, were almost nonexistent to his senses.

Chapter Thirteen

POWER

She stared at the bubbling black liquid, its clear smoke flowing over the bowl's cracked, aged rim. Hesitancy distilled the notion that all was well, for she had the strangest inkling it would not work no matter how many times the dimmed Friandria Vivery whispered that it did. That it was complete.

A large bubble expanded atop the liquid's surface and popped loudly, echoing in the dim, vacant tunnels, the far reaches of her home. Places she had not cultivated yet.

The table was old, pushed up against the wet, dark wall, barely standing on its old legs. Taken, she knew from the Enchanter's home in Pinnett, the Enchanter whom she had killed.

A necessary sacrifice to know what the Enchanters schemed.

Wondering what the Enchanters knew, what power they held, for that white light would not blare so periodically on any mere whim, indeed. Equis Equinox was granted his power. She felt it in her blood.

But no matter, she thought, bristling, focusing on the bowl before her, *my power will far surpass his own.*

For here, she smiled, *was the answer to my long held truth. My ultimate power.* She stared at her pale hands in the light of nearby torch high against a wall. *The power to transform fully at will.*

For she needed a way to hold the transformations at bay, at least until she could *hold* them. Finally show Xavier the truth of her power, for she felt he was to join her soon. Yes, quite soon. *The Calling of Void* had only been strengthened with their kiss, and she would see to it he agreed to be her King.

"*Xavier,*" she thought, aiming her thoughts. She waited but a second before she tried again. "*Xavier.*"

Cool, clear silence teemed on the edges of her mind.

Nothing.

Damn.

She had heard not heard from in a day, now, and she was worried for the first time in a long while. *The Calling of Void.* . .she had not given him an order, told him what was best to do and as such he would feel the connection between them. . .but be lost without her word. It was why her voice would reach him. Pull him to her.

Bring him at last.

"Your Grace," Friandria whispered, and she turned to eye the red-haired Vampire, pulled from the depths of permanent death with magic most untouchable. "Won't you drink it?"

Eleanor smiled uncertainly, unsure if she should, if she were truly ready. She stared at her hands again, remembering the way they had turned large, finished with black claws, the skin thinned. . . .

I can't let that happen again.

Friandria smiled vaguely, her skin duller, paler than a Vampire's, her back against the other stone wall, her red hair falling haphazardly around her shoulders and back, the frayed Elite Creature robes she'd been gifted far too large upon her body. They hung loosely down her shoulders and arms, gone were the silver robes she'd been given when being versed in the Enchanting Arts.

Human again.

She stifled a snarl at the former Vampire's new state, but smiled after a time, for she had done it, she with her Elite power—true power—had brought someone back from the dead.

"Not yet," she answered after a while, "I feel it is not yet time."

The dull gaze turned to confusion, and in the light of the torch, she stepped forward with a bare foot. "You wait for something, something I did not place in that Potion, your Queen."

She stared. "What are you talking about?"

"You wait," she went on, continuing to step forward, "for his blood. The blood of the one that can push your true form through. His blood was not enough before, you did not have enough, but now with the mixture," and her absent gaze drifted to the bowl behind her, "and his blood. . .the unwanted transformations will stop."

"You presumptuous Creature," she said with a snarl, anger flaring in her heart that her secrets could be so readily *seen*. "How dare you profess to know—"

"How dare I?" Friandria whispered, suddenly, her voice low in its dullness, but still somehow menacing. "You made me. Brought me back. With your magic—I am tied to you. You did not think I would know your innermost desires? The truth that the Vampire you seek holds the blood that fuels your transformations."

What in the World? Eleanor took a forceful step towards her, a hand outstretched to grip her throat—

Friandria waved a hand and Eleanor's fingers curled in the dim, hanging in the air just inches from the woman's veins.

"Do not pretend, Miss Black," Friandria said, and her voice was suddenly cold, threatening. "I can feel the weakness in your blood, the things that pull your brain, Eleanor. You made me," and she spread her fingers wide, wisps of black smoke lingering around her nails. Eleanor eyed it, transfixed. "And you made me with your essence. I am yours, just as much as you believe Xavier Delacroix to be—"

"Shut up! He *is* mine!" she said, wrenching her hand back from the spell placed upon it. There was a crack, like a whip being waved through the air, and Eleanor spread her hand before the woman's face, the steady stream of rage pushing itself up through her body, spreading to her hand—

The sound was sudden, a gasp whispering through the air, and she dropped her hand, turning at once to eye the surprised, beaten face of Damion Nicodemeus gripping what looked like his burned cloak in a Goblet-less hand.

"Da—how are you free?" she breathed, turning to eye him in full, Friandria completely forgotten.

He stepped forward with a grace, a swiftness she knew could not be contained, and as he drew level, she realized he had a glow to him, a prominence, and at once she eyed the bundle tucked under a dark arm.

He couldn't have, she thought in panic, yet she knew he hadn't. She, after all, was still an Elite Creature, still held the form of Vampire. *He had not taken the blood from the Goblet. Yet.*

Wondering what kept him from doing so, she took a step away as his gaze found the table, the bowl, and the bubbling liquid within.

His brow furrowed. "What is that?" he asked, his voice low.

"Nothing of note," she whispered. "Damion. . .how. . .how did you—"

He turned to her again, and the cruelness of his gaze struck her hard. *He hated me*, she realized with a start. *But of course. . .of course he would. . .* He flexed a shoulder, his shirt singed greatly, and he said, "I had. . .help."

Help? "What kind of help?"

Friandria cleared her throat bringing both gazes to her. She had pressed up against the wall with Damion's appearance, but now seemed more sure of herself, and took a step closer to Eleanor. "He smells," she said, in her same barely-there voice, "of greater blood."

Eleanor eyed her, eyebrow raised. "What?"

"I said," and her vacant stare roved to Damion, "he smells of greater blood, the blood of the first Vampire—no, no—the blood of those that fly in the sky."

"What on Earth are you talking about?"

And much to her surprise, Friandria stepped towards Damion, shuffling her feet against the hard ground as though she could not move fast enough, and lifted a hand, slashing him across the throat with her fingers.

Blood sprayed from the wide cut at once, and Damion bent double, the bundle of cloak falling out of his hand to land with a dull thud against the hard floor. Quickly, Friandria moved to the table where the bowl sat, picked it up, and turned, stepping for the snarling, pained Damion whose blood seeped past his gnarled hands and fell in large drops to the floor.

Eleanor watched in further amazement as Friandria knelt before the Vampire, holding the bubbling bowl high, directly under the drops of blood. The red fell into it with sucking hisses, and after seven drops were attained, Friandria removed the bowl, rose to her feet, and turned to Eleanor, something of a smile upon her gaunt face.

Eleanor stared at the mixture now, and could almost feel the implication hanging low over her shoulders, within the woman's distant eyes. That if she did not drink, if she did not take the Potion now, she would never—truly, control her transformations. But why had the woman moved to slice Damion and place his blood in the bowl? Surely he wasn't one of special blood?

But as she looked over Friandria's red head towards the still-retching, stumbling Vampire, she remembered what the woman had said.

Could it be, truly, that the Vampire had—somehow gained special blood? It had been a day since she'd left him alone in her throne room. What on Earth could have happened, and in her sanctified home no less, to warrant such a quick, stunning change?

She thought once again of the Goblet, but could not see how the man would have drunken from it without all Vampires and Lycans, and perhaps even her own, reverting to. . .*ugh*. . .humans.

So what—how was this possible?

"Your Potion is truly complete, my Queen," Friandria whispered, shaking the bowl slightly so that the thick black liquid sloshed against its high sides. "All that is left is to drink and you will get the Vampire you seek."

She blinked with these words, the overwhelming scent of Dragon's blood, Vampire blood, various herbs and unspeakable objects mixing just beneath her words, demanding she inhale. She could have chosen not to, in her state, indeed, but what the woman said wiped all thought from her mind.

"I will have Xavier, truly?"

Friandria blinked and it was as though she was not seeing Eleanor at all. "Your essence, Eleanor. . .is my essence. I know. . .what you know. And deep down you know the curse placed upon him, that settles in his blood even now calls him to you. With this," and she raised the bowl higher beneath Eleanor's nose, "he will be yours—as will the ultimate power."

And with these words, she grabbed the bowl from the woman's thin hands and lifted it to her lips, and drank. Almost as soon as the thickness of it touched her tongue, she regretted it: it was revolting, vile, nothing like blood, like flesh at all. But once she had swallowed, she suddenly found she could not stop. Something was pulling at her throat, her tongue to continue to drink, to take, to inhale this Potion, the thing she had fashioned out of what little was left of *The Immortal's Guide*. And once it was all gone, she dropped the bowl, not hearing it clang to the floor.

She did not hear the Vampire's growls, though she saw him push Friandria aside, eyes murderous and red in the dark, and with his blood still falling in droves, he reached out a hand for her, but she stepped back, able to see what he had become clearly now.

Deep within his blood was layered a sheen of golden fire, fire not of this World, of that she was sure. She could not smell the blood, indeed, somewhere in the back of her mind she felt she was kept from it on purpose, through some spell or curse. But with another glance into his red eyes, she could see they were glowing now, they were changed, greatly. Yes, he *had* had access to great power whilst within her throne room. But not of this World, not of this World at all.

Surveying him for moments more, she decided that he had access to another. . .someone that knew her secrets. . .and Dracula's as well. And with greater focus now, she recalled Javier Theron, how the Vampire had not been able to take the form of Lycan, yes, she could pull his image to her mind's eye, see the truth of his blood, where it stemmed from.

And indeed, she was not upset, no, he had been a smart young Creature, to heed Dracula's word to the very end. But that was just it. . .he would meet his end at her hand.

She stared once more at Damion, who had fallen to his knees, a bloodied hand clutching the bundle of cloak just before him. He opened his mouth, his tongue lapping against the roof of it as he spoke, but whatever words he said, she could not hear.

And in a haze of great fire, sparkling with the tinge of something more, he disappeared from the narrow tunnel.

She knew she should have been mad the Goblet had been taken in truth, she knew she should have been furious Javier Theron had been a spy, a greater means to Dracula's seemingly endless hand on her affairs. But all she could find within herself as she kicked aside the burning bowl and turned to a quite unconscious Friandria lying limp against the wall, was pride. For Dracula, in his quest to see Xavier succeed, had given her the edge she required to finally see the truth of her power revealed to the Dark World. An edge from Damion Nicodemeus's blood.

She almost laughed as she lifted Friandria from the floor and slung her over a shoulder. She almost cried, indeed, as she realized Xavier was just—just beyond her reach.

But she extended a hand and pressed against her veins, her blood, and willed it to change, and she watched with great amusement as it lengthened, the nails growing long and sharp, black against the dark of the tunnel, the skin stretching, thinning, graying to accompany the size. . . .

And with another smile she willed it away, watching as her arm returned to normal, and with a chuckle, that sounded somehow deeper to her ears, she pressed forward through the vacant tunnel, back toward the populated areas of her caves, eager to give her men the gift she had been given. Eager to reclaim the power that was the birthright of all Creatures.

※

Aleister Delacroix opened his eyes, the light of a brilliant sun blinding him at once, and then as moments passed, his location was revealed to him:

Jagged rocks protruded from the ground wherever he could see, and he realized with a start that he lay stop them: Several hard points pressed against his already aching back.

Snarling, he rose to stand, losing his balance slightly, but he was not alone:

The Order of the Dragon were here, as were Amentias and Aciel, Lillith Crane, all rising from the ground as well, hands clutching their midsections or caressing their heads, all holding looks of utter defeat.

Flashes of light filled the sky amidst the gold, and for a wild second panic filled him. I should be aflame! But blinking upon the other Creatures, he saw, indeed, that Aurora Borealis held her hands high, a large shroud, invisible at first against the ceiling of blazing sun, was being held above their heads, keeping the rays from truly reaching them on the ground.

He took a step forward, the pain fresh, but how had he received it? He remembered Xavier, and a flare of anger flashed in his dead heart. Betrayed! Blinking harder still around at the passage of rock, the walls on either side of them, his brow furrowed. Xavier was not here.

But before he could question just where he was, a burst of colored light shone from the mountain's peak and all looked up, gasping as they did.

"Xavier?" he breathed, as the others let out concerned whispers of shock, fear, indeed.

The light died as quickly as it had come, and Aleister could smell Xavier's blood clearly now. But where in the World was he?

"Aleister?" the surprised voice whispered, reaching him even against the voices of the others, the low buzzing that filled his ears. Turning quickly, he eyed her again. She was walking toward him, stepping swiftly over the rocks, eyes watering with tears. Her hands, still held aloft to keep her spell in place, trembled slightly, but she wrapped her arms around his neck all the same, sobbing loudly into his chest, and the smile lifted his lips, the warmth only she could afford him blanketing his cold heart.

"Keep the spell steady, Aurora!" Peroneous shouted from near the mountain's base, his gaze hardened on them.

Over her head, Aleister could see the dark Enchanter's brow was furrowed deeply, a heavy scowl upon his face, but a thumping vein in his face gave away his fear.

Should we be scared? he thought as Aurora pried herself from him at last, wiping her face with her shoulders, still holding her hands high.

"Enchanter," he said, staring at Peroneous. "What's happened here?"

"Seems our *mighty* King has taken it upon himself to face Equis all himself. But I feel another's presence," and he eyed the large crater in the ground to his right. "It appears the woman. . .Philistia Mastcourt has risen and taken it upon herself to join the battle. If she fights alongside Equis or Xavier. . .I cannot tell."

He moved from Aurora, her relief gladdening him, yes, but what madness had Xavier gotten himself into now? "What do you *mean* you cannot tell? And why are we still here?" he asked, stepping for the Enchanter, aware all eyes were upon him as he stumbled.

Peroneous tensed, but Aleister did not care: Xavier was lost once again, and no one moved to his aid? *How long indeed had I been under?* he thought as Peroneous opened his mouth begrudgingly to say, "We've only just woken up from an attack by a Cleaner, Aleister. But you, Aleister, you were harmed by Eleanor. How are you feeling?" And his dark gaze looked quite concerned as another burst of colorful light filled the sky, only this time numerous screams filled the air after it.

"I. . .I ache," Aleister said, keeping his gaze on the Enchanter despite the thought, troubling though it was, that Xavier may have just been blasted apart by magic, "but I am fine. But Xavier," and his gaze once more found the mountain's peak where the brilliant sun was shining brightest, "he isn't. He hasn't been for a long time."

※

Xavier Delacroix was stunned. He felt quite powerless as he lay behind the barrier created by Philistia Mastcourt's hands some hours before, only bidden to watch what happened with wide, astonished eyes.

She had conjured a staff from the depths of her mind, and it glowed brilliantly in the light of the sun. And somewhere, in Xavier's greater mind, he knew it was truly night, but here, on this magical mountain, the matters of the Dark World did not seem to hold sway:

Equis roared mightily and waved large, trembling hands just then, sending yet another brilliant haze of colored light through the sky. They reached the second barrier Philistia had created just before herself and smashed against it, creating cracks in the fixture. But the powerful woman did not falter. A low, guttural sound protruded past red lips as she heaved with her hands, pushing the barrier that resembled a solid stone wall toward him.

The sound was deafening as it slid across the ground, streaks of black covering the once pristine floor of the city, and several Fae and Elves jumped out of the way as it moved with ungainly speed toward the towering Creature in the center of the city.

He had fashioned steps, protruding haphazardly from the ground just before his feet, and it was these he stood on as his gaze hardened, his stance tense, preparing, Xavier believed, to do away with the wall before it could reach him.

He never did anything.

Several Elves, badly bruised, indeed, jumped before the steps, and with glowing eyes, they held out their own golden staffs, and said in unison, "*Malach ach pol!*"

Xavier watched from behind his translucent wall as the solid one shattered into many pieces, a triumphant laugh barreling against his ears next. "Madame Mastcourt, stand down!" Equis said, calming down, but only slightly: he still held his hands high, prepared to cast another spell. "This foolishness has gone on long enough! You are not fit to fight me! You are not fit to be the martyr for those bloodsuckers! Do not let your mind be clouded by their charming ways! They are monsters and you are not making the World a better place by attempting to help them!"

"I am helping our World, Equis!" she shouted in return, waving her staff, and from its tip a powerful burst of red light blared and it zoomed on the air, headed straight for Equis's heart.

An Enchanter stepped between the line of Elves and the red light, said something Xavier could not quite catch, and turned his back on the beam. Xavier sat up higher, intrigued as the red light reached the Enchanter's back and sank into it without a sound, much like Equis's light had done to Nathanial earlier.

Xavier looked to his right, not surprised to see the Vampire still out cold. Whatever the strange light had done to him had kept him that way. Coupled with the few other attacks that had skimmed him before Philistia had pushed them away with a hand, and set up the shield to keep further attacks at bay.

He could not smell his blood, and this unnerved him. All he could smell was the magical blood of the Enchanters, the Elves, the angry Fae. The Fae that held glowing eyes, unseeing of what was currently taking place, but surely each seeing quite different outcomes.

And the longer he stared at them through the ruined, burning, smoking city, the more he saw several begin to run away, back toward the still standing palace at their backs.

What did they see?

And just as he thought this, the sky opened up, a giant circle appearing directly over Equis's head, and all manner of light, of shouts, of magic ceased immediately.

All was terribly silent as they watched in abject terror, the sun, false though it was, fade into the recesses of a thickening blackness that was beginning to overtake the sky.

Lightning flashed though no sounds of thunder accompanied it, and the longer Xavier watched, the more he felt as though he should rise, should run, but he could not move. All stared at the swirling sky, and then, before he could think of what more to do, gigantic balls of fire began raining down from the hole, slamming into remaining buildings, setting all ablaze.

Screams filled the air, and indeed, all Creatures began to realize the threat they faced. While many began casting shields over themselves and others, few others disappeared on the spot, yet Equis and Philistia, much to Xavier's surprise, remained where they were, staring up at the sky in equal terror.

It was not long before the balls of fire ceased, and a grand figure appeared within the hole's vast depths. He heard the audible gasp, felt the tremble of the ground, and at last he sat up. The Ascalon remained at his side, shaking atop the ground as well, and he gripped it, eager to use it should he have to. For a terribly tall man, dark as he was frightening landed atop the debris-riddled ground in-between Philistia and Equis, and even Xavier found it odd how the strange Creature seemed even older than Equis, but still retained a youthfulness.

Figuring it was some sort of magic, Xavier rose slowly to his feet, not surprised to find them shaking, but still he stared through the barrier Philistia still held in place, and watched as Equis let out a sound like a sob, a tear leaving an eye. His long black hair whipped in the wind the strange new Creature had created with his landing, grand fear in Equis's eyes.

The Creature turned to Equis, giving Xavier the impressive view of large black wings resembling black fire folded into his back, his hair long and black, slightly wavy as it fell alongside his equally black robes.

Whatever he was, Xavier decided then, *he was a warrior.*

The dark-skinned Creature held a sword on his person, its hilt silver, protruding from the black strap at his waist, and when he clenched a dark hand around it, Xavier felt himself tense in fear. Whatever he knew of battle would be no match for what this Creature could do, he was sure of it.

"N-No, no, please," Equis was whispering to the Creature who had begun to advance upon him.

"Please?" the Creature said, and Xavier sank to a knee at the voice. "You have disobeyed our word at every turn brother. Stealing power from the Elves, bemoaning your loss of power at that Creature's hand. . .and now that you have your power back, what have you done with it? Interfere in our affairs!"

"I—I have not—I would n-never—" he began when the Creature took another step forward, the sword still clenched tight in a fist.

"But you have—you did," he said, and Xavier found it troubling how the voice stuck in his head though at the same time felt so very out of reach. "You knew what would happen if you interfered in his matters, Equis."

And the sword, at last, was withdrawn. The blade was black, and though Xavier thought it metal, he could not be sure: it did not gleam in the light of the fires that still burned around them.

Equis's eyes were held on the sword, and Xavier found it a troubling sight: the powerful Ancient Creature seemed almost a child it was so frightened he looked. As if matters were far beyond his head and he could not fathom it. A look Xavier knew well.

"I knew Syran would be most cross," he whispered, eyes still on the sword, "b-but I did not—" He gasped suddenly and his gaze moved to the swirling, dark sky, and it seemed he remembered something long forgotten. It was there he spoke as though he could see someone no one else could. "Forgive me, brother. I only wanted what was best for our world."

The dark Creature raised the sword, blade pointed to Equis's heart. "Syran does not hear you, Equis. He did once. But he never will again." And he plunged the blade through Equis's heart, the blood gushing from the wound as though a river, and Equis's eyes widened, rolling in their sockets. A rattling gasp left his open lips, and Xavier's eyes widened as the Ancient Elder went up in brilliant orange flame sparkling with a touch of something more Xavier could not readily place.

But he could see no more before the wall that kept him safe was dispersed and he smelled the death on the air, felt the rush of heat and flame from the burning Equis, and heard, at last, the screeching call somewhere above that sounded strangely familiar.

And as he stared up at the swirling sky once more, the gasp left his lips, for a man with large wings of fire was descending from the hole, his gaze serious, blue within the dark that seemed somehow darker with the man's presence: he glowed with a golden light, his wings of flame flapping steadily within it. His chest was bare, the bottom of a white robe held around his waist lined with golden thread, and as he took his place beside the dark Creature who was still staring down at a still-burning Equis, Xavier saw the Creature's hair fell to the beginning of his neck, blonde against his light skin.

And as the Creature began to share words with the darker one, Philistia moved quickly to his side, and motioned with her hand for him to be quiet. And just as the newcomer turned his gaze to them, Philistia's eyes flashed a vibrant color and Xavier knew himself to be pulled along the dark, away from the penetrating, dangerous glare of a bloody Phoenix of the Nest.

Chapter Fourteen

BURDENED BLOOD

It was morning by the time Alexandria, Christian, and James reached the familiar trees and stepped carefully up to the stables behind Delacroix manor, Christian letting out a snarl of disbelief as they stepped through the stables, the horses neighing as they passed, to eye the full content of the manor beyond it.

It had crumbled in the day Victor had attacked, all that remained were decaying stone, and a crude, burned outline of the foundation. All was ash within the foundation, even the white living room, previously held up by magic had been completely destroyed.

"What the bloody hell happened here?" James asked, aghast. He gripped tight the bloodied cloak Christian had given him a while before. He'd wrapped it around his waist without further to-do and they'd pressed on.

"While you were off with Lore," Christian said with a snarl, not bothering to eye him, "Victor paid my home a visit. Alexandria and I just made it out with our lives."

James blinked. "Victor did this?"

"Yes," Christian answered, "a lot has happened since you were bitten."

The Lycan stared at the manor with incomprehension for moments more before Alexandria stepped to him, placing a comforting hand upon his shoulder. "We are sorry, James," and Christian stepped toward the manor slowly, leaving them behind, "for your loss."

He froze with the words, the truth of them reaching him in a flurry of new grief for the man. *Of course. His aunt had been in the manor with everyone else. There was no way she survived.* He turned slowly to eye them, not surprised to see the look of great sorrow on James's face, and he remembered what the woman had shared, how deep in the throes of Dracula's hand she had been. How deep they all still were.

Alexandria's expression was soft as she gazed at James apologetically, his own riddled with tears, and it seemed he was prepared to open his mouth to say something, when Christian heard rustling from the manor and shushed them, ushering them back into the recesses of the stables.

From behind the dark wood of the archway, they saw the many Enchanters, Elves, and even humans muddling through the ash and singed debris, looking, it seemed for any sign of life amidst the mess.

"What do we do?" James asked, his voice breaking.

Christian stared at him, wondering if he would survive the trip to the Vampire City at all, the many horses in their stables behind them whinnying nervously. He stared again at the badges gleaming from the humans' chests back where the manor once stood and snarled. *Scotland Yard. Damn. We don't need this.*

He recalled the all-too fresh sight of Scotland Yard officers before Damion's land, the sight of their shocked gazes as they lay eyes on the three Elite Lycans, Darien Nicodemeus, and Alexandria Stone that month before, and his brow furrowed in concern. It would not do to relive that fiasco. Especially with Alexandria pale of skin, brilliant of blood. . . .

"We need to get past them," Christian said, turning his thoughts to the here and now. "I haven't had blood in a day now, nor have you, Alexandria. And James, how well are you feeling? Do you think you can make a run for it?"

"No," they said together, Alexandria's brown-green eyes held on the several humans that had begun to leave the manor and step, with haste, towards the stables. Christian heard something like, "Such a shame. . .we need to find the brothers, Archibald—and put a stop to Lord Victor Vonderheide, though how he could have done all this in a single night is beyond me," as they approached.

The man named Archibald nodded grimly, but said nothing, and the horses let out yet more whinnies of fright. Rarely used though they were, they were not at ease with Vampires and Lycans: Animals seldom were.

And Christian turned to them, the large beasts in their stables, and motioned with a hand for the others to follow his lead. He'd just had a very wild idea, and he hoped his brother would not hate him for it. *But then*, he thought, stepping for the largest stable of them all that held Xavier's black stallion, Knight, *Xavier would have enough to contend with, indeed.*

Opening the stable door, he whispered words of encouragement to the large beauty, though it never fully settled, and swung a leg over its bare back. Releasing the creature's rope from a hook near the swinging door, he whispered words of encouragement into a large ear, even as the voices from outside grew closer. A worn sheath hung from a rack most near the stallion, and Christian grabbed it, eager to be free from holding the damned thing aloft. It was most upsetting when it glowed red and he could do nothing but drop it. Placing the sword's blade within the sheath, he secured the strap to his waist and eyed the others.

Next to him, Alexandria had just swung a leg over a Hanoverian horse, its light brown mane almost matching her own prior to becoming a Vampire, for her hair had grown slightly darker, and further down the stables James swung his leg over a saddled gray horse Christian understood as his own. A gift from Xavier.

The voices were just outside the stable's entranceway now, and he held Alexandria and James's gazes, seeing their readiness to move. They gripped the reigns of their horses, staring upon him expectantly, and with a nod, he dug the heels of his boots into the creature's side, sending it bounding out of its stable. It turned sharply, running through the archway, and at once the scent of human blood reached Christian's nose as they were just there, mere feet from the stables, thrown back in surprise.

He flashed them a smile, showing his fangs, and before a cry could leave their lips, Knight had pressed on faster, now sensing its complete freedom, turning for the beach. Christian could not turn to eye whether the others following him, but smelled her blood, and by extension James, for she was making it so.

Silently thanking her, he urged Knight forward, eager to be free of the sight of the ruined manor. It pained him far too much to stare directly upon it, yet he could hear the shouts and exclaims from the Dark Creatures that remained within its debris.

Knight reached the beach at last, slowing down slightly, yet still moving at a blinding pace, and once they reached the grass of the front yard, still singed from the attack, Knight whinnied in what sounded to Christian like a whoop of joy, and jumped over the high black gates of Delacroix manor.

Once its hooves pressed against the cobblestone street, Christian felt something within him shift, yes something became quite clear, but before he could truly figure out what it was, the sword began to glow with a red light.

As they passed various horse-drawn carriages, humans, Vampires, Elves, and Enchanters on the busy street Alexandria drew level with him, a seriousness in her now-red gaze he could not ignore.

"What's going on now?" he asked, their horses level.

The wind whipped at their hair, sending it to blow before their faces, but even through his curtain of black, he could see her eyes, held on him with something of impatience. It was a look he suddenly imagined the intimidating Dracula held on his face many a time.

"We are being guided to the Vampire City," she said as they maneuvered as one around a carriage with ungainly speed. Several Vampires Christian once recognized as respected members atop the surface shouted curses at them from the sidewalk, but upon seeing Alexandria drew silent. He felt their gazes follow them as they rounded a corner, heading toward the edge of London, the grassland several yards ahead where the road ended abruptly.

"Guided? Or pulled?" the voice of James asked harshly, and for the first time Christian turned on his horse to eye the frustrated Lycan who had been gripping his horses reigns far too tightly, as if in attempt to control its speed and destination. It did no good: the horse determinedly pressed forward with their own, loud snorts leaving its nostrils.

"Definitely guided," Alexandria said, snapping her reigns, bolting ahead as they entered the woods south of London, a place Christian had never ventured to before.

They rode endlessly for a time, the sun shining through the trees, and Christian marveled at the cold of it his skin beneath those rays. *I can walk in the sun,* he thought in astonishment, eyeing the hair of the woman in front of him. He had not truly thought on it so lost he had been in Dracula's calls, Alexandria's red light.

Her red light.

He recalled again the sight of the green light that had trailed on Dracula's fingertips as he'd stood in the room with her those many years ago, and all at once he found himself eager to fly off his horse and land upon the back of hers, at her back, at her side, even if he could not protect her. *Truthfully,* he thought, a smile tearing at his lips, remembering the way she had handled the Elites back in those strange woods, *she had protected me.* And a flash of sadness reached him, and he almost pulled back with his horse, but it would not slow if he desired it. The trees blurred past, and he kept his gaze trained on her long, dark hair. *What if I am never able to protect her again? What can I do against her blood, the blood of Dracula?*

Inadequacy returned in a harsh wave, and he remembered himself as a young boy, always at his brother's back, eager, even then, to prove he could be just as strong, just as capable as Xavier. *But nothing,* he thought, as they pounded against the hard ground, *had changed, truly. I've traded in my brother for the woman.* He chuckled to himself, ashamed at his own realization.

"*But you listened to your instincts far more than you know,*" the cool, cold voice said suddenly, and he almost let out a cry of surprise, but stopped himself. The sword's heat seared against his leg, the familiar heat he could feel, and he eyed the glowing handle, the gem in the guard protruding against the leather as though desiring to be free.

"Dracula?" he whispered as several birds flew high overhead, their high songs sounding faraway suddenly.

"*You are far more capable than you give yourself credit for, Christian. The way you have assured my granddaughter reached her destiny is more than admirable, and believe me, if I were still with you all, you would be rewarded highly,*" the voice went on.

He blinked hard, the voice making it difficult to focus on what he was now doing, riding a bloody horse sans saddle to reach a city he'd never been to, meet a Vampire he'd never met, with a human that used to be his brother's servant-turned Lycan, and a woman he'd been bidden not to kill now a Vampire—at his bloody hand, and still he said to the sword, "But what you did to her—you used magic to make her blood the way it is, didn't you?"

There was silence, though the sword still glowed, and Christian took this to mean he was right. "I thought Vampires could not do magic, Dracula," he went on after a time of riding.

The sword let out a single strong pulse of red, and then dimmed considerably, and Christian knew the Vampire was done sharing his wisdom.

Bloody liar, he thought with fresh anger, knowing indeed that Vampires could do magic. He had seen it the night Nathanial Vivery flew from the cottage in Cedar Village, fury in his heart, sending bolts of lightning to the Elite Creatures above. *So what,* he thought, pressing his heels into Knight's sides once more, *had he done to Alexandria, exactly?*

✳

Alexandria Stone gripped the reigns tighter, the voices swirling within her mind. *"Protect the Dragon. . .blessed with magic as you are, you are the key to controlling the blood of all Creatures. . . ."*

Magic, she thought, remembering the stare of Christian as she rose from the ground, forever cold, terribly numb. She blinked in the light of the sun as her horse leapt over an overturned tree whose roots had been ripped up from the ground. *What magic has he placed upon me?*

And as if on cue, her horse let out a strange sound, much like a cry of fright, and she pulled on her reigns, eager to settle the creature, but as soon as its front hooves landed on the leaf-strewn ground, they rose again, and she pressed her bare feet against the horse's side, and down into its stirrups.

"What's wrong?" she heard James ask, and with a rush of wind, her control slipped, and she could smell his Lycan blood strongly.

A snarl escaped her throat with the scent, and her horse's heart beat a thunderous rhythm beneath her with the sound, and she instantly regretted it.

It rose high on its hind hooves, and in her surprise she lost her balance, sliding from the beast's back, the reigns slipping quickly from her hands which were beginning to glow once more with the red light.

She landed roughly atop her back as the horse bounded through the trees ahead of her, letting out sounds of fright while it ran, never once turning back. "Bloody hell," she breathed, rising to her feet, her many skirts swirling about her legs as she stood. She suddenly found her outfit quite encumbering in a strange, new wood now that she had the mind to smell—and strongly—the multitude of cold blood that filled the ground beneath their feet.

The Vampire City really is this way, she thought, eyeing Christian at last who had drawn level with her just minutes before and had watched her horse gallop off through the trees as well.

She blinked at his extended hand before taking it, pulling herself up onto his horse's bare back. The seat was uncomfortable, the animal's spine moving beneath her, her legs swung, not over both sides, but upon one, and was instantly reminded when her grandmother would have her sit this way atop a horse she would frequent often when visiting the elderly woman's home. A sudden sadness claimed her heart, heavy and complete, and she blinked in the gaze of the Vampire in front of her, realizing where she was, indeed.

She had felt, for a wild, stupid moment, that she still needed to eat, needed to drink things that were not red, for her grandmother had been eager to remind her to do these things, and do it often whilst in her strict presence.

But now, with her Vampire mind, the cold it spurred, she could not help but feel the memory of her grandmother was strange, as though it came through muddled, the woman not able to be held in clear imagery. Yes, her memory had been touched, and the realization startled her, for what was so threatening about her an old maid demanding her grandchild eat?

But even as she perused her mind for more, Christian's voice cut through her trance, "Alexandria, are you alright?"

She blinked, and he was staring upon her in hard concern, the sharp gaze of James Addison atop his own unsettled horse piercing her in equal worry, and if she could have blushed, she would have. "I'm. . .fine," she said at last, staring past Christian through the trees where she could still hear her horse's hooves padding the ground furiously. "I got distracted. . .she got scared. I believe that's all it was." Though she weren't sure if that were entirely true.

Christian looked as though he wished to protest, but James said, "I could smell your Vampire blood—both of yours for the slightest of seconds, Alexandria. As I understand it, you can keep it from us?"

"I can," she whispered, "I mean—I should be able." She sighed in frustration and James pulled on the reigns of his horse to steady it. "There is much about my power I wish to uncover. I feel there is still so much I don't understand about it—how I can use it—why."

"It's why we travel to the Vampire City, Alexandria," Christian said, and his eyes were dark, though held telling admiration. "Westley Rivers should know how to help us." And before she could say another word, he pressed the heels of his boots into the horse's side and with a jolt, they were off, James letting out a growl of alarm, snapping his horse into following close behind.

※

Victor Vonderheide gripped tight the burning stone. He had not returned to her, could not find it within himself to do so. To see her pleased gaze. . .the thought disgusted him. He could not bear to return to her home after what he had done. He had ordered the remaining

Creatures to return back to Eleanor, the Enchanter most of all, and had returned, as those guilty often do, to the scene of the crime.

He'd watched the crumbling remains of Delacroix manor, returning only when the fires finally died, and in the light of the sun he had watched as the officers of Scotland Yard had arrived, mixtures of grief and shock upon all their faces.

He had thought of pressing forward, to greet these Vampires, these humans, many he had known for his entire death, when he smelled the new blood to the woods at the back of the manor, and wishing for cover, for he stood several feet away from the stables, shrouded in the trees, he gripped the stone with the hand that held the always-burning ring. And all at once he found himself encased in a strange bubble, yet everything around him was still clear to his ears, but, he knew, by pressing from the leaves and into the light of the sun, he could not be seen, nor could the sun's light reach him:

No one looked up from their dismal perusal of charred remains to see the Vampire so boldly walking on Xavier and Christian's property, and he thought this very curious, until he'd heard the voices at his back.

He'd turned in his alarm, to see Christian, Alexandria, and of all people, James Addison maneuvering through the stables, grief and fear on all their faces.

It was here he'd watched Alexandria the most. Yes, he had not been wrong in watching her two nights before, when she'd placed her hand on Christian's shoulder, disappearing in a gust of wind. She was truly beautiful, truly terrifying, truly. . .filled with Dracula's blood.

For he could smell it plainly, and how curious it was that he could.

And so lost in his thoughts he had been, he had not noticed the two human officers stepping from the manor to head to the stables, indeed they passed right by him, not sparing him a glance.

He pulled his thoughts from her blood, curious to see what would happen next, when all three Creatures came bounding out of the stables, all atop horses, Christian flashing a smile of all things to the human officers, sending them falling back in fright.

The Vampire is truly happy, he'd thought then, noticing clearly how pleased Christian was. It was in his eyes, his voice, and even, Victor noted as he watched them gallop off towards the beach, in the way he rode Xavier's horse. *It's as though he is free,* he thought wistfully, and blinking upon the confused, frightened humans who were peering past the stable's archway as though scared another horse-ridden Vampire would appear, he smiled, for he knew Christian was. Free from Xavier's terse eye, free from the watchful gazes of the Vampires atop the surface, free, indeed, but not, he thougt with a frown, from Dracula's desire.

For it was clear Dracula still had a hand on the Vampire, it was clear Dracula still held the ropes as it were, binding all Creatures together to complete his will. He saw this in Alexandria, her blood, her purpose. One that could still the blood of Lycans was powerful, and he had heard that the ones he had sent after them had never returned, so it was clear she could do more than just still the beasts' blood. Though he was not against Christian having killed Eleanor's Creatures. After all, even he seemed changed. *Much more capable, much more sure. . .very,* he thought with a sudden pulse of heart, *much like Xavier.*

But as he watched James's horse leap over the black gate that led to the streets of London after the others, and the officers, Elves, and Vampires moved from the manor to reach their companions, he felt the stone burn fiercely in his hand, and heard a voice, clear and cool against his ears.

"Protect the Dragon. . .and spare all."

Desiring to know just who this Dragon was, who on Earth he was supposed to protect, he focused on the burning stone, which had only grown hotter in his hand, and he saw Alexandria in his mind's eye, riding swiftly through familiar woods.

He opened his eyes in shock, no longer seeing the exasperated, bemused gazes of the humans that sputtered endlessly, barely getting out the words, "Christian," and "sharp teeth," to the more than shocked and troubled gazes of the Vampires and Elves that did their best to console them, but instead felt a flurry of fear.

She was heading to the Vampire City. And he thought of the withered corpses of Sindell Black, Julius Dewery, and Armand Dragon, within the hidden room of the manor, sickening worry replacing all reasonable thought.

They will know. . .know everything, he thought hurriedly, ignoring the glowing eyes of the Elves as they placed long-fingered hands on the humans' heads. *I can't let them. I can't let Dracula win.*

For if there was one thing he desired more than to hear Dracula's voice again, it was to never be human again. The life he'd lived was one riddled with illness, with death, and he'd found new life in Dracula's bite, no matter if the Vampire in question had not paid true heed to his creation.

Staring around now at the glowing humans, the Elves that cast their Spell of Forgetting, he eyed the crumbled manor, and then looked down at the burning stone in his palm. It seared against his skin, the pain unbearable, but he was not truly feeling it.

With this, he thought, remembering the ball of fire that had passed through the window's glass, the balls of fire that had rained down from the skies at his anger, his rage, *I can make it right. I can stop them from destroying what Dracula has built. I can remain,* he thought, his eyes beginning to water, the memory of Dracula's brown gaze, cold and hard returning swiftly to his mind's eye, *his Creature forever.*

Chapter Fifteen

THE NEW FORM

Philistia Mastcourt sank to the floor of the cottage, a shaking hand pressed to the wood of the floor, but she rose before long, limping slightly, doing her best, through tears, to cast spells of protection around them.

She'd had barely enough energy to get them to Cedar Village, and even here she did not trust in their safety.

Her leather gloves had burned off with her last spell, and now her long, dark fingers weaved intricate shapes through the morning sky, as she did her best to keep the cottage they remained in quite invisible. They had landed just outside it some hours before, and had begged the Enchanter that lived there entrance, and upon seeing her the Enchanter had relented. As it was now morning, the Enchanter, a balding man with a large belly, slipped out of his sleeping robes, and shuffled on his day robes with a something of a harried, sheepish air: he barely looked any of them in the eye as he slipped through the door.

Nathanial and Xavier rested in beds above, Nathanial still unconscious, Xavier. . .well, not able to speak. He'd been shocked more than anything at what he had witnessed atop Merriwall Mountain, and she could not blame him. She, herself, was rattled immensely. The sight of the sky, opened and thickening with a new strange air, one she had not felt in a very long time, had stunned her, and Equis as well.

Her breath hitched as she stepped from a window, drawing the curtain, and letting out a breath of exhaustion, she sank into an already depressed armchair most near the door, and let the tears fall in full.

The sobs wrenched from her throat, her gasps deep, desperate. *Equis, you fool*, she thought, banging a fist against the arm of the chair. *You damned fool. Always mad for power. And now you're. . . .*

She heard the footsteps descend the small stairs and straightened at once, wiping her eyes hastily. She blinked upon the diluted figure through her tears, and watched, blinking hard, as he sank onto a small couch nearer to the center of the place.

"That Creature," Xavier said, and his voice was quiet, angry against the silence. There was no fire to puncture the dark. The Enchanter had left without setting one, too unnerved he was to move with normalcy. "That Creature. . .the winged one. That was a Phoenix, wasn't it?"

"Yes," she said once the lump in her throat was somehow less. "I tried to. . .I should have moved sooner."

"Moved sooner?" He looked as though he desired to sleep for a very long time, his eyes, once vibrant and green, were now dull, tired.

"You are not ready," she said, "and it is said, whispered, really, that if ever the Phoenixes were allowed passage to ground again before the Vampires reached the Goblet, he would kill you all."

A look of remembrance passed across his eyes. "He. The one with. . .the eyes. . . ." He looked as though he could speak no longer when he went on. "He looked downright murderous. . .I've never felt so. . . ." His mouth closed when he could not find the words.

Philistia regarded him for moments more before clearing her throat, knowing though bewildered they all were, that they had to move, that Xavier had to become what his creator needed him to be.

She sat up straight, leaning over the arm of her chair to eye him seriously in the dark, the snarl leaving his lips as she did. She sank back at once, the thrill of fear at his gaze now red passing through her quickly. Alone with a Vampire, she thought sarcastically, again. This does not bode well for my desire to live a longer life.

"I thirst," he said suddenly, and he shifted, almost hanging precariously off the couch, ready, should he desire it, to spring forward.

"And you have not had blood in quite some time," she said, sensing it on his skin. "Yet I am too weak to give you mine. And besides. . .my blood is laced with magic, it surely cannot taste good—"

He had stood from his place atop the couch, and had moved swiftly, leaning low over her armchair, his hair just before her face, his fangs pressed, though she hadn't the faintest idea when it had happened, against her neck. And then, with a breath of her surprise, he bit down, the pain piercing as it flashed along her vein, and in eagerness, grand need, he began to drink.

He was weakened, angry, confused, and sad, but it was his desire for another that struck her hardest while he drank. But this desire was dark, twisted, and as Nathanial appeared at Xavier's side, a hand upon his shoulder, pulling him back, Philistia felt this desire encumber her for the slightest of seconds. But as Xavier straightened, blood flying from his lips, rounding on a furious, equally tired-looking Nathanial, Philistia knew the foreign desire to vanish.

Placing a hand on her neck where the blood still poured, she focused her best on conjuring the power needed to close the hole. With a breath, she felt the heat at her hand, and did her work, while Nathanial snarled angrily in Xavier's direction.

✳

"You cannot just take the blood of the one that saved your life, Xavier!" Nathanial shouted, gray eyes wild. "And she's saved mine too. Unlike you! What's the matter with you?"

Xavier stared at the Vampire for a long time, smelling the magical blood of the woman beneath his nose, tasting it upon his tongue, and he fought the urge to turn and continue his meal. *I've gone far too long without blood as it is*, he thought coldly, not desiring to focus, indeed, on the madness of the mountain, nor on what had happened to him at its base. . . .

"I needed blood," he said simply, the blue eyes of the strange Creature continuing its odd barrage behind his lids every time he'd dare close his eyes. With them open, he could recall only the feel of his arms as they extended and lengthened as he writhed atop the jagged rock. . . *Abomination, indeed.*

"You need a good thrashing," Nathanial spat, stepping around him, moving to the woman whose wound had healed. Her eyes were closed, her head resting languidly against the back of the chair, and she looked to be asleep, though Xavier knew better.

He could feel the low hum of power that teemed through the room, then, and knew she was regaining herself, though why she did not sleep he did not know. Figuring it had something to do with the fact the Phoenixes were now on Earth, and were going to hunt him down, he sank back onto the couch, forced, if only by his own mind, to come to terms with the fact that Dracula had been right back in *The Immortal's Guide*. He was not ready. Not to face them.

He recalled the way he could not move as the sky was opened. It was as though the World had stopped, nothing else mattered, indeed, but the power emanating from that hole, and then they appeared, far older, far more powerful than what they, mere Vampires and Lycans could ever hope to be.

He pictured a winged Dracula climbing up an endless mountain to reach the long-lauded Nest to speak to these mysterious Creatures. Their creators. A fresh wave of fear crept over him, and he turned his thoughts to Eleanor, for she, terrifying though she was, was not the prospect of taking up the torch for someone else's redemption. She was cool, cold, and direct. She was power he could at least see, power he could understand, if only through their fleeting kisses, scarce touches. . . .

He blinked. He could not feel her. Truly, not anymore. Hadn't, he realized with a start, since he'd climbed Merriwall Mountain.

What had changed?

And grief came next as he recalled the dark Enchanter, the two former Elites, and members of the Order of the Dragon that perhaps still remained at Merriwall Mountain's base.

"What about the others, Enchanter?" he asked her, not caring that her eyes were still closed brow furrowed in concentration.

Nathanial shot him a look of disbelief, but he was rewarded when she opened her eyes, stared directly upon him, and said, "They remain at the base. And no, Vampire, I do not know what has befallen them. My only concern is seeing you Vampires to your Goblet. Do you any idea where," she said, Nathanial keeping a hand on her shoulder, "it can be?"

"No," he said, angry that he had never known where the damned Goblet was. *At least,* he thought, *Dracula could have shared that in his book.* Thoughts traveling once again to what he was kept from in *The Immortal's Guide,* he did his best to focus on Eleanor Back, dismayed when he found the connection gone.

The thought of Eleanor dead reached him in horror, but he quickly calmed himself, reasoning that if she were dead, he would have definitely known. Her Creatures would run amok in the World, issuing chaos wherever they saw fit.

Or perhaps not, he thought, recalling the Phoenixes, their ability to land within the Dark World most horrifying.

"Then we must find it, Xavier," Philistia Mastcourt said tiredly, "and do so quickly. I am not sure how much longer my spell can hold upon this home. The Phoenixes have much better gifts at magic than I, a mere human."

"Do you deem us to go find it, Philistia? Leave you unattended?" Nathanial asked, and Xavier narrowed his eyes upon the Vampire's words.

She looked positively exhausted, as though she wished for nothing more than to sleep, but she said, "Yes. We can't let the other Enchanters, especially those in Shadowhall begin to start executing Vampires and Lycans at their will. I risked my life to defend you Vampires," and she sighed. "And I intend to see it through. Evian Cross awaits us in Lane. If we move now we can be there in about four days."

Nathanial made a sound of protest. "You're surely not well enough for the trip—"

"I used a bit of my power defending you both back there, yes," she said, heading him off, "but I did not become Equis Equinox's right hand by being diminished in power." And she flexed a bare hand, the nails finished with dark red paint. "I can control it far better than we could when Dracula held control of the Art."

Nathanial looked as though he wished to say more when a loud bird's call issued through the cottage, and they all looked toward the door.

"If that's what I think it is," Xavier said, rising to stand, gripping the Ascalon at his waist, "they move fast."

"We will need to be faster," Philistia said, and Xavier stared at her as she waved a dark hand through the air, a trail of blue around her fingers, and all went black.

✳

Thomas Montague lay atop his bed within her caves, replaying it over and over in his mind. The sight of Alexandria Stone, just there before his paws. The young Lycan, freshly turned. His father staring upon him in disbelief.

I should be dead, he thought again, rolling over atop the stiff mattress, staring at the stone door which had not opened in days. He heard the others rustle about, whispers words of excitement, sometimes fear, but he never opened it. Did not desire to see them, did not desire to hear Eleanor's words that he had failed, that the woman had become a Vampire. He did not desire to be reminded, miserably, that he would never see his wife again.

For Alexandria Stone, her blood swam through the air, and no amount of dreams, of pleading, of visions of red would bring Mara back.

He had been used. By her. By Eleanor. By his father. All of them, indeed. And he did not desire, nay, could not bear stepping outside that door to be used by anyone else ever again. So he lay atop his bed, the only thing fresh about him his clothes, but still he could not find it in himself to rise. . . .

And then his door swung open and he blinked in the light of the torches moving beyond it.

An Elite stood there, her brown eyes deep, hair brown as it trailed down her back. "Her Grace is requesting everyone to the main hall. She has something very important to show us," she said, before slinking back through the door, though she left it open.

The noise from the halls clamored through his ears, and he stared at the doorway, wondering what more could have happened now. The word 'show,' stuck to his ears, however, and he stood from the bed, stepping slowly to the door, the tunnels beyond it.

All Elite Creatures, hoods upon their heads and not, roamed the halls, heading in one direction deeper into the caves. He hesitated for a moment, remembering the last time he took heed to the excited whispers of newcomers, but after a while, he stepped with them, ignoring some curious glances cast in his direction.

They walked for what he deemed far too long a time, quite sure he had never been this deep in the caves before, indeed, he had never known they'd existed: the walls looked freshly dug, these tunnels narrower, but still they moved.

And just when he thought they couldn't possibly walk anymore, lest they get lost down here forever, the tunnels opened up to a grand hall, larger than he had ever seen:

All tunnels spilled into it, its circular shape offering more holes within the walls around it so as to allow more Creatures to enter it. It was high, the ceiling curving, still stone though it was, but there was a strange light that hovered far above their heads, and dark though it was, it cast a brilliant glow that shed light to every part of the hall so that none of it was lost.

There was no throne here, no podium, no stand upon which to pontificate, no it was quite bare, and Thomas almost wondered what Eleanor was getting at now, when she appeared in the center, all Creatures giving her a wide berth. Thomas thought he knew why.

She was different. Something in her eyes, her smile, the way she sauntered forward, as though capable, at ease with something no one else knew was telling of whatever power she'd unleashed.

For Thomas felt she had unleashed something.

In her presence now, he felt as though he lacked something he had not ever though he'd lacked before. With the murmurs and looks of concern all about him now, he saw he was not alone in this assessment.

"Some of you may have heard me mention here and there that our power. . .although great, is not complete," she said, and he shuddered against her voice, a grand sensation of falling accompanying it. Steadying himself, he focused on her, not liking at all the gleam in her eye.

"And some of you," she went on, ignoring further the louder voices now, voices of question, of burgeoning fear, "have even begun to doubt my power. Favoring Victor Vonderheide, indeed, over me to lead you." She watched them all, and waited, it seemed, for anyone to come forward to either rebuke or prove this claim. No one did. "But I wonder, my dear Creatures, if we have gotten too big for our purpose."

"And what is our purpose," one fresh-faced Elite said from somewhere behind Thomas, "not to simply capture Xavier Delacroix, is it?"

A hush fell over the large crowd, and Thomas felt they were much too packed should she decide to kill them all with a wave of a hand, for that was exactly what she looked prepared to do.

He breathed a sigh of relief, when instead, she resumed her beautiful smile, the necklaces at her chest clinking together as she stepped closer to the crowd. "That is one purpose, yes," she whispered, "but it is not the only. No. I have been taking what is owed to us, as you know. . .and that is not just to hold the form of both Vampires and Lycans when we choose, but to take it further, undo the spell of encumbrance Dracula has had placed on we Creatures, and be what we truly are meant to be."

"You speak, as always, in riddles, Eleanor," another Creature shouted into the quiet, "tell us straight what we do, and what we do it for. We know we've a compulsion to Xavier Delacroix, but we don't know why. What is so special about his blood?"

"It is what's made you what you are," she said calmly," and Thomas applauded her for not snapping at the man with his words so carelessly spoken. "When Xavier Delacroix gave me his blood, I had just returned from the book and took with me, before it closed, a page. With this page, and with some help from the Enchanters brave enough to aid me in this venture," (at this, several Elite Enchanters let out cheers), "I took the blood between we Creatures and bound it. Together. Though to make it accessible with sheer will. That took Xavier's blood. Another of Ancient blood.

"And once I'd had it, I focused on the blood of the Lycan, got to thinking with words Xavier and I had shared previously, why it was the blood of the Creatures sent Vampires' blood to boil. And then I transformed for the first time. Though it was sloppy, messy, and not done entirely well at all, it had been done. And in that state I lost myself, unaware the state of a Lycan is so. . .raw, pushing one to kill. To those of you turned by Lore, I congratulate you on taking well to the transformation. It is a difficult one to master for those more used to a. . .colder air.

"Either way," she said as some laughs and cheers left a few Creatures, the tension seeming to dissolve with her words, "the blood of the beast alluded me. It was not until Xavier slashed me with the Ascalon, a sword embedded with great power, that I was able to cling to that power, bide my time until I could regain what little power I had lost."

Thomas found his voice now, not understanding what she'd said. "But you were dead, last I recall, Eleanor. Truly, utterly dead."

Her gaze found his own, and his heart grew cold in his chest with her stare, and he felt himself tense, ready for her to reduce him to ash, but instead her brow furrowed slightly, and she said, "I transferred my essence, the power of *The Immortal's Guide*, into my necklaces, and when all was clear I reversed the spell, able to regain a human form."

"A tricky bit of magic," and Enchanter said to Thomas's right, "but nothing we former Shadowhallers can't work out." And he grinned darkly.

Eleanor smiled appreciatively at him. "And without those Enchanters versed in the darker arts, I would not stand here as I am. And without Damion Nicodemeus's blood. . .I would not stand here, gifted with my true power as I am."

Whispers of confusion filled the hall as all Creatures looked around, the utterance of Damion's name not helping matters. Thomas's brow furrowed. *Damion?*

She stretched her hands out directly before herself, then, her nails beginning to elongate, her fingers beginning to grow longer, her skin going from pale to a color Thomas found to be a sickly gray. She groaned as her eyes hardened in concentration, the bones within her arms beginning to fill and grow, the skin around it appearing to stretch to accommodate its now massive size.

Cries of fright filled the hall, but Thomas could not bring himself to speak. He had heard from Lore quite a few times, that the Vampire form was lesser than it used to be, but he had never questioned it— only thought it strange his father would mention such a fact with no explanation if only to brood over a past where Dracula always slipped past his gnarled fingers.

Now Thomas thought he knew why.

She bent double next, her spine elongating, stretching against her skin, her shirt, and he watched in further horror as the shirt ripped, no longer able to accompany her size. Her feet tore through her boots, her toes and nails now resembling claws as she shifted her footing atop the stone ground.

And as her torso pulled and grew, two thin films of skin stretched from her back, hard, black bones appearing there as well, and he watched as one bat-like wing, scattered throughout with what looked like fur, elongated fully while the other grew, stretching down her back.

Her clothes had long since ripped in places, whatever material she wore able to withstand her large size: She stood tall in the hall now, her black hair barely clinging to her large, round head. As she stared at them all, he found she looked quite sickly: her chin had pulled, pointed to a tip, her eyes had become completely back, large as she surveyed them, and how they did not seem to gleam in the strange light above.

Her skin was now completely gray, almost translucent against the light, her veins able to be seen as she clenched and unclenched her long claws as if basking in the power she now held, tufts of black fur appearing atop her thin skin though not fully covering any part of it.

Two large wings protruded from her back in full now, and as he stared up at her with the others, a grand sensation of nausea filled Thomas's throat, and he turned from her, retching what little blood he had taken many days before from his system. He did not notice that others did the same, that others, those closest to the tunnel's entrance ways had turned to leave, tears filling their eyes.

No, he did not notice this because the moment he looked up again, a spout of blood, black as it left her lips, gushed from her large mouth as though a deranged fountain. He watched in incomprehension as it flew into the air, reached the light high above them, and then split off, a shower of black blood dousing them completely.

And the moment it filled their ears, entered their mouths, for their screams were mighty in the grand hall, they too began to change.

And Thomas Montague could only see his wife's caring eyes, before she was turned into an Elite Creature one last miserable time before he felt his bones begin to painfully expand within his body, and he doubled forward with the others, a snarl of fear, of terrible anguish leaving his lips in full.

Chapter Sixteen

THE GATES

Christopher Black felt strange, though he knew it his natural state now that he was out of his tower. But this strangeness was not one borne of his desire for Lillith Crane to notice him in truth again, to forgive him for what he had done, no, it was borne of the swirling sky, the immense power that filled the air.

They had watched all night as the bursts of light filled the air, and then ceased abruptly. And the sky had opened up, the darkness prominent. They had watched in bemusement as the dark Creature landed first, and then another, this one lighter in appearance.

They'd heard a terrible scream before long, and shaken though they were, for they all hoped it was not Xavier, regardless of how strange he'd had shown himself to be, and now they moved, wearily, back toward Cedar Village beneath Peroneous's and Aurora's shield. Aleister grumbled to himself off and on, Christopher hearing words like, 'Xavier,' and 'must help,' though the scarred Vampire did little more than look pained as he stared straight ahead, the many days' distance to the small village seeming overwhelming now.

Christopher did not speak, not anymore. He knew Lillith would not take it in kind, knew the others were all lost in their own thoughts, so he remained silent. Forced to think, only, on what he'd just seen, been through, and how drastically the World had changed from what Dracula had bothered to tell him. To know the Vampire always seemed rushed, scared, during his visits. Christopher chanced one glance back toward the mountain, and knew why. He'd been terrified of those Creatures, their power. . .their hand.

No wonder he moved as wildly as he did, no wonder he controlled magic, gave the Creatures most a threat to his plan lesser space in the World. . . .

Christopher Black wondered about Xavier Delacroix, and if the Vampire knew just what he'd gotten himself into, what Dracula had, undoubtedly, pushed him into.

He remembered the green-eyed Vampire, embracing Eleanor before they'd landed, and he recalled what Xavier said. He desired to know what she knew. How she had gained her power. Used what she'd been shown in some book to her advantage.

And he wondered, for the first time, if she had been right to do so as he looked up once more at the still-swirling sky, feeling the medallion at his chest burn hot.

※

He flew atop the trees, the Goblet tucked safely under an arm, and he did not slow, not even as he eyed the large hole in the sky to the north, the sky there black, flashes of lightning filling it.

He continued on, feeling his cloak burn beneath his arm, but he did not slow. He headed back toward London, his home the most important place to be now, yes. He had to get to Dammath, had to warn Xavier. His blood still stained his clothes, but his wound had healed before long, the only thing that harmed him now, was Eleanor. Her mad quest for power.

The look in her eyes when he'd appeared. . .he could see her for what he was, then. Truly corrupt. Mad with a quest for both a Vampire, and an overwhelming desire to placate her fears. For she was scared, immensely so, this thing that scared her something she had gained on her journey through the book.

He remembered Damion's new face, and searched the skies in alarm now, no longer able to dismiss the Creature as not of his concern.

Even if Darien was changed, Damion could not deny the Vampire had moved to see it through that Dracula's, nay, the Phoenixes' desires were done. He recalled the sight of the hole in the sky though he flew away from it now, and the burning voice in his mind once he had done what Dracula had needed him to do, recite the oath over the blood. Become, finally, another hand in his ancient quest.

That voice, he knew now what it was. When he had stared into Eleanor's eyes back at her caves, he had realized it. The Phoenixes had spoken to him, and if their words were to be believed, he was not the one to drink from the Goblet, he saw that now.

Look what it had done to her.

Dracula was merely a pawn in all of this. The sword, the Ares, merely a tool to ensure greater power was held, given to those to see the path to peace through.

And he pressed on, eyeing the sky for his brother, for Xavier, anyone, indeed that was designed, forged in the Phoenixes' ancient fires to rid the World of the bloodsuckers, the beasts.

And as he recalled Eleanor, the purpose with which she held herself once his blood was taken, placed into that damning Potion, he had a feeling they would need all the help they could get to see the mission through.

✳

James snapped his reigns as the sun began to dip below the tops of the trees, his gaze trained on the Vampires atop their horse ahead of him. He had no reason, now, to doubt their power, most importantly the power of the woman.

And how it seemed the Lycans' power was greatly diminished against that red light.

He recalled how Lore's long snout, and sharp fangs gleamed under the moon as he dove upon his leg, ripping the skin and muscle from the bone.

A wave of sick rose in his gut, but he turned his thoughts awake, determined to focus on her. She'd saved him that night. Emerged from the manor bathed in a soothing red light. Had merely lifted a slender hand and told the beast to go, and it had listened.

The rest of that night a blur, he recalled how he had felt himself slip with his great loss of blood, into the reaches of death's embrace, but soon Damion Nicodemeus had appeared. A jar of Unicorn Blood in hand, and he James, had been forced to drink that thick, foul-smelling liquid only to awakening a few days later within Xavier Delacroix's bed.

His thoughts turning to the green-eyed Vampire in had not seen in weeks, in months, he gripped the reigns tighter, eager to draw level with Christian's horse, his blood burning hot in his veins as he did.

The smell of the Vampire's blood trailed on the air, and he eyed Alexandria, confused when she did not eye him back: her gaze was focused, far too intently, over Christian's shoulder, the brown-green irises piercing in the afternoon light.

What did she see?

He turned his attention to his own horse as they moved as one, attempting to sense anything, be it more of Eleanor Black's Creatures or Vampires. Nothing reached him at all, nothing but the scent of the Vampire beside him, Alexandria's blood not arriving to his nose, strangely enough.

And then, with a short intake of breath, he smelled something new.

It was old, powerful blood, a seed of anger within blanketed by righteous cause. A soldier's blood. Though how he knew that, he hadn't the faintest idea.

It was not until several large, beautiful birds flew overhead, that he felt like he was being watched, and the Vampires appeared from around trees.

Some held black bows, their arrows trained on them, and Christian skidded to a stop, James doing the very same as their horses let out even more unnerving whinnies beneath them.

Some Vampires held swords, others multiple daggers, and even still others thin staffs, all weapons trained on them, but James found it remarkable he could not smell their blood.

Nor did it seem, could they smell his: they looked wary, but not threatened. Their eyes were not red, their lips not pulled into perpetual snarls. They were merely combat ready. And the more he looked now, the more he saw the darkly robed Enchanters, two of them on either side of the slew of Vampires, hands raised high, an invisible barrier keeping the sun from reaching the Vampires' skin.

"Vampires. . .and. . .beast," one Vampire said uncertainly, stepping forward, her bow and arrow still trained on Christian, "dismount and step forward." Her eyes grazed the sword at Christian's waist. "And place your weapons on the ground."

He eyed Christian for guidance, the Vampire motioning for Alexandria to dismount Knight, and with this, James moved, sliding off his horse just as Christian did the same.

Once they were all on the ground, Christian stepped forward, eyes hard, though he undid the strap at his waist and threw it on the ground, the gem still protruding painfully against the leather. James could tell it still glowed, although dimly now.

The Vampire from before stepped forward, sliding the sword back toward her with the heel of her boot, her arrow mere inches from Christian's nose as she did. He did not blink or appear concerned, but his grip upon Alexandria's hand did tighten, James saw.

"Wait, Elisa," another Vampire further back in the trees said now, but the woman did not turn.

"What is it Gregor?"

"Isn't that Xavier Delacroix?"

"Nonsense. Xavier's eyes are not as black as. . . ." but her voice trailed as her eyes widened, and her mouth hung open in slight surprise as she withdrew her arrow, placing the bow at her side. "My word. . .I. . .Lord Christian?" she breathed in astonishment, timid fear.

He nodded.

"Bloody hell stand down!" she said, motioning with her bow and arrow for the others to lower their weapons. Once they did, she lifted the Ares from the ground and handed it sheepishly back to him. He took it with something of a smile, placing it around his waist once more. "Forgive me. I didn't realize—"

"Think nothing of it," he said quickly, and James could sense the urgency on his tongue. "Where is Westley Rivers? I was told he looked forward to greeting us."

"The spell of protection has been replaced since Eleanor Black took the Vampire City from us, my Lord. Though it is. . .not as strong as it was because we don't know what exactly Dracula had done to place it. The Enchanters we are familiar with moved to secure the City all the same. We're actually at the limit to appear there now. When we felt the barrier become disturbed, we moved as we could— as we should in these strange times to observe the threat." Her eyes moved to Alexandria slightly behind Christian. "Who is that?"

Christian stepped in front of her slightly, his hand never leaving her own. "Westley mentioned her in his letter. If he knows, I daresay that is all that matters, is it not?"

How protective, James thought, watching as the Vampire named Elisa gave him a curt nod, before stepping back, and with a nod in Christian's direction, disappeared from view, all other Vampires following suit.

As the brazen wind died, James eyed Christian and Alexandria, the question deep in their gazes as well. But with a resigned sigh, he did not resist as Alexandria placed a hand on his shoulder, precisely where the Lycan had bitten, and felt himself be pulled along darkness.

When he opened his eyes, he stared at large black gates set into what looked to be the mouth of a cave, large chains tied around them, a large, rusted lock holding the chains in place.

Elisa moved to the gates, and placed a hand on the lock when a voice, low and drawling reached all their ears and they tensed considerably as one:

"There is a first time for everything, isn't there, Christian?"

James whirled around as the many Vampires rushed forward, drawing a line between themselves and the newcomer. Elisa remained where she stood behind them, her hand, for all James knew, still on the lock.

He could hardly see over the heads of the Vampires that stood, white cloaks flapping in the sudden harsh wind, but when he heard that voice again, he eyed Christian to see if it could possibly be true.

Victor.

"Oh come, you bar me from passage to my very creator's domain? How rude."

Upon realizing who it was, some Vampires at the line dropped their weapons, but Christian said, "Do not be fooled—he is not with us—he is not with Xavier."

Elisa was at his back in the next second, eyes red. "I saw him side with her when they overtook the City, my Lord, but are you sure he is still with her?"

Christian's eyes were hard as he glared at Victor over the shoulders of the Vampires. "Positively. He burned down my manor with her," and he shook the hand that held Alexandria's arm slightly, "inside. He is no friend of ours, not anymore."

Elisa looked as though she couldn't believe her ears, but soon straightened, and with a commanding air told the others to raise their weapons, prepared to fight if need be.

"There will be no need for that," Victor said, and much to James surprise he began to step forward, ignoring the Vampires' snarls of warning, their raised weapons. "I merely wish to apologize to my dear boy here, for destroying his home. It wasn't me, truly, you see. It was this," and as two Vampires parted against their best wishes to allow him passage, James saw the small circular stone the Vampire held in-between two fingers, holding it high for Christian to appraise.

As the others raised their weapons again, Christian shook his head slightly, bidding them to stand down, and with a furrowed brow, said, "How could that have caused all the destruction that night, Victor?"

A look of grand confusion filled Victor's violet eyes then, the eyes James had always thought were strange. Once he considered the older gentleman to be a kind man, albeit pale, but now, he saw the Vampire looked immensely out of place, terribly sad, even.

"I hardly know. I was pressed to it, wasn't I? She told me to—I was told to—forgive me, my boy. *Please*," and the last word left his lips as a strangled hiss, "she desired me to prove my loyalties but I fear I can never be *of* her. Not truly. Not after what I've done to you."

Christian's mouth twitched though his eyes were still cold. Alexandria placed another hand on his arm, still gripping his hand tight, and she seemed to be telling him something through the mind.

His eyes flashed red after a time, and Victor's eyes widened though he did not step away.

"Why are you here, Victor?" Christian asked.

"T-To right the many wrongs I have wrought upon your head."

"Truly?"

"Yes, of course."

"Yet how could you do that when you delivered us to Eleanor on a silver platter? Alexandria all but stabbed and tortured?"

His violet gaze moved to her, but not for long. It seemed he could not stare upon her in truth. There was pain in that prospect James deduced.

"I regret my transgressions," Victor said quietly, and his hand wrapped around the stone, the pale skin catching in the light of the sun, and James wondered how it was the Vampire was able to walk in the sun without aid, for the rings no longer worked.

"You will regret far more if you don't leave this sacred ground, traitor," a new voice, deeper this one, said from behind them.

James turned, as did everyone else, to the rusted gates, the dark-skinned Vampire that stood behind them menacing in the dark of the large tunnel. A hand was on a sword at his waist, his clothes reminding James of a most celebrated soldier, and as the man lifted his hand and tapped a finger against the lock, he smelled the blood of a soldier, and knew who he had smelled but several minutes before.

Thinking it strange how Alexandria had not kept this scent from him, he watched as the Vampire stepped over the fallen chains, past the gates, and marched directly up to them, all soldiers kneeling immediately where they stood.

Up close now James could see the dark Vampire was handsome, if not terrible cold: his eyes were black in the light of the sun, his hair wavy and black, settling at his shoulders, and his right arm's sleeve was folded in on itself, pinned behind his shoulder. *Must have lost it in battle*, James thought.

"I rue the day Dracula let slip his orders to you, Victor Varick Vonderheide," the Vampire said to him now, his voice vicious on the afternoon air.

Victor looked quite hurt with these words, but said, "Rue the day all you desire Bronzechair, I do not fault my creator for creating me. Not anymore."

"Indeed?" the Bronzechair asked. "Then why, as Christian has asked, have you come?"

And at this Victor seemed to gain himself for all sadness, all fear dispersed from his person, and he said, "I wished to speak with Christian on a matter most dear, I believe, to both our hearts."

The Bronzechair shifted his footing with interest. "Oh? Do go on."

"I will not speak with the entire 3rd Army present!"

"But you will Vonderheide," the dark Vampire said. "Now begin."

Victor looked as though he wished to resist, but said after a time, "Christian, it has come to my attention that Alexandria holds great power. Yes, we knew she would as a Vampire, but how strong do you feel it is? And to what end? I have reason to believe Dracula was not truthful when sharing her power with us, what little of it he would." And he placed a hand on Christian's arm, all eyes roving to it. "The answer is in her blood. How much do you truly think he did to see her as she is now? Think Christian." And the hand was squeezed. "We have seen what great power does in Eleanor Black. It corrupts."

The dark Vampire grabbed Victor's wrist, pushing his arm away from Christian's, and as the Vampire stumbled back, shock widening his eyes, he said, "Do not attempt to fill Lord Christian's ears with such nonsense!"

"Nonsense?" Victor breathed, and he placed the stone in a pocket of his cloak, and James saw the red glow even through the dark fabric. "I don't speak nonsense, Westley. I speak truth. Everything Dracula did was for his own selfish gain. To become human? Think Christian, do you really want to be as they? Weak, defenseless, at the mercy of greater Creatures?"

"Need I remind you," Christian began, "Alexandria was human but almost a week before—"

"And she was a bane to your existence as I remember it! Weren't you the same Vampire that could not wait to be rid of at my ball those months before?"

Christian's mouth closed abruptly, whatever words he'd been prepared to say taken clear from his tongue.

He did not eye Alexandria as a cruel smile lifted Victor's lips, but Westley Rivers placed a hand on his shoulder, and stepped ahead of him, blocking him from view of Victor, but the damage, James thought, had already been done.

Christian looked as though he'd been slapped, a darker truth he did not wish to realize beginning to fill his eyes, and he stepped, although slightly, away from Alexandria, her own brow furrowed heavily in confusion.

Westley had just finished shouting obscenities at the violet-eyed Vampire, before ordering his men to rise and attack at his word, but as they raised their swords, drew back their arrows, and pointed their staffs, Victor disappeared in a burst of wind, a knowing smile upon his face as he went, and James fought back the fear that the Vampire had just caused something that could not easily be undone.

Chapter Seventeen

REWARDED

"They're here! They're bloody well here!" Nicholai screamed as Arminius waved long-fingered hands through the reddening sky.

"I can see that, *Vampure*!" he yelled back. "Get to Rore! We'll be safe there!"

Nicholai Noble pressed onward with the Elf's words, terror pushing him forward. *The spell is broken*, he thought frantically, eyeing the lavish city several, several miles away. *They will kill me, they will—they must—*

The sky darkened suddenly just before him, blackening the field, and in swirl of brazen wind, and lightning, a large hole opened in the sky.

No.

As he watched, transfixed, a large bird, larger perhaps than the one that followed, emerged from the dark, and flew with terribly large, sweeping wings down to the field. Nicholai could not move as the Creature flapped its long, deep blue wings gracefully, and then landed softly atop the grass, its eyes black as, (he thought), they surveyed him. It was all he could do to not scream.

"Vampire," an extremely deep voice said next, and he blinked, hardly daring to believe the bird to speak, but he knew, with a quick nod of its long head, it was so. "You must stop running."

"And let you kill me?" he whispered, as somewhere behind him he heard another bird's cry, heard Arminius's voice wheeze something like, "Damn."

"I will not kill you, Vampire," the Phoenix went on, bristling its large wings, "but Syran desires to."

Syran. The sight of the strong, almost kind Phoenix returned to his mind's eye, then, the blue eyes stern, and how he could imagine them enraged, disappointed even, placed upon him in clear contempt.

He shivered but not from cold.

He opened his mouth to speak, but no words could form, his tongue lapping against the roof of his mouth, but no sounds would protrude.

His hands shook at his sides, his sword long forgotten at his waist, and he was aware, once again, his medallion was cold, still black against his chest.

I have no protection, he thought suddenly, and the World seemed so much larger then. The sky, it still swirled with its strange darkness, and how quickly what little of the sun remained dispersed completely. All was dark.

And if he had the mind to move, he would have run in the other direction, done his best to distance himself from the waiting, watching Creature before him, but he knew it useless to try: no matter where he went, indeed, he knew they would find him. Always.

He had disobeyed their word; he had failed where they deemed he triumph. He had shown compassion, and knew it futile for a Vampire to even toy with the emotion, for if this was the outcome, it was better that Alexandria Stone never be turned at all.

What good did it do? Her power swirling about? The Phoenixes? The Enchanters?

What good was any of it, indeed, if all it did was bring him here, before the very Creatures he could not stand (quite literally) to be near? What good was all the plans, the medallions, the red lights, and blood, if this—staring death, true death, in the face was where it led?

Something heavy landed atop the ground behind him, and he turned, feeling uneasy at giving his back to the Phoenix, but quite pleased he did: He stared up at the Creature Darien had become, the black eyes gleaming through the dark, and fear, and something else Nicholai could not place held him there, merely staring.

And before he could think to do anything at all, before he could think to protect himself, the Creature held out a long, black clawed hand, and placed it atop his head, the nails cutting through his cheeks and ears, and Nicholai could barely see the alarmed look of Arminius as he hobbled forward from many yards away before the Creature squeezed, and Nicholai felt no more.

※

Arminius could not breathe, the body of Nicholai falling to the ground, his blood spraying against the Creature's arm and middle, his head. . .what remained of it falling in chunks to the grass.

He wailed, or at least someone else did, for he was certain that was not his voice, but yes, even as he stared at the unmoving, headless, body that lay atop its stomach before the large Creature, he felt his lungs constrict as the need to breathe returned.

He gasped, inhaling as best he could, another sound quite like rage, anger protruding past his lips, and all he could see, all he could hear was Nicholai's voice to him back at the cottage, the words they had shared: *"There is no time to explain, Arminius. . . He is no more a Creature of sanity than he was a Vampire of true merit. He was a tyrant, ensuring all obeyed his orders or succumbed to his wrath. . . ."*

And he sank to his knees, and it seemed the World met him eagerly: the ground was soft beneath his legs, almost a cushion, and he beat the Earth with a fist, no longer caring if the Phoenix at his back set him aflame, nor if the Creature Darien had become moved for him. He cried for Nicholai, cried for Xavier, cried for all the others that wore medallions, and even those that didn't. For Alinneis and the other Etrian Elves, once his brothers, now outcasts still. And he cried harder for himself, no amount of magic, indeed, able to stop anything now, or so it seemed. Such was the World.

We are nothing, at their mercy, unable to move on our own. He tried to save Alexandria, do what he felt was best, and this—this was his reward?

He chanced a glance up at the body of Nicholai, quite shocked when he found himself incredibly alone, the city of Rore shining quite a distance away, only the corpse of the Vampire atop the grass.

There was no sign of Phoenix: the sky was normal for the night, now, and he turned his head quickly to see if the Phoenix that had chased them had gone as well. It had.

Knowing he should be worried, and immensely so, for himself, for the others, he did nothing but stare at the mass at Nicholai's ripped apart neck, tendrils of the silver hair waving slightly in the wind beneath a pile of red.

※

Javier Theron ran as quickly as his legs could carry, far, far away from her caves. She was changed. They all were changed.

They were all monsters.

He'd felt the shift in her blood shortly after he'd visited Damion, and knew his time at her side was at its end, but as he ran, he felt slowed: he suddenly could not move fast enough.

Continuing to press forward, though the wind, the air began to crawl, he was finally thrown back off his feet. He stared up past the trees, the moon's light not shining anywhere past the leaves, but still he noticed the greater darkness that swept across him as the large. . .things flew overhead, flapping what sounded like great, heavy wings.

Fear blanketed him in earnest, but he rose once more to unsteady legs, unable to do little more than snarl as he felt the wind blow at his back.

He turned and there she was, her eyes wide, seemingly unseeing, bent forward slightly, her wings stretching outward and closing against her back as though she needed to get used to the action. Her breasts held no nipples over their places, and he thought, strangely, that they needn't. Never did need to be there. Vampires, after all, had no need to feed their children through way of milk.

But he was pulled from this notion when she stepped forward, and in her movement, he saw her intention, felt it pass across the cold air, reaching his blood as if he could drink it through his skin.

She means to kill me, he thought wildly, stepping back as quickly as he could, yet unable to take his gaze off her eyes, how cruel, how dark. . . .

And with a flap of her wings she moved forward, a clawed hand reaching out for him, and in a wild, desperate moment, he searched his mind for Dracula, searched his mind for the blood that once drifted across the air only two months before.

He found nothing.

Her black claws pierced his chest, and he stared in disbelief as her large hand squeezed around his cold heart, and pulled it from its place.

Chapter Eighteen

THE NEW BREED OF CREATURE

Xavier Delacroix ducked as Philistia's hands weaved their magic through the air. A strong pressure pressed against his head as the spell was cast, and he did not turn to look and see if it had hit its target.

They had left Cedar Village before night fell, and moved north, up past the empty plains and to, where it was said, sat a lake of ice, caught in the falling snow of Lane's mountain.

Philistia had said Merpeople lived within it, but as the Merpeople of one lake had recognized him as their King, these Merpeople should do the same, though her voice had shaken as she'd said it.

And now he could see the white surface, tinged with deep blue here and there as they ran, balls of sparkling fyre leaving the Phoenix that chased them, smashing against the ground beside them, sending the grass to go up in flames.

"We can't swim across it!" Nathanial shouted, the roar of a nearby fyre almost drowning his words.

"We can walk!" Philistia shouted back, sending a giant burst of blue toward the large, persistent bird.

"Across it?" Xavier asked in shock, not understanding how that would be achieved. It looked sturdy enough but he remembered how Aleister had been pulled under, how he had moved to rescue him. And there in that dark water, he had believed he'd seen Eleanor Black, hadn't he? But he'd blinked and it was simply a Mermaid.

He feared what he would see should the ice crack beneath his feet, and as they neared the large lake in earnest, he felt it like an arrow to his heart.

She was back. But something, no, everything was different.

He could not hear her voice, nor could he feel her passion, her desire, all he felt was a twisted sense of righteousness, cold as it had been within his mind those weeks before.

She was his queen again, yes, he felt it strongly in his blood, but where, and he searched the skies for her, any sign of her, for it was so resoundingly close he felt her, where was she?

"Xavier, what's wrong? We must move!" It was Nathanial's voice screaming through the cloud that had appeared within his mind. Pulling, enrapturing, thickening. . . Yes, he could barely feel the Vampire's hand as he pulled at his cloak, sending him stumbling across the burning ground to reach the ice.

Nathanial already stood upon it, and Philistia was farthest, a large shield of protection around herself and Nathanial keeping the balls of shimmering heat from reaching the ice below.

But Xavier could not bring himself to cross the lake, nor did he care about the bird that was attempting to burn him alive with its fyre, and a voice, quite unlike her own, but so very much familiar, said,

"Come. It is time to join me, my love."

And he blinked, but he was no longer before a burning field, he was no longer being pulled by the hand of frantic Vampire. He stood now, in his room back in Delacroix Manor, and as he stared around at the pristine placement of everything within it, he smelled her, naturally, before he saw her.

She entered the room, closing the door softly behind her, her eyes brown, holding the coldness he had come to enjoy as her natural gaze. Her curled black hair was wrapped fashionable about itself atop her head, loose curls hanging from the sides of her face, and as she stepped deeper into the room, she clasped her hands with his, and kissed him full on his lips.

"Something serious troubles you," she said when she pulled away, and he could not believe how soft, how calm everything had been back then.

"It is Joseph Gail," he admitted after a time of staring into her pleading eyes. "The Vampire gets to choose how she shall rule while I am merely placed to train under Dracula. We are nearly the same. Am I not worthy of being King?"

Her brow furrowed and she stepped back slightly, folding her arms beneath her chest. He took the time to admire the black cincher clasped over her abdomen, hiding the red fabric there, the tightness with which it pushed her cleavage, ample it was, up. He blinked as she opened her mouth and said, "Do you truly want to be King, Xavier? Or do you just want the title? You have taken the mantle of leader for the Order wonderfully, better than most, I imagine, but to truly be King—King of what? Of Vampires?"

He eyed her hardened stare, feeling the slightest bit foolish, but he knew she would not laugh if he voiced it.

"I wish, one day, to be King of the entire Dark World."

And there was silence, but not for long. "If you are King what will that make me?" A coquettish smile playing at her lips, red though they were.

He pressed a thumb to them, and they parted slightly, her stare becoming heady. Wrapping an arm around her waist, he drew her closer, her arms undoing themselves to clasp at his back. Close to her now, like this, he remembered how she made him feel. Strong, wanted, capable.

And he stared her straight in her wanting gaze as he said, his voice shaking, though he had to be said, for this woman, this beautiful strong woman, had wrapped herself around his dead heart, and he had believed it then, that he could never be without her.

"Eleanor. My Queen. You will be my Queen. Forever."

And he thought of his mother, his father dead as he believed them to be, dead on the floor of their modest home, and he thought of staring upon the World with the eyes of a Vampire, never to breathe again if he truly did not desire it. And he thought, most longingly, of seeing Eleanor Sindell Black for the very first time within Dracula's training room, her favored attire of blouses and breeches, boots and scabbards drawing his eye at once.

But it was her beauty that held his gaze, her viciousness as she trained.

Her quest always, to know how everything was done.

And with a cold gasp, he was pulled from his mind, and brought back to the world afire to see Nathanial upon the ground at his feet, Philistia kneeling atop the ice bleeding profusely from a wound to her abdomen, and he looked up just as the numerous winged, slightly furred Creatures filled the skies, their bat-like wings flapping together in momentous unison: the wind it spurred blew his hair and clothes from his face.

And as they neared, and quickly, Xavier eyed the one that appeared to lead them, hardly daring to believe it to be true.

But as she drew closer against the dark, her dread nowhere to be found, he knew it was her.

The silver glint of her many necklaces swayed across her chest, and as she let out a horrific screech, blowing up the grass and dirt below her, shifted vertically in the sky, and all the others did the same.

There were thousands of them behind her, hovering within the dark, and he noticed for the first time that the Phoenix had fled, its strange fyre still burning around him.

And as he stared up at her, unable to sense her within the thing that stared at him now, he could hear a faint voice, terribly familiar, but one he could not truly recall, whisper in his ear, *"The blood of transformation. Power. Passed to us from our mothers, them from their fathers—I've said far too much already."*

No, he said to the voice that was flying from him the more he stared at her, expectant, though for what, he did not know, *you haven't said nearly enough.*

About the Author

B esides being addicted to vampires, blood, and a good, steaming cup of tea, S.C. Parris attends University in New York City, and is the author of "A Night of Frivolity," a horror short story, published by Burning Willow Press. She is the author of *The Dark World* series published by Permuted Press, and enjoys thinking up new dark historical fantasies to put to page next. She lives on Long Island, New York with her family and can be found writing ridiculous articles for CLASH Media.

PERMUTED
PRESS
needs *you* to help

SPREAD (THE) INFECTION

FOLLOW US!

f | Facebook.com/PermutedPress
🐦 | Twitter.com/PermutedPress

REVIEW US!

Wherever you buy our book, they can be reviewed! We want to know what you like!

GET INFECTED!

Sign up for our mailing list at
PermutedPress.com

PERMUTED
PRESS

14

Peter Clines

Padlocked doors.
Strange light fixtures. Mutant
cockroaches.

There are some odd things about
Nate's new apartment. Every
room in this old brownstone has
a mystery. Mysteries that stretch
back over a hundred years.
Some of them are in plain sight.
Some are behind locked doors.
And all together these mysteries
could mean the end of Nate and
his friends.

Or the end of everything…

PERMUTED
PRESS

THE JOURNAL SERIES
by Deborah D. Moore

After a major crisis rocks the nation, all supply lines are shut down. In the remote Upper Peninsula of Michigan, the small town of Moose Creek and its residents are devastated when they lose power in the middle of a brutal winter, and must struggle alone with one calamity after another.

The Journal series takes the reader head first into the fury that only Mother Nature can dish out.

PERMUTED
PRESS

Michael Clary
THE GUARDIAN | THE REGULATORS | BROKEN

When the dead rise up and take over the city, the Government is forced to close off the borders and abandon the remaining survivors. Fortunately for them, a hero is about to be chosen...a Guardian that will rise up from the ashes to fight against the dead. The series continues with Book Four: *Scratch*.

Emily Goodwin
CONTAGIOUS | DEATHLY CONTAGIOUS

During the Second Great Depression, twenty-four-year-old Orissa Penwell is forced to drop out of college when she is no longer able to pay for classes. Down on her luck, Orissa doesn't think she can sink any lower. She couldn't be more wrong. A virus breaks out across the country, leaving those that are infected crazed, aggressive and very hungry. `

The saga continues in Book Three: *Contagious Chaos* and Book Four: *The Truth is Contagious*.

THE BREADWINNER | Stevie Kopas

The end of the world is not glamorous. In a matter of days the human race was reduced to nothing more than vicious, flesh hungry creatures. There are no heroes here. Only survivors. The trilogy continues with Book Two: *Haven* and Book Three: *All Good Things.*

THE BECOMING | Jessica Meigs

As society rapidly crumbles under the hordes of infected, three people—Ethan Bennett, a Memphis police officer; Cade Alton, his best friend and former IDF sharpshooter; and Brandt Evans, a lieutenant in the US Marines—band together against the oncoming crush of death and terror sweeping across the world. The story continues with Book Two: *Ground Zero.*

THE INFECTION WAR | Craig DiLouie

As the undead awake, a small group of survivors must accept a dangerous mission into the very heart of infection. This edition features two books: *The Infection* and *The Killing Floor.*

OBJECTS OF WRATH | Sean T. Smith

The border between good and evil has always been bloody... Is humanity doomed? After the bombs rain down, the entire world is an open wound; it is in those bleeding years that William Fox becomes a man. After The Fall, nothing is certain. *Objects of Wrath* is the first book in a saga spanning four generations.

PERMUTED PRESS

A PREPPER'S COOKBOOK

20 Years of Cooking in the Woods

by Deborah D. Moore

In the event of a disaster, it isn't enough to have food. You also have to know what to do with it.

Deborah D. Moore, author of *The Journal* series and a passionate Prepper for over twenty years, gives you step-by-step instructions on making delicious meals from the emergency pantry.

PERMUTED
PRESS